ANANDA: BOOK I

Primordial Zenith

A. Rose Mapstone

This book is dedicated to my soul siblings; especially Jamie White, whose spirit reflects mine so brightly, it's blinding.

Also, to my many teachers – in this dimension and others – who inspire me endlessly.

Thank You. I Love You All.

TRIGGER WARNING – Although its characters and events are purely fictional and meant for entertainment, this book contains themes of mental illness, self-harm, and relationship abuse. Reader discretion (and extra self-care) is advised.

Table of Contents

One

When the ship's belly brushes the landing pad, my toes curl. The walls vibrate as a magnetic field claims the couple thousand square feet of space-traveling beauty.

It's nearly impossible to get lost in my ship because it's a chrome crop circle. Every path is connected. No matter where you wander—from my bedroom to the empty guest rooms—you end up back in the center cockpit, where I'm usually lodged. It's surrounded by an ellipsoidal wall of buttons, levers, and screens, so it's my favorite place to pretend that I'm in control.

Clouds of dust skid over external cameras and lift in a gust. Screens clear and reveal a dozen different Earthen flags stuck in barren ground.

"Syzygy, report."

Her speakers crackle to life, emitting a low female voice. "Destination: Oracle, Mars. Sector six. Arrival time: 7:14, Eastern Volcanic. Ship status: Brilliant. Welcome, Captain."

"Thanks, G." I take my shirt off, ball it up, and wipe my neck. "Request to upgrade your interior with a massage chair?"

"Denied," Syzygy responds. "Your trove is extremely low."

"Not after today." I kick my feet up on the control panel, careful not to knock toggles. "After this gig, I'll buy myself out of my work contract with enough left over to get six massage chairs. Maybe some starworks for the holidays."

I grip my shoulders as if holding on for life, kneading knots into submission. They roll and wobble under my fingers like pebbles in boiling water.

After a few seconds, the speakers chime. "Incoming signal from Oracle Spirit Center."

1

I gather my small braids into a bun and don the Sens-Com goggles. "Accept."

A pair of cat-like eyes stare at me from behind a mask of feathers and tangerine quartz points. Madam Tauris sits like an empress, hands folded in her lap, shoulders draped in green silk. My senses are submerged in her space—her oily skin smells like cinnamon and the room is thick with dragon's blood incense. I can almost feel her hands grasping mine.

"Zenith Lin, to see your face is a gift," she purrs, resting her chin on laced fingers. A Nova-Indian accent is woven in her voice like string through beads—a fading hint of her ancient Arabic ancestors and their sandy tongues. Her head bobs up and down while she scans me. "Perhaps this is a bad time."

I force a laugh. "Excuse me, Madam T. It's been a long journey."

"Yes. I expect, after a while in the stars, you tire of wearing shirts," she teases, then waves a hand. "But the state of your body does not matter; it is your soul I'm eager to see."

"Great." I lace fingers behind my head, only mildly offended. Her philosophies have always left my ears ringing in alarm. "When do we start?"

Tauris inclines her chin. Her throat bulges in the shape of a waterfall, muddy and smooth. "Your soul must have been lost for many cycles—it doesn't know when to rest."

A shrug moves through my whole body, almost a shiver. "I'm a traveler. Always have been."

"Seeking answers?"

"Sure."

"And adventure?"

"Is there a difference between the two?"

Tauris' pale fingernails run over the mask. Her smile waxes like a moon. "Fate tastes good for you today, Zenith Lin. I'll have my boys come for you, after your ship enters our level."

"Thank you." I remove the S-Com with fidgeting hands. A fierce wind smacks the side of my ship, whistling against star-proof metal.

"Well Mars, I didn't miss you."

I stand and stretch, enjoying the crackle of my spine. Blue floor lights guide me through the circular, maze-like hallway. To the left of this giant cell, I reach the bedroom door.

Syzygy coyly asks, "Password?"

"Anulos."

The door slides open, revealing a low-rise bed frosted with blankets. Despite having the desire to throw myself on top and pass out, I open the wardrobe. Inside, a mirror and breath-screen display popular Martian trends and what I would look like if I wore them. I flip through the database by exhaling sharply on the glass through pursed lips, humming idly. My view is plagued by gemmy sweaters, long skirts, and toe rings.

"Deimos," I swear. "Martian-humans. They're not so practical, are they?"

I swipe away suggestions and tap on a gray crop-top sweater, white jeans, and fluorescent rainbow sneakers. Humming becomes singing as I strip out of sweatpants and climb into the wardrobe.

My bare ankles are met with the familiar cool sting of liquid polyester as shoes morph to my feet. On either side of me, claw-like machines sew plastic fibers into a customized outfit, from an extra-protective hood to copper belt loops.

After about ten minutes, the wardrobe finishes its fusing and weaving. Fiddling with my braided bun and unruly scruff, I step out and sigh. "What do you think, G? Too Earthen?"

"According to recent trends on Cosmigram, your outfit isn't Earthen enough, Captain."

I snap and shoot finger-guns toward the ceiling. "I like the way you think."

Finishing touches include black eyeshadow, silver blush, a quartz belt, and a lapis-colored jacket. "Much better."

"Entrance into Oracle's underlevels will commence in three minutes," Syzygy announces as I depart the bedroom. With each step, light bounces off my new shoes and hits the walls.

"Love it when you talk dirty," I joke, pocketing a few small items from the captain's compartment.

A flash of my tattooed hand over the ignition pad turns off and locks the ship's controls. Every light dims, except for the exit, which waits for me, blinking like an all-knowing eye.

"Entrance into Oracle's underlevels will commence in one minute."

"Oh, G, you tease," I moan, throwing my head back. Laughter bubbles from my lips, but she ignores the commentary. For the fifty seconds that follow, I amuse myself by feigning sex noises.

"It's my duty to remind you that Oracle's underlevels have a minimal noise policy, Captain." Her walls shimmy and we slide underground.

When I reach the exit, I pat G's walls. "Thanks, babe. Always a pleasure to be inside you." My inked handprint opens the exit and I begin the descent.

Under Mars' surface, shadows douse the ship's discus body in dark silk. Despite this, the atmosphere feels heightened, more electric. Breathing becomes syncopated with a distant song, echoing off cavern walls.

The tunnel-like darkness of Mars' underlayer is punctured by several small lights—homemade constellations. The ground dribbles and glistens with what smells like ammonia.

Behind me, Syzygy's door seals. Every step has my body lurching, thinking it'll fall and splatter on slick ground.

Nah…I got this. I'm safe.

Two men meet me at the bottom of the stairs, identical emerald eyes glowing.

"Hello, Zenith Lin." Their unison voices echo.

"Pan's orbit," I swear, rubbing my hands together. "It's freezing down here…guess I dressed well for it…and where's the big lights? I can't see a damn thing."

"Oracle is currently in a cleansing process and lacks usual utilities. We will make the necessary adjustments for you." Their perfectly manufactured bodies flash like paper lanterns, transparent skin revealing ribbons of wiring. Synthetic muscles stretch and shimmer like comets from their groomed hair down to their toes.

"Wow," I chuckle. "And I thought my ship was sexy."

Their light tints pink. "Welcome to Oracle, Zenith Lin."

I sift sweat and worry between my palms. "Lead the way, beauties."

Their skin illuminates the floor and they exhale heat, creating a comfortable bubble for us to walk in. It's nice, but with every stride, the distance from Syzygy feels like tightening cords.

She'll be okay, I reassure myself. *No one can enter her but me.*

In the rust-colored wall ahead of us, there's an arched entrance, embellished with vibrant, metal-infused crystals. Stone angels spout incense from their eyes and mouths, catching rays of impending light and casting it in every direction.

"A mystical fiesta," I muse.

4

The sexy cyborgs ignore me and place their palms on either side of the entryway. The smoke thickens momentarily, and our light bubble flickers.

My nostrils flare. Frankincense, cannabidiol, and chocolate. The entryway alone costs more than the best massage chair I could find. I'm practically drooling.

She must be richer than the RSA presidents…

When the smoke dissipates, Madam Tauris appears under the archway. She leans against the wall, eying me through an ungodly number of fake lashes. Swirls of black hair blend with her robe. A red pendulum dangles from her bottom lip like a drop of blood. "Ah, Zenith Lin. Do you enjoy my boys?"

I nod. "They're lovely. Do they have names?"

"Not yet. They're brand new. Finished them this morning. Although I can see you'd like to keep them, they're not for sale." Swaying her hips to one side of the archway, she makes room for her creations to enter.

When I try to follow them, she places a hand on my chest. "Of course, we could make other arrangements." She hooks a meaty arm around my waist.

The woman reeks of stale witchcraft and misfired faith. I laugh and jerk away. "Tempting, Madam T. But that's not why I'm here."

"Of course." Bourgeoning lust is replaced by a childlike smile as she bows. "I apologize, Zenith Lin."

"Call me Zenith."

Flashing teeth, she retreats inside. I follow her under the archway, where the stream of vapor continues to tickle my nose. The floor is coated in blinking puddles of polished amethyst. Bright stalagmites jut from the ceiling and shed light on our path. It's like walking through a kaleidoscope.

When we reach the end of the hall, Tauris rests her pearly claws on a pair of brass doors. "Well Zenith, if you like my boys, then you'll love this." Arching her back, she pushes the doors open, revealing a room made entirely of glass—a transparent theater box.

Just outside this cubicle, a glittering, dripping dome holds a dozen astrobatic performers, lit by strings of lights and crackling torches. Bodies sheathed in ribbon and lace, dancers glide through no-gravity air like dandelion fuzz.

Noticing my suspended jaw, Tauris snickers and shuts the door behind us.

I close my mouth and take a seat in one of the arm chairs. The table between us is covered in decks of Tarot cards, with a hole in the middle. But none of that holds my attention, as I'm continually dragged to the sight across from us—the beautiful dancers, their slick skin, and frothy bodies.

"Aren't they enchanting?" Tauris sighs. "I made them myself."

My heart twitches. "They're like the boys? They look so…lively…"

A flippant wrist-flick frames her smirk. "Oh, they're almost as organic as you and me. Their stem cells came from some of my clients, whose pretty DNA spills on my sheets now and then." She giggles.

"They're your children?"

Her eyes meet mine through a veil of flyaway hair. "Oh, no. You misunderstand." Her chest rises and falls. "They're products of business, you see, not lovemaking. The organic matter comes from clients who are indebted to me, who owe more than they financially possess. So, they give me their vitality. But I owe them nothing, and so nothing comes from me. I can assure you—my life force remains untouched." She rubs her hands together.

"So, these aren't your children?"

She nods.

"Just…synthetic clones?"

"Ex nihilo."

I glance at the ballerinas and sigh. "Isn't that kind of cruel?"

"Full of questions, aren't you?"

"And you're full of surprises." It emits harsher than intended, rainbows streaked in bitter shade.

"It doesn't stop here," she promises. "You know I like to keep my clients…entertained." She taps the glass and the performance begins with a series of drumming and chanting. I can hardly focus on her face through the thrum of music and firelight. A half-naked woman swings in front of our box, toes pointed. Copper-colored hair runs in rivulets from her pale scalp.

Focus, I remind myself. *You're not here for the dancers.*

As she shuffles the first deck, I scan the room, searching for a compartment, drawer, or even a crack. *Nihilo.*

"First, there's the matter of who you are," Tauris begins, pulling a Tarot card and laying it on the table. A mechanical, skinless hand lurches from the hole to display the card. The Fool is depicted—a bright-eyed homeless man balancing a bloodied heart on his fishnet sleeve.

I can't help but laugh. "Looks about right."

"Who you have been," she continues, as a card tumbles from the pile. Another bone-and-muscle hand snatches the new card and holds it under the first one.

"Seven of segments," I read aloud, raising an eyebrow. The man on the card balances three jagged pieces of glass on each arm, and one on his head, in the middle of a circle of candles.

"Finally, who you will be." Her wrist flicks violently as she shuffles. When the last card is spit out, two tinny, robotic hands hold it in silver palms, as though presenting a gift.

"The Skyscraper," we speak in unison.

On the card, it's a beacon, protruding from a moon. People and creatures throw themselves out shattered windows, but some sprout wings and fly. In the background, meteors fall, igniting the top of the skyscraper in a halo of yellow flame.

Vertebrae cinch my lungs. I cross my legs and lean to one side of the armchair. "Does this mean I'm screwed?"

Tauris cackles. "No, it means you're ignorant. Despite your expansively curious nature, you lack perspective." As she presses her lips together, the droplet jewel catches my eye again. In the dim light, it looks like a bead of amber, simultaneously heavy and weightless.

When I lean forward, Tauris presses my hands into the table. Stray cards from other decks slip and fall.

Her voice crawls in my ears while her spidery fingers slide up and down my forearms. "You seem to be an ambitious fool, exploring simply for the sake of experience. You could still be carrying too much that isn't yours. Balance is skewed because of this. You're talented and sharp, but you continue to spend in excess. You lack authentic understanding of your position in the universe, and you vainly put all your hopes into wealth and possessions."

Laughter splits my tightened lips.

Her smile falls. "The universe isn't a possession—it's The Skyscraper." She plucks the card and it twinkles in a beam of bright purple. "Always under the influence of powerful forces, but since it made these forces, it is in fact the structure that chooses to fall. Order out of chaos."

I retract. "So, I'm…the universe?"

Nodding, she says, "The body is a skyscraper too—a tower for your soul. Constantly evolving under the laws of Nature. Once the smoke comes, and the flames reach too high, you must open a window and jump."

7

"You lost me." Out of the corner of my eye, a petite dancer balances himself by one hand on another man's chest. I lick my lips. "Am I the universe or am I a body?"

Her knotted fingers press into my cheek. "You are both."

"Not possible."

"Hm. You're so literal."

I shrug. "Capricorn sun."

She smiles and retracts her hand. "Ah, but cusping with Sagittarius. Don't even get me started on your Vedic and Andromedin charts."

Rubbing my neck, I look at the dancers again. They're in pairs, hooking elbows, holding black lights between their teeth. Or maybe the blacklights *are* their teeth.

Tongues of fabric swing, quiver, and project spiral silhouettes onto cave walls.

"Zenith." She says my name like it's a curse.

In a beam of black light, I can see leopard spot and dragon scale shapes staining the gem hanging from her lips. My heart dives into the depths of my guts, rolling like seas. *She's right—I am a fool.*

Clearing my throat, I drape my arms over the chair. "I'm sorry, Madam T. With all due respect. This isn't really working for me. May I have a different kind of reading?"

Her laughter stirs my nerves. "Always asking. Never receiving." She snatches my left hand, tracing ink-laden lines with the talon tip of her thumb nail. "Do you know how beautiful identity is?"

"What, my chart?" I snort. "Madam T, it's just a tattoo…everyone gets them when they turn eighteen…"

"Zenith," she chides, shaking her head. The blood opal swings and bounces against her chin. "You're still too literal. Identity is beautiful. Not just our natal charts"—she gestures to her own hand splashed in powder blue—"but the skin they're engraved in. The body and all its organs are vessels for the complex mind. Each cell is an intricate expression of the same self."

Exhaling, I try to lean back, but she snags my wrist. Her smile is sickening. "Humans are so easy to read."

"Well. Yeah." I snort. "We tattoo our bodies with the cosmic details of our birth."

Glitter lingers under her eyes, deepening bruise-colored bags. "We're all reflections of each other."

In a quick orange blaze, the torches go out. Tauris gasps and releases me. I squint and turn, searching for a stray light or pulsing music. When I find nothing but sizzling silence, I produce a blade of titanium kyanite. "Alright. This is some warped fuckery. T, I'm gonna have to ask you to—"

From beyond the glass, a shard of white light wrenches my irises and send me reeling. Tauris shrieks. The floor rumbles and a loud crack punctures the air. Cards scatter like feathers, flickering into flame as gas caresses the room.

Ears numb to everything but a ramming heart, I throw on my hood, fumble with the kyanite, and blink hard. When I enclose the metallic blue rock in my tattooed palm, it lights up, as it's programmed to. In a shroud of blue and orange firelight, Tauris falls to her knees, gawking at the spliced glass wall.

Elsewhere in her sacred space, explosions continue to storm.

Out of time to be sneaky, I fling myself toward her, aching to claim my only reason for being here—the blood opal, the last treasure I'll ever need to steal.

But from outside our prism, a choir of screams erupts.

I look up as towering wet rocks ignite and explode. A new performance has begun. Eyes widening, I yank Tauris by the arm and drag her to the door. I press her tattooed palm to the master-pad. As the door opens, a thundering gust of explosive gas shoves us into the hallway, haloing us in broken glass.

"Shit!" I duck behind a glob of quartz points protruding from the wall. In the same instant, a large piece of glass shoots through Tauris' skull. Her body hits the floor like a boulder. Rouge blood litters the amethyst floor.

"Shitshitshit."

When I roll her over, a red puddle settles between her petrified cat-eyes. From the blossoming wound, blood drags down the middle of her face like war paint, settling in the space between elliptic lips.

Somehow, the opal remains untouched. I thank my holy stars, pull the chain taut, cut it with the kyanite's sharp edge, and stow the gem in my pocket.

"Sorry, Madam T," I murmur, and book it for the archway. Crystals crumble and flake into the air, as if gravity has stopped. All I can think about while squeezing through the shrinking archway, swirling incense, and falling crystal shards, is Syzygy.

My stomach seizes. I barely feel my feet touch the ground. The sopping air stings my throat and lungs. The kyanite's light is stifled by clouds of dusty gas. I yell to make sure there's not a wall in front of me. Legs and arms pumping, I ignore the continuous blasts from behind me and focus on moving forward. Under the false sky, my sense of navigation is slowly restored.

Something hot and sticky leaks into my soles as I run through puddles. *Cleansing,* they'd called it. The whole underlayer stinks of artificial fire, chemical warfare.

I imagine a shady robot opening its tubular mouth and spewing the place with kerosene, or an even more powerful and dangerous fluid. Dozens of dizzying conspiracies clink against my skull.

"G," I pant, shaking out dark thoughts.

She stands out like a biofluorescent stone in the darkness, silver panels reflecting the kyanite's blue light and my psychedelic shoes.

White spots splatter my vision and my knees tremble, but I make it up the stairs like a rock in space—no resistance.

At the door, I hover a sweaty palm over the pad. She opens with a soft pop of air, interior lights swelling in silent welcome.

It isn't until after the door seals behind me that I feel my bare toes clenching the cool floor, shoes half-melted by a chemical reaction.

Two

After we leave Mars' atmosphere, I set coordinates for Earth and check the cameras. At this distance, the planet is a harmless sunstone sphere suspended in black powder.

A sour rock of doubt pulls me from the screens. I turn autopilot on and lean back, thumping my bare heels to the engine's warm, strumming pulse. The louder it gets, the faster we go, and the deeper I breathe.

Rotating from the controls, I dig elbows into knees and rub my face. Soiled skin and scruff move like plaster under my clammy hands. Tauris' lifeless, scarlet-striped face flashes in my mind's eye—perpetually gasping.

Inhaling through tight teeth, I dig into my pocket. The lima bean-sized blood opal sizzles with warmth. I pull it out to inspect it, but the special spots are hidden in regular lighting. Now, it looks like a common drop of amber—stiff and depthless—or some knock-off garnet-ruby hybrid. But the longer I stare, the more the fleshy marbled surface makes the veins in my palm look like watercolor, tattoo streaks of acrylic. My body feels false and grotesque. Scarlet waves roll over thoughts, washing my mind in sudsy blood.

Syzygy's beeping ruins the trance. "Incoming signal from City Isle, New York, RSA, Earth."

"Forgive me for resting," I mutter, then clear my throat so Syzygy hears me. "Accept." With a free hand, I don the S-Com, tendons still twitching from strain.

Senses projected through a cloud of metal-laced marijuana, I cough. The room cools and stiffens like oil paint. From the ceiling, little

11

chandeliers glint. A man in a blue velvet pantsuit sits on the edge of his chair, balancing a bong between his knees.

"Pleiades, Jaal." I shake my head. "You know I hate that smell."

Jaal flourishes a hand, flashing obsidian cuffs. "Did you get my messages?" His usually bronze eyes are electric green.

"Messages?"

He snorts. "Must've signaled you a dozen times."

"I was busy."

He flashes bleached teeth. "Busy succeeding, hopefully."

I nod and hold out the gem. It wobbles, frightened to be displayed.

Releasing air through puffed cheeks, he frowns. "Thought it would be bigger."

"It's still worth a lot, though…right?"

"More than you know." He narrows his eyes and taps his temple.

"Good," I sigh. *Worth enough to let me quit this job.*

"Very." His irises shift from green to honey-yellow.

"Are you wearing S-Contacts?" I pocket the gem again.

"Newest edition. Zoom and all. Can get right up in your face. Pretty spiffy." He twirls the bong between his palms and leans back. "Not as spiffy as that opal, though. Deimos. Can't wait to get my hands on it." A gnarled eyebrow raises. "How'd you snag it? Thought Tauris kept it on a pussy ring."

I clear my throat. "I didn't have sex with her, if that's what you're asking."

"Nobody does it for you like me, huh?"

I grip the chair arms—the only sensation keeping me grounded in the ship. After a careful breath, I say, "She's dead. Her cronies are too, I think. The place went up in blasts, and not the festive kind." Biting my lip, I lean forward. "Did you…I mean…the explosions weren't yours, right?"

With sun-colored eyes and blonde dreads, he looks like a lion when he grins. "Zen. You're a smart boy, aren't ya? You know I don't do business the clean way."

I launch out of the chair. "You could've killed me!" My body goes rigid with rage, popping a double-jointed shoulder. "And your little chemistry project wrecked my shoes!"

Shrugging, he clicks his tongue. "Plastic sacrifice. You can make new ones. Not my fault they have to soak their planet in flammable chemicals to keep it fresh." A manic grin. "But Zen. C'mon. I'd never

12

kill you. Not when you got the finest ass and quickest hands in the Milky." He takes a long hit and sends the smoke rolling off his pierced tongue. "Not to mention—you got my blood opal."

I want to scream, *it's not yours*—frighten the lion—inject vaporized fear into the bong, so his lungs collapse, send every vein and artery into shellshock, and suffocate his heart. But as usual, his oil-slick voice wriggles inside, and my organs fail instead.

Wiping gems of sweat, I sigh. "Is this why you called? To check on precious cargo?"

"Everything's under control. I just like to see your face."

"You killed a lot of people, Jaal."

He wags a white-inked finger. "Decommissioned a lot of *copies*, Zen. Huge difference. Anyway, Tauris left me no choice. I was nice to her, and she fucked me over, big time. But this blood opal...it's what we need. We'll do better with it than she ever would've." Smoke circles his head like a crown. He bites the bong's glass mouthpiece.

"Whatever." I dig thumbnails into my biceps. "You're gonna pay me in full, right?"

"Of course. The closer you get, the more moon-cheese trickles in your trove. When you get to San Fran, the transaction'll be complete. Don't even sweat it."

An invisible claw clamps my throat. "San Fran Isle?"

"Yeah." He sighs. "Changed the HQ. If you checked your messages, you'd know. By the time you get to Earth, we'll be partying in the Pacific."

"Oh."

"Problem?"

"Nope." I snatch the kyanite blade and spin it between my fingers. "See you then." I touch the S-Com, but he holds up a hand.

"One more thing, baby." His voice rakes my inner ear. "Know you think this is just formal business and shit, but it's more than that. Got a big surprise for you. You're gonna love it." I flinch, feeling his beaded tongue run across my earlobe.

"Thanks." My voice shrivels and scatters like dead leaves.

I remove the goggles and cast them onto the controls. Stars strobe and wink through the cameras, as if they want my body too—more than I do.

"Shit." I feel like a spirit changing hosts, hanging my head off the back of the chair and listening to the drag and flow of breathing.

The kyanite blade buzzes in my hands, begging me to use it. If not on Jaal, then on myself. It's an old hope, that cutting my body open

13

cuts the ties we've shared. It's old and unhealthy. I know that. Still, it plagues me.

Better safe than sorry, I stow the knife in the weapons compartment and shut it, then dig my fingers into the oily roots of my hair.

A muffled ache stretches from the back of my neck to my forehead. Instead of Tauris, Jaal rises and hurls like a flood, leaking through brain tissue, soaking scalp, and ruining braids.

The last time I saw him in person was an Earthen year ago, just after we broke up. S-Coms make it easy for him to get to me, to make deals and ruin my mental health, but nothing is as bad as being with him in person.

My heart rams into bones until it's exhausted, pulse flushing out the nervous system, squeezing memories that ooze on rain-soaked thought-webs. Maybe it would feel nicer to be drooled over—begged for—if I was one of Tauris' half-baked clones, a real object.

I struggle to lift the veil of his breath—the last echo of his presence in my space. It reeks of steely weed, toffee, and tar.

Gotta get what's mine, he used to tell me. *Mine.*

I rise, tilting on an axis of vertigo. "Syzygy, change coordinates." Hands rest on my expanding belly, the ebb and flow. "San Fran Isle." On the exhale, shoulders roll and fingers wiggle, stirring sensation back into limbs. My limbs.

I own myself. No one else. I am myself.

"Next destination: San Fran Isle, RSA, Earth." Even G sounds disappointed in me, for giving into the promise of hard, coded cash. "Travel time: about 72 hours on supraspeed. I recommend getting comfortable, Captains."

My next breath unravels in a cough. Every ounce of Jaal or Tauris is sucked down a black hole. "What did you say?"

Silence etches the air.

"Syzygy. Repeat."

A light whirring, like spinning fan blades.

"G," I sing, thumbing the wall. "Don't be glitchy. Talk to me."

It's betrayal—my dearest friend and companion ghosting me while I'm on the edge of another breakdown.

I consider the possibility of an actual glitch, but can't shake the suspicion that she's doing it on purpose.

I walk along the walls, fingers brushing screens, buttons, and knobs—hoping to soothe her into speaking. But nothing comes of it. Now I know she's ignoring me, because the engine's ethereal sound stretches up and down in a wave. She's pulling herself together, composing a new song of nuclear fusion and fission, atomic bursts energizing, but it's not just for me.

"G, babe? If you answer me, I'll get you a special cleaning." I press my palms together, pleading. "I mean, real special. Finest you've ever had."

Whatever frantic, fragmented train of thought I have left is flattened by a singular, sweaty sensation. Something falls from above, splays softly like frayed rope, and glides across my forehead, swiping my frizz.

I look up.

From the pentagram-shaped arrangement of metal beams, a woman hangs upside down. Her milky skin divvies shadows like moonlight.

"Sweet Pleiades!" I reach behind me, open the weapons compartment, and scramble for an electro-handgun.

The start of an avalanche, she flips and lands on the floor, long red braids swinging to her hips. In the dark, her eyes were magnet-black, but now they're glossy garnet.

Steadying my arm, I aim the gun at her head. "How the hell." A breath to sanctify. "Did you get in here?"

She adjusts the waist of her white leggings and grins. "Easily."

I cock the gun. "You're one of Tauris' toys, aren't you?"

Her smile slips. "She used me, but I was never hers." She tilts her head. "From the looks of it, that's something you and I have in common."

"Trying to get on my good side?"

Sighing, she rolls her pretty eyes. "I'm trying to make friends," she says, holding out a hand. "My name's—"

"I don't have time for introductions with clones."

"You had plenty of time for them when they were hanging in front of you like Christmas ornaments." Her eyes harden and soften in a span of seconds. After wiping her steaming forehead, she lifts a white lace sleeve and flashes her forearm. In gold ink, the natal chart barely diverges from the rest of her freckled skin, but it's an authentic stain of proof that she's unique—nobody's copy.

"You're human?"

She nods. "As much as you are."

When she covers her tattoo again, I gaze at the elaborate copper plaits that tumble from her head.

15

"That doesn't explain how you entered my ship undetected. Or why you're here in the first place. You looking to steal or something?" I hyperfocus on the blood opal held snugly against my thigh. It burns like a drop of acid.

"I need a ride." She twists the end of a braid around her wrist. "Your ship's pretty old, just waiting to be broken into, and the bombs gave me plenty of time to penetrate the system." Her muddy eyes search mine as she steps closer, slender nose aligned with the barrel.

"So, you're a techie."

Her eyes wander to the ceiling. "Kind of."

"If you've done any permanent damage to Syzygy, I'll kill you."

She laughs and shakes her head. "I haven't damaged anything."

"You broke into my ship," I seethe. "How can I trust you?"

"Well, for starters, you can lower the gun."

"No."

"But you're going to."

"How do you know?"

"Because I know you more than you know yourself." She shrugs again, as if it's casual, common knowledge. Then, she does the unthinkable—she sits in the captain's chair, bending her knees lotus-style. When I try to protest, she swivels to face the screens and spreads her arms.

"Look at it. Doesn't it feel too big for you, a dress that doesn't fit?" She glances at me, corners of her mouth twitching. "Maybe the galaxy's made for two."

I press the gun to her temple. "Don't fuck with words. I've tangoed with enough tongues today."

She unlaces her legs, bare toes brushing the floor. "I know. I'm sorry. You live in dirt long enough, you start to speak like the snakes." When she looks at me, her eyes glisten. Not with fearful tears, but globs of sticky regret. "I shouldn't have spoken to you like that. What kind of guest am I?"

I snort. "The not-invited kind."

She leans into the gun, sniffling. "Can we please start over?"

Despite the cranking gears in my brain, I lower the gun, arm screaming. "Fine. But if this is some wicker-basket-witchery, I swear to Pan…"

"I'm Reiki." Her lips bloom and she offers a hand again.

"Zenith." I extend my hand, which quickly turns into a pointed finger. "Listen. When I land, you're off. I'll help you find a place to stay or whatever, but after that…" I shove my thumb behind me.

Her head bobs. When our palms touch, a throng of energy ricochets between us. Hair raises on the nape of my neck like little white flags. Chewing the inside of my cheek, I pull back, but her smile is wide. "Thanks, Zenith." She wipes her eyes. "It's just that I'm…headed back to Earth and I…just want to be safe and free, y'know?"

I tuck the gun back in its compartment and rub my other hand. "You can't have both. That's not how life works."

She opens her mouth, but before she can say anything, the ship jolts and sends her flying off the chair. I snatch her wrist and peer at the screens. Space glitters like bejeweled fabric, but no debris.

"What did you do to my ship?"

"Nothing," she insists, trying to pull away. "It was probably the bombs. Shrapnel or something."

"That's impossible."

She laughs nervously. "Your boyfriend practically blew up the planet's core. What did you think would happen? Ol' Syzygy would leave unscathed?"

My grip tightens. "He's not my—"

Syzygy's engine wails under us, structure wobbling, briefly gelatinous.

"Shit." I release Reiki. "Stay here." I roll up my sleeves and head for the center of the room, to a transparent trapdoor. When I stand on the pad next to it, it lights up and opens.

While I descend into my ship's smoking center, I realize I'm backing myself into a corner—or rather, the basement of my own home. Reiki tricked me into lowering my gun with nothing but glossy doe-eyes and static electricity. If she wants to, she could flay me alive down here, with a mere click and twist of the controls. If she gets past the ID pads. Again.

Vertigo hits me when I step off the ladder. I grip the poles to steady myself, sucking in hot air and letting it turn to mist at the tip of my tongue. Despite everything, I smile at how intimate it is down here, in a round mechanical belly that smells like singed licorice.

The room is almost a replica of the one above, but half the size, lit only by the engine—a miniature star, caged by nuke-proof metal and stellaglass, rotating in the middle of the floor. Not only does this mechanism power the ship—when I ask politely, she thrusts—but it also literally pulls every piece together. Hot, gravitational, cosmic glue. An array of external vacuums collects interstellar fruits to feed the human-made star and maintain its cushy life. (And mine.)

But something's off. Impatiently, the ball of light and gas hisses.

17

I throw on a pair of work goggles and approach it the way I approach all hearts—with as much protection as possible.

Hands gloved, hood up, I explore what I can. All seems to be well, except for the fact that nothing's obtained from outside. Nothing's recycled. The star-engine is stifled, starved, lacking in proper nutrients to blaze. It coughs when it spins, instead of whirring, sickened. This should disappoint me, but instead it sends vertigo spinning for the hills and puts my mind on the forefront, in high gear.

"Don't worry, G." A doctor about to operate on his lover. "This won't hurt a bit."

More than anyone though, I feel like my Mama—the way she was when I was very young. All soiled hands and salty teeth. This hood is her headscarf, protecting milky skin, bearing a slate of black hair and a cornucopia of determination. Behind these goggles, my eyes are hers—heavy-lidded, turning violet under infantile sunlight. Her bangled wrists flex in mine. Even her coffee-coated throat sits behind my Adam's apple, dark and grainy.

No force can stop you here, Zen. Out here, you're free.

I rub my hands together and lean forward, fiddling with wires and tubes, pressing my forehead against a strip of warm metal. A puff of cool air spoons my curled spine, interrupting the heated high, the deep and gritty mechanical focus.

"I can help." Reiki's voice clinks like crystals.

"I told you to stay put," I say, glaring over my shoulder. "You've done enough."

It doesn't surprise me when she disobeys a second time, tracing fingers over the star's dusty capsule, but it shocks me like lightning when she kisses the same panel I rested my head on. Her lips linger, as if pulled by gravity. Then she reaches for my face.

I swat, eyebrows converging. "What the hell are you doing?"

She points to my forehead. "Your third-eye's filthy."

I wipe my face with the back of a glove. Despite her ice-tipped words and hands, she overboils me, splattering my focus in rivulets of steam. My bottom lip retreats under teeth.

She giggles, then covers her mouth. "Sorry, sorry." She pats my shoulder and circles the engine like a satellite.

I sit on the floor, arms crossed. "There's not much you can do. I think the external vacuum's warped."

"You'd think so." Leaving smudged handprints all over the metal, she continues to smile. "It's hotter than a supernova in here."

"Hm, I wonder why." I take off the gloves and fiddle with the wedge of curiosity she's stuck in my skull. "What are you gonna do, a techie thing?"

"Mmm. More like an energy thing."

I've never seen anyone touch my ship so lovingly, not even myself. At first, I think she's being condescending, mocking me. But it isn't meanspirited. It's like she couldn't care less about what I'm doing. She has a strange, meditative posture. She breathes, strokes, and listens. Without speaking, she seems to know Syzygy more than I do. Ship whisperer.

"I was raised in conditions like these," she explains, almost reading my mind. "I know what it feels like."

"To be trapped?"

She gestures to the small flares and heatwaves coiling into stellaglass. "To burn constantly, without resolve." In a clump of dust, she carves symbols, ancient Kenji Japanese.

I can't help but laugh. "What's that? It looks like something my moms would've had on their spirit altars."

She blows on the symbols, letting pieces of dust crumple and puff. "Your moms are smart, then."

"If you think that's gonna help—"

"Shhh." Her arms raise in a cruciform pose and she shuts her eyes. Another cool breeze saturates the room.

Evidently, with knees tucked to my chest, I'm completely unprepared. The breeze intensifies, shoving off the hood and sending me onto my back. Vertebrae rolls with a crunch against hard floor.

My first instinct is to reach for a gun, but when I remember it's upstairs, I sit up with a grunt. I feel for the gem in my pocket, feeling a sick kind of relief when it stings. If this is how I die, I at least want to remember the dicey success of my final job.

But even as I brace myself for another blow, all is calm. The room that burned so harshly it almost cracked open like an egg is pleasantly lukewarm now. Syzygy's heartbeat isn't sputtering—it's thriving. Somehow, the engine's powerful focus is restored.

Reiki did little more than a fancy dance to replenish the engine's nutrients, and all my brainpower could accomplish was to scramble for a gun.

She flashes a smug, pearlescent grin. "How's that for wicker-basket-witchery?"

Three

Without another word to Reiki, I retreat to my bedroom. The door locks automatically, just as Syzygy announces: "More air traffic than usual. Meteor showers expected, but they don't stand a chance against my stabilizers."

Despite my gratitude, I ignore her and burrow into blankets, fully aware of dirty denim scratching cotton. Every skin cell protests for a shower, or at least a change of clothes, but all my mind wants to do is smother itself to sleep.

Unsurprisingly, I find it difficult to relax when a redheaded space-siren haunts my ship. I imagine her stroking G's walls and whispering Japanese folklore into the metal. Invisible magnets pinch my stomach, shooting pain through organs, to the skin of my back, where there's probably a significant palette of dirt. My limbs sprawl and anchor like roots. I can't move, but I can't rest either.

Instead, I shake my head and make a noise between singing and groaning into a pillow. My throat throbs like I've been choked, and I try to pretend I really am suffocating, to stop the flow of oxygen to my brain and shut off its power system. It doesn't work like that though, because the brain's part of the body, and the body's programmed to keep itself irrevocably conscious. To my continual dismay, I'm not a cyborg.

Heaving a sigh, I roll over and examine my soiled hands. Broad, sweeping palms—the whitest parts of me—glimmer with sweat. Cerulean veins and tendons tighten when I flex. My left hand is its own masterpiece—a crooked pinky, unusual calluses from clasping a paintbrush or plucking sitar strings, and of course the natal tattoo.

In fluorescent light, it looks like harmless pen ink, as if I got bored one day and scrawled angles and aspects myself. Eyes slide over each shape and symbol, settling on the sun in the center. I haven't analyzed it like this since receiving it for my eighteenth birthday, but Tauris' words are nailed into me. I can't shake them, the same way I can't shake off Jaal's greedy, corkscrew hands or Reiki's copper braids. No space is safe. It's all plagued by a carousel of intruders. To prevent a dizzy spell, I use the tattoo as a point of reference.

At first, circles and dashes form a hatch-marked tree trunk—a scroll of ancient, patterned guts, a neatly measured life-line. But then it throbs and pulses like an array of visible signals, or a hypnotist's spiraling clock, singeing photoreceptors and sending me outside of myself. Contrary to my intentions, the more I stare, the further I drift.

Eyelashes are pulled like shades, but it isn't quite sleep that greets me. It's a fluid, meditative back-and-forth, in which consciousness spills and refills itself. Somewhere in this in-between, I find harmony. It reminds me of tuning the sitar during a meteor shower, with nothing but my own voice. Only, my voice is gone. Replaced by wandering urges and fading feelings.

Drifting, sinking, floating. Fragmented, whole. Suspended by strings of starry abyss. A wet throat constricts. I'm the center of a crushed velvet mandala, or satin spiderweb. Disconnected and intertwined. Fingers gripping fibers. Saturated with free will, but unable to move.

Ahead, a spark spirals like starworks. Raw beauty at its best, in its origin. Must chase. Must find. Seek that heavenly body. Aim for it like a diver, bending and twisting to kiss the unkissable. Untouchable. Unthinkable.

I tilt like a planet, waiting, spilling, fading. Inside and out of this tricky, atomic regime. Hold for a second, a mouthful of light. Careful. Brace. Release.

But the spark has a face; it's a star. Crushed carbon nose. Stirling lips. Must seek. Must chase. For I have lost.

Finally forward, blurry beams propelling. Cosmic stilts for dysfunctional roots, wandering vines. Hacked at birth with ink-swept blades, inches apart. Itch the scar. Follow that star.

I want to scream the name I don't remember. The face I forgot. But the more I heave to speak, the less I receive.

Come to me. Please.

Ebb and flux. Reach and release.

So close. Energetic edging. A little piece of death. Helium balloons swell behind ribs. Fill, diffuse, give in, rest.

The star has wings! Prismatic shades laced in vertebrae.

Rivulets run—tongues of rain slipping down a panel of glass between us. Cosmic condensation teases me. Fractals steady themselves on blood-smothered hair. Violet, brown, black braids. Translucent bronze flesh. Eyes like silver mines. Mine.

21

The star is me.

I wake with a shuttering gasp, soaked to the veins in sweat. Vertigo greets me first, snagging the side of my head and rotating the room clockwise. Lips part, fashioning a bubble of spit. I feel like a teen again, brooding in puddles of saliva.

Reiki ushers me back into consciousness, rubbing my shoulders and helping me sit up. At first, I receive her aid with the same elation I felt in my subconscious, but then cranial bolts readjust. Something clicks, snaps. In a sweaty, bloodshot haze, I shove her off the bed and pin her to the tilting wall.

"Whoa, Zenith, chill." She raises her hands in surrender, knuckles hitting metal.

"How…why are you in my room?"

Her laughter is breathy and weak. "I just wanted to help. You seemed…sick."

"I'm fine." My forearm presses into her clavicle like the blunted side of a blade. "You can only get in here with a password. This is the third time you've broken into my ship."

"I didn't do anything. The door opened for me."

I look at the open doorway, then glare upward, as if bashful lashes are flitting in the ceiling lights. "Syzygy. Report."

Silence.

Reiki flinches when I turn back to her, and for a moment I consider letting her go.

Instead, my grip tightens. "Did you ruin the vocal system when you fixed the engine?"

Wetting her lips, she says, "Healing requires extended periods of repose."

I slam my knee into her thigh, but she doesn't react. "This is a ship. Not a person."

Her eyes dance. "Says the person who flirts with her."

I bite my lip hard. There isn't a hint of terror in her. Her chin juts defiantly and her hands are steady. When I sigh, warmth radiates past my ribcage, mimicking the echo of a dream-feeling.

"I flirt with everyone," I mumble, releasing her. "And everything." I want to throw up, purge the warmth out of me.

"You haven't flirted with me," she says, hands on her hips.

"Oh, give it time," I deadpan. "I'll be all over you in a few hours."

A weight wrangles my body, sending energy plummeting. I sit on the bed and rub my eyes. "Now if you'll excuse me, I need to take a real n—no way…what the fresh hell?"

Her entire body is outlined in rose gold. It flickers when I blink, like a broken screen. But it's there. Clear as solar flares.

"Holy Borealis. It's official. I'm losing it." I stand, but she grips my wrist. The color surrounds her like a full-body halo, stinging my eyes.

"You're not losing it," she promises, trying to ease me back on the bed. Throwing side-eye to no one, she giggles. "Well, actually, you're finding it…"

"Did you mess with my head too? Is that why the star came to me?"

Apparently, I'm moving a lot, because she grunts, trying to hold me in place. "Listen, Galileo. That's not how energy work…works."

"Oh, and I'm guessing you're the expert?"

"Well—"

"I thought you were a techie."

"Well, no."

Something clicks. "Oh, fuck me…you're a Conduit, aren't you? An energy healer?"

"For the love of Sun, yes. Now just…lie down, okay?" She guides me back, where I rest on a hill of pillows.

The mattress sighs when she lies next to me on her stomach, palms pressed in prayer.

I eye her suspiciously, but the room spins again, circling me back toward sleep. I want to fidget or roll away, but vertigo threatens to sever the head from my body, and the heat in my chest anchors me to the sheets.

Her mouth is next to my ear, breath splashing my neck. "I know you don't trust me, and that's fine, but will you at least give me the benefit of the doubt for a few minutes? Just breathe, and this time, I promise you won't regret it."

Opening my eyes as wide as I can, I try to focus on her face through a shield of light. "Fine. Heal me with your witchery."

The light intensifies, forcing my eyelids shut. Behind them, phantasmal faces splay in a color wheel—Mama, Mother, Jaal, Tauris, and a few others—each a different shade of pain.

At first, the faces sharpen, slicing my mind.

A used, banana-colored condom hangs from Jaal's crooked smile. His eyes constantly change color, and I find myself guessing which hue comes next.

23

Tauris grins with sharpened teeth, perpetually bleeding between the eyes. Her hair moves like a black sea until it spills over, and a stream of playing cards exits her temples. Coins are pushed through her teeth like a casino game.

With one blink, Mama bursts into flames, starting with the prayer shawl and ending with an ashy roll of blueprints. Next to her, Mother's face smolders and crumbles. Both faces strain, eyes like blackened almonds, until they become gusts of powder and glass beads—tricks in a Sufi-Buddhist magic show. Homemade jewelry clinks into abyss with fallen silverware and smashed dishes.

I grip my stomach, suddenly feeling like I'm on a waterbed.

But when Reiki touches my head with an icy palm, the visual shifts, and nausea dissolves. Everything's replaced by the sole sensation of unnaturally cold fingertips resting in the exposed scalp between braids. Amid flat darkness, snowflakes spray.

In the lucid leftovers of my consciousness, I feel her hands move to my throat and chest, where warmth scatters. From there, energy massages blood and muscle like hot stones, glossy and steaming with lemon water and lavender. The rocks soften into bubbles, tumbling up and down, back and forth. Breathing fades into the background.

At my naval, the inner vision is restored and bodily sensations morph into memory—*an old skyscape quilt, the scent of ginger, fidgeting limbs. Mama places a cold compress on my feverish forehead.*

"Sweet lamb," her voice pours over me, out of memory. "I love you lightyears."

My jaw crackles when it relaxes. I want to respond, but downy knuckles brush my mouth.

"I'm going on a trip," she says. "I need you to get better soon and help Mother while I'm gone, okay?"

I whimper. I couldn't speak through a swollen ten-year-old throat, and I can't speak now.

"Zenith Lutfi, never fret." A piece of lemon-yellow silk tickles my nose as she leans over me. "My colleagues and I are visiting the Venusian Quadrant for a few months. There'll be rainbow meteors. I'm going to Sens-cap the whole thing for you and Mother." Her breath smells like coffee and every type of oil I know.

In the memory, I nod and fall back asleep.

But in real time, sobs simmer from my chest in waves. As the memory evaporates, I realize Reiki's hands aren't cold anymore—they feel like freshly used oven mitts on my bare feet.

I try to wiggle, but she digs into my joints, holding my feet in place. Coolness blurs into heat. Although I want to focus on one feeling, I can't. I'm a boiling puddle in a tornado. Ignited globs of cottonwood. A real fucking mess.

Sniffling, I stare at the ceiling. I can't remember the last time I cried this hard. A gray wisp leaves my mouth when I exhale, rubbing the ceiling like a tendril of sage smoke. Every shape is hued with smudged color.

"Thank you." Reiki's voice sounds granular, like brown sugar in a wooden bowl. My words...channeled through her throat.

I wipe my eyes. She's still dressed in a midsummer sunset, but as she finishes praying, her skin soaks the glow like a sponge, and it becomes a subtle, almost cosmetic part of her.

Her gaze connects with mine. "Wanna talk abo—"

"No." I sit up, scratching my scalp. Shakily, I inhale and wipe my face on my sleeves. "You look like LSD and DMT had a baby." I laugh because there's nothing else left to project.

Her mouth spreads. "A side-effect of opening your higher senses."

An eyebrow twitches. "I thought the HolRevolt began by claiming there are no side-effects of energy work."

I expect a philosophical quip, but she punches my arm instead.

"Ow! Since when did you get so tough?"

She smirks and stands. "You haven't known me long."

"Okay, but your fist feels like a rock, and minutes ago you were healing me..." I rub my arm and stand, relieved by the lack of vertigo.

She leans against the wall, smoothing her fraying braids. "My aura. That's what you're seeing."

"What?" Brows tighten. "No one's been able to see auras for centuries. And it's...not like the books say. Not just color. Yours has shape, form, texture. Like you're made of it. Or it's made of you."

She clears her throat. "Contrary to popular belief, the ability to see auras doesn't come and go, but it does change form. You may not always see, but you can always feel. Haven't you ever caught a vibe?"

I laugh and shrug off the chill of her words. "No, but I've caught lots of other things."

She rolls her eyes, lips tightening to resist a smile. "I'm sure your occupation is riddled with vibrational warnings, but until now, you may have ignored them."

"I'll have you know, my senses are stellar, and I'm a great judge of character." A hard grin accompanies the bullshit.

"Oh, right. That's why you work with mad scientists like Jaal Nadir."

Her words splinter the conversation. A wave crashes the back of my skull, melting in the space between brain and eyeballs. I hang my head.

An azure light bursts and spreads from my palms like a steady stream of flame. "Pleiades!" The visual is enough to distract me and block the incoming white caps. "What the hell did you do to me?"

All warm amusement, Reiki pats my wrist. Liquid rose quartz encircles vaporized lapis. "Relax. I enhanced your energetic flow, the same way I did with Syzygy's engine."

"So, you *did* mess with my head!"

"Actually, I cleared it." Her smile unravels. "Eventually, you should be able to see everything and everyone as they are, including yourself."

Forehead still crinkled, I stare at the heated color that curls from my fingers like aluminum shavings—a second, constantly changing skin. "Is this what they taught you in Conduit College?"

"Please, Zenith. *Life* is my school." She reaches to pat my wrist again, then retracts, lacing fingers in her lap. "You should know…to see your own aura is to witness perpetual self-healing." Her smile swells. "Congratulations."

I roll my wrists. "It's amazing, but…" I sigh and tug my braids out of their bun. A nagging ache erupts as the rutted ropes of hair fall to one side. "It doesn't feel like healing."

"What does it feel like?"

Next to the bed, my sitar rests. It's the only thing in the room other than blankets that makes it feel like home. Without touching it, I can hear the strings vibrate, feel strumming graze my ears with metal-laced tongues.

I shudder and mask it with laughter. "Honestly, it feels like someone else is inside me, and not in the sexy way."

An extra flicker of rouge light shoots up from her chest and settles in her face. "Oh. Well. That's. Probably the trauma—"

"Nope." I want to laugh again, but it's gone. I'm an empty cup, and she's tipped me too many times. "I'm fine."

"Okay, but the first step of healing is recognizing—"

"You're not my therapist."

She looks as though I've hit her. "No, but I *am* trying to help you."

"Why? You just met me. You're probably looking for dirt to dig up, finishing what Tauris started." I throw the words like knives, or bits of a broken mirror. *Deflect, deflect.*

26

Gloss coats her eyes and she looks down. From this angle, her copper braids are a pair of ram horns, threaded in thick ridges on either side of her head. Rose quartz light darkens, as though bruised or cracked.

She clears her throat. "You remind me of myself." Then she looks up again. "Play me something."

I tilt my head. "What?"

She raises her freckled chin toward the sitar. Her eyes still glitter like prisms, but her smile perseveres. "Play me a song. I know you want to. Music's the fabric of your being."

I cross my arms and snort. "You're either very intuitive, or very nosy."

"Please?"

Rubbing the back of my neck, I say, "Alright, but only because you're my stalker—I mean, biggest fan." Soft laughter returns as I crawl on the bed and reach for the instrument's onyx neck. The veiny bundle of strings feels foreign in the blue aura, almost stinging my new skin.

With the body cradled in my lap, and a brass wire around my index finger, I pluck a few strings and mess with the moon-shaped tuning pegs. Wood and metal create a blend of warm and cool, yin-yang manifested. In the back of my mind, an om chant begins.

For a third time, spiritual experience ensues, but this time it's on my terms. An invisible layer of energy cocoons me in silk, lavender, and sesame oil. Without the hum of technology or nagging words, I submerge into the safe place I forgot about—song.

The thrum of metal keeps my spine straight, but muscles relaxed. Balance restores itself between plucks. It's been a while since I've released the performer in me, who sings through the hands, plays with glossy entrails, the deep and long tunnels of the heart and its supplemental organs. I'm an instrument for instruments, a singular orchestra.

When I look up, Reiki's eyes are bulging, glowing like sunlit drops of maple syrup.

The echoing, gritty sound is punctured by my grumbling stomach.

Dripping giggles and sunshine, she pokes my belly. "Sounds like healing to me."

Four

Hours of sleep induce meta-jetlag—red, swollen eyes and sluggish dissociation—which Reiki says is "totally normal for this sort of thing." I can hardly stand it. Having her around mimics the irrationality of constantly slapping myself in the face and then apologizing profusely and kissing my hands.

I plop into the captain's chair and rip open a bag of dehydrated mangoes with my teeth. With each soapy sweet wedge, I become more grounded. Taste dominates my developing sixth sense.

Reiki sits on the floor beside me, posture impeccable. "An old-fashioned astronaut's diet, huh? When was the last time you had a home-cooked meal?"

"No more personal questions."

I wait for a scowl, but her laughter continues to bash my expectations. Her teeth shine like the insides of seashells.

On the wall of screens that surrounds us, space looks close enough to touch. We're almost home, if the tree-ring-pattern of light is any indication. Soon, the blue ball will rise into view, a cosmic skyline.

I turn on all the screens, so that the room is only lit by starlight peeking through tangled irises, eyeing us as we scoot by.

Stuck to the screens, I toss Reiki the bag of mangoes and dig into some trail mix. Reiki's energy work changed not only my external sensations, but how I perceive myself internally. Mere hours ago, I wanted to shed this body and project my consciousness into the stars, hide in the folds of oblivion.

Now, I'm almost fully comfortable carrying these clothing-hanger-bones back to Earth—the planet I grew up on, where I used to feel this good. My mood helps me remember. I'm the incarnate action of cooking dinner with Mother, chatting about Mama's many adventures over a steaming pot of rice, painting recycled canvases on the porch, having picnics with friends on the beach, and scrawling anonymous poetry into walls with laser-blades.

Even as I sit in the captain's chair, pretending to sulk, my mouth begs to be stretched, arms craving to pump a fist in the air. It feels like success, but it's not.

You're not done with the job. Finish, get out of this contract, and then you can celebrate. I throw back the words like shots of sake.

"Do you have a bathroom?" Reiki asks.

I peer at her through my water bottle. "No, we piss on dark matter."

Her scowl is warped into a clownish grin by the plastic.

"Since you find it so easy to get into my room," I say, flourishing a hand. "You can use mine."

She leaves the control room. I enjoy the quilt of silence that follows.

But all feelings and thoughts halt when I notice the incessant stripes of grime tucked under my fingernails. Suddenly, the need to wash my hands is overwhelming.

I drop an almond back into the bag, nose wrinkled, and saunter to the bedroom.

The door's still open. I wonder if Syzygy knew I would follow Reiki, if she senses my suspicions.

I knock on the bathroom door, receiving no response except running water. I roll my eyes and neck, crackling vertebrae. The light tap of my knuckles turns into a hard rap.

"Are you almost done? I need to shower."

"Oh!" Her feet patter on tile. "What a coincidence—so do I."

Groaning, I press my forehead into the door. "Reiki, c'mon. Syzygy's hydro-cycle is slow. I only have so much clean water in the system at one time…"

"That explains why you smell."

"I do not!" Pounding the metal only coaxes more laughter from her.

"I didn't say it was bad." I can hear the shrug in her voice. "Why don't you join me? Save water."

"You're doing it again," I yell, my face heating. "Teasing, like you want something, like everyone else does…"

A soft beep sounds, and the door slides open.

Reiki rests her hands on her ashen hips, squashing freed hair against speckled skin. Naked and backlit by fluorescent light and an indoor waterfall, she looks like a proper celestial being—something to be imitated, worshiped, and then destroyed.

Hastily, I avert my eyes.

"Has it occurred to you that maybe I don't want *anything* from you?" Her cold fingers lift my chin, like a doctor checking for swelling. "Maybe I just enjoy your company." She catches my gaze with garnet fists and holds it, sending ripples of heat down my core.

I want to hit her, to replicate the sting in my face and neck. "I don't care. Just get out and put some clothes on. This is still my ship."

"Aye, aye, Captain."

I blush harder under the pressure of her earthy irises, ignorant to what she's thinking or trying to say. But I still feel different—ridiculously, impossibly calm.

Sighing, she pats my arm and gathers her clothes. "You need a shower more than I do, anyway." With a soldier's salute, she leaves me in a swath of steam.

Her comfort in my home is disturbing, but I only nod in thanks, muscles detangling, dropping the strict act. At least now, I can admit conscious pleasure in bathing, regardless of whether it's induced by the thrill of dopamine, lasting serotonin, or some other-worldly force.

Before I close the door, Reiki adds with twiddling fingers, "Oh. Just so you know. There's a certain…presence lingering near the tub."

I press a palm to the door frame, looking over my shoulder. "Are you saying my bathroom's haunted?"

She shrugs. "Spirits love water."

Unconvinced, I feign a smile. "Is it someone I know?"

Her voice turns icy. "No." The first word of hers I recognize as a distinct lie.

With the flick of a switch, I shut the door.

Finally stripping out of these dirt-caked, blood-smudged clothes is therapeutic, and like the strange enjoyment of Reiki's energy work, it leaves me nearly skinless.

I toss the polyester clothing into a recycling laundry shoot, sighing. The blood opal feels like a hot coal in my hand, so I place it on the back of the sink, where forgotten jewelry clusters.

Vulnerable and momentarily unburdened, I unlace my tiny braids, letting hair kink like black lightning bolts.

While showering, I scan the pieces of my reflection I can make out in the mirror—hips jutting above slick thighs, child-like toes wiggling in suds, and a chest so flat it's almost concave. I try to stand taller, to look more intimidating. The only tough look comes from the scruffy jaw and dark circles under my eyes. There would be nothing wrong with that, of course, if it didn't mean people saw the childish parts of me as their physical and emotional playground.

Determined to release some tension, I drag a soapy hand between my legs.

Then I sing. Not soft and breathy like earlier, but with a tense belly and embraced vocal chords. I belt so that even the water seems to shake under the weight of my voice, working my way toward a passionate, musical orgasm.

An elongated note fizzles into a soft yelp when Reiki knocks on the door.

"Sorry," the Queen Invader of Privacy calls. "Just thought you should know—a ship's coming. I don't know why Syzygy didn't pick it up, but it's moving pretty fast."

My piping stomach jolts. *Shit.* Unable to finish what I started, I lean against the wall and rinse off.

Already, from beyond my ceramic cavern, a much larger ship clutches mine with a tight, false-gravitational fist. Subtle clicking vibrates the air.

I pound the tile in frustration. "Sweet, glittering Pleiades! Can't I have five goddamn minutes alone?" I turn off the shower and shake my head, spraying water.

With the jab of a button, I enact the ceiling vents. They vacuum steam and water to be reused later, leaving me mostly dry, staring at my pathetic erection in the defogging mirror. With unfocused eyes, I see a blood-red block of energy twisted in my pelvis, and I can't help but laugh.

Reiki kicks the door. "Stop laughing and get dressed. I think they're—"

Syzygy's voice breaks through. "Incoming signal from the Reunited States Astropolice, Ship Number 221."

An acidic fist grabs my throat. I bound through the door before it fully opens and push past Reiki.

She sees my groin and laughs into her hands. "Oh, that *is* pretty funny."

31

I clamber into the wardrobe. "Shut up and hide."

While the machines compose jeans and a t-shirt, I breathe through the nose and out o-shaped lips. Fresh polyester sticks to my skin, masking my imploding mind, leaking sweat, and scattered heartbeat with synthetic confidence.

"Incoming signal from the Reunited States Astropolice, Ship Number 221. I suggest you answer promptly, Captain."

I roll my eyes. "Good to know you're alive and well, G."

As soon as I'm clothed, I fly out the door, heading for the cockpit, not bothering to wait for Reiki. If there's anything I trust her with, it's keeping herself hidden.

Sitting in the captain's chair and turning on the lights, I wipe my face and sling my hair into a damp bun. "Syzygy, accept the signal." With trembling hands, I don the S-Com and greet our captor with a flamboyant wave.

"Salutations, fellow expatriate." Grinning stings.

Like an old film, the man on the other end is dressed head-to-toe in black, except for glasses, which shield his eyes in blue. Enhancing his credibility, the room is covered in RSA flags with strawberry stripes and black-and-blue stars.

"Howdo, travele'." The cop extends three lazily flexed fingers in a wave. "You're approachin' RSA zones, and accordin' to protocol, we gotta conduct a random safety scan. You know the rules."

I almost cringe at his accent. Clearly this guy isn't from my spine of the woods. All show, I tilt my head in the most innocent way possible, licking my lips slowly. "Of course, sir. Zenith Lin, age 22, Capricornian sun—"

"That won't be necessary, Mr. Lin. We're already scannin' you and the resta' the ship. Just hang tight for now."

This time I can't hide the cringe. Not only does he refer to me like I'm someone's father, but he has the nerve to invade my body and home without consent.

The worst part of this process is that I have no idea how or what they're scanning, and I know Reiki's somewhere, giggling under her breath, energy blazing like a comet. Sweat puddles on my hairline and the base of my spine. Despite all the "work" she did on me, my anxiety still manifests through ticking tendons and thumping veins.

"So," I try to distract myself with small-talk. "Have you been in this position long?"

He turns from what I assume is the scanner screen, raising an eyebrow and peering over his glasses. "You flirtin' with me, Mr. Lin?"

I ignore the urge to facepalm. Not wanting to dig myself a deeper ditch, I say, "No, sir, of course not." I chew my lip and inhale deeply, catching a whiff of cigar smoke on his end. "Just a curious person, floating in space. It gets pretty boring out here."

The policeman chuckles, adjusting the black netting around his mouth. For some reason, they all find it necessary to hide their identities behind ninja masks. "Lookie, Mr. Lin. I ain't here fo' to chit-chat. We've been 'formed of a bad accident in the Martian sector, and while we don't know all the details yet, it's 'mperative that we—"

A mechanical chime makes me jump. He laughs harder, shakes his head, and presses a few buttons on his control panel.

Another police person walks behind him, also cloaked in black. "He's clean."

A long-held breath tumbles out. I have no idea how—even my gun surpasses legal standards—but I made it. "Thanks. Are we done here?"

The man pushes the blue glasses up his nose and nods. "Thanks for your cooperation. Move along, Mr. Lin, and have a spectacula' resta' your day."

I can't get out of their magnetic field fast enough. As soon as I toss the S-Com aside and feel the RSA ship loosen its grip, I ignite the controls and skid away, toward the aquamarine ornament ahead. It's still a few hours' journey, but continental details become pronounced like wrinkles.

"No matter where I go, for however long, I always end up crawling back to Earth," I muse aloud, "like a little bitch."

Laughter trickles into the room as Reiki makes herself known again, wearing nothing but a white oversized t-shirt. Her wet hair clings to the material and droplets glide down her like small rivers. "You're dripping with humanity, Zen. You can't run away from who you are." She leans against the control panel and pats my hand. "That being said...Earth isn't your real home, anyway."

I ignore her metaphysical philosophies and cross my arms. "You smell like my soap," I note, eyeing her strange outfit and its severe lack of material. "Did you use my wardrobe too?" Upon closer inspection, I notice the RSA flag on the shirt's breast pocket and wrinkle my nose. "Girl. What the hell?"

"What?" she laughs, swinging her hair to one side. It's like a waterfall of ancient pennies. "I figured I could make myself at home, and I want to look my best for my country when I return."

33

I pinch the bridge of my nose and shake my head. "Contrary to popular belief, most Americans wear pants and shoes."

Her eyes widen. "Wait, really? Again?"

I change the subject with a flip of my hand. "How did you bypass their scanners? Mine are one thing, but theirs are powerful."

She licks her lips and presses her palms together. "Some forces are more powerful."

"Like what, some spiritual cloaking device?"

Tapping the side of her nose, she grins and shakes her head. "Here's a better question for your bourgeoning noggin—why are humans so territorial?"

At first, I want to turn back to the controls and ignore her spurting aura like the scanners did. But I can't look away from the pair of clay beads that are her eyes. I swear she snags me like this on purpose. Deciding to play along, I shrug. "Animal instincts?"

"No, I mean really," she insists, digging palms into her thighs and leaning forward. "Why are there segmented territories? Why should the RSA hold one area of space for itself? The sky is no place for imperialism. Come to think of it, Earth isn't either."

"Calm down, star-hippie," I chuckle. "Without order, there's only chaos. That's just how it's always been."

Her mouth stretches somewhere between a smile and grimace. "No, it hasn't. You don't even know. The universe *is* order out of chaos. It doesn't need humanity's regulations." A spark falls over her eyes. "You say you left Earth to get away from humanity, but you're more human than most. You can't see past the blue ball you keep going back to."

I scoff. "Ha, ha, I see what you did there."

She tilts her head. "What do you mean?"

Is it pity in the taut lines of her face, or humor?

With a lump in my throat, I swivel to face the controls and turn auto off so I have something else to focus on. If it's one thing I'm good at, it's pretending to be busy.

Five

The closer we get to Earth, the more my anxiety bites down. As much as I hate to admit it, Reiki's right. Every word out of her mouth sends me reeling into another dimension of thought, and I've silently decided to agree with her—humans *are* too territorial. Why should we be split by sections of land and sky? The freaking States had to be physically split into three landmasses before they realized how important unity was, and even then, we all resonate differently depending on where we grew up. Why should we carry our tribal seclusion into future millennia?

I don't want to look at the enlarged globe ahead of us yet, and I refuse to settle on Reiki's eyes because the solace in them is terrifying. So, I shut my eyes. With a tight throat, unable to sing or scream, I sink into myself like an anchor without a chain, unwilling to be pulled back into something that isn't—can't be—good for me.

Rolling my shoulders and stretching my calves, I find a weird peace in the awkward silence between us. Although she's combing fingers through her slow-drying hair, I know she's watching my every twitch with interest.

"Are you okay?" she asks.

Whether it's because I'm overwhelmed or simply lazy, I say nothing, hoping she'll forget about it and go wander the halls.

But even in my short span of knowing her, it's obvious she's relentless. "Zenith, if you're not okay, we can take a break before landing. You're still ahead of schedule, aren't you?"

My eyebrows merge. "What would you know about my schedule?"

"I'm on your ship," she laughs, crouching on the filthy floor. "I've heard you speak to your so-called superior. I know how people like you work."

I rub my temples. "People like me?"

"Capricornian suns." She smirks.

"I have a dab of Sagittarius," I mumble. "Anyway. If you really knew me, you'd know that I'm actually behind schedule."

She lies in corpse pose and closes her eyes. "See, that is the most Capricornian thing I've ever heard."

I roll my eyes 'til they ache. "Whatever. Even Jaal knows I prefer to be early."

"Does he know that because you're business partners, or ex-lovers?"

I can't tell if she meant to throw shade, but I hate how she talks about Jaal like she knows everything, digging at my personal life, stupidly clever but pretending to be clueless. Choosing to be the bigger person, I swivel back to the screens and let her feel like the smug yogi she appears to be.

Earth's aura looks like spilled gasoline on water—a technicolor haze that's only flattering until I blink. For as long as I've been alive, the planet's surface has been unappealing—riddled with large scars and ancient ruins from atomic wars—but it was still blue. Now, I see that it's energetically clogged. Clouds and oceans are obscured by inky bruises and heaps of smoggy vomit.

My awakened sixth sense has made it even harder to love home.

"Humans were her children," Reiki whispers, making me jump. I turn to look, but she's still on the floor, eyes closed, tears pooling down her temples and into seashell-like ears. Freckles shimmer and she sniffles. "Babies are almost like parasites, you know. Young and inflamed. They take and take and take… but everyone grows up. Maladies can become remedies. Everything transmutes." She clears her throat, cheeks splashed with embarrassment. "Is it still getting better, the human-Earth relationship?"

Stinging knots tighten behind my eyes. "Mostly," I insist, biting my lip. "San Fran Isle, where I'm from, is actually pretty nice after millennia of filth, with so much pro-nature tech—"

"Nothing can grow with chains," she says, eyelashes separating like a newborn bird's sticky feathers. "You of all people should know that."

"Yeah, well, you barely know me," I huff, reaching for the controls to dodge a satellite. "Sometimes we need chains to know we can grow in the first place."

Yes, that was Capricornian too, but surprisingly, it shuts her up.

A little too pleased with myself, I start to hum, tugging Syzygy gently back on track, as she had tilted off course due to my distraction.

While I still try to look past the global wounds, a flicker of maroon light catches my attention. Red, orange, golden yellow. Breath halts in my throat while I pause to find the source of the explosions. Every sensation I've experienced in the past couple of days floods back full-force, so that even the floor quakes and wobbles.

Instinctively, I lurch out of the chair and grab a gun. *Jaal, what the fuck!*

But it's not Jaal. They're not even explosions. At least, not the kind I thought they were.

With my hands pressed against the control panel, I stare at the screens, sweat forming under my nose. A collection of colors spews from Earth's satellites like sparkling paint bombs, breaking my fixation on the aura and decorating blueness with vibrant, human-made fire. Starworks.

"Are you afraid of celebrations?" Reiki teases with a soft laugh, sitting up. She wipes her eyes with the hem of her shirt, effectively flashing me. Again.

I release a long, dizzying breath and slide onto the floor. "I just want to relax for longer than it takes to sleep."

She pats my shoulder. "I know, Cap. But you don't have to rush. What better time to relax than Earth's New Year?" As usual, she continues to do the unthinkable, rocking onto her knees and cupping my face in her hands. Before I can react, her lips are moving on mine like leaves skidding across water.

Weakly, I push her off, but her smile is infectious.

"Happy 4444," she giggles. "Did you know that's a huge angel number?"

Stunned, I lick my lips, which now taste like the sea. "What does it mean?"

"Depends who you ask." Her veil of color darkens to rouge as another starwork goes off and lights up the screens around us. "Some say balance, or an alignment of galaxies. Others will insist it's the end of the universe." She snorts and shakes her head. "But constant balance means no evolution, and every end is just another beginning." Her eyes settle on my mouth, like she wants to kiss me again. "Really, four-fours is an alignment of souls. Emotional inflammation and release. An infection of cosmic love."

I lean against the wall, insides spiraling. Ruminating her words, I look up and imagine a pair of Chinese dragons circling the pentagram of rafters. They lick the peaked ceiling with serpentine tongues, clasping tails.

"You're uncomfortable with the metaphysical," Reiki says, dragging my gaze back to her. "But I promise it's worth the confusion."

"Wow," I say through tense laughter. "You're a living, breathing fortune cookie."

Her blonde lashes flutter. "A what?"

I eye her in disbelief. "Are you sure you're from Earth?" One moment, she's preaching like the next goddamn Buddha, and the next, she's asking questions as though she's lived on Mars her whole life. Which I'm starting to think is probable.

"You're breaking your own rule again," she says. "Asking personal questions."

Fed up, I wave my hands, accidentally cracking my wrists. "Screw the rule. If I'm stuck with you, we might as well talk." Hearing myself say it feels like a hypocritical slap in the face. *What is she doing to me?*

"Well," she exclaims, lacing her fingers. "I'm glad you've come to that conclusion, because I have a lot to say."

"Wow, really? Shocker."

Our strings of laughter intertwine, hesitance turning to ecstatic energy as it moves through our stomachs and throats. Caught up in the moment, I touch her knee. "Get dressed. For real this time. I want to show you something."

When we're in my room again, there's less tension; I've softened.

In front of the wardrobe, she flicks through clothing options on the screen with her breath.

"So, where's the underwear? I couldn't find it earlier..." She looks from the screen to me with an incomprehensible amount of childlike curiosity.

"It's in the program. Choose whatever you like. Just make sure it's an actual outfit. The machine measures you and everything fits like...well, kind of like an aura, actually." Self-consciously messing with my hair, I feel like those stylists on S-TV shows, submerging my imaginary audience in a sensory space to witness the redesigning of someone else's life.

But this isn't me. My preference for weird clothing doesn't justify playing fashion expert. I don't poke around in other people's affairs, except under business terms. But being this close to her—giving her a reason to listen to me, even for something so trivial—is like entering a rogue planet's caverns and finding a new kind of gemstone. She's beautiful, strange, and crumbles in my hands.

Tell me what to do, the crystals would cry, *because you discovered me. I have no identity without you*. Without even slipping into meditation this time, my mind gets carried away.

While listening to the sound of whirring plastic fibers and spinning clouds of dust, I lean against the wardrobe. Even if she wasn't here, even if she hadn't invaded my ship and my life, I would probably still be pathetically, neurotically imaginative.

"I can feel you overthinking," she announces. "Give your brain a break."

"Why did you kiss me?"

The machine continues to stitch, buzzing softly. Then, I hear her sigh. "I mean. No reason, really. Just to celebrate. New Year and all. People still do that, right?"

"You know," I say, folding my arms. "I can't tell if you're always full of shit, or if it's just how you say things."

"Thanks," she deadpans, opening the wardrobe and exiting. Hands on her hips, she looks at me expectantly. "Well? What do you think?"

My jaw relaxes at the sight of her. She's thrown her hair in a messy top knot and it bobs like a loose tiara. She wears colors remnant of the RSA flag—a marbled red and white tank top with a blue and gold jumpsuit that cinches at the ankles.

"It's still too patriotic," I critique. "But much less homeless." My eyes rest on her bare feet. "You'll really fit in on the coast."

When her aura blushes crimson, the crystal metaphor comes back into my head, making me chuckle. Something about helping people...but it isn't really helping. If anything, this is the kind of help that selfish people use to inflate their egos, to distract. The kind of philanthropy Jaal does to make up for "accidentally" killing people every month. The kind of hypocrisy that makes my teeth bolt to one another and grind.

"Here." I hand her the kyanite blade. It turns from black to bright blue immediately, and her aura hums.

She blinks profusely. "What's this for?"

I close her fingers around the handle. "Self-defense."

39

Her eyes are ridiculously glossy when she looks at me. "Thanks." She tucks it like a pin in the bun of copper strands.

"One more thing." Together, we stand on the bed. "Don't get weird," I say, pressing my hand against the ceiling. Recognizing my tattoo, the sensor blinks and a secret door opens. "I'm only showing this to you because…well, you've shown me a lot, and I have to one-up you."

She looks at me, caught between a scoff and a beam, as a ladder unravels between us.

I rest a hand on her lower back. A brow quirks, daring her to climb. Some stupid part of me wants to impress her, to give her more reasons to do as I say.

But she shocks me into submission, and with great vigor, shoves me in front of her, patting my butt as I take my first step on the ladder. Irritation spikes and then melts when we reach a small bubble-shaped room full of equipment that's never been used.

"What's all this?" Reiki asks, ducking under a hanging bubble mask.

"It's the emergency storage pod," I explain. "Most ships have two or three on all sides, but G's a special model, much smaller." Absent-mindedly, I pat the wall. "Everything here can be used to escape if—Pluto forbid—something bad happens to the ship."

She fiddles with a space suit, crumpling its shiny material. Everything she touches seems to liquify between her fingers.

"I thought we could…well, I'll show you." I blot a stripe of sweat on my forehead and find the mini control panel, switching it on and lighting up the pod with the rays of billions of surrounding stars.

She gasps and I can't help but grin. "The pod's made of stellaglass," I explain, blowing on the curved wall and tracing a heart in condensation. "Lightweight, lovely, and transparent. You can see everything from here. No screens, just stars."

Outside our transparent dome, Earth looks like a tumbled larimar sphere lodged in cloudy resin. From various satellites and official ships, starworks continue to go off, creating colorful puddles in space. I've seen it plenty of times before, from both inside and outside of the atmosphere, but with Reiki, and my opened third-eye, it feels different. Newfound electricity ricochets through my limbs like I'm a circuit, and when I look at her, it all halts.

Her dark, round eyes are the perfect reflection for the pops of distant color, glossy tears reflecting hues of purple, orange, and yellow. For a hot second, all she is becomes color and energy, like her body's an

40

illusion and her true essence intentionally explodes. Then she looks at me with wet eyes and a trembling lower lip, and I look away.

"Thank you," she whispers.

My laughter ripples.

Without explanation, I start to hum. Eventually, words form between tongue and teeth, and I'm writing a song as I go. At first, she continues to watch the splattering starworks, and while I sing, she speaks.

"I've butted into your life, pushed your patience over the edge, and scared you senseless." She shakes her head, flicking tears onto the glass. "You should get rid of me. But you hold on. It's like your soul remembers, reaches in, and opens a door."

A violet starwork ascends and sparks, silhouetting her in white. I keep singing, silently begging her to join me, to sew her voice to mine. I have no idea what she means, talking about my soul, but I don't mind. Something clicks between us, and even though she's babbling and I'm singing a broken ballad, it feels right.

"You don't have to be kind to me, but you are. I thought it would be harder. I thought you were lost from me forever, but I was wrong."

It takes her a few moments to join me, whether from embarrassment or something else, I can't tell. But her energy shifts when I hold her hand, aura erupting to match the starworks. When she opens her mouth, the sound drifts like loose petals on a spring breeze. It's sweet, but it's in pieces, not lingering and filling the space like my voice does.

I squeeze her hand and place it on her stomach. "Try singing from your, uh, belly chakra."

She giggles. "Solar plexus?"

I snap my fingers in vague recollection. "All the tension should be held in your tummy, not your throat or chest. Let it move through you like energy. Channel sound with your body."

"Like an instrument."

"Yeah, exactly." I nod. "The higher the note, the deeper the tension goes, and it builds." To exemplify, I sing a quick vocal run she probably couldn't replicate and end it with a billowing C. My aura erupts, and a deep red snake of light curls bashfully around my hips and ankles.

Her laughter is extraordinary, wrinkled nose and flushed cheeks. "So *that's* what you were doing in the shower. Pleasure comes from the roots! 'Cause you feel safe when you sing, right?"

41

Sheepishly rubbing my neck and clinging to a semblance of confidence, I clear my throat. "Yeah. I guess. Now, just. Sing."

This time, I'm not Mama, but Mother—the one who taught me how to sing with my whole body and being, as if every fragment of existence is a vessel for fluid life, and sound is just another drop.

Reiki improves tenfold, her voice renewed by the building pressure in her stomach. Her range still isn't as wide as mine, but while I was singing in showers and hallways, she was silently swinging from satin ropes like a child made of clockwork.

In a way, we've both come from places of performance. She's had to keep a flexible posture, while I've had to maintain a professional poker face.

As we sing, she becomes bolder, trying to hit higher notes while I dip into lower ones. It isn't quite the harmony I was hoping for, but I'm not disappointed. This is just another excuse for her to listen to me, another reason to keep her around.

Singing lessons, I ponder, gazing at red and white sparks shooting from the western hemisphere. *Maybe that's what I'll do after I get out of Jaal's contract...*

Reiki follows my gaze and stops singing. "Whatcha thinking about, Cap?"

Shrugging off the idea, I glance at her, massaging a shoulder knot. "I didn't realize, until today, that planets have auras too."

The corners of her mouth curl down when she smiles. "Well, yeah. It's a collective glob of conscious life."

"How does that work, scientifically speaking?"

She laughs. "Well, it's not science, really. It's more like a parallel system. Beyond it."

"Right, but how?"

She turns to look at the revolving ball, chin resting in her palm. "Well, you can see it, can't you? There's something called an auric field, and it emanates from all physical forms containing energy, all living beings. It comes from within and can be used as protection."

"Mmm, an energetic condom." I grin. "But what about stars?"

"I mean, stars are concentrated auras, in a way. Pure energy. Souls floating without bodies to tie them down. Even our sun has an auric field. It keeps the whole solar system from falling apart." She flutters her fingers to mimic planetary motion and splays them to depict apocalypse.

I bite my lip, retracing the heart on stellaglass several times. "Why do we get hurt if we get too close, though?"

42

The question pinches the air between us, and at first, I think I've hit a wall. But after banishing my own silly rule of no questions, I'm not going to let her silence slide.

After a moment, she shrugs. "If you were the seed of an entire planetary system, you'd want to protect yourself too. You hold everyone, and yet no one, in your billowing body. Forever. We all came from sunlight, and we can go the same way."

I grind my teeth, lingering on the many nightmares and flashbacks I've had of Mama staring at herself in the mirror. Under fluorescent lighting, when the Fever first sprang, she looked like death itself—pale and dark at the same time. An empty vessel, a body without a soul. If I had been able to see auras then, I'm almost positive she would've emanated no color, but a thick gray mist that terrorized the spirit from her cracking shell.

Thoughts snag the backs of my eyes, building and stinging.

"She didn't even get that close," I protest quietly. "She only went to the Venusian sector, not the Mercurial. She shouldn't have lost her hair and fingernails, her energy, her...mind."

Recognition falls on Reiki's face. "You're talking about Gemini Fever, aren't you? The illness caused by solar flares."

I rub my eyes, frustrated for giving into the flow of tears. I haven't thought about it this hard in years, and never with this new metaphysical perspective. It makes my brain feel like lava hitting an icecap.

"Zenith, it's okay."

"Pleiades, why am I even talking to you about this? It doesn't matter." I push off the wall, palm sticky with tears and condensation from our breath.

She grabs my wrist. "You're not alone anymore. You can talk to me."

I sigh and shake my head. "I haven't seen my moms in four years. One of them got sick and it didn't end well, so I left. That's it." I try to tear away, but her grip is strong. She holds my wrist with both hands, thumbs moving in circles against rebelling veins.

Now I'm sure she's using witchcraft because the small motion is enough to soothe me back into sitting on the floor with her. She holds my face again, and I wince when she kisses my forehead. A blue, energetic ice cube collides with my third-eye and melts down the entire chakra network. My throat, jaw, and mouth relax into a communicative puddle.

43

"I know more about energy work than you think," I confess, cracking knuckles against my thighs. "Or at least, I used to. I grew up surrounded by that shit—crystal beds, altars, oil fusion rooms, Feng Shui, you name it. We went to mosques and temples, because Mother believes in Allah and bodhisattvas, and Mama believes in her." I sniffle stubbornly like the child I never got to be.

Reiki tries to smile, sliding onto her back and resting her head in my lap. "That makes a lot of sense."

"I actually…wanted to be a Conduit." I shrug.

"Aw, that's precious," she preens. "Everyone's a healer at birth, Zenith. You wanted to be what you forgot you were."

I clear my throat, brain waves breaking. "Well, whatever…I was never able to…we were too busy taking care of Mama. Like I said, it didn't end well."

"Did she pass away?"

I'm suddenly all too aware of her warm, glass-stem neck pressing against my calves. "She went lunatic and tried to kill her wife."

Her body goes rigid and she stares up at me with an obnoxious cocktail of pity and discomfort. "That's…awful."

"Yeah, well."

She drags her fingertips across my legs, tickling hair. "I'm sorry for prying. I know how much that hurts."

I swallow the desire to spit, *you don't know anything,* to mumble *shut up shut up shut up* into her hair, to make her see that whatever she's doing to me—this plastic kindness—isn't okay. Can't be okay. Won't ever be okay.

Instead, I throw her a wink. "At least you know a little more about your captain now."

Upside down, she cranes her neck to scan me, full of icy concern. "But you still know nothing about me."

"Not true." I tap my forehead. "Mother used to do something like what you can do, on a smaller scale. Old Japanese stuff. 'Hands-on healing,' she said. Guess what it's called."

Her eyes widen as though she's been caught, and then she laughs. "Your mother was a Reiki healer?"

"Reiki Master, I think. Of all kinds, too." With the side of my mouth, I blow a frizzy flyaway. "Which is almost the same as a Conduit, huh? Just less official."

She clears her throat. "I was named for the kind of energy I embody."

"Kinda literal for such a meta girl."

44

"Well. You're a space-pirate named after a seemingly fixed planetary position." She reaches up and pinches my chin. "The universe loves irony."

Behind her, the starwork finale fizzles into light-dust, layering her aura like a blooming lotus.

Six

"Can we sing outside?" Reiki asks, tip-toeing after me into the control room, stuffing her face with dried fruit and cheese.

I swig some water and raise an eyebrow, the back of my skull still buzzing from the sound of our briefly braided vocal chords.

"On Earth, sure." Resting a knee on the captain's chair, I inspect the surroundings as we begin entering the atmosphere. Everything looks normal, aside from the cloudy remnants of starworks. Bigger, newer ships follow mine toward Earth's surface, returning home from their pricey New Year vacations.

Reiki harrumphs. "But I want to sing with the stars."

"You can do that on Earth."

"I want to sing *with* the stars. Arm-in-arm. Aura-to-aura."

I grind my teeth. "With bubble masks and a false gravity field, we can. But I have a job to finish."

"Don't throw me out when we land," she begs, catching my eye. "Please. I can help you finish. The job, I mean."

I choke on a gulp of water, coughing with laughter against the bottle's rim. "I'd like to see that."

She spins the chair so that I face her and straddles my lap. "Look, Cap. I may have worked with Tauris, but I'm not like her. I won't take advantage of your hard work, because that's what she did to me. I can help you be independent, so you can make a new life for yourself. You won't have to work under Jaal's filthy thumb anymore."

Instead of lashing out or saying something dirty to make her blush, I hide my own flushing cheeks behind another sip of water. "Why do you care so much?" I mumble.

46

It takes her a moment to respond, as if the question has fried her brain cells. But then she inhales deeply and exhales with, "I have a job to finish, too. Healing people. Helping them grow. It's who I am. Helping you helps me."

With every word, I can practically taste the strawberry in her breath. The sweat on her neck smells like sage smoke and pine. She's too close to me, in every way. I couldn't throw her out if I tried. If I wanted to. If I knew how...

Before I can build a clever communicative cage to hide my lack of a spine, a streak of red light bleeds across the screens.

Panic starts in the arches of my feet, coursing up my legs and into my guts. Every part of me screams for retreat, except for my brain, which pleads for the money.

"Encore?" Reiki inquires innocently, tilting her head.

The shivering walls say it all. For the second time today, my ship is snagged by another. What's more, only one kind of ship moves as fast as the police and casts a reddish pink glow. Only one ship would emerge from the shriveled west coast to chaperone me into the atmosphere.

"Get the opal," I command, a stony edge in my voice. "It's on the sink."

She stares at me. "You left it in the bathroom? What kind of pirate are you?"

"I'm not a pirate."

"Not a smart one." She waltzes away to reclaim the stone—my ticket to more than just a massage chair.

Despite all the chaos and frustration, Reiki's arousing promise gives me hope. Maybe I can do something else. Be someone other than this chrome puppet I've made myself into.

But the hope is squeezed out of me when a dematerialized body phases through the ceiling.

Well-accustomed to rude interruptions, I react as though following protocol. Body before mind. Wiping sweat from my forehead, I retrieve the gun, eyes moving between the door Reiki left through and the newcomer. I thought I knew all Jaal's cronies, but this broad-shouldered drag queen is entirely unfamiliar.

His dark, leathery skin is coated in technicolor feathers, beads, and the tackiest mesh suit I've ever seen. Black hair sticks to his scalp in zig-zagged plaits, except for a flowing rainbow faux-hawk littered with glitter and crystals.

In stark contrast to the wardrobe, his aura is a foggy gray. When I tilt my head, it glistens yellow-green like phlegm. I can't help but feel sorry for this poor sap, but pity is soon replaced by rage when he reaches for my crotch.

"Tread off!" I swat the hand away with my gun. His natal tattoo is surrounded by a circling snake eating its own tail.

A garbled string of words plummets from his mouth, and for a moment, he sounds drunk. But then he rises and looks at me with eyes bluer than planet Earth. "Oops. Heh. Sorry, 'migo. I could phase in and out a thousand times and it would still feel like caca. It's confusing at the end, when particles smash back together."

As he brushes himself off, I notice faint burn marks on his belly and thighs through the mesh. The inner scream to get the hell out of here returns with a vengeance.

He eyes me with an uncomfortably white smile, wrinkling winged eyeliner and pinching blade-like cheeks. "Guess I was reaching for the whole package, eh?"

I hit my forehead so hard it stings.

"Hey, 'meegs. Don't be so hard on yourself. A good pun takes a hot sec to get, especially after molecular 'trusion." He shimmies and cracks his neck. "Ah. Better."

I adjust my gun. "Who are you?" I've had to do this too much today.

He stares down the barrel and licks his lips. "Mmm...J-baby told me you'd be feisty, 'specially since you don't know me."

"Yeah, well. I don't like strangers."

"He says you're defensive."

"You haven't answered my question. Who are you?"

He pops his tongue and laughs. "No manners, either. Doesn't even treat a guest right. No wonder he stopped giving you the D."

I've never been so tempted to shoot someone in my life.

His laughter warms. "Oh, cool your expired polyester, Zenith. I'm just messin'." From his chest pocket—the only non-mesh material in his outfit—he produces a piece of glittery sandpaper.

I accept the offering and cringe, recognizing the handwriting as Jaal's:

This is Obsidian. He keeps precious cargo safe. I know you like it rough, but play nice.

Every bubble of self-expression I'd popped in the last few hours suddenly reseals and clusters in the shadows of my insides, getting stuck in weak intestines. I hate feeling my old coping mechanisms come back, only to collapse and fail. This self-awareness could kill a bitch.

Lowering the gun, I crumple the sandpaper and enjoy it scraping my palm. "You can't even introduce yourself, but you can phase through my ceiling with illegal tech?"

"Just 'cause it's new, doesn't mean it's illegal." He crosses his arms.

"Whatever it is, it's extra." I toss the paper in a bin. "Jaal could've sent a com."

"You know he loves a good pun."

I rub my palm. "Is that your magical connection? Puns?"

A shadow passes over his face. But while I internally congratulate myself for being clever, he laughs hard and slaps a muscular thigh. "Ah, Zenith. Cut the caca." Laughter ends harshly. "You know like I do—J's ready to finish the job."

"Is that why he sent you? Because I can't land my own damn ship?"

He shrugs. "You took too long, and we can't risk coppers knowin' what you did."

"I didn't do anything." The gun quivers at my side. "It was all Jaal."

"You saw it through to the end," he corrects me. "Couldn't even save the client."

I resist a full-body shiver. "She wasn't his client, and that was an accident."

He shrugs. "So's this."

Before I can react, he unclips a black crystal point from his mane and aims it at the doorway. A stunned yelp echoes off the metal walls, and an invisible energy field is lifted. In its place, Reiki stumbles and slumps against the wall, sending the blood opal soaring toward us like a spark.

Obsidian spins on his toes to catch it. "You ain't supposed to share, Zenith."

My gun is aimed at Obsidian again, but my eyes are on Reiki, who clutches her face in pain. Instincts are put on hold, as I find myself conflicted between running to her and killing him.

"You were given strict orders," Obsidian says, voice climbing in pitch. "What the hell, man?"

A whirlwind of red burns through my aura. Body before mind. I pull the trigger, sending a bolt of blue lightning straight for his heart. But he stops it with another beam from the dark energy crystal, head cocked.

"Was she hiding the opal this whole time?" He flicks his wrist again and the electric pulse is consumed by the crackling crystal. "Man. This don't look like good business to me. J's gonna have your ass on a plate."

I shoot again, this time at his feet. He jumps like a clumsy dancer. "I've been working for Jaal way longer than you," I seethe. "I know how he works. If I want…if I want a friend, then by Deimos, I'll have a fucking friend." I glance at Reiki again, heart banging to be free of its cage. She curls against the wall, staring past my head.

"Damn, 'meegs. Alright. Just trying to do my job."

I roll my eyes. "She's not a threat to you, or the job."

"This ain't a team thing, 'meegs. You were supposed to work solo."

"After Jaal intervened on Mars, I had to make adjustments." I raise my aim to his swaddled balls. "Now. Apologize."

"Pleiades, sure." He puts his hands up, laughing uncomfortably as he looks at Reiki. "Lo siento, chica. Look, there's a good healer in San Fran. Best we know. When we land, they'll handle it, okay? J-baby pays me good for what I do, and—"

"I'm sure he does." My voice reaches a new low pitch, bearing a dark undertone of *I fucking dare you* that I won't be able to replicate in a few minutes. It shuts him up for now. He leans against the wall and stows both the black crystal and the opal in his hair nest.

Unsatisfied but unable to fight any further, I stow the gun in a back pocket. Thank the stars it only needs my natal tattoo to be activated, and my ass is literally safe.

When I reach Reiki, my hands are surprisingly steady. Under her breath, she laughs. Tears roll down her face like glossy, deflating balloons. Her gaze is loose and unfocused, irises wobbling. I wince, not used to seeing her so vulnerable.

"You okay?" I offer a hand.

She doesn't take it, staring past me. "Negative, Cap," she says hoarsely. "I can't see. Anything. Not even auras…" Her trembling chin brings my hand to the gun again.

"It's okay," she insists, sniffling and patting my thigh. "I'll be fine. Just…" Her nose wrinkles. "Don't act so obsessed with me." Strangely grateful for her advice and the fact that she can't see the raging blush in my cheeks, I help her stand and lead her into the room.

"Told you I'd be all over you within a few hours," I joke weakly.

With a melancholy smile, she pushes me away.

50

I don't want to move from her, but she's right—I can't act too attached, even if I am. As soon as Jaal sees my attraction to her, he'll melt her like an ice cap and that will be the end of my newfound hope. My newfound friend.

After sitting her down in the captain's chair, I keep a wary eye on Obsidian. He's cleaning his teeth with an unusually long pinky nail, apparently ignoring our exchange. The blood opal sits in his hair like a demonic bird's egg.

I hate everything about this situation. I know how to land a damn ship—I don't need Mr. Feathers and his flashy Star Vixen 600 ushering me to the place I grew up in. Sure, it's been four years, but that doesn't matter when it comes to the fractured foundation of a childhood I had on that island. The fault lines will lead me back home just fine.

"When we land, we'll bring you to the new HQ," Obsidian announces.

"We?"

"My sister and me," he replies. When I look at him, he's grinning behind thorny fingernails. "You'll like her. She's the pilot keeping your ship safe ri'now."

I shut my mouth. He's right—without the aid of Jaal's money and authority, I would have no authority to slip past so many regulated sky sectors. Obsidian and his sister are like free passes through the most fucked up rollercoaster line in the solar system.

On cue, Obsidian's bedazzled serpent ear cuff beeps, and when he picks up the call, his eyes turn from brown to blue. All this expensive tech makes me dizzy.

"We were just talking about you," he chuckles, looking up and nodding. "Mhm. Sure. There's four of us now, though. Zenith y amiga. Don't worry about it. Already scanned her and all."

A lie, but I wonder why. Maybe I zapped some sense into him. When I turn to the screens, my heart trembles. Hover jets and energy balloons replace the glow of satellites as we sink into the wounded-but-healing arms of Mother Earth. As the atmosphere thickens, so does the anxiety. It's such a beautiful, almost tranquil place, but the only slice of promise here now is Jaal's deposit in my account.

While Obsidian banters with his sister about the heinous process of landing two ships, Reiki takes my hand. Her energetic pulse caresses mine, sending a ripple of familiar light through me. At this rate, I'll have nowhere to hide this infatuation.

"Don't get too cozy, 'migos." Obsidian says, causing us to break apart. He looms over us, S-contacts turned off. Teal flecks fade from his natural brown irises. "We're about to land."

Seven

All the stars in space cannot compare to midwinter sunlight on Earth's northern hemisphere. Even Syzygy's engine pales in comparison—quite literally, as the ball of fire must be almost completely dissolved before it can touch Earth's sensitive surface. That kind of energy can only be sustained outside the planet's atmosphere.

"I wasn't lying," I remind Reiki, trying to cheer her up. "There's environmental protocol for everything. Earth's not as bad as Mars."

"Not anymore," Obsidian butts in with a cough, leaning over me as I fiddle with the controls. After putting the S-Com goggles around my neck with great reluctance, I turn everything off and give the other ship total control. It stings, but I need to show Jaal that I'm loyal. One last time.

The star-engine cuts off, pressure is released, and a landing bubble brings us gently to the ground. When the screens fall into sleep mode, I do the same with my panic.

The door opens without my permission—like everything else— and in place of Syzygy's usual announcement, a swelling alto echoes off the walls.

"Touch-down!" A broad woman enters, dressed head-to-toe in white pleather. Her accent is more like Tauris', laced more with Indian than her brother's, which is more on the Hispanic side of Hisphindi.

Also unlike her brother, she has platform military boots and a bleached buzzcut. She wears no makeup except for navy blue lipstick, and when I look at her, she sticks out an artificially forked tongue.

Her curves are so plentiful, she practically spills out of the pleather suit while saluting me. "Onyx Khatri. At your service," she says,

53

then flourishes a hand, reconsidering. "Actually, you're at my service. But let's not get technical. It's not even noon."

Overextending my capacity for kissing ass, I flash her a smile. "Thanks for taking care of my ship. That's the smoothest landing she's ever had."

I expect a blush or a smile, but she just shrugs. "That's my job." Her yolk-colored eyes twinkle when she spots Reiki. "I gotta say though, you have great taste."

Pulling Reiki out of the chair and heading for the door, I ask, "Can you give us a few minutes to change? We're not exactly Earth-ready."

"You're readier than most," Onyx says, while her brother slinks to stand next to her in the doorway. "C'mon, Zenith. Make this easy for everyone."

I hate passive aggressive threats. If someone wants to fuck with me, they can come right out and—

A string of slurs lodges in my throat when Reiki squeezes my hand. Their silent threat is met with silent compliance.

My mind keeps fixating on Jaal's lust. When he sees Reiki, he's either going to want her or want to kill her, and both reactions would ruin everything.

While I lock and exit the ship, Obsidian and Onyx watch me like hawks, and with how much taller they are, Reiki and I might as well be their prey. My throat burns. The only thing preventing me from shooting the stars out of their eyes is Reiki's clammy hand clasping mine. It's weirdly comforting that Miss Spirit is just as anxious as I am. Now, her needing me isn't just a metaphor. She literally can't see without my guidance.

Outside, we're met with a gust of lukewarm seawater and iron.

Reiki wrinkles her nose. "Well, Cap. Is the natural environment well-supported?"

The view leaves me speechless. From this angle, the city sits in pieces. It's always been like that, but it's even more apparent from the top of a landing tower, through the lens of my cracked-open sixth sense.

Mimicking ancient Venice, each block is defined not by roads, but waterways which are constantly filtered and recycled. I always find it hard to imagine what it was like when the roads were solid, coated in plastic and piss, millennia ago. Earth used her own blood to wash away landmarks, and now there's only scars in pockets of energy that line the city.

To the east, the Golden Ruins of an ancient bridge float like rose petals on turquoise water. Decorative tourist boats and jets zip around, full of people blinking photos and belting holiday hymns.

Midday sun highlights skyscrapers. Strips of redwood forests are laced with colorful projected advertisements and alloy-coated sustainment vines. Capitalist nature pumps everything it's got into controlling the masses and feeding impoverished plants.

"It's been so long," I say numbly.

"Not long enough." Onyx marches forward. "Necessito una vacación."

Usually I would stop to touch Syzygy's landing stairwell one more time, but having to guide Reiki keeps me focused on what's ahead. The closer we are to the ground, the more familiar our surroundings become.

This is the most tightly packed part of the city, where wanderers go for shelter and support. From above, everything looks insignificant. The deeper you sink into the beast, the less it gleams with pride. Under every sanitized bubble of apartment complexes and homeless shelters, there are layers of wine and grime that seep past skin and taint lonely hearts. Pristine filth at its finest.

"Tell your coworkers to check Syzygy's programming," I say, hoping to distract from the intensity of our upcoming encounter. "Her vocals are a little…slow."

Neither of them responds, which irks me, but as I look over my shoulder, hot irritation turns to a block of ice. Wearing an array of black and white jumpsuits, Jaal's advanced techno-puppets scale my ship and usher her into the facility to be restored. It's a bioengineered dance of a different kind. *Fingers crossed they don't destroy G for good.*

We follow the Hisphindi siblings across the tower's flat roof, into an elevator. Squeezing into a slim glass pod with three odd but attractive people would usually make my day, but this day gets more unusual by the minute. Especially since, as we descend past the ground floor, light fades into a deep blue abyss.

"Alcatraz?" I splutter, my attempt to act casual failing.

Obsidian laughs and crosses his arms. "Hang tight, 'meegs. A lot's changed since you been gone." He puckers his lips while he and his sister share a tube of lip gloss.

I wrinkle my nose. "Clearly."

"What's Alcatraz?" Reiki asks.

Lips pursed, I tear my gaze from the creepy siblings. "An ancient underwater prison," I say, hiking a quizzical brow. "You don't remember learning that in history class?"

She shakes her head but gives no explanation.

"You know about the Schism though, right?" *How the land cracked into three parts and so did the people, before the Reunion.*

The look on her face reminds me of the face I made at teachers when they asked me if I did the homework. I chuckle and rub a thumb across her palm. "It's okay, most Americans don't know their history either."

"The past has passed," Obsidian lisps, spreading his arms as if he's about to break into interpretive dance. "Alc is our new Atlantis!"

"Nerd," Onyx coughs, smirking.

"But it's true," he whines. "J-baby says it's our personal paradise. We do a lotta good here. You don't gotta be historical to know that."

Somehow, I'm not convinced.

We pass floors and floors of what seem to be underwater office spaces, a business center pulsing with technological development and innovation. It's the sheer opposite of Mars' organic, rock-encrusted caves. These layers are paradoxically watery and electric. Dually alive.

Reiki clings to me like a child, grabbing my shirt. Despite being a couple inches taller than I am, she's hunched, shrinking her body and energy.

"Can you feel it?" I whisper.

"All of it." She sounds surprisingly strong. "Even those weird, metallic vines."

I shake my head and chuckle. "I told you—it all works together. Those help protect the plant life and keep it alive, while supplying energy to the city."

Her eyes wander, searching for reason in blurred blackness. Mars must've been biochemical hell for her.

Onyx flicks her forked tongue toward Obsidian. "The fuck'd you do to her sight?"

He smacks his glossy lips and spins a cloudy crystal between his fingers. "Lo siento."

To my surprise, his sister smacks him upside the jaw, causing his head to hit the glass. "Idiota." Her eyes are fierce like harvest moons on the edge of a silky horizon.

His groaning turns into laughter and he rubs his scalp. "I always do something wrong, don't I? J-baby might…punish me again." His

56

eyes lit up by the thought, he takes the blood opal from his hair nest and sticks it under his tongue.

I don't know whether to feel disgust or pity for this guy. He's obsessed with Jaal, possibly even more so than I was. His words only push Reiki closer to me, and now she's shaking. Trying to comfort her with soft touches only seems to make her shake more.

Onyx's glowing eyes seep into Reiki's aura. As if entranced, she reaches out to grab Reiki's chin. "No worries, bruja. You're doing great." My grip tightens, but Reiki stops shaking. Something in her shifts, and her aura accepts the intrusion.

I search her face, only to be met with hazy brown eyes and a knowing smile. Even when blind, she still smashes my expectations.

Barking a laugh, Onyx wrenches open the door and stares us down as we walk out.

We follow a transparent tunnel through swirls of seawater, where fishy creatures and robots mingle and swim. Lights on the floor guide our way. This isn't the cozy atmosphere of my ship—it's stifling. I'm used to the breathless vacuum of space, but this tunnel makes my skin crawl. Gallons upon gallons of saltwater slosh over us like blue beer, intoxicating our senses and drowning out the light.

"The silence is nice," Reiki muses, "But I can feel the water pressure from here."

"Me too." I release her hand, only to find her gripping my elbow a minute later.

Not caring that Double-O walks behind us like a two-headed dragon, I lean into her slightly and say, "Listen. I know we haven't known each other that long, but—"

"Aw, look, Nyx," Obsidian taunts, fanning his face and flipping the faux-hawk. "He's proposing!"

I throw a sharp look over my shoulder, but it only makes them laugh. Cracking my knuckles, I whisper, "Reiki. I won't let anything bad happen to you again. Okay?"

Gratitude emanates from her before she shows it, a warm amber energy washing over us. She squeezes my arm, accepting my sentiment even though I completely avoided using the word "promise." Once we walk through the brass-colored doors ahead, my sense of control will be nearly obliterated. I can't even guess what they'll want to do with us.

Emphasizing that fact, Obsidian shoves me into the door while Onyx presses her inked hand over the scanner pad.

"Just so we clear," he says, broad palm pinning me to brass, "You ain't walking out 'til the deal is sealed. If J-baby wants something, he gets it."

Acutely aware of the gun stashed in my back pocket, I remember what Jaal told me seventy hours ago. I move the S-Com from my neck to my eyes and get online to check my account. Numerous colorful ads throw themselves at me, but I blink them all away, focusing on the new and shiny amount of cryptocurrency.

Zero.

That fucking bastard.

Swiftly, I throw a backwards kick at Obsidian's groin, spin around, and slide Reiki safely behind me. She yelps in surprise, but Onyx is apparently unfazed. While her brother groans and stumbles, she looks at me like a crow staring at something shiny.

"What's got your rocks in a knot?" She tilts her buzzcut head. "What, you think you're gonna murder your ex with the gun he let you have?"

Enraged, I take off the goggles and aim the gun for her head. "You people act like he gives me everything, but all he does is take. He thinks he can just take what he wants and then slather me with 'gifts', but that's not how I work. Not anymore."

"Zenith, wait—" Reiki tries, but I'm too pissed off. The only reason I sunk this low (literally) was to get my hard-earned cash, not have it all stolen from me. There's no reason to stay, to put up with this charade anymore. This is it. This is the final straw, the absolute deal-breaker.

For a moment, Onyx truly seems to be at a loss. She sighs, folding and unfolding her arms several times before leaning against the wall and shaking her head. "You're making this hard, homie."

A blunted edge strikes my skull. Her face and words blur.

Eight

When I return to consciousness, the first thing I see is Obsidian plunging his tongue down Jaal's throat. They lean over me, half-naked. The dimly lit room reeks of weed and fried electrical cords, and the first thing I feel—aside from disgust and rage—is the tightness of shiny chrome plates on my wrists and ankles, magnetizing me to a bed.

"Christ and Kronos," I try to say, only to realize they gagged me with a crystal sphere.

Drizzled in my saliva and theirs when they part, I attempt to yell more profanities, muscles straining against the bonds.

"Zenith, babe," Jaal says, stroking my knee. "Heard you was worried about the transaction going smoothly. Now you know." He sticks out his tongue, revealing the blood opal balanced against his silver piercing.

I cringe, spit dripping down the sides of my chin.

Laughing darkly, he takes out the gag, scraping my teeth, and hands it to Obsidian. "Sid-baby, leave. Me and Zen gotta talk. Alone."

Ever the obedient slave, Obsidian retreats into the shadows. I hear a door slide open and then shut, and when Jaal turns back to me, he snaps his fingers. Chandeliers fill the room with light. He casts a fluorescent gold gaze while demagnetizing the bonds with his mind-powered tech. Although I can move freely, the bonds stay on my body, making me feel more like a pet than a prisoner.

"What the fuck," I cough, sitting up.

"It's fun doing business with you," Jaal purrs. "But still want more. You know that."

59

I roll my eyes and rub under the bonds, where bruises are splattered. Every violet-brown mark is just another one of his fingerprints.

"There is no more," I relent. "You took all my money."

"You know what I mean, baby."

I roll my eyes so hard they ache. "You have a new bitch," I hiss, wiping my mouth with the hem of my shirt. At least he hasn't stripped me. "Give me the money and let me go."

"Oh." Jaal pouts and clicks his tongue with a pitying shake of the head. "You think you're done. That's cute."

Tears boil at the brims of my eyes. "I'm done. It's over. I have enough to buy...freedom."

"Nothing's ever really over, is it?" He straddles my hips. Above him, the glass ceiling reveals sharks and robotic fish chasing each other in a confused, sparking mess. *I'm so sick of glass rooms.*

"You said. I'd be rich. Free. Doing this job for you."
I turn to scan the room for my gun, but he pulls my chin so hard my jaw cracks.

"You can't resist me anymore," he says, craning his neck to lick mine. "I'm in charge of your funds, and I'm in charge of you. You oughtta beg me to—"

I slap him across the face, leaving an auric imprint of bright blue in his black fog. It's like pouring paint over several layers of tar.

He knees me in the crotch, and I yell, only to be shut up by his tattooed hand. "Better fuckin' relax, or I ain't gonna get to show you the best part. Have another deal for you, impossible to say no to. Meditate on that."

Meditate.

White spots swimming through my vision, I bite down hard on his palm, to which he yelps and backs off.

I squirm out from under him and search the room. There's no sign of my gun, or even the kyanite blade. On my feet, I feel lighter. Distance from him helps me reassess the energy. He looks unfazed, but the auric stain spreads. I've wounded him, somehow.

"Where's Reiki?" I demand.

He brings a hand to his mouth like a lion licking his paw, hiding a smile. "Who?"

"My friend. Where is she?"

His bleached eyebrows raise. "That what you call the girl who hit you over the head?"

60

A punch to the jaw would hurt less. My eyes narrow. "You're lying."

He sprawls on his stomach and rests his chin in both palms. "Nope."

I'm searching desperately again, this time for something metaphysical. I try to stretch my aura outward, seek out Reiki's warmth. But it's dark and heavy down here. My energy can't scatter like it wants to.

"You're an asshole," I mumble, balling my fists. Tears glaze my eyes while I return to the breath. Determined to feel whole again, even briefly, I sit on the floor in lotus position.

"You're actually meditating," Jaal says in disbelief.

I glare. "I've always meditated. You just never noticed."

"Noticed when you stopped, actually." His face softens, muddy lips parting in a half-grin. "Zenith. Baby. Everything comes together for us now, with this new plan I got. Lemme tell you about it. It's everything we wanted."

I sniff, refusing to be afraid of him. Seeing his aura in such a clogged state makes it a little easier. Reiki was right—I see him for what he is, even when he's right in front of me. But now, I'm not only repulsed by him. I pity him too. He's a shadow of someone else, a chaotic puppet of dark matter.

"I'll listen to you," I sigh. "After you tell me where Reiki is. Because if you've hurt her, or if any of your cronies—"

"Space and Time," he swears, rolling his eyes. "If I knew all it took to ignite your passion was a little snowflake, I'd—"

"Tell me where she is, or all deals are off. I'm not fucking around, Jaal." Too fidgety to meditate, I stand.

"Ooh," he chuckles, rolling onto his side. His hand rests on a satin-wrapped hip and glides across to twirl pajama drawstrings. "Why don't you come over here and prove it?"

I spin around and head for the door, where Obsidian left his desperate stench.

Jaal's voice plagues me. "Wouldn't do that if I was you, Z."

My palm stings when it hits the door. "Shut up!"

It slides open, and across the hall, open for everyone to see, there's a vast training room lined with weaponry. Warm lighting pools from panels in the floor, making everything glow.

In the center, Reiki hops from one foot to the other, swinging a pair of crystal nunchaku, sparring with Obsidian and Onyx. Her aura sizzles with electricity, contrasting sheets of yellow light with a storm of silver and blue. When she sees me, it fades. Quicker than I can blink, she switches to the knife I gave her, and throws it at my face.

Yelping, I duck and snatch it between flat palms. A thin line of blood crosses each hand, obscuring the tattoo like graffiti.

"You can see me?" My words fall flat on the floor.

Her auric cloud shifts from blue to pink, a rising sun peeking through dark haze. She looks at me directly, garnet gaze tumbling with something unreadable.

"Pleiades." I shake my head in disbelief. "I guess I was the blind one, huh?"

Tight-lipped, she rests the nunchaku over one shoulder. Snowy quartz glitters over her RSA-clad chest. Frost on the flag. Her hair sticks out from its bun in mad bouts of frizz like chopped wire. The look she gives me is painfully stunning.

Yet I stare at her dubiously when she approaches me and reaches for the knife. I pull it out of her reach. "What happened? Did they make you do this? Say something."

"She doesn't have to say anything," Onyx interjects, arms folded.

I could stab her with this knife. Instead, I squeeze the handle so hard, my knuckles crack. Blood decorates wrists. "Reiki, you're freaking me out. Don't be like G. Don't leave me in silence."

In an infinitesimal amount of time (or maybe it was space), her aura bursts and throbs in tendrils of every element and color known to Earth. But only I see it, and it passes so quickly I can't even tell what it means.

"Did you see a healer, like Obsidian promised?"

Another soft, pitying smile. Another emotional punch in the face. "I *am* the healer, Cap."

All at once, every fond moment we spent together in the past day twists into something monstrous. Every time she healed me becomes a wound. Every smile is a clenched jaw. Every question was a coy answer. Even the kiss was a play, a lie. She sussed her way into my heart, and I was dim enough to fall for it.

Blinded by scarlet rage, I drop the knife and go for her throat with my thumbs.

But an invisible force tugs my limbs backwards, yanking me back into the bedroom, where the magnetic field glues my bonds to the bed. I yell so hard, my throat splinters.

Jaal laughs, eyes fading from oil spill to amber. "Bad boy."

The door closes again before I can even think to look at her face, before her aura has a chance to explain itself.

Fuming, I tuck my chin toward my chest. "Don't touch me. Don't even fucking look at me."

"We can change positions if you want," he says, licking his lips. Heated rage is my only shield, but it's fading fast. In its place, only fear remains. Saltwater spirals down burning cheeks. Still, he reaches to unzip my jeans.

"Please," I beg, hating myself and everything that ever comes near me. "Please, Jaal. Just leave me alone."

A sun-colored brow twitches. "That's more like it. Now. Tell me you wanna hear the deal."

This is worse than having to look at Reiki. I want to open the door again, talk to her. Figure out her motives. Calculate the past few hours with higher wisdom. Not fear. I want to crack open her body and examine the organs, then throw them on a table for divination. I want to check her natal chart again, make sure she's human. *Please someone tell me I'm still human.*

"C'mon, Z-baby," he purrs, anchoring fingers in the belt loops and dragging. "Know what you want and know what I want. Makes us a great team."

I look up at the shadows of sharks and underwater robots, tears blurring with water. I could be swimming. Drowning. "Please, just. Get off me. And. Tell me about the deal."

He kisses me, open-mouthed, exhaling his rotten soul down my throat, leaving the taste of blood and pot. Somehow the opal stays under his slimy tongue. Then he peels himself off, leaving my jeans hanging off hips. "Strikin' a hard bargain, but I never liked it soft."

Tears and snot coat my face like makeup. He makes no attempt to care.

"Wanna know the real reason you got the blood opal?" Smirking, he removes the opal and holds it between thumb and forefinger. It looks like a scab and darkens his aura. "This ain't just a money-maker, Z. It's a life-saver. And there's only so many in our solar system."

I open my mouth, but he hushes me. "Watch."

He reaches under the bed and produces my gun. Automatically, I try to reach for it, forgetting about the magnets. To my surprise, he places it in my hand, allowing it to activate at my touch.

"Shoot me," he says, in the same voice he once used to lure me to bed.

I cock the gun. "You've actually lost your mind."

He cackles, a sound I've never heard lurch from his throat. "Not yet! Still plenty of time for that. Just do it, Zenith. Shoot me."

And I'll be safe.

He doesn't have to ask twice.

Just as he aligns his chest with the barrel, I pull the trigger, sending volts of electricity into the chasm where his heart should be.

Momentarily, he's a flailing bone diagram, a joint-rattling skeleton with ever-changing eyes. He seizes on the bed like a broken machine.

I shut my eyes so hard, more tears burst from the corners. It takes a few trembling breaths before I have the courage to open them again. When I do, he's lifeless. No movement, no sound. Not even an aura.

I stare in disbelief, letting tears continue to spill from my face to my chest, staining cloth. The room reeks of fried flesh. I bite my tongue to ward off gagging.

But then, warmth prickles my ankle, where Jaal's limp fist rests. The blood opal glows so intensely, light leaks between unfurled fingers. His aura returns like swamp fog—glossy, green, and darkening as it intensifies. With a swooping cough and gasp, he reanimates.

I don't know what makes me sob harder, the fact that I thought he was dead, or the fact that he's returned. A selfish part of me, hiding under the uncontrollable blubbering, hopes his soul's been cleansed somehow. Maybe the purgatory between this level and whatever Hell awaits made him a better person. But the lustful glint in his eyes debunks that theory.

He kisses me again, licking snot like a hungry dog.

"You *are* crazy," I hiss, turning away. Bile shimmies up my throat but I swallow it back down, clinging to a semblance of control.

"Maybe," he muses. "But the opal can fix that too, with a little help. If it's powerful enough to restart the heart, just think"—he taps my head as if hitting a button—"about what it could do to the brain."

I spit on the sheets. "What do you mean? What did it even do?"

Blinking sends the last tears rolling.

His barrel-shaped nostrils flare. The blood opal goes back into his mouth, giving him a lisp while he rolls it under his tongue. "I'm sick, Zenith."

I bark a laugh. "Yeah, no shit."

"Sick of the world we live in. No massive wars in a while, sure, but we're getting lost. Dragging our damn feet out here…we lack

64

inspiration, innovation. But the blood opals. They're not just science, baby. They're miracles." He wags a finger. "Do you know where blood opals are harvested, why they're so hard to get?"

I don't know, and I wouldn't give him the satisfaction even if I did.

"Star-caves. The only caves in the solar system that can handle and hold an abundance of solar energy."

I start the breath technique I always use—deep inhale through nose, long exhale out mouth. Urgency floods through me quicker than oxygen. "So?"

His breath hits my neck. "*So,* they're beads of cosmic fire. Perfect little capsules for channeling the most powerful energy source in the system."

Silence, other than our ragged breathing. If this was a few years ago, I'd be so turned on, unable to speak. This time, speechlessness stems from a harsh comprehension of my ex-lover's warped reality.

"You want to make more unnecessary weapons for your personal heists?" I ask, monotone.

"Nope. Nice guess, though." A grin splits his blistering lips. "If I work my magic, and everyone pitches in, we can make a vaccine for Gemini Fever."

I scoff, sick of hearing him speak. I lean back against the pillows and sigh. "That's a load of vom. Why are you telling me this?"

He squeezes my thighs. "Because this is what we need. What our people need. High-grade healing."

"You know nothing about healing."

"Bruja has helped us plenty, more than you have in the last few months." He lifts the shirt to kiss my lower stomach. My sacral chakra roars—attacked beast in a fleshy cage. "She knows more about healing than any of us, and she's willing, but her insight misses a few...matters." Low laughter rolls off his mouth like smoke. "I ain't crazy, Z. Not yet. But I'll be as batshit as your mama if this theory doesn't work." My muscles clench when his nails dig into my hips.

Corruption isn't the only thing corroding his mind.

My lips part, shoulders slack, limbs relax. I give in, not to him, but to the truth. "You're Feverish, aren't you? When you said you were sick, you meant—"

"Smart boy."

"You don't want to help people. You're just in it for yourself."

"It ain't just me who needs this, Z. There's a whole flock of humans out there, waiting for our help, including your mama."

"You can't cure her," I say, zoning out on the blackened spot of energy between his eyes. It's like a second silent mouth, screaming for help into the void of his being.

I'm not sure if I mean he can't cure Mama because she's incurable, or because he shouldn't be the one to do it.

He looks less like a lion and more reptilian every second. "Worth a shot, ain't it?" After shoving me playfully, he swings his legs over the bed's edge and does a shot of absinthe. I hadn't even noticed the bottle was there, but its sharp green collides with his numbed aura.

The shot glass makes a popping noise when it hits the bedside table. He ejects a wheezing cough. Fluorescent green leaks from his mouth. "Anyway." He turns to me again, irises churning. "Thought you could use a family visit."

Shivers etch my spine. "How considerate of you."

He inhales a rattling breath. "This ain't a remedy we're making. It's widespread prevention. The Galaccine."

If I could facepalm, I would. "Are you serious?"

"Deadly." His tongue flicks over glistening teeth. "Goal is to strengthen, immunize, immortalize—at a cellular level. Saturate our cells in pure energy." He thrusts the blood red bead in my face 'til it blurs. "With Saturnine aurorae packed in 'em, these'll make us so adaptable, our bodies beat the Fever before it even starts. Almost like we become the Fever, embody it to battle it." A brow quirks.

I scoff. "You're gonna fight flares with flares? That's the stupidest theory you've ever had!"

Jaal watches me for a moment in calculative silence, tilting his head like a robot. He could unhinge at any moment, gears cranking 'til they clatter on the floor. "Been researching this for years, Z. Bruja told you about auric fields, didn't she?"

Heat floods my face. "Y-you wouldn't know anything about that. It's not science."

I hate his smile. "Wrong, brother." He tugs a loose earlobe. "Everything is science."

He used to tell me that late at night, when I stared through his bedroom skylight and questioned the universe. He never made room for anything but science. Even religion was something he thought he could yank by a leash, dominate, and simplify.

Unable to sit still, Jaal gets out of bed and paces. I remember this tick too. He did it when the mind finally took over the body. Intellect versus ego. He gestures wildly while he speaks. "Saturn's rings and moons create a special kind of aurorae, stuff our people have been wondering about for centuries. But ancient scientists never knew what was really going on."

My face hardens with skepticism. "And you do?"

He punches the glass wall, causing the sound of a crack, but no marks. "They're more compatible with our bodies, and more compatible with blood opals. Have a whole fuckin' trove of opes now—since bitches paid their debts—ready to be happy little pills. Immunize the body and mind with a spark of sunlight in each weak cell. Fortification. Sending immunity into superhuman overdrive." He claps, his eyes changing color rapidly, flicking mainly between obsidian and dwarf star red.

I scrunch my nose. "Jaal, come on. You're a scientist—a stellarfucking weapon maker—not a Conduit. Not God. You can't…you have no right…to do something like that."

"That's what skeptics said when Conduits cured cancer."

"No," I shut him down immediately. "It's not."

He huffs. "Well. Your bruja's a Conduit. She has the right, don't she? That's why we're working with her."

"Her name is Reiki," I say carefully. "And you're not working with her. You're using her. She's probably too naïve to understand that."

In a dash, he smacks me upside the head, causing my teeth to clatter. Blood thumps against my temples, trying to get out.

"For your info," he seethes, "she signed a contract, like you did four years ago. Read the whole thing, fine print and all." His eyes narrow and he points at me. "You need to take this seriously, Z. She knows more of what she's getting into than you did."

Boiling in his blatant hypocrisy, I take a long, slow breath and rub my jaw. "That's the truest thing you've said so far." Another breath to bring the boil to a simmer. Cool the steam. I'm the one in control. I must be, because he's finally lost it.

"Zenith, please," he whines, knees bent like a begging child. This is new.

"You're not giving me a choice. You haven't even told me what I'm supposed to do!" I protest, blowing a sticky strand of hair out of my hot face.

He straddles me again, dwarfing my face in his broad palms. Calloused fingers snag my loose curls. "Baby, it's simple. We go to Saturn with some blood opes and the best technology in the fuckin' galaxy and capture some aurorae. J-Daddy cooks you up somethin' special and you head home with a big grin and an antidote for your mama."

I shake my head fiercely, curls brushing sticky pillows. "A vaccine is not an antidote."

"It's not a vaccine; it's *the Galaccine*. Fortified, superhuman, cellular immunity. For life." He kisses my neck, letting breath avalanche. "Quit being so jumpy. This ain't a Pharm; it's a damned miracle. Think on it, Z."

Nine

I do think on it. And I think it's fucking insane.

Despite his efforts to make me comfortable—undoing the bonds completely and offering me privacy to shower and change—I've never been more out of my comfort zone.

It's been a few hours since he pinned me to the bed and made me listen, and now I'm alone in a different room. I stare at globs of fish that glide outside transparent walls. How ironic that I'm the one caught in a tank.

Despite having showered again, Reiki's scent still haunts me. It's as if the sweet part of her aura melted into mine and lingers there for safekeeping. At least Jaal's sweat slid off with ease, for once.

It wasn't always that way. I used to scrub my skin in boiling water 'til it bled, obsessed with exfoliating every dead cell that still swelled with Jaal's orgasms.

Reiki's scent isn't carnal, but it's just as painful. Maybe even more so because it took to me so quickly, punctured holes in my soul as opposed to my body. Somehow, she reached deeper than Jaal ever did in the smallest span of time.

I try to remember what it was like to be relaxed, to breathe as though it's my first string of breaths.

It's like a shitty song on repeat, all of this, and I keep falling for the pause in between. Every salvation I follow leads to another personalized Hell.

A knock echoes from the door, making my spine jolt. I blink and run my hands through my hair, pausing to make sure I heard correctly. The knock comes again, softer this time.

Without speaking, I rise and open the door, my palm splayed on a glowing green pad.

Reiki's coppery hair is plaited in mandalas, letting loose at the nape of her neck, tumbling down her back. She wears a gray bralette and joggers, wrists and feet wrapped in cerulean ribbon. A holster around her stem-like waist supports my knife and a pair of jasper nunchaku. Ballerina warrior. Her freckles are mud splatters under the hallway's shoddy lighting, but it's nothing compared to the deep, wet caverns of her eyes. I sink into them like a victim of quicksand.

"Hi." Her smile stings worse than the cuts.

"What do you want?"

"May I...um. May I come in?"

When I observe her aura, taking full advantage of the gift she gave me, it shimmers like a fading mirage. A dysfunctional S-Com scene.

Something's missing. But the natal tattoo winds across her palm and wrist, reminding me she's still human. Something good could return.

Stepping aside, I let her in, watching her every move as I take my hand off the pad to close the door. She sits where I was before, pulling knees to her chest.

Her aura billows outward, a cloak of smog. I yearn to hold her but ignore the feeling. Even if I can help, I shouldn't. She did this to herself the moment we met. Instead, I sit across from her, limbs folded in repose. Regret.

It takes her a moment or two to solidify what she wants to say. With her hands folded, she hides truth in the solar plexus. When she finally speaks, a beam of lime light hits me so hard, every sense is stimulated.

"Give me your hands," she says.

Laughter erupts from my chest, harsh and uncomfortable. "What?"

She chooses the words carefully. "I healed myself, and now I'm going to heal you." Her eyes melt. "Please, Zenith. Let me do what I'm meant to."

I grit my teeth. "You were meant to be on my side, not his. You lied to me. Why would I let you touch me ever again?"

"Because you like it when I do." I expect a teasing smile, but all I get is painful transparency.

Seething, I throw myself to my feet. "You're impossible. I trusted you so much, so quickly! But you're just like him. You reel me in with all your promises, claiming to have my well-being in mind, and then

70

you throw me back out to fend for myself. You guys make a fabulous team." I stalk across the room and press my forehead against the glass. A humanoid fish bot winks as it passes.

Reiki doesn't move, but I feel her energy spreading, cradling me in warmth.

My breath fogs the glass. "Stop it."

"I'm not doing anything."

"Then stay away. Keep doing nothing. I don't want your healing anymore. All I want is the money and my ship. The rest can drown for all I care."

A sensation like honey trickles down my back. I see her move in a dim reflection on the wall. Each step she takes toward me makes the room spiral. What you need is to heal. You've started now; you can't stop—"

"Everyone talks about healing like they know what it is!" I yell. "Like it's possible. For me."

I'm not crying for me, but for the child I used to be.

He's so far from me now, I almost forget that we're the same person. His heart was too big and open for such a slender chest.

Something settles between Reiki and me, a sheet of sparkling air, cosmic dust. Our souls whisper without knowing exactly what they say. Although anger still rumbles in the drums of my being, her thumbs wipe tears from my face until her touch is all I feel. Through her hands, liquid gold seeps into pores and follicles and scars, regenerating the feelings I thought I'd abandoned. Brief moments I'd lost.

"It *is* possible," she says, her voice like the wind, "for everyone." The music we made last night laces us—a pink-and-blue imprint of our fresh companionship—and lingers after she retracts. She faces the wall like it's a mirror, staring into her own eyes longingly. "You think you can't trust me. But once you stop thinking, all you'll *feel* is Truth." Her whispers make my scalp tingle. "Not only am I on your side, Cap. I *am* your side. Always have been."

I sniffle, unable to count the number of tears I've shed recently. "That's either very Biblical, very stupid, or super sexual. I guess I'll take it." Dabbing my nose with a sleeve, I throw her some side-eye. "You talk like we've known each other for a long time."

For a second, her eyes flash multicolor, and I wonder if she has Jaal's contacts too. But it's so quick, it can't be. Just another dysfunctional perception.

Pulling my hair back into a bun, I clear my throat. "I don't want to feel the truth, Reiki. I want to know it."

She looks down at her hands, fingers trembling. "Same thing."

Frustrated with our dancing banter, I ask, "Why did you lie to me? What the hell is all this about?"

"Jaal told you, didn't he? He's trying to prevent and cure Gemini Fever."

"Yeah, but what I can't figure out," I ponder, cracking my knuckles, "is why you're working for him. You're more intelligent than I give you credit for, so what gives? You don't actually believe his theory, do you?"

Her aura spills. She's still hiding behind layers of energy, but they're fraying. After a moment of thought, lips knotted together, she nods.

I rub my eyes 'til they burn, hands sliding down in exasperation. "That's why he sent you to me, isn't it? To persuade me. Lie to me, or with me. Whatever worked to get me here."

Silence sizzles where there should be an explanation. I want her to say, *I chose to follow you. I like being around you.* I want her to pledge loyalty to me, not Jaal, and not some ball of energy. For once, I want someone to look up to me, not the other way around.

"Jaal has done terrible things," she sighs, taking out the knife. She inspects it under a low-hanging bauble chandelier. Dots of whiteish light lodge in its blade. "But even he deserves to heal."

The words are a stab to the gut. Not only does she ignore the question and what it insinuates, but she has the nerve to victimize Jaal. "How can you say…"

A long, slow inhale cleaves the space between us. "I didn't lie to you about everything," she says, releasing the smallest sliver of blue truth. "I still want to be safe and free. Like you do. We can still help each other. I still know you more than you know yourself." Every word of hers is another jagged thorn in my forehead. If only they could make me bleed.

"That's my knife," I say, holding out a hand. "Give it back, and I'll think about trusting you again. Looks like you don't really need it, anyway."

Embracing her unofficial role as "Queen Invader of Privacy"— or maybe "Goddess of the Unexpected"—she strides forward, slides the knife into my jean pocket, and takes my hands. The scrapes burn, opening afresh. Steam-like energy escapes the snarling red mouths. I suck breath between tight teeth.

72

But when she turns my palms upward, liquid light puddles in crevices, dousing the wounds and drowning pain. Strips of skin sew themselves shut with supernatural stitches.

Here we go again.

"See?" Her voice lingers a notch above a whisper as light restores skin cells. "Healing is always in reach. Especially for you. You just need to be open to it." She kisses each hand like Christ's disciple honoring the stigmata, but she's the one who does the miracle work. As the light fades, I have the irritating urge to genuflect.

"Zenith," she says, dark gaze sharpening. She holds my shoulders square. "Whether you like it or not, our paths are aligned. I can lead you back to yours, if you'll let me."

"How many times—and with how many metaphors—are you gonna beg me to trust you?"

Her nose scrunches, warping freckles. Her gaze floods when it falls to my hands. "I'm sorry I threw the knife at you. Training is…intense, but that's no excuse. Being around these people just makes me…"

"Fucking crazy?" Uncomfortable laughter falls, our giggles merging and growing like throbbing gongs.

I want to laugh with her like we did when we were on the ship, like it was a feast. Now it feels more like throwing up—expelling all the blockages that keep me from seeing what's true. If I exorcise all this fear, then maybe I'll have room for something else. Something better.

I clear my throat. "You still haven't persuaded me."

The mischievous smile rises like a peeking sun, flickering across her eyes and settling in her chin. "Would you like me to?"

It's the first time she—or anyone for that matter—asks for my consent. I feel so warm, so shocked into silence, all I can do is swallow and nod.

Stupidly, I expect her to keep preaching about healing, but instead she closes her eyes and holds my head by the temples. Pressure builds between our merging foreheads, melting synapses and fusing wavelengths. I can feel everything again—highs, lows, and every notch in between. But I'm fine, safe in the gentle embrace of a body I barely know, but a recognizable soul.

Instead of hearing her voice, I feel an inner speech leaking through cells and fibers. Wordless and wise, it whispers to bodily and cosmic systems, mending broken pieces and hacking up needless cords. Together, we shift through this lifetime, feeling every choked scream that begs to erupt. Time unravels again, renewed.

73

Mother and I used to meditate like this at bedtime. We sipped chamomile tea and wrote down all the gifts we were grateful for and all the burdens we would release during sleep.

When I was little, the universe was loving. I didn't only have two mothers. I had infinite parental influences. I was connected to the cosmos before even exploring them. But when Mama contracted Gemini Fever, I was filled with prepubescent rage. I called the universe a cold bitch and consequently labeled myself the same.

Mama was my ocean—something so vast, I could barely understand, but wanted to embody. Eventually, I sank, not because of her nature, but because of the sky's nature—uncontrollable storms that shook saltwater out of its crater and turned it to blood.

Returning to the present with a shake of my head, I realize one painful fact—I'm always going to be Mother, cleaning a maniac's messes, simpering after unattainable approval. I could never be how Mama was in her prime—a starwork among cooling coals—and I will never be what she became. The fact that Jaal wants me to visit them paints my tongue with brine.

I don't want it. I don't want any of this.

Yet, the thought of an antidote sticks. A whisper of hope, like a shooting star that someone else sees first. If I keep looking hard enough, maybe I'll find my own, because this wish is hardly mine anymore. To heal others is a gift beyond comparison. But to counteract Gemini Fever at its core? It's like angels killing demons—nearly impossible, because the demons were fallen angels to begin with.

Reiki's hands shake when emotions cusp, as if we've lived the same life. Mutual understanding swirls between us. Instinctively, I place my hands over hers, holding them steady. Her smile glows, light bleeding under closed eyelids. There's still a tug in my gut and a gnawing in my chest, but it all drowns in the weight of letting go.

When she does speak, it sounds distant—the room has expanded and we're on opposite sides, an ever-swelling balloon of the universe.

It's a process, she calls from beyond space, jumping through energetic hoops, amplifying sound and meaning. *All your life, all you've done is take that which isn't yours. But when you let go, you'll feel it. You'll know why it's worth the wait.*

I don't know if she means the *wait* I endure or *weight* I carry, but I'm comforted regardless. The words sizzle and echo like a spell, chanting to cells new and old. They course through my DNA, to the core of what makes me human, and I can just begin to detangle strings of Truth.

Her lips move against mine, speaking words into action, reminding me that she's here. Even when she's not. I can't tell if it's real or imagined, but in this place, both are the same.

You don't believe in a remedy because you don't believe in healing, but you're always searching for it. How can you find and keep something you don't believe exists? Belief is Truth, before it manifests. Make space for something you've never seen. Make space for healing.

I'm not a pirate of treasures, but emotions. I steal people's feelings before they have a chance to process them. I glom onto their toxic glow.

It's not a broken S-Com scene—it's transcendent of every sense. Physicality and spirituality are one. I've never orbited so close or retrograded so far.

In a quiet room underwater, practically held captive, I start to feel more fully, for the first time in my life.

Ten

Hours later, in a room none of us want to be in, throngs of smoke bluster and billow in a grounded storm. Little coughs scatter the air and puncture speech. Crystal bongs clink like glasses in toast. Ash litters the floor and table. Everything is glossy, fragile, and too expensive to look at, let alone touch. (No wonder he "needs" my trove to fund Project Galaccine.)

This is supposed to be a living room, but there isn't much room for living.

On his makeshift throne, Jaal leans forward, eyebrow twitching. "We got a deal?" He asks, plucking a blunt from his mouth and waving it at us like a wand. Aluminum fabric crinkles over his bulging muscles. At his heels like pampered hounds, Onyx and Obsidian sit in bean bags.

"N-not yet." I cough only to hide my trembling tongue. "I need to clarify a few things first." I flourish a hand, hoping to move the flow from words to body, solidify a confident façade.

Under Jaal's sluggish but interested gaze, I aim to find a slice of comprehension. A seed of agreement. It's just another song, another performance life demands of me. But even an actor needs some wiggle room for improvisation. This room is like a stage, carrying my voice up and dropping it back down. Even breath echoes here. "You want Reiki, Obsidian, Onyx and me to go to Saturn. You want us to capture aurorae for you, so you can combine it with blood opals to make an impossible vac—Galaccine for Gemini Fever."

He claps, the joint dribbling ash on the corner of his fat mouth. "So, you do listen. Good to know."

Ignoring a twinge in my neck, I continue. "Saturn is days, maybe weeks, away. There's no way we can get there and back before…" I

76

pause to feel the words between my teeth. "Before impatience takes over." I raise a skeptical brow. "This isn't a quick trip, Jaal. You'll lose your damn mind waiting for us."

Obsidian and Onyx chuckle. Their auras attack mine and Reiki's like smoke mixing with vapor.

It's not like I trust Reiki entirely now, but she makes me feel free. When it comes to Jaal, I don't really have much of a choice. But at least I can pretend I do when Reiki's with me.

"Not to mention," I add before Jaal can insert his two-gems. "There's a reason no one's captured Saturnine aurorae before."

When silence is all I get, sharp laughter juts from my unhinged jaw. "C'mon. Don't play stupid. The Saturnine sector is just as dangerous as the Mercurial. It's so far away, nearly on the outskirts of the system. There are gallons of dark energy bubbles, black holes, ice comets…"

"Your point?"

"Anything could happen. Someone could…" I glance at Reiki, but she's staring at Jaal with a placid gaze.

"Die?" Jaal butts in, sneering. "This ain't my first floatin' lotus, Z. People die every day. Death's easier than the Fever. You know that." He takes a deep drag before tossing the blunt on the floor and stomping it out with a bedazzled heel. "Told you a hundred times before—science means sacrifice. Takes a dozen deaths to save a hundred lives."

On that uplifting note, I turn to leave. Rethink the situation, propose a different deal. I need more time to ruminate. There must be a compromise, and this isn't it.

Jaal leaps to his feet. "Zenith." His voice drips like hot wax.

"I'm not negotiating with you if you're going to talk like that." I blink, almost wishing my eyes weren't so dry so I could release the bullshit. "I never wanted our…this work to be long-term."

He covers a chortle with a reflective sleeve. "Retiring early?"

When I look at him, my throat chakra ejects a royal blue icicle of energy. It hits his aura and sends spiderweb cracks crawling over the metallic sheen.

Seemingly unaware, he raises his hands in placating defeat. "Okay, look. It's not Pluto or Andromeda, baby, just Saturn. Will ease all your worries later. For now, let's eat."

A lump in my throat wobbles, melting the ice so that it slides down my spine. "Okay." I mainly give in so he'll stop talking.

When Jaal's contacts shift from yellow to blue, a mind-powered symphony activates. Whizzing maid-bots rise from the floor to clean the weed den. They tint pink when Jaal slaps them to speed them up. I can't help but think of the two men from Mars.

While the robots perform software-driven slavery, the room changes from glass to chrome and fake wood. Theater to restaurant. Only the classiest technological advancements for the nastiest man.

The table glows white and stretches to fit our space, molding itself as if made of animated water, molecules shifting with the blink of Jaal's eyes. Icepick-thin robot fingers ignite holographic candles. Yellow-green light makes Onyx and Obsidian look like painted demons. I wonder if they dress that way to distinguish themselves from the robots.

Reiki giggles, trying to cover up her shaking. She might even be more uncomfortable than I am.

Lazily, Jaal pokes an enormous chandelier that lowers from the ceiling. Without leaving a trace of mechanical power or physical change, the robots finish their duties with bowed heads.

I wait a few calculated breaths before asking, "Where's the food?"

From the depths of his tin foil wrapping, Jaal produces four S-Coms. My grime-coated goggles stand out like a bolt among feathers. I was unaware he'd taken them at all.

"Sens-Eating? You're joking."

Jaal shakes his head, and with another shift of his irises, summons tiny drones. They hover like dragonflies to drop dissolvable capsules into a flute of water for each of us, before disappearing back into their shadowy compartments. If I cared enough, I'd try to find where all these critters come from, but I'm still distracted by the fish— that, and the general pressure of an encroaching business deal.

Breathe, I tell myself, or maybe it's Reiki's voice bundled in my hair. *Play his little game, and then you're in the clear.*

Jaal stares at me while he activates the S-Com, eyes shifting from dark to absolute white like puddles of milky vodka. I pretend to do the same, holding the goggles loosely over my eyes. As soon as he's knee-deep in the illusion of consumption, I lower them and scan the company.

Obsidian and Onyx slurp their infused water like giddy children on vacation, each wearing an outrageous mask, but Reiki is as apprehensive as I am. We look at each other, siphoning yet another soundless agreement. It buzzes like music between immobile lips. I wipe the goggles off and put them back around my neck, where they wait to be used for something more mindful.

Reiki sniffs the water, wrinkles her nose, and grips the bottoms of our glasses. Slowly, the water morphs from liquid to gas, heated only by her palms. My jaw hangs open as liquid simmers, boils, and disappears.

That can't be good to breathe in, I think. *But that was so cool.*

My train of thought is jostled by the choir of noshing moans at our table. I lean back and fold my arms, stomach cycloning.

Under all this tension and rage, I still have so many questions for Reiki. Our exchange of energetic empathy seems to be worth more than all the words or gems in the solar system.

Bolts and screws clatter in my brain while I try to work out the kinks of our sudden closeness. It's not perfect, by any means, but I need someone on my team, and at least this time it's a twenty-two-year-old space witch instead of a twenty-eight-year-old sociopath.

Speaking of the Devil and his demons, the three of them deactivate their S-Coms and belch in satisfied unison. Empty glasses, empty grins.

Jaal rises like a king, irises glittering black, and cracks his spine. "Bruja told you what you needed to know, but I can show you." He reaches for my hand, and I avoid it by holding onto Reiki's.

"Where I go, she goes." A lifting wind of hope circulates. I may be grateful for her wisdom. I might enjoy the softness of her touch. But I'll be damned ass to head if I let her play double-agent again without my knowing. The soul knows she's always close, but the ego needs her here to make sure she doesn't betray me again.

Pretending it doesn't knot his nerves, Jaal shrugs and stalks ahead, leading us to the source of his grandiose promise. Colorless shadows surround him, whether from irritation or the Fever, I can't tell.

On our way through tinted glass hallways, my grip on Reiki's hand tightens, skin tugging like suction cups. Mirroring the sound, psychedelic squids follow us on the other side.

Jaal's tin foil cloak whips in front of us, reflecting yellow dome lights. For a moment, I sympathize with him, trying to reach his stoned level of comprehension. Clearly, his power has never been questioned before this, and before Reiki, he never had a reason to be jealous. Now, he can't stop from glancing at our laced fingers, practically drooling. It sets every vertebra on edge, and yet the pink smugness in Reiki's aura keeps me aware of the truth—I don't need to be afraid of him anymore. Simultaneously, I'm hyperaware of his current disposition. Gemini Fever isn't something I want to stick around. It's not technically contagious, but the madness that erupts isn't healthy to behold. Not again. I keep my mouth shut while we continue to wind our way down to his labs.

"We're like blood cells in a vein," Reiki muses aloud, and I quietly admire her for it. "But who's red and who's white?"

"A better question is: who's the infection?" I'm shocked by how low my voice is.

Even Obsidian and Onyx titter with hands over their mouths, but when we approach a door, Jaal punches it. Instantly, the sound of crackling joints and dented metal echoes down the hall we came from. Tiny, light-powered fish startle and scatter like stars.

"An underwater lab," I say, eager to divert his attention. Return the lion's mane. "How…innovative."

Jaal turns as if his body is made of clockwork, face twisted in a clownish grin. "You better be impressed. Had this worked on for ages before you came along, and now look at it." He spreads his arms wide in praise, pushing open the double doors. A priest in his domain. "Everything we could ever need." Despite his reverent appearance, the greed in his aura is unmistakable—tinted, swashing vomit colors. He moves between sin and synthetic so quickly, I doubt that even Saturn's flares can save his crazy ass.

Inside, blacklights filter the room, causing every object to glow. When I look at him quizzically, he explains, "Makes it easier to clean."

At first, I don't understand what he means, but with the door closed, neon smudges stain every surface. A haunted cathedral, it's equipped with advanced scientific tools, enabling Jaal to screw with the structure of the universe in a small space.

Walls are lined with cupboards of vials, each highlighted by fingerprints and streaks of leftover experimentation. Ironically, nothing is sacred. It's a perpetual crime scene, decorated to seem holy.

Rubbing my wrist, I relate to this bruised room. We both have the kind of injuries that can only be seen in certain lighting. We have become vessels for everything that isn't ours.

"It's just a lab," I think aloud, unsure if it's directed toward myself or Jaal. When Jaal whips his head to look at me, dreadlocks swooping, my throat cinches.

"Watch your mouth when you're inside her," he says with a smirk, patting the walls. "She's sensitive."

I glance at Reiki, whose milk-colored face glows like a moon in this light. Her chapped lips stretch. "He talks about this room like you talk about your ship."

With the flick of a switch, Jaal turns on a generator, and the room rumbles to life. A machine in the center buzzes and spits fire behind a glass tank. Despite our initial jump of shock, the glow adds warmth to the space. Even without tuning into my third-eye, I feel dozens of different energies tumbling in segments around us, metaphysical chunks oozing and bleeding through shifting light.

"Well, whatever this is, it is like Syzygy's engine," I say softly, only intending Reiki to hear.

But Jaal has the ears—and face—of a jet-powered jackal. "Close. But no." He walks the perimeter of the tank. Under a spark of yellow fire, his hair looks white. "It's a transmuter."

"Like a star," Reiki persists.

"No," Jaal says, teeth grinding. "Less heat and mass. More empty matter. Fire so physical, it almost acts like the human body, simply speakin'."

Brows bridging, I lean to peer at it from a different angle. Behind the cubic cage of stellaglass, fire floods, shifting between lava and pink vapor.

"Organic like flesh, hot as blood," Jaal continues, preening himself on being so toxically clever. "Absorbing and reacting to substances in a way that mimics human bodies, human immune systems." Shadows shift over his face, but I can practically hear his ridiculous eyebrows lift like wings. "This is our constant variable— Phoenix Compound. Safe for cellular regeneration. Perfect for testing our Galaccine."

"Oh, so you are planning on testing it before you inject it," I mutter, receiving a slap across the back of the head from Obsidian. His rings tug my split ends. Despite his joking beam, I bite my tongue.

A bubble rises from the mass, morphing into the shape of a fetal head, complete with a mouth, nose, and eyes. When Reiki gasps, it sinks back into a glowing mush, but I swear I heard it scream. It takes a lot of willpower for me not to scream with it.

"Where did you get it?" Onyx beats me to the question, but I hear the stupid grin without seeing it, signifying that she already knows the answer.

"Aw. But I wanted them to guess." Sighing, Jaal slaps the top of the tank, sending steam rolling off his palm. "Same place I got your friend here." His eyes dance. "Before Madam T broke our deal, she was a great gift-giver."

I bite the inside of my cheek. "What?"

81

He nods toward Reiki, arms folded across his chest. "Surprised she didn't tell you."

Next to me, her energy ebbs and surges in chaotic waves. Onyx and Obsidian feed on it like blind, rabid dogs. The lack of true vibing is extraordinary—I don't know how he expects us all to work together.

"Tell me what?" I squeeze Reiki's hand so hard, knuckles pop. I have a feeling I'll be doing this a lot—holding her so tight that inevitably she runs away. Or I do.

Scoffing, Jaal rubs his hands together. "Tauris has been denying me the last opal for months. Said it was too special to be in my hands. Coveted commodity. That's why we sent you in, to be sly, y'know?"

"And?" I wipe sweat off my Cupid's bow; it stings.

"Before she paid for her negligence—"

"—with her life," I interject. Biting my tongue keeps me from spitting at him.

"She paid with someone else's." His chin tilts toward Reiki.

Yanking away from my sweaty grasp, Reiki pulls her elbows close to her chest. "I'm sorry, Zenith. I should've told you."

But I'm not mad, I think. *How could I be? It's like I thought...We are both slaves to this madness.*

Even though she feels my thoughts, she curls further into herself, denying my empathy. Such a hypocrite.

Clearing my throat, I press on, trying to ignore the fact that he treated her like a pack of trading cards. "So, you expect me to drag this lava-clone all the way to Saturn and inject it with even more unnecessary pain, for the sake of scientific discovery?"

Jaal cackles and holds up an index finger. "Wah-wah-one. It's scientific salvation. And two." A peace sign. "It's not alive. It only acts like it is."

"Do you hear yourself when you talk?" I ask, trailing the tank's perimeter. Obsidian reaches for my wrist but I tug away. "Is that what you said about Reiki, when Tauris handed her over like a...what was it, commodity?" I scoff, phlegm raking my throat. "She's my friend, not your bargaining chip. We both work for you, sure, but that means nothing in the face of..." I bury a trembling fist in my jean pocket.

He tilts his head, a brow raised.

"This..." I gesture to the tank of redness, its swirling and ever-collapsing mouth burning my heart from the inside out. "This isn't just new technology, Jaal, it's...unethical. I don't have room for this thing in my moral compass, let alone Syzygy. This is the most irrational, unscientific thing you've ever proposed!"

82

He coughs. "About your ship, ah…Syzygy is…temporarily decommissioned. Fixing that bug in her programming, like you asked."

Unwavering, I walk right up under his big, scrunched nose and say, "Then I'll wait. But I'm not doing this without my ship." The low voice strains my vocals, but the deep blue that it generates is the most intimidating thing I have.

At first, his eyes surge like broken power sockets. But then he laughs heartily and slaps my shoulder. "Cocks n' comets. The witch and the ship, sure. Whatever you want."

"Thank you."

Jaal smirks and sprawls his arms wide. "Been a while since you thanked me. You think your pretty little possessions are so important, that the money is crucial, hah. As usual, I'm here to take you under my wing, little boy, and teach you about the bigger picture. Sure, I'll give you what you want. Always do." His tongue piercing clangs teeth. "But you'll be giving the galaxy what it wants. What it needs."

There it is—a dazzling fractal of compromise. My new motivation. We say it in unison, speaking it into being: "Healing."

Eleven

"Do you really think it's gonna work?" I ask for the hundredth time. "The Galaccine?"

Reiki sighs, swinging our arms as we stroll down Main Street with entwined hands. "I think it's worth a shot."

I ignore the accidentally recycled pun. "But like, is it preventative or is it a cure?"

"Both."

I raise an eyebrow. "You sound so confident."

"Well, I'm confident in Jaal's confidence." That almost makes me let go of her hand. But then she adds, "and I have the utmost faith in you."

We have this pseudo-couple thing going on, and maybe it's just part of the façade we've built, but I'm starting to like it. To Hell with whatever Jaal thinks.

"Thanks, but. I'm sure someone in a few galaxies over already has this cosmic cure thing figured out, and as usual, humans are a hundred steps behind."

Her chin trembles, releasing a burst of giggles. "Shh, don't tell Jaal."

The warm moments shared like secrets are my favorite. Even the saddest saps who lurk under buzzing lamps can't help but smile when they see us.

"People used to look at Jaal and me like that," I muse, quickly tossing my gaze to the side when a pair of gentlemen tip feathery hats at us.

"You think a lot about how other people see you," she observes. "There's nothing wrong with that, but there's nothing right about it either. Nobody's judging you as harshly as you judge yourself."

"Doubt it," I reply as my eyes lock with the green orbs of a tall, reptilian woman.

At night, San Fran Isle is cloaked in metallic frigidness. A sharp curfew of seven o'clock reels in most crime, enforced by silvery jet-hounds policing sidewalks. It's like the damp caverns of Mars, in which everyone depends on false sunlight and synthetic companions. Moral authority comes from strict code and calculation, not subjective bystanders or a brainwashed cop.

Justice and order are predators lurking in the same shadows as their prey.

Impoverished criminals are masked in dirt, seeking sensation, hoping for trouble—money, tech, sex, drugs, or even a glance. Anything to make them feel more alive than their cold-nerved hunters. When we pass one of the taller skyscrapers laced with electrical vines, a hound emerges from the wall panels and stalks past us on hind legs.

"Say what you want about Jaal," she says, reacting to my full-body shiver. "But at least he keeps you off the streets."

It's such an old-fashioned thing for her to say, it makes me do a double-take. Even though I'm looking at a freckled snowflake of a girl with petrichor eyes, a veil of antiquated masculinity falls, a faded photograph. *It's like I've seen her soul before, in a different body...*

Needles prick my forehead when she giggles. "What?"

I shake my head. "Every path is a street," I argue stubbornly, hiding peppered blush. "Jaal just keeps me on the wrong one."

She nods, balancing my pain and hers on each shoulder. "He must be changing, though. He let us out for a walk."

"We're not dogs," I snap, crushing orange energy in our squeezed hands. "We can go anywhere, whenever we want."

Her eyes crinkle. "I've been trying to tell you that for..."

"As long as we've known each other."

Genetically engineered bugs drop from trees, cleaning and lighting up the air around us, keeping it fresh. Underwater systems activate, glowing to boil and purify waterways. The whole road is like a cleansing fountain, changing color with each stage.

I suck my lips against teeth. "Reiki, what happened with Tauris? Why did she hand you over like transited cargo?"

Her hand goes limp, falling out of my grasp. She walks ahead of me, touching each tree we pass. Every stroke sends pearlescent light

85

scattering through half-synthetic branches, down biomechanical roots, and into the earth and water thrumming under us. Only she would aid the flow of systems she can't fathom.

"Humans separate themselves from Nature, especially in science, so they can use her as a scapegoat. But we don't heal by forcing Nature to adapt to us...that's like cultural assimilation. To heal is to recognize the mutuality between Nature and humanity—gradually integrating, like your city has done with its climate—to explore differences and share common essence. Energetically, we're already one. We don't need to interfere. We just need to listen, let the processes unfold..."

I snag her waist, spinning her to face me.

Stewing in the rant, her irises sizzle like burnt rubber. "Tauris knew that wise dynamic. That's why she left Earth when she was young, to remember Oneness...and you did the same, subconsciously." She kisses my cheek with cool lips, leaving a periwinkle stain and bubbles in my stomach. "See, Tauris was Jaal's counselor for a while, and he only turned against her because he couldn't digest his own Truth. He wasn't ready. But you are." Her thumb brushes my lips before she pulls away again. "Tauris basically gave me to him so he would shut up."

I shake my head. "Stars..."

"Maybe subconsciously, she knew my role in his life was more crucial than it seemed...but...honestly? I think he saw me as your replacement, his next fine treasure."

My stomach squirms, bubbles turning to rocks. "Pleiades...he hasn't—?"

"No, but he wants to," she says, shrugging. "He wants everyone and everything he can't have, naturally. But anyway, it's no use...I'm a difficult gem to mine." She gazes at the ground, giggling at her own metaphor. My stomach lurches at the possibility that she knows it's my metaphor too. Her deep sigh accompanies a gust of ironclad wind.

She itches her throat. "He finds my freedom intimidating, terrifying even, and so he stays back. He was probably used to your...devotion." A fleck of glitter falls from her eye and hits the ground. Metaphysical tears. "He's kept me lightyears away until now, using me only for knowledge of Tauris'...plans. Now that you're here, I can tell he just wants to heal. But even I can't eradicate the Fever. I can only aid in the creation of its remedy."

I swallow and chuckle, cloaking nervousness in silky amusement. "Wow. This is the most you've talked in a while."

Her nose wrinkles when she takes my hand again. Our steps syncopate. "It's the city air."

86

"It's not that bad, you know," I insist. "It used to be way worse—no water or trees, just concrete and trash. Literal shit and piss. At least now, things are working together…even if they don't have to, it helps a little, doesn't it?"

She sighs. "The trees say so. But the physical air is fine; it's the atmosphere that worries me, the personal and cosmic clogs that rise and—"

"Hold up. You talk to trees?"

"I commune with everyone," she says, aura unfolding in rose petals.

While the city's systems keep air clean, she makes it sweeter with every step. But then, she trips over nothing, and even though I laugh when I help her stand, her aura flickers like a candle stifled by its own melting wax. Freckles blanched, she looks ill.

"What's wrong?" Instinctively, I touch her forehead. Violet energy oozes between twitching fingers.

"Um. Just…tired." Her chest swells and deflates, knocking a bralette strap off her shoulder. Biting my lip, I slid it back up.

"We need some real food," I sigh, kissing her scalp. I can't help it. Maybe it's stupid, but showing affection feels like a display of power. Not with dominance, but freedom.

She searches our surroundings and leans on me. "Anywhere good?"

"Yeah, I know a place." I smile weakly, keeping an arm around her waist while we walk. "C'mon. Hopefully they're still in business."

Keeping her upright helps me focus, but the deeper we go into the city, the heavier I feel. Even in eerily peaceful streets, the energy is repulsive. Almost toxic. Vibrant color leaks from every waterway and tree, but the auric fields are tinted gray, bleached into oblivion, as if outer space settled on the ground to rot. I keep trying to justify it, but it's just more cosmic decomposition, another quietly abused place for the universe to wilt. I wonder if it was always like this, if my whole planet has always been this fucked, and I'm just now noticing it.

My faith wavers and returns in turbulent cycles, punctuated by ear-stabbing howls that echo off chrome and crystal buildings. Jet-hounds sweep by, splashing us.

Reiki's teeth chatter. "S-someone's in t-trouble…"

"We'll be in trouble too if we don't book it. C'mon." We duck under the next lamp, down an old set of stairs, sheathed in flickering gray light. Wet soles make my head spin with memories of Mars, but the hazy red hologram, *OPEN*, is a beacon.

It's still here, I think triumphantly, exhaling a puff of fog. I press a shaking palm against the pad and the sign changes to *WELCOME*. The door slides with as much ease as my ship's, and we enter to be greeted by the steam of warm food and drink.

Porthole windows in the restaurant mimic Jaal's HQ, allowing patrons to be entertained by fish-bots and underwater light shows. Unlike our glass prison though, this place is made to look ancient and sunken, like a wooden sea ship.

"This is neat." Reiki breathes deep and leaves my grasp, fueled by the warmth.

"It's called Ananda, after the Sanskrit word for 'bliss,'" I explain, wandering toward the bar. "A place that feels different, and yet the same, for everyone. This time it's a pirate's ship, but I've seen it decked out like all kinds of places. The White House, The Black House, Taj Mahal, you name it. A lot of culture comes in, so a lot of culture is reflected. I came here often after school." *When I had nowhere else to go.*

She scans the room as if she's been here before. "Is it always a setting from the past, or do they do futuristic stuff too?" Her child-like awe attracts the locals' wine-soaked smiles.

"Not sure." I shrug as we sit on barstools and loom over the touch-screen menu. Flipping through options, I ask, "You in the mood for seafood?"

"If by 'seafood,' you mean kelp chips, then sure." I feel the smirk in her eyes.

I nod and select a few tasty treats, plus the tallest glasses of water they have. Lamps overhead look like globs of gold, pearls, and rubies. One brushes my hair and I swat it out of the way.

"Was it always this quiet?" she whispers, leaning in.

I pull back from the waft of caramel on her skin, chewing my lip. "In here, or the city?"

"Both." She digs elbows into her knees, rubbing her chin thoughtfully. "I thought Earth would be…busier."

"Well. Don't let this sad scene fool you," I chuckle. "It wasn't always like this. When I was a kid, there wasn't a curfew. The jet-hounds were only for specific situations."

"Really?"

"Then I graduated high school, and a huge shift happened. Probably not as huge as the Reunion of the States, but for this city, it was pretty wild."

"You lived here your whole life?"

Scratching the back of my neck, I'm put on the spot. This feels too much like a date. "Yeah. 'Til I turned eighteen and met Jaal." I wave over the screen, but it beeps at me, denying access to the trove my tattoo is connected to. "Oh shit, right. I don't have money."

"I've got you." She winks, wiggling fingers. The natal tattoo glitters in gold light.

Eyebrows arching, I watch her palm glide over the screen. Light morphs from red to blue.

"Well." Clutching my elbows, I lean on her shoulder to receive a pat on the cheek. "Thanks."

Two tall glasses land on the table with soft clinks, deposited by floating eel-bots. I salute them with a peace sign and Reiki guzzles water like it's her job.

She splutters a satisfied exhale, holding the empty glass like it's the most beautiful thing she's ever touched. The most fragile. "Thanks for…bringing me here…and listening to me…and all that jazz." Breath fogs the rim, blurring the swirled octopus etching.

I shrug. "Well. We're in this together, aren't we?"

Although she's as still as the glass she holds, her aura unfurls into mine. Laughter bubbles in my chest, but my gaze is dragged toward a streak of creamy yellow fabric on the other side of the bar. A woman with coconut husk skin tugs on her headscarf, metal rings clanging nervously. For a second time tonight, I do a double-take, but Reiki tries to draw me back.

"Zen, what is it?"

I stumble off the barstool and approach the woman, mouth agape. The sun-colored headscarf clings to her curls and looms over her shoulders like a boa constrictor. She radiates magnetic ruby waves, prompting me to touch her.

But she grimaces with pinched, peppery eyes and a mouth too wrinkled to be Mother's. Up close, her body's a crust of burnt bread, the shell of a carbon dust doll. I realize the headscarf is stained and her skin is scattered with ash. Clearly offended by my approach, she tugs harder on the fabric, hiding her shrunken cheeks.

"Oh, I'm. Sorry. Thought you were someone else." Quickly I spin around and return to Reiki's side, face burning.

"It's okay," Reiki says softly, squeezing my hand. Our food is served by some friendly cyborgs. Mediterranean spices and fishy scents tickle my nose, but a yearning ache swarms behind my eyes.

I look at the plate in front of me and accidentally sprinkle drops of saltwater on my salmon. It glistens pink like freshly peeled skin, and suddenly my appetite is gone. "Sorry," I mumble again.

Reiki's hand on my thigh makes me jump. "Drink some water, Cap," she whispers. "You're gonna get dehydrated again."

"Thanks." Every ounce of fake confidence I built around me crumbles. Pieces collapse into the food with tears.

Reiki inhales deeply, rubs her hands together, and places a palm on either side of her plate. As usual, she tugs me from my self-implosions.

I tilt my head. "What are you doing?"

Beads of energy drip like sweat from her palms and encircle her salad, dotting green with gold. "You seasoned your food. I'm doing the same."

My laughter springs behind the sting.

"Maybe we can visit your moms," she offers, gazing at the seaweed. "Before we leave."

I shake my head.

We eat in silence for a few minutes, wordlessly agreeing to focus on nothing but the food. Sometimes the simplest human processes are the most important.

By the time I look up, the woman I mistook for Mother is gone. Impoverished ghost. A reflection of the emptiness inside me. *Breathe.* I inhale. *Release.* I exhale.

"Jaal's furious," Reiki says, nonchalant, noshing some spinach.

I begin to ask how she knows that, but I know better. "He's always furious."

Swallowing, she sets her fork down and looks at me. "You understand, then. You know that his aggression comes from something else."

"Displacement?" I scoff. "Sure, I guess so. I'm not really into psychoanalysis, but if I had to put a label on it, I'd call it an insatiable lust for the unknown. Everything he doesn't understand needs to be dominated." I tap a fork against the glass. "Everything's just a variable to be controlled. He's a user, Reiki. We both know it."

"There are independent variables too. Things that even he can't put in a box."

One side of my mouth lifts, at odds with the other. "Are we independent variables?"

"More like out of control," she laughs, shaking her head and taking my hand.

90

I take her in, the way I drink a final sip of water, savoring satisfaction. Part of me wants to scoop her up and run away, stow ourselves in the farthest cosmic puddle and get lost in shadow. But then, I guess we already are.

Always dramatically on cue, the S-Com around my neck beeps. Brows furrowed, I throw the goggles on, holding my breath. But instead of a cloud of marijuana smoke and Jaal's demon eyes, Onyx greets me through an ancient Venetian doctor's mask. I lurch back, to which she rolls her eyes.

"Save your lunch," she drones. "I bring news: Jaal has…changed his mind."

"Oh?" Hope expands in my stomach.

Her dark lips fold into a sneer, shadowed by the beak of her mask. Black licorice pinches my nostrils. "See…there's no reason why he shouldn't come with us. He's the head of this project, a victim of la fiebre."

Harsh laughter almost shoves me off the barstool. Reiki's hand is clammy in mine.

"Great joke," I chortle, wiping my forehead. "Hilarious."

"Basta ya," Onyx snaps, playing with a copper earring. "We'll need him to make a dose large enough to expand beyond our…borders. He's coming with us."

"Well then," I say loud enough for the whole restaurant to hear. "He can kindly fuck off." The pungent scent of licorice dissipates when I take the goggles off and look at Reiki. Her eyes widen.

"C'mon." I pull her away from the bar, the gawking people, and confused cyborgs. We head outside. "Those sluts ain't got a thing on us."

She tries to go one way, but I direct her toward the opposite, embracing the sudden need to lead. Thunder rumbles, and I can't tell if it's from the pit of my stomach or the sky.

"What are you doing?" she asks shrilly, struggling to keep up. For once, she can't read me. I'm dozens of paces ahead of her sixth sense.

As night swallows the city, lights brighten in contrast, some even more white than the comical halo on Reiki's head.

Half-way to our destination, hands still firmly clamped, we couldn't look any sketchier. It doesn't help that the sky cracks, dabbing the streets with ripples and waves. Metallic wind claws our backs, pushing us further toward the city's black-and-blue middle.

91

"I don't understand," Reiki calls over the tumult. "Jaal's place was the other way. Where are we going?"

"I'm surprised your intuition hasn't figured it out," I reply, wiping sticky hair strands out of my face. When she responds with nothing but teeth-chattering, I give in. "I decided you're right, as weird as that is. I'm going home, Reiki. You don't have to come, but I'm going. I need to see what...what's left to save."

"I want to come," she insists, beaming behind slates of rainwater.

Between the double entendre and her hopelessly adorable face, I can't help but smirk. Her lips tremble, downpour giving the impression that she's drooling. She's so hyperaware of my humanity, and yet so oblivious to her own.

"Okay, but just. Be cool, I guess. We don't know what to expect. Even you can't possibly know."

Through blue-coated pills of rain and yellow slaps of thunder, I hear her speechless questions. There's no offense taken to my words, but curiosity lingers in the back of her throat, dancing and bobbing with tonsils. She cares about me, probably too much. She wonders if I'll be okay, if I'll ever feel okay for more than a few minutes. She wants me to heal—I can feel the yearning. Now I'm just waiting for myself to want it too.

I shake my head, flicking bits of water left and right. "It'll be fine."

But will I?

If the streets were empty before, they're hollow now. The storm could've been programmed, it scares people off so efficiently, sending even the boldest streetwalkers back into the shadows. Beyond chrome and glass, old brick-and-mortar places are still safehouses for desperate misfits. Reiki's right—I'm grateful to not be one of them.

Jet-hounds continue to patrol, gliding through water like long-snouted submarines, scanning molecules, sniffing for subterfuge. The only thing scarier than the government is Jaal, and so I push through wet wind like the eye of a hurricane.

"We're not running," she reassures as the rain flow slows. Water settles in our hair but rolls off polyester clothes. "Jaal's not gonna chase us. He's too preoccupied."

"I know." I lick my lips, surprised by how salty it is. "But we should get out of this rain." I look both ways before crossing a bridge in the street. The glowing red glass vibrates under us. "I'm just. Sick of his bullshit, and the people who work for him. I'm veering from that and

92

going back to what I'm familiar with. Happiness starts at the roots, right?"

Uncannily, she grins, teeth glinting like flecks of stardust. From the taste of rain, to how she brightens when I repeat her words, everything is a shock. My whole system is shaken to its core, and I'm not screwing around with Jaal's surface-level thinking anymore.

Beside us, a torrent of water encircles a submerging hound. Its mouth opens and howls, too humanoid. Too familiar. It almost sounds like me.

My feet bolt to the ground by the panic of an impending flashback.

"No." I slip out of Reiki's grasp, knees crunching against pavement. Even as the weather clears, everything blurs, skewed by a hectic timeline, scratching out my vision and replacing it with the cold husk of memory.

"Ugh." I clench my head, trying to stop the spinning. Agony is the salty liquid on my skin, coating me, labeling me *tasty*. Devouring me. I'm shaking harder than the earth did when it split this country into pieces. Parts of me float away and make their own islands, pretending to be safe in solitude, ever-shrinking. Scattered against the ocean, I'm lost.

Trying to remember and ground myself only makes my root chakra burn. I'm soaking wet, practically drowning, but dying in fire.

Hounds howl, yelling in pleasure, passion, retching all over my bedsheets, all over my walls. Hunting me down, taking me down, pushing into me, down down down…

From the distance, a pair of gold hands hurtle.

"DON'T TOUCH ME!" Flames that anchor my knees turn to puddles of blood, glistening a violent brown like a vat of melted crayons—every color together, forcibly meshed. Every unique shade is lost. Every color drowns itself.

"Please," I sob, sinking into the mess. "Don't."

My chest fills with liquid rage, fluid betrayal. The whole universe weeps with me.

Somewhere, Reiki cries too, but the curling palm lines leak light onto my head, replacing salt with medicine, pain with peace.

My jaw clenches so hard, it pops. She speaks words I can't recognize, a light-language I've never heard, words that aren't really words.

After a shuttering inhale, I collapse into a pair of broad, bulging arms.

The last thing I hear is a low, gruff voice. Someone louder and earthier than Reiki, with holo army boots and a paintbrush beard.

"For the love of Sun, mate. It's the fifth millennium. Where's your bloody umbrella?"

Twelve

I'm in my childhood bed. I only know this because it smells like spilled wax and the ceiling is an interactive map of the Milky Way. The last time I slept here, I was eighteen years old. Every time I held still, I would hear nothing but ragged breathing. Either my own from the shock of nightmares, or Mama's in the room over, struggling to let go of illness. Solar flares clung to her lungs and other organs, forcing her to donate pieces of herself to the cosmos. The memory causes me to shoot upward in bed.

A full body mirror lined with string lights projects from the opposite wall, mocking me and my bony frame. Someone dried my clothes, but they still hang on me like I'm a mannequin.

With the edge of a downy sheet, I dab my face and neck, where a cold sweat replaces rainwater. Someone also dried and took out my hair, leaving it a nappy mess. I tug the curls, wishing I could be as persistent—and hard to control—as them.

I look at my hands. The mirror neglects to show how damaged my aura is, the gray crispiness of a traumatized vessel. Overused, overspread energy. I sigh, lacing fingers in my lap and closing my eyes. I can still meditate myself back to wholeness.

Behind closed lids, everything is scattered. Pieces of a multidimensional brain slide into my stomach and guts spill between curled toes.

Slowly, sensations like breathing, perspiring, and skin against cotton bring me back. Tiny stitches of energy sew me back to life, a scientific experiment of metaphysical monsters. Self-induced, quantum healing.

It hurts like a bitch, coming back together, so I go slow. I take my time. With every breath, I stretch against the fabric of being, and with every lick of lips, I remember myself.

But then it hits me hard—*I'm home.*

Ignoring dizziness, I launch from the bed and open the door, listening for signs of life. While my ears ring with strain, I scan the hallway. It's exactly how I left it, from the montage of family images on the touch screen walls to the lavender candlelight in the bathroom. The same antique rug lines chrome floors—an elephant-clad homage to Mama's Japanese roots.

In the foyer, altars have changed. Entryway tables are speckled with holographic Kwanzaa candles, tiny tapestries, and star charts.

Each step I take feels stranger than the one before. My bedroom was so perfectly intact, full of old clothes, instruments, and journals, but the rest of the house is a shapeshifter. At least it means someone still lives here.

But when I enter the living room, my jaw dangles in surprise. I rub my eyes 'til they ache. "Lutfi? What are you doing here?"

The man looks and smells like coffee with too much cream. Still carrying the half-assed British accent I remember, he scoffs, "Zenith, you're my namesake. The least you could do is call me 'uncle.' The most would be a gentle embrace. One man to another." His Vitiligo lips peel in a grin. "You've grown to be a good one, I hear."

He sits in a ruby-tinted armchair, legs kicked up so that his boots glint in lamplight. Reiki sprawls, corpse-pose, on the floor. She smiles when I look at her, although her eyes are closed.

Lutfi swirls a glass of red wine that matches his chair. "Sit and tell me what you're doing, skulking the streets with a Conduit friend and a fit of impulses."

"I'm sure she caught you up," I reply, leaning on the door frame. It even creaks the same way. "What are you doing in my moms' house?"

He raises a wicked brow. "Am I not welcome here?"

"Pleiades, don't talk down to me. I've had enough of that for one...millennium." I drawl the last word in a mocking accent, to which he only chuckles. "Where are they?" I persist. "Moms."

His silver irises—the only represented gene we share—are bowls of a scale, weighing the balance between the value of truth and me. After a moment of tight-lipped consideration, he leans forward, ankles hooked. "They're fine. I'm worried about you."

I snort. "Join the cult."

Reiki opens her eyes and scans the room. I follow her gaze from muted blue walls to chunks of amethyst and malachite on the windowsills. Dreamcatchers hang against stained glass. Never noticing how old and eclectic this place was, I smile.

A string of tension pulls me to sit in the chair across from Lutfi.

He clears his throat. "I wasn't expecting you today. The stars whispered otherwise."

I shrug. "I rarely do what the stars say."

Catching air between his palms, he exclaims, "You take after me, then!"

Skin crawling, I cross my legs, hiding the rouge roots of an unreliable family tree.

He exchanges a wary smile with Reiki, aura thickening. "Your friend and I have been sharing stories."

"Lovely."

"You remember some of my stories, I presume?" He asks.

I feign a laugh. "Sure, L. What kid doesn't remember story-time with his beloved uncle?" Even though he's my mother's half-brother.

"I taught you more than your bloody teachers did." Cracking his knuckles, he leans back in the chair and sighs. "I'm not prepared for this, by any means, but I have another story for you. One I wish I'd told sooner. I advise you to pay attention with the same avid curiosity you had as a child."

It crushes me that he never acknowledged my admiration of him until now. *Where've you been?* I think. *With all your fatherly love and support? Where were you when I needed a real savior?*

Resting my chin in a sweaty palm, I glance at Reiki. Her smile is weak, but the silver lining in her aura seals the deal. "Okay." I gesture for him to continue.

While he swallows the rest of his wine, sediment and all, I inspect his aura. A dull glow is sheathed in spots mimicking that of his skin, but red and black like the inside of a rotting pumpkin. His graying beard and hair are braided loosely with no pattern, which Mother would disapprove of. He's a rickety frame of the man I once knew. I can't help thinking: *Same.*

"You left your mothers in quite a state." He covers a belch with his sleeve. "And during Mercury Retrograde, nonetheless." Badges line his tattered jacket, outlining the scholarly accomplishments of his youth. His white-man accent, Rasta-style, and obsession with old school astrology got me heckled a lot in high school.

"I didn't abandon them, if that's what you mean." Despite the fierce words, my inner voice is searing with guilt, unknowing who to blame.

I should have stayed, gotten help from someone on Earth. I could've done so much more for them. We could've done so much more together.

It's been months since I've had these thoughts. But a few hours ago was also the first time in a while I've panicked to the point of blacking out, drawing myself further inside. Reiki mentioned that this would happen—traumas and treasures unfolding in a paradox—but I didn't expect to be dragged back home by my uncle's waxy fingers.

"My sister was taking care of your Mama," he explains. "But there was only so much Imani could do. You know what the Fever does. We needed more than just therapy after that predicament."
I try to reel in the rage, douse the flames in water. But Lutfi's words persist with swirling gasoline.

"After you left, well…I've never seen Imani so dependent, not just on Soluna's approval, but on her own suffering."

Nobody asked me to stay. Nobody said a word. Nails dig into my forearms. I'm not sure if they're mine. I don't think anything here is mine. Reiki slinks next to me to cool the simmering, keep me from exploding.

"It's not Zenith's fault," she interjects, only touching me with energy.

"Well, no," Lutfi agrees. "Of course not. But family is everything. What do you have without us, I wonder?"

Freedom. My hairs stand on end.

I glance at Reiki, choosing words carefully. "I didn't come here to be patronized, L. I came here to find my moms and…I don't know. Make amends."

"Is that so?" Lutfi strokes his beard with both hands. "Reiki says you're working with Jaal Nadir. Do you know him well?"

Fire floods my face. "I've known him for four years. So. Yeah. You could say that."

"Oh, I'm sure." There it is again. That condescending rattling in the back of his throat, oozing from heavy lids and wine-stained lips. "You no doubt know, then, who taught him everything he knows?"

Brows crinkled, I look from him to Reiki. Her colors fall on the floor and ripple across the room, sheathing us in a safe space. All the right shades for truth-telling.

"No, I don't."

He tugs his braids. I recognize the gleam in his eyes. If this was the only segment of childhood I truly enjoyed, he would have Aunt Prue at his side, sharing tales about stars, planets, and everything in between. It wouldn't be a blame game, or a trip around fanciful family ideals.

Lutfi would hold a candle in each hand and tell us ancient stories about humanity, and how we reached this era. He would give a historical run-down of the developed higher consciousness, synthesizing the ideals of Mother and Mama, linking the fabric of existence with raw meaning. He would lead us through an explorative meditation and divinate with star charts and planetary maps.

I wanted to be like him, once. Before idolizing Mama, I was devoted to the idea of him. But then he settled with watching stars from behind a telescope dome, and I wanted more. I wanted to embody the stars he studied.

He restores my focus on the present by speaking.

"Zenith, you know I'm a man of inspiration." He slaps his chest. "Feeling. Not unlike Imani, and not unlike you, in fact."

My frown must cut like a sword because he wags a partially pigmented finger. "Don't deny it—you are your mother's son." He sighs heavily, hands falling into his lap. "While Imani was a freshwater stream, Soluna was an overpowered nebula. Nothing could penetrate her aura, and nothing stood in her way. She burned through everything… including you."

Stomach clenched, I hold my breath. As a child, I found his flailing braids and hands exciting, but now I know he's skirting around the truth. It's stuck, lodged in his chest like a pearl.

"Passionate people are dangerous," he continues, gazing at the empty wineglass. "Especially those with strong fire placements in their many natal charts, like Soluna. They love and lust for so long, until they forget what they seek. This made her mad even before the Fever, because although Imani and I warned her, she dove into the depths of heliocentric hell and never left." There it is—the word-playing blow to Mama's scientific work, hindering my attempt to find him charming again. If family is everything, then I don't want anything.

"Teaching was a passion of hers, as you know, but a faint one compared to discovery. Unlike Imani, Sol was never satisfied with staying home." He folds hands in his lap, twiddling thumbs, as if the discussion is trivial. "Now. Does that sound familiar to you?"

A smirk clips my lips to the side. "Well. I am my mothers' son."

He returns the smile, but only briefly. "Before you left, you witnessed what the Fever did to your Mama. But do you know how she got it in the first place?"

"Sweet Pleiades. How does anyone contract Gemini Fever?" I run a hand through tangled curls. "She got too close to the sun, a natural-born Icarus. If you're trying to say that I'm gonna burn the same way she did, then…" I trail off, distracted by the energetic earthquake in the soles of my feet. Bloody cracks trail up my legs, but when I blink, they disappear. A deep sigh tranquilizes me for a moment. "You keep prompting me with questions, but you don't answer them. I'm not here to shmoos with old crews, Lutfi. I just want to know where my moms are."

His lips lose all pigment when he tightens them, strained by the truth that begs to be thrown up.

Ushering it out of him, Reiki circles back to the first question, even though I'm pretty sure she knows the answer. "Who taught Jaal everything he knows, Mr. Azda?"

Lutfi keeps his eyes on me. "You must understand—there are many circumstances in the universe even stargazing can't predict. Astrology is useless without meaning and…so are we." He releases a blustering sigh, shaking his head, calling his own personal wind. "I'm sorry, truly, I am. I'd always hoped Imani would tell you, so that you wouldn't end up making the same mistake Soluna did. But alas." His many rings are lost and entangled in the fallen-out braids of his beard. "Soluna was Jaal Nadir's tutor. She was the origin of his scientific success, and he was the downfall of hers."

Ears ringing, I shoot to my feet. "No way. Jaal would've—or Mama would've told me. Someone would've…" Finding no one else to accuse, I point at him. "You're making this up to scare me."

But one mud-stained look from Reiki instills reality. As usual, she knew and I didn't. I've been shuffled through the dark by people I thought I loved. That's why they talk to me like I'm a child, too fragile to comprehend truth, too damaged to grow or make a change. Even mirrors look at me like I'm twelve.

Who am I to a universe that never stops growing?

My muscles twitch. Blood thuds against my shaking head. I can feel Jaal's teeth sinking into veins, dirtying DNA. "Holy, fucking shit. Absolute, big-bang-balls-in-the-mouth fuckery." I pull so hard on my hair, pieces break off.

100

I expect Reiki to hug me, comfort me, but she doesn't even say anything. Hands outstretched, she continues to swirl the room's energy, stabilizing and maintaining the memories that inhabit it.

When I look at Lutfi again, asymmetric tears trace wrinkles and settle in his beard. A hand covers his mouth, tugging his bottom lip before pulling away. "I'm sorry, Zenith. It's bad business. Toxic, really. If I'd known you'd trail after Nadir, I would've said something. I've been a poor excuse for an uncle." He dabs his eyes with a sleeve. "In a way, the stars have been guiding us here all along. At least you're not alone."

We gaze at Reiki, who shields herself from our emotional overflow with a soft giggle. A fluorescent pink bow of energy wraps us, sealing the room, healing the space between us.

"Um. Apology accepted." While releasing my hair, I could cry, but I don't. Numbness plays with my fingers, settling with the dirt under nails. I stare beyond aura and skin, desperately analyzing quantum particles. "I, uh…think I'd feel better if you told me more about…what happened."

He clasps his hands. "This calls for more wine." He looks between Reiki and me.

We shake our heads graciously and watch him flee for the kitchen. After a beat of silence, I follow him.

My old home is unlike most—the downstairs is practically all one room, separated only by furniture and utilities. Every wall bears an old-fashioned hologram system that displays photos like the ones in the hall or customizable paint colors and designs. Most people opt for Sens-Houses with their flashy personalized settings and sensory overloading. Mama and Mother liked to keep it simple, and from what I see, Lutfi has maintained their wishes.

The kitchen is especially plain, except for the rose quartz countertop and stained-glass windows. Windowsills are lined with petri dishes of sage and Palo Santo. At least a dozen bottles of wine sit in a row under old-fashioned wooden shelves, but the rest is untouched.

"Since when did you become an alcoholic?" I joke, leaning against the island.

Uncorking a particularly large bottle that matches the counters, he flashes me a smile. "I was born that way, Cheeky-Z."

My chest aches. "You haven't called me that in a while."

"You haven't been here in a while." With a brusque sigh, he takes a pitcher from the cupboard and fills it with rosé. "It's alright, though. I'm taking care of the house while they're away." When he reaches for a knife, I flinch, thrown back into a memory I tried to scrub clean.

"Sharpen your wits!" Mama screams, flailing a knife in Mother's face.

It should be funny banter, a joke. But it's not, and I'm desperate to help, but if I get in the way...

Mother glances at me from across the counter and reaches for a towel.

"You can't make messes just to clean them, Imani," Mama drones, bloodshot eyes bulging. A maniacal smile hangs off her chin as she twirls the knife. "You could get hurt."

Mother sops up the steaming mess, careful not to splatter Mama's bare feet. I can almost feel the terrified rap of her heart. "Soluna. Could you please move so I can clean the rest?"

In one fierce motion, Mama kicks a glob of tofu in Mother's face.

Clothes and cheekbones splattered with curry, Mother looks up at her wife helplessly. "Have you taken your medicine today, my love?"

"Medicine," Mama spits, throwing the knife aside. It ricochets off wooden shelves and spins on the floor. "Medicine's for the weak of mind. I'm strong—mind, body, and soul." She punches her own chest defiantly.

After glancing at me again, Mother winces and hangs her head. She and I both know the medicine only delays the symptoms anyway. Sooner or later, Mama's illness will develop a tolerance. Her mind and body will decay, and her soul will gladly escape.

"What about your heart?" Mother asks, desperately hoping a piece of her beloved Sol is still in there somewhere.

That gets her a firm smack across the head. "I'm a scientist, Imani. Not a fucking poet. And certainly not a housewife." With that, she yanks the headscarf off her own head, revealing a clumsy patchwork of bald spots, and tosses it on the mess. "That's your job."

Mother's fingers quiver when she picks up the scarf and brings it to her lips, curry and all.

"Oh," I whisper, partially in reply to what Lutfi said. Then it hits me, while he plops freshly sliced grapefruit into the pitcher and adds a dash of clear liquor. Something strong for the strongest man I used to know. "Mother left? Was Mama with her? Where'd they go?"

A vein protrudes from a pale patch, tension clasped between skin and jawbone. He gestures for me to follow him back to the living room, where Reiki lies on the couch, apparently asleep. Her aura ebbs and flows, a calm ocean of foam. Needing to fidget, I sit on the floor and touch my toes, tugging the backs of my calves and thighs, playing the strings of my being. *I miss my sitar.*

"They left to get help." He refills his glass, sloshing pink punch with a slowly rotating wrist.

"What kind of help?"

In the corner of my eye, Reiki flinches, her mind sinking into REM.

"The kind she couldn't give Sol on her own," he replies, taking a long gulp. The vat of pink blurs his cookie dough skin. I want to add that color to his aura.

"So, she *is* still alive," I confirm, flocks of icy energy rolling off my shoulders like liquid nitrogen.

He nods. "Just barely, last time we spoke."

It takes him a moment to gather his thoughts again and redirect the train. "Sol was too weak to move anymore, so Imani finally had time to come to her senses and seek help. It hasn't been easy, but important duties are the most difficult to perform." He chuckles. "I'm sure you've learned that, after working with Nadir."

"But who can help her?" I demand, biting a thumbnail. "If there's only so much we can do, who can do much more?"

"I'm not sure. She was...unspecific." With another swig and a shake of his head, his cheeks flush. "Look here, Zenith. You and I have a lot of regrets. Big burdens. But your mothers do too. When they left, Sol wanted to heal. Anyone with an intact third-eye could've felt it. Imani was desperate." He leans forward, elbow balanced on a bouncing knee. "Reiki told me about Nadir's grand scientific discovery, and the experiment he's swindled you into." His pinky wiggles against the glass's stem. "The Galaccine. Dodgy name, don't you think?"

A helpless laugh rolls off my tongue. "Yes," I say, the only thing I'm confident about.

"D'you reckon it'll work?" He raises a fluffy brow. "I mean, I assume you do, since you came all this way with so much guilt in your chest."

Gears in my head shift smoothly, lubricated by his gentle curiosity. "Reiki has faith, and I'm starting to. It's complicated, but...it's worth a shot, isn't it?"

"Ha!" He slaps a knee, dribbling drops of wine. "A shot that's worth a shot. Bet he made a joke about that."

"How'd you know?" *Can he sense my thoughts too?*

"Well, that's the rest of the story, isn't it?" He sets the glass on an obsidian coffee table and breathes sharply through his nose. "I met him when he first started working as Sol's apprentice. Sharp boy, obsessed with explosive chemicals. A bit wonky in the head, but who isn't? Loved puns more than his own cock, and that's saying something."

I lick my lips to stifle a giggle. At least we share a raunchy sense of humor too.

"I know I wasn't always around, Zenith, but when I was, I saw things unfold more clearly than anyone. Wretched things. You must understand." Another clearing of his throat sends a blue ribbon of energy unraveling between us. "There's always been more than what meets the five senses with that one." A heavy veil of gray rests on his aura. "Unfortunately, I never did anything about it. That's why he was able to push your mama so far, right into the sun…"

My brows converge. "You really think he's the reason Mama got sick?"

"I don't think, I know." He scratches his beard. "He's what, five years older than you?"

"Six," I amend. *Not that it matters.*

"And he probably never mentioned his schooling, or the project he spearheaded with your mama. Probably treated you like a child, an ignorant infant. Right? Why d'you think that is?"

"I don't know." I gesture helplessly. "He's a pretentious pedophile?"

Lutfi doesn't laugh, probably because he knows it's not a joke.

To my left, Reiki turns on her other side. Cerulean coils of light spill onto the rug.

"He knew who you were from the beginning," he says gravely. "But he never told you a thing, 'cos that would give you power over him. Freedom. He wants ultimate control. One of the many people I've met who labors under the delusion that they can control Nature." If Reiki was facing us, I'm sure I'd see a smile on her face.

"Pleiades, how do you know all this?" I dig a fist into my hair.

Pressing his palm against the side of the coffee table, he projects a multicolored diagram on the wall behind me. My neck cracks when I peer at the concentric circles laced with lines. Each point is labeled with a name and degrees. Our Sun and his loyal planets, beloved celestial bodies. Jaal's natal chart.

For a moment, Lutfi is a doctor sharing the fatal diagnosis, solemnly nodding his head and folding his arms. "Sun in Aries explains the aggression. Mars conjunct Mercury and Chiron in Scorpio. Secrecy. Venus in Capricorn. Passion, determination. Heliocentrically, he's a bonified, unevolved Libran Earth. Kid's got issues, evidently."

I turn away, scorched by an image I always saw but never analyzed. "He would be balanced as fuck if it weren't for..." I trail off, staring into space. "Wait." I blink myself back to a semblance of focus. "What about the project he spearheaded?" Snatching in the dark for a string of hope.

"That's the worst part," Lutfi replies, emitting a bitter laugh. A gulp of wine splatters down braids like beads of blood. "Project Sagittarius. The first documented exploration for the cause of Gemini Fever, in hopes to rectify it. Not so different from the trip you're embarking on." He clears his throat aggressively, eyes watering. "I imagine this is Phase Two, or has Jaal neglected to inform you how he obtained information on solar aurorae? It wasn't firsthand, my boy. It was all from Soluna's notes. A calculated flaw in her scientific study spurred him to fix it and continue."

I choke on my own spit. "How do you know this?" Repeating the question doesn't make it easier to ask. I dig into the arms of my chair 'til my palms are numb. "Astrology can't give you the knowledge you're supplying; even you admit that. Analysis...speculation...it's all bullsh—"

"If I know anything, it's that there's no better experiment than a failed one," he interjects, pointing at me, holding my gaze. "'Cos then you know what to change. How to proceed."

"But she got the information they needed. And now we...we're making a cure."

"Precisely. But she failed to stay safe. No amount of scientific discovery is worth sacrificing personal health."

Echoes, echoes, so many repeating sounds between people I love and hate.

"Sol's failure was the greatest lesson he retained." He swallows, frightened by his own words, or stifling another belch. "Now, you'll be his next test subject."

My jaw suspends. I have no words, no sense of language. I watch his mouth make shapes and focus on breathing, trying to avoid passing out again. But Truth is like cold water dumped on a deep sleeper; it shocks the body before hitting the brain.

"Make no mistake. Project Sagittarius was your mama's idea." The volume of his voice raises with his BAC. "But Jaal helped her create a plan of action. He was the first to know the results, when she came back on that fated day." A hand goes to his mouth, wiping wine and regret. "I can't believe we let her go...I mean...After all those weeks of trial and error, error, error…Christ, she was her own bloody test subject, wasn't she? I can't believe she ever came back at all."

Reiki inhales sharply and rises from slumber. Her copper hair is a mess of tangled wires, sticking to her sweaty brow. She turns, dragging a spit-soaked piece of hair from her lips. "Don't worry, Cap. I'm here for you."

Lutfi grins, eager for distraction. "I'd take her over Jaal Nadir any day." I know it's a joke, and I know he's trying hard to stay on my good side, but I'm fucking skinny. My good side is slight.

I rub my eyes, ironing out tears. "So. You're saying. He stole Mama's sanity before he stole mine."

After downing the glass, he goes to pour another one, but stops when Reiki stretches and yawns. "It's a great story, Mr. Azda," she says. "But it's missing Jaal's prequel."

Sun-shaped grapefruit chunks slosh when he sets the crystal pitcher down. "You reckon he needs a bloody backstory?"

On the galaxy-colored rug, among tribal crests and sacred shapes, Reiki sprawls. "He *has* a backstory, just like we all do." She tosses me a sleep-laden wink. "You read his natal charts, you should know. Where's his Lilith? Pallas? Eros and Psyche? What about his multi-system charts? How did those energies unfold? These are important celestial aspects that could affect a human child. Can you imagine what happened to those energies when he became a man?"

"I don't care what any of his charts say." I rise, hips and knees crackling. "I'll drag him by the dick if I have to so that he sees this project through to the end."

Reiki grins like a horizon line.

Lutfi sends his glass spiraling on the rug at his feet, slapping both knees in a fit of laughter. "His…mothers'…son!" Energy rolls to the ceiling, stalled only by Reiki's vibes.

Cooled off for now, I exhale a long-held breath and meet Lutfi's old, mischievous eyes. "So, Mama and Mother. Where are they, exactly?"

With tight lips, he reaches for the pitcher. "Told you, I dunno."

I snatch his wrist, milk chocolate against yin-yang swirls. "Find out." Holding him so tightly only reminds me how exhausted I am. "I'll go on this trip with Jaal, but only so I can make sure it works. It's the only hope we've got, Lutfi. And if what you said is true, then the project's original plan was to heal…Mama's hope was to heal."

Reiki's cold fingers squeeze my knotted muscles. "Mr. Az—"

"Lutfi," he insists, trembling. "Please."

"Lutfi," Reiki says, slowly pulling my body against hers. "I'll take great care of your nephew." Hips aligned, she spoons me the same way Jaal once did, but laces fingers with mine and rests her head on my shoulder. A gentle wave washes over me, making me part of her ebb and flow, in sync with her gravity. "If there's anything we can do to help your family and save you all from grief, then we'll do it. I promise we'll at least try."

Wetness leaks across my collarbone. She's crying.

Smiling warmer than he ever has, Lutfi takes both of our hands and kisses them. "God Bless the mad ones." He shakes silvery tears from his eyes. "Thanks, both of you."

I nod, swallowing in a desert-dry throat. "Find out where they are, and I'll bring them back, with aid. Jaal can have his fame and fortune. All I want is the remedy. Then we can go back to how things used to be, except maybe with more family therapy this time." A wry smile pins my cheeks in place.

Thirteen

The next morning, after a hasty breakfast of oats and fruit, I'm back at Jaal's complex with a hankering to cut something. While Reiki skips around in Syzygy, helping the others finish repairs, I'm in a colossal Sens-Room, slashing villainous simulations to bits with an electric katana.

Unfortunately, I haven't trained with a sword since I last met up with Jaal in New York. Muscles strain with each dodge and duck, but luckily the sword is so high-tech, it moves like a feather on breeze.

Everywhere I turn, simulated rock monsters come at me with barreling fists. The walls depict dark, glistening caverns dripping with poison-infused crystals and dwarf-red eyes. Each monster I slay with a tap of the blade—a bash of blue-and-green electricity—is another symbol for everything I hate. Everything that's made me sick. Everyone who betrayed me and fucked up my life.

Behind a mad haze of sapphire, emerald, and yellow lightning, I fixate on the insanity of Jaal's lies. Not only did he manipulate Mama. He programmed me to be the perfect self-destructive machine like these rock monsters, like the bombs he so ambitiously creates.

"He's a stain on my existence," I mutter between tight teeth, spinning on the balls of my feet to dodge an attack.

When the fake monsters hit me, the room amplifies my pain receptors, and every blow becomes more gruesome. They're intentional hallucinations, perpetuated by crystal-clear code, foggy blue fear, and a pile of rage.

Just as the tip of the blade casts ricocheting bolts on a beast's chunky forehead, the simulation shuts off.

Twitching, I scan the walls as they fade back to computer-mirrors and recount the details of my failures and triumphs. Numbers pan across my sweat-slick face while I stare at the gaunt reflection. Black leggings, sneakers, and a crop top cling to my glossy brown skin. Branch-like arms extend and fold slightly as lungs gather and release air. Reiki's clever plaits pull my hair in tight loops at the crown, making me look royal and strong. But the designer bags under my eyes tell another story.

Energetically, I look decent. A fluctuating system of rainbow chakras swarms my body like Chinese dragons, orbiting this clingy flesh-prison. I'm jolting with adrenaline, trembling electrons, and flirtatious spirit animals. For once, self-care practices are aligning with my ever-changing life.

Behind me, Jaal claps, dressed in a white satin jumpsuit. Already, he's outfitted for success, eyelids and lips painted magenta. His bundled hair changes from corn wisps to nebulas when he tilts his head.

Having spent most of my anger toward him on this simulation, I grin and bow flamboyantly. At my squeeze, the voltage disappears, leaving a traditional katana blade in its smoky wake.

Jaal approaches me and rests a hand on my shoulder. His aura is different today—steadier, more open. "Impressive, Z-baby."

Shirking the nickname, I add, "Not as good as you. It's been a while." Hoping he'll take the bait.

"Psh," he scoffs, waving a hand. "You're used to swordplay, but not like this. You like the beta?"

Scratching my neck where sweat continues to pool, I force a laugh. "Sorry for snagging it from your storage. I couldn't help myself." If this was the past, I'd tack on a moist-lipped *I've been a very bad boy*, but this time the urge is crunched between the fangs of energetic dragons. Confidence and self-esteem burn like a sun.

Surprisingly, he shrugs. "Knew you'd be tempted. Why d'you think I left it unlocked?"

"Wow, shocking."

The pun sends a chuckle rolling off his pierced tongue. His irises swirl like the edges of a black hole.

Leaning against the wall, causing a crinkle in the program, I clear my throat. "So. What's up?"

Making me jump, the door slides shut automatically. Jaal flashes pearlescent teeth, ring clanging against bone when he licks his lips. "Admire your boldness, baby. Reminds me of an old teacher of mine."

I plaster a grin, perfecting the masquerade. "Thanks. Y'know, you look good, Jaal. Did Reiki do some healing for you?"

Without warning, he wrenches my hips against his, hands disconnected from the calm pair of yellow eyes. Rage rises from his root.

I flinch and blink, knuckles stiffening over the sword's hilt, unable to tell if it's him or me who's shaking.

Rank, staggered breath assaults me. "Know you think you got me figured out. You think I'm a failure, catching the sickness that spites my scientific advancement." The energetic wall he builds is thicker than his skull. "You ain't seen what I've seen. Nobody has. Been to Hades and back."

I raise a brow, craning my neck to avoid the stench of smoke-soaked bodily fluids. Pretending to care, I squint and scan. "Jaal. Pal. You seem scared. Totally shook-nasty." I tilt my head. "Is everything okay?"

A scabbed fist slams into cellophane walls. Half of the lights flicker and die. "It will be." Our silhouettes separate in the mirrors. His energy weakens when he pulls away.

Lowering the sword, I rub my temples with thumb and middle finger. "Pleiades, Jaal. Maybe you should rest for a while."

"Rest?" he cackles, tongue-bauble gliding over teeth. "No time for resting." A hand moves over mine on the hilt, squeezing 'til electricity pumps into the blade. "Only training. My body's gotta be at its peak when I take the Galaccine."

Strangely, my pulse is steadfast. I move the blade out of his face, shifting its glow to the floor. The damn thing makes auras difficult to see, but the blurred lines beckon me. "Alright. Show me up, for once."

He likes this side of me. Ironically, the raging hatred that boils in my guts is the same thing that turns him on. If I ever did love him, that was when he wanted nothing to do with me. Our relationship was always inverse—a stupid paradox, bad for both of us. I see that now, clearer than stellaglass.

Beaming, he takes a step back and hyperextends his arms, activating electro-leaf blades in his sleeves. That's what I assume they are, anyway. A newer, multi-edged version of the sword I grip, sprouting in sharp feather shapes at his wrist.

Forearms barred in front of him, he winks. With one eye red and the other navy, he waits for me to make the first move. His aura swirls and rumbles—a collision of yin and yang, cloud and thunder.

110

I walk a few paces before he's on me like wildfire, muscles bulging as he aims for my neck. A zap of lime green electricity cuts him off, scorching a plastic sleeve. Synthetic whiteness melts like marshmallow onto the floor, and he cuts the excess with a leaf blade.

A crazy giggle escapes my mouth. But he stays quieter than a grave while he bends and bobs, trying to cut my legs.

For once, being smaller is a strength. Light and zippy, I dodge his blows with more ease than I did with the simulations.

I yelp when a petal-thin blade skids across my thigh and leaves an inky red mark.

Jaal cackles. "You know my weapons like your taste."

Abundant with rage, I enhance electric pulses, hacking up his auric shield.

What he did to me for years, packaged in a few minutes of sparring.

Knuckles roll and crack from gripping the sword too tight. If I just let it go, let everything go, maybe fate would make the final hit. He'd go down in a blast of stormlight and I'd never have to see his damn face again.

Remembering I already killed him once, my knees buckle.

Just before he nicks my neck, I slide out of his range, plastic leggings making my shins slick. Aches spread and scatter, forcing me to stay in my body and attend to the pressure of a dozen blades continually launching at my throat and thighs. He aims for places he likes to nibble, but instead of hickies and bite marks, he craves a cut straight to bone.

"UGH!"

Dodging turns to flailing, but I keep up with him, deciphering every move a millisecond before making my own.

Jaal says between breaths, "Doctor says…thirty minutes of cardio a day…keeps him and his pills away. Do you feel…less depressed…'cause of this?"

Metal and skin lick each other.

With the same rhythm of making love, we build a bridge of hate. When I blink too much, I lose my stability, and he snatches both of my wrists with one hand. An array of blades hovers over my nose. I tremble in his grasp, caught in the web of our tangled limbs. Again.

"The fight isn't between a rainbow and sharpened cufflinks," he drawls, dragging my hands and sword to the floor, forcing me to squat. All the while he looms over me. "It's between your inner selves. Even Bruja knows it."

111

Pinned to the floor, my sword is useless, and so I spit at his face. A glob smears over his magenta lips, but he sneers. "See what you don't wanna see, Zenith. You're obsessed with me. Always felt it, now I know for sure."

"Get off me!" I snarl.

He guides my weapon to his head, hovering the electric blade over a temple. His hair sizzles and blackens, only making him smile more.

"Stop. You're fucking feverish. You don't know what—"

"Oh, I know." He nods, lower lip trembling in false empathy. "Given you so much. You don't wanna hurt me. You wanna hurt yourself." Flashing his teeth, he morphs into one of my nightmares, shuffling through sheets, adopting the voice my own brain used to turn against itself.

He readjusts the blade's angle with a crunching bend of my wrist, making me whimper. Frizzy flyaways at my hairline crisp and break off.

"All you want is pain. You wanna explode to be reborn. So. Let J-Daddy help. You zap your pretty body to ribbons, and I'll hang it with the tapestries."

A surge of lilac color diffuses the plight of bloodlust. Panting, I blink and turn to the door.

Reiki enters with her palms open, white and purple light gushing from every fleshy line and wrinkle.

Jaal whips around to look at her. "Ah. White flag. Fair play."

I drop the sword with a bone-rattling clang and fall to my knees. It deactivates—and so does the urge to electrocute my own spinal cord—spinning 'til it hits the wall.

Reiki's wide, compassionate eyes lock on mine.

Jaal's blades ring when they slide against one another, metallic bodies retracting and dissolving into electron-filled sleeves.

As if a switch flips, he shoves past Reiki and stalks out the door. Silence trickles. Numbness expands, replacing the thump of blood.

As she approaches me with outstretched arms, I shake my head. "Don't. I smell like him."

She holds my temples and bends to kiss my forehead. "I'm proud of you, Cap," she whispers, lips dragging in sweat.

"I'm not," I mutter, staring at my hands.

Her breath rolls in icy waves over my face. "You're working so hard. You're more aware than he'll ever be. More connected."

I shake my head, a whimper still hanging from my lip. I rub the quivering from my chin. "It doesn't feel like it."

She sighs. "Take a break. Come see—"

"You don't get it," I hiss, tears flooding. "No level of empathy can make you understand." If I shake any harder, I'll dematerialize.

To that, she says nothing, but pulls me into her, filling my ocean with freshwater. In the calm fizz and flow, I remember myself, and all the feelings that make me human. Worth a life. Even if it's a crappy one.

Sniffling, I lean into her chest. When she holds me like this, it feels like a thousand eternal columns prop me up, build a sturdy foundation. "He surpassed my auric field, Ki. Got inside my mind and stuff. How did he do that? How does he always do that?"

"You probably let him in."

"I didn't," I insist, collapsing into her embrace, letting every muscle liquify. We sit sideways together, stabilized by a cornucopia of healthful energy.

She smooths sticky hair from my face. "Not on purpose. But even experienced energy workers have trouble maintaining boundaries. It's not your fault."

My eyes roll so hard, the space between flesh and bone aches. "Never is."

"Just another habit to break and release." Her hand falls. "C'mon. Rest with me."

I sigh and rub my face.

"Please?" Her face is too close to mine; I could count the fibers of her irises. "Come see your new and improved Syzygy."

"Improved?" I pull away from her, shakily getting to my feet. "There was nothing wrong with her, except for that vocal issue..."

Rising, she steadies me and kisses my cheek. "We made a couple changes, but I think you'll like it."

Fourteen

At higher levels, San Fran Isle glints like fish scales, but nothing shines like Syzygy.

"Is that my ship?"

She laughs. "Yeah. They upgraded the exterior with new interstellar alloys. I added some crystal prism layers for a personal touch."

I glance from her turquoise grin to the rainbow-tinted beast of a ship. It could be made of the same material as the shoes I ruined on Mars.

"Holy shit," I laugh, unable to contain the excitement. "Thanks, Ki."

"That's not all," she adds in an amusing infauxmercial voice. I almost forget about my bloodied, shredded leggings and bruised ego, too distracted by how cute she is.

"'Grats, 'meegs," Obsidian greets us at the bottom of Syzygy's stairs. He bows and flourishes a billowing green sleeve. "New ship is ready and rearin' for take-off." Seeing the chocolate crinkles under his eyes—likely from stress, since he can't be much older than I am—makes me want to drown in a vat of concealer.

"You're a fuckin' mess," Onyx tells me, grinning. Her forked tongue protrudes from black lips.

Teeth grinding, I ignore them and stride up the stairs, enjoying the familiar tap of rubber soles against polished metal.

I run my fingers through my hair. "I guess this makes up for all the times you messed with her programming."

Reiki laughs nervously. "Oh, yeah, well…"

Even the ID pad is tinted various shades. It glows a soft dusk color when I press my palm to it, and the door glides open.

The interior smells like a new ship, wafting with fresh pleather and sweet aluminum, but most of it is the same—at first.

Five massage chairs are clustered in a circle in the control room. Wireless fairy lights hang from star-shaped beams.

"A Conduit's touch." I smirk.

"Oh, that's nothing," she snickers, pushing me further into the room. "Take off your shoes."

Overly amused while I unlace the sneakers and set them aside, I toss her a salacious grin. "Anything else you'd like me to take off?"

While her eyes roll, her aura returns to a burnished sunset. Brushing stray hair out of her eyes, she points to the newly installed flooring, where I leave bioluminescent footprints.

"What's this?" I look down and spin, creating a lotus-shaped lightshow.

"Thermodynamic health scanner." A bite of her lip captures giggles that beg to be released. "Automatically detects and tracks body temperature and auric field stability. To keep you and your passengers healthy and whole." Hands rubbing together, she tilts her head. "Y'know. For when...I'm not around."

I shake my head, palms outstretched in awe. "Well, I can't really kick you out now, can I?"

After the scanner finishes, a delicious bass voice rumbles the walls. "Welcome back, Captain Zenith Lin."

My lips part, releasing a fit of chuckles. "Oh my. You made her a man." A hand roams the walls, shifting metal from silver to pink. "A really, really sexy man."

She rubs her neck, blushing. "Yeah, it was kind of an accident at first, but I think he feels better this way."

Gratitude roaring in my chest, I look at her and laugh. "How did you do it? The walls light up too. This is more wicker basket witchery, isn't it?"

"Basically."

"He's the same, but different."

"Just like his captain."

"Oh, and these chairs!" I exclaim, flinging myself into a chair's plush embrace. Feeling the fabricated stir of a sandy beach and smelling saltwater, I blow a finger-splayed kiss of approval. "It's a belated birthday gift! Thank you."

The dreaminess in my voice evaporates when I recollect the current situation. "Jaal gave me lots of gifts when we first...dated. That's not what this is, is it?"

"Heavens, Cap." She raises a hand, releasing topaz bubbles. "If I wanted to manipulate you into falling in love with me, I would've succeeded by now."

"That." I point at her. "Is not even slightly reassuring."

Even with all the similarities, the relationships I've destroyed and created are as different as earth and sky. My frown deepens when another unsettling thought surfaces, replacing the last one. "I'm sorry Jaal and the others call you a witch."

Her laughter's so loud, it scoops when it hits the ceiling. I want her to sing with me again. "Oh, so they can't call me a witch, but you can? You act like we know each other so well." A wink, making fun of me for the anxieties that lace us. Puffing a hair out of her face, she adds, "Who cares what they call me? This is 4444, not 2222."

"Say 'toot' one more time," I tease, tapping an ear.

She runs at me and pins my shoulders to the chair. Our eyes lock, exchanging stardust in frozen chaos. I see myself in those garnets, and I like it.

A mess of emotions enhances the cords we share, and we wash it all down with laughter.

After a deep sigh and a shake of her head, she continues to explain their progress with Syzygy.

"The cronies fixed some program bugs and made him more life-like. But I dove deeper. See, their work was short-lived, but not because of Jaal's fancy technology. My work is what helped theirs take less time." A nose-wrinkling snort. "It was pretty fun...I've never done so much to a ship."

She clears her throat, tugging her gaze away. "Don't get mad, but I went to the engine again. Only this time, I expanded his auric field, flourished his protective flame." Her irises lighten a shade. "He surrounds this ship and inhabits every button and toggle. You, my friendly thief, are the captain of a living, breathing starship. Be nice to him."

One would think by now all her surprises would roll off my back like water, but instead my jaw hangs. In the span of a few hours, with nothing but Jaal's cronies and her witchy spirit, Reiki has turned my ship into an animate, holistic haven.

"That's one way to apologize for all the chaos you've stirred," I breathe, blushing when her fingers brush the back of my neck.

116

"It's not just programming…it's a life. Syzygy's life. You two have a bond that no one, not even I, can interfere with."

Out of nowhere, the engine heaves and wheezes, as if it's being started. Which shouldn't be possible while it's idling.

"Are you sure about that?"

Together, we descend back into G's innermost workings. The deeper we go, the more dark clouds scatter our vision and seep into our lungs.

At the bottom of the ladder, Reiki flips a defogger switch, activating a system that causes the gas to scatter and dissolve like magic.

"Thanks, Ki," I sigh, only to cough as the remnants dissipate.

Work goggles suctioned to his eye sockets, Jaal dangles from a makeshift swing in the ceiling, bundles of wires balanced on ankles.

I approach him with crossed arms, but he doesn't acknowledge me. Black sparks soar from the tangled glob of material in his hand, staining the floor with tar-like drops.

"Honestly, Captain," Syzygy's voice rumbles, finally speaking out. "It's…not what it looks like."

I can't help but laugh at G's new expressiveness. Reiki trails beside me, patting the wall reassuringly.

"Is that a dark energy fuse?" I shield my eyes from the flicker.

Too focused to acknowledge me, Jaal suspends the fuse over his head. Blacklight strobes over his forehead. Carnelian rays from the engine highlight a grinding jaw and bleached lashes like an old chiaroscuro painting. The face I used to fawn over is warped, waxy, and wicked—turned inside-out.

"Jaal, I'd like to know what you're doing to my ship." I brush past a flock of frayed wires, examining the damage. Despite still idling at a safe, Earth-bound level, the star engine revolves and flourishes more fluidly than ever. "Harassing me is one thing, but you don't want to know what happens when you hurt my ship."

"So full of threats." Jaal inclines his head and inspects the wires above him. Each one is a different texture and color like a variety of plant vines. He adjusts the goggles to release some steam. "It's a fuse alright, but not what you're thinkin'." A dusty sigh drifts from chapped lips. "It's protective, not offensive. Helps your ship not explode."

"Explode? Why would it do that?"

He shakes his head. "Think you'd hammered it in your pretty head by now." When I continue to seethe in silence, he clears his throat. "Aurorae'll be channeled through the engine into the Compound. Efficient, but tricky."

117

I rest my hands on my hips, resisting the urge to throw something. "You can't keep doing things without my permission, Jaal. That's not how a team works."

"A team works when a boy lets a man do what's gotta be done."

I throw my hands up. "Everyone thinks they know what's best for G, but he's mine. Reiki's the only one who seems to understand—"

"That's your problem, Z!" He snaps his fingers and points without looking at me. "You pretend objects are animate for your benefit, but claim to own them. Bit hypocritical, don'tcha think?"

"Oh, *I'm* the hypocrite?"

His shoulders rise and stoop. "Possessiveness doesn't suit you. Think you prefer to be possessed."

Heat creeps up my neck. "Well. You're wrong, and that's not even the point." I feel Reiki's hand next to mine, aching to grab it, but refraining. "Exactly what are you doing to protect G's engine from auric explosions?"

"Oooh, big boy uses big words." He laughs and rolls his shoulders to cover up the fact that a particularly large spark made him jump. Sweat glistens on his honeycomb skin. "You're lookin' for simple explanation in a complicated scientific process. Hard to explain." In the metallic crackle of light, I'm starting to think he's fully transitioning into a bloodless drone-man.

He gasps when a black spark smudges his plastic shirt, charring transparent fabric. The charcoal-like sound and appearance of the electrical chemicals inspires the feeling of chalk between my teeth. He brushes blackness off the shirt, sniffs fingers, and goes back to work with a shrug, braiding each wire with its counterpart. Flexible alloys and rubbery vines mingle.

"So, what is it, like, a protective weave or something?" I try to joke, change the mood with words and energy.

Reiki secures my fingers with hers.

Jaal chuckles and swings his legs. A firm shake of the head unravels a dreadlock from his ponytail. It drapes over a flexing temple and jaw. "Nah, it *is* a fuse. Same thing I use for J-bombs but reversed. Kinda." He waves a hand, revealing several burns and lesions in the casted glow. "Don't know if you remember how dark energy works."

I clear my throat. "It's hidden everywhere, right? And it acts like a repulsion jet, spitting everything out of its wake so that the universe continually grows."

He nods. "Destruction for the sake of creation."

118

"But J-bombs were made to cause minimal damage to the overall universe, not tiny humans." I eye him, ripples spreading behind my naval. "They're not meant to be used in tight spaces like this. If you think you can control chaotic energies with nothing but brains, reminding me again why I can't stand to work for you, then you're—"

"Crazy," Jaal cackles, leaning so far forward, the stray dreadlock brushes stellaglass. "Know that. Discussed this. Point is—we've hacked the system. You saw Obsidian's toys, didn't ya?"

"The dark energy crystals?"

"Yeah. Why d'you think they work so well? Crystalline structures make energy transference more defined. Higher the vibration, stronger the flow."

"That's why he used it on me," Reiki realizes. "Sid knew my vibration could handle it."

Jaal ignores her. "It's kinda like a magnet—goes both ways, attracting and repelling. If I can use dark energy to wreck, then I can make it flow inwardly, create a compact casing for aurorae and opals to combine in. A guide for light energy."

I guffaw. "This isn't Shiva we're talking about."

"You're right. It's basic metaphysics. Energy can't be made or destroyed, only moved. So. Basically. Manipulating dark energy to move light energy."

I press my palms together 'til my wrists crack. "Okay, this is extra-stupid, not to mention super dangerous. Is life just one big experiment to you?"

He snickers, oblivious to my rage. "You that concerned?"

After finishing the final wire, he hangs them on a hook above his head, completing the whole rig. From my vantage point, it's a hoarder's room, substantial evidence of an unhealthy obsession.

With each slick, colorful tube connected, potent dark energy moves through the flaming ball of an engine, and into the vat of Phoenix Compound that protrudes from the wall like a fish tank. Another fetal head whimpers in the mess of humanoid skin and lava.

"Oh, I'm concerned, but not for you," I answer finally.

Syzygy steps in again, voice crackling only slightly. "Rest assured, Captain. I am fully capable of handling this."

I look away from Jaal to hide the tears in my eyes.

Jaal tugs a pully rope to descend his little swing and sighs. "You care more about a hunk of metal and star juice than your man?"

Instinctively, my fingers curl, nails snagging Reiki's knuckles. "You're not my man, Jaal. For once, will you please just talk to me like we're equals?"

"Bruja's got you thinking big, doesn't she?" His voice rolls over the alloy floor like thunder on placid water. His boots land with a soft thud and he looks at me expectantly over a beam of yellowing light. "Only not in the right way."

"Reiki's not like anyone else." Vocal chords stitch themselves like these wires, stiff and sparking. "She doesn't think like you, but she doesn't think like me either. She only thinks small when someone needs quantum healing. Infinitesimal hope. And even then..."

Even his aura is stained with used and abused dark energy, making him the deepest black hole I've ever seen.

"Didn't get her for you," he muses, biting his tongue's tip. "But glad to see she serves more purposes than one."

Fifteen

"*I* can't believe he spoke to us like that!" Reiki hollers later in the day, slashing a fake enemy with nunchaku. We're training in Jaal's Sens-gym again, back to back, holding our stance against a dozen red-eyed rock bodies. "He talked about me like I wasn't even there."

Metaphysical sweat the color of an oil spill puddles at our feet. She grabs my thigh to lean and get a better swing at an oncoming boulder. There's so much I could say, and yet nothing at all.

I sigh and lower my sword. "We should rest."

Electric blue light waltzes over her face when she whips her head and lowers her weapon. Garter snake braids that were standing on end from the accumulation of electrical energy go limp.

I resist a chuckle.

Her dark eyes plead while she holds my wrist. "You were never an object of his affection, were you? Just an object."

"C'mon, Ki," I say gently, coaxing the nunchaku out of her hands and setting our weapons aside. The walls shimmer back to mirrors. Seeing our intimacy reflected clearly is almost scarier than the monsters. "It's okay."

"No, it's not okay," she exclaims, digging into her scalp. "I felt it before, but now I've seen it firsthand. Madness. Pure insanity. I can't fathom the cruelty, the inhumanity…or perhaps it *is* humanity…"

"It's the Fever," I say, but we both know that's a lie.

We sit in mirrored lotus position, knee to knee. I don't want her to feel my pain, but it's too late—it's been lodged in her since she met Jaal.

"He gaslighted you," she continues, eyes flashing rouge. "He abused you, and what's worse, he made you think you wanted it. Now,

121

he smugly awaits your validation, even though he's doing exactly what was inflicted upon him. How does he expect to heal in this kind of environment? It makes no sense! It just...makes me so...AGH!" She throws her hands up and sprawls back on the floor.

"You've got to stop caring about me so much. It's not good for your health."

Craning her neck to stare at her reflection upside down, she allows tears to etch her forehead. "It's not just you and Jaal, Zen. It's the collective. I've never felt this kind of communal betrayal. I'm just so sick of it. So many millennia, and we're still hurting each other like it's law." A lip-trembling scowl. "When really, the only law anyone should be following is Love!"

Her words sink in while I lay next to her on my side, bending an elbow to hold my head up. My thin hips are rigid against the cold floor. "You're the one who said Jaal deserves to heal."

"And I stand by that," she hisses, "but it doesn't make it any less painful to perceive."

I bite my lip so hard, it stings. "What happened to him? Despite having known him for four years, he never told me anything. You said he does the same things that were done to him. You think he was...abused?"

She eyes me through the mirror. "You can tell a lot about a person by the state of their auric field. Just like planets with contaminated atmospheres, or moons that rarely see sunlight... I don't even have to look at them. I can feel the pain from lightyears away." As she exhales sharply through an o-shaped mouth, tears evaporate.

I look at my hands. "Is that why you're overly kind to me?" My shoulders curl inward. "'Cause you can sense my pain?"

A glare pummels my energy as she sits up. "Why does there need to be a reason?"

"Everyone always has a reason, an end-game, a...plan." I swallow deep-seeded nausea. "You're perceptive. You know that."

Smiling smooths her jagged gaze. She puts a hand on each knee. "Cap. Listen. Nothing I feel from or for you is your fault. Just like how any feelings you might have aren't my fault. In fact, no one is truly at fault for any emotions that bubble up in another person. We're all just experiencing, moving through energies. Reacting to events, chemical and otherwise. And anyway, while we're on the topic of motivation..." She huffs a sigh. "I'd do a lot of...things...to you, but hurting you isn't one of them. I promise."

122

To emphasize her point, she holds out her pinky and ring finger, a gesture of goodwill.

I laugh, hooking the two fingers with mine and shaking our fists in agreement. "So, you do know some Earthen fads."

She gathers her reddish mane to one shoulder, combing through unbraided pieces with trembling fingertips. "I may have lived on Mars, but I wasn't under a...oh wait."

Her laughter is a wave of seafoam, coating my bellows in bubbles.

"Hey." I lean and touch her knuckles. "Wanna sing again?"

"Is that why you grabbed your significant other?" She asks, referring to the sitar perched next to the door.

"Yes," I reply, getting up and retrieving it. My joints rattle in rebellion, a lack of flexibility on all counts. "Music is really all I have right now. But we can share it, I guess." I grin to match the brightness in her face.

"I'd like that."

Tuning the sitar brings me a new kind of peace. Bones hum with a prelude, sweet caresses and thrums of the insides. This is what I need. This is what I want.

After a few perfected strums, I start with a mantra that Mama and Mother used to sing to me—something Kenji for "love" and "light." As usual, a collection of mental instruments plays with mine, from the soft, earthy pat of drums to a dozen different types of string. Sounds weave a hammock-shaped throne around us.

Tentative at first, her voice barely differentiates from the strums—she's too nervous to stray from the melody.

I can't hide the smile, fingers too busy threading life into metal and wood. She can animate my ship, but I animate the air.

Together, we wander through a patchwork song, stitching and fixing our spliced souls and burrowed-into bodies.

A multidimensional, synesthetic experience ensues, broader and crazier than last time. I don't know if it's her breath or mine, but my lungs fill with pine sap. Ears ring from sonar overflow. Every ancient word I emit leaves a different flavor—tarragon, sage, olive, vanilla. We soak ourselves, bask in dew-trapped sunlight, float on ghostly breath.

My fingers and vocal chords halt when fierce, frigid hands rake my ribs. I gasp, startled by the intrusion. I cling so hard to the sitar, it makes a garbled noise.

When I open my eyes, Reiki's on the other side of the room, backed against the wall. I turn around, expecting an intruder. Nothing.

"What's wrong?" I flick curls out of my face.

Her buttermilk knees quiver as she slinks to the floor, eyes peeled. "Someone…attacked our aura." With a hand on her heart, she slows her breath and blinks profusely.

"You didn't touch me?"

She shakes her head. "I don't know who or what it was, but I think it was an accident."

"Attacks are pretty intentional."

Palms pressed against the wall, she scrunches her nose in focus. "It felt accidental…like someone was trying to communicate with us but couldn't pinpoint how."

"Wild," I say, tapping my chin. "Does that mean this place is haunted?"

"What an antiquated idea," she scoffs. "No, it's like what I felt in your shower. Peaceful, but confused. Lost."

"But you didn't recognize it?"

"It was so physical," she breathes. "So cold. Stuck in suspension, frozen, out of time… I don't know. It's hard to explain."

"Can you protect us?"

She shrugs. "It's gone now, but whatever it was…it's struggling. It doesn't want us to hurt, it just wants to be free."

"Sounds familiar."

"Sorry, I just…got a little carried away with the…" Her hand flourishes, insinuating that she channeled energy while we sang, which comes as no surprise. What does surprise me is when her lovely eyes roll back into her head and she slumps onto the floor.

"Reiki!" I rest the sitar on its case and scramble to her side. Relief washes over me when I feel her steady pulse and breath. "Sweet Seven Sisters. You're turning into me, fainting like that."

I hold her head in both hands and gently usher her into my lap. Up close, her skin is polished moonstone. Flyaways stick to her temples, blending with freckles like peach-and-white swirls of spirit jasper.

"For someone so cosmic," I whisper, thumbing loops of hair away. "You look like you were birthed from Earth's core."

Our song still lingers in my belly. I could kiss her, but it wouldn't be out of lust.

I play it all up to annoy Jaal and cater to his one-dimensional brain. But when she's tranquil like this, immobile in my arms, suspended between the conscious and the subconscious, something realer resurfaces. More familiar, and more distant. Somewhere under those seashell lids, there are fragments of a smashed past I want to invoke.

124

Kissing her would be too simple. I want to swallow her energy—not for glutton, but to keep her safe—encapsulate her essence in a rose gold throat, sanctify the bright being inside with bodily relics. I wouldn't hurt anymore, if her systems communed with mine.

Her eyelids flutter open. She strings up a weak smile. "I heard your outer space," she whispers, head bobbing. "I didn't know you were a poet in this life too." Trying to focus on me overwhelms her, and her body shuts down again to compete with dizziness.

What are you? I mouth, unable to bring myself to speak aloud again.

Everyone speaks in riddles, either from clarity or insanity, and it's starting to get to me. Not only am I diverging from everything I know, but I'm becoming obsessed with everything I don't.

Gingerly keeping a hand under her skull, I move to pick her up. I may be shorter than her by an inch and skinnier by several, but to my surprise, she feels lighter than the sitar. My mind harps on the endless possibilities, about how simultaneously delicate and powerful she is—more energy than mass.

I'm dying—no, living—to know where she could take me, where we could have been, and to comprehend the quantum mess our spirits create.

I let go of so much just by holding her.

Giving in. Not just to thought, but to the power of thought, the leering flirt of hope. Without it—and here's the hot tea of a millennia—I'm just another pathetic pansexual lost in the abyss.

When her arms wrap around my neck, I have a sneaking suspicion that she's messing with me. But the rest of her body is limp, and her aura is saturated, weighed down by all the energies she sponges from other people.

With her head on my shoulder, long legs collapsed over my arm, I rise, almost dropping her when the door opens.

"The fuck'd you do?" Onyx's black aura splatters, streaking her blonde buzzcut and carnelian eyes.

"Nothing."

Her violet nails thrum against black pleather hips, disbelieving.

"First of all," I hiss, readjusting. "I'd never hurt Reiki. Not now, after all she's done for me." Heat rises to my ears from the combination of effort and embarrassment. "Secondly, it's none of your business."

Her hips jut to the side, leaning on the doorframe. "Obviously you wouldn't hurt her, Zenith. You're a masochist, not a sadist." Just when I think she's on my good side. "But accidents happen."

"Could you help me bring her to a room? She just overextended herself."

"Y'think?" Onyx deadpans.

Sixteen

If returning to Earth launched my guts into trachea, then leaving for Saturn threatens to expel my entire digestive system.

"You can do this," I say to the bathroom mirror. Under a swatch of foggy breath, my reflection stares back with a flushed, sunken face, unconvinced. "You have Syzygy, Reiki, and a semblance of sanity." I raise a trembling index finger. "Didn't sleep well, but that's normal. Big trip. Whatever. Point is—you're safe. With her, you're safer than you've ever been…"

"Ten minutes until ascent," Syzygy announces. "I am more than ready, Captain."

Charred knots lodge in my crown and chest, settling in sweaty palms that slip when I lean on the cold sink.

"Breathe. You're a strong, healthy individual, and nothing—not even Jaal's Fever and his backwashed army—can change that." Hopefully, the more I say it, the truer it'll be. My own personal, polished mantra.

While I wash my hands, I imagine the water circling past the drain, into its recycling chamber, repeating a process it never knew it needed.

Somewhere in these cycles, there should be an answer to my woes, a healing force I can use more readily than Reiki's. If she's anything like Mama's first round of medicine, my body will kick her out before she's performed optimal functions.

Mentally, I kick myself. "Lunatic," I hiss. "Don't turn into Jaal. She's not an object to be used…not medicine…"

But she is a gift, a vast voice echoes in my mind.

At first, I react to the bombarding voice as if it's Syzygy's.

127

Slowly, I realize the voice is a projection of someone else, possibly the presence Reiki and I felt. It's not quite violent, but it sends me reeling almost as bad as Jaal's.

Downy, invisible fingers tap the cluttered space between brows.

Keep her close, even when it feels like death.

"Tauris?" I blurt in speculation, lurching.

Love is the only Truth you need now. Pick up your pieces and give them Peace.

Voices cluster until they barely differentiate from my own poetic nature, circling senses and leaving me exposed.

I return to deep breathing, calm logic swaying me more than a disembodied voice. Sensations detach, not mine, not anyone's. A simple physiological phenomenon.

Dipping my head into the sink, I drench my face in cool water, but stop when another presence sweeps through my body and mind.

Lights flicker. The sink sputters off. One of the shower nozzles drips.

"I'm not a haunted house." I rub my temples with the quivering bones of my inner wrist. "I'm not crazy."

But maybe Gemini Fever has become so potent, it's contagious, and I caught it from Jaal, and I'm losing my mind, body, and soul, and everything will crumble if I don't do this job right for once just do it right you stupid little—

"Cap?" Reiki drags me out of myself, opening the door. "Zenith." Her brow shrivels and her arms open, but I move away in a cold sweat.

Don't come near me. If I'm losing it, if I've already lost it, I don't want to keep dragging you with me.

"You should be resting," I scold, not giving her more than a glance. If do, I'll probably burst into tears.

"I feel better. Besides, I could say the same for you."

"Thanks for the concern," I try to be genuine, but it comes out like staged lines. "But I'm fine. Just trying to spark some motivation. This ship still needs its captain."

Her smile goes from bright and proud to green with guilt. "Um, about that…"

"What did they do?"

At the bedroom door, she tries to block me, but I shove past her, into the hall. Rainbow fairy lights guide my way—another artistic touch of Reiki's. They flicker when I walk by, motion sensing the patterns of breaths and steps.

"One minute until ascent," Syzygy bellows.

I slap open the cockpit door.

Obsidian sits in the captain's chair, fiddling with controls. Screens buzz and blink with a dozen different and new settings. Mere colors overwhelm me. String lights above tremble, either from my energy or the ship, I can't tell.

"Done fucking yourself?" Jaal asks, leering from the chair next to Obsidian. His chin is balanced on an open palm, ever the thoughtful bystander. I should roundhouse kick his wrist and jack-up his jaw.

Sprawled in a chair with numerous blankets, Onyx laughs 'til she coughs. A veil of smoke floats between them.

"Don't talk to me like that." I march right up to him.

"Zenith." Jaal's placating makes my teeth clench. "Know you're accustomed to a certain level of…comfort and control." He tilts his head, laughter slipping off a string of pearlescent smoke. "But this tech isn't your biz. Sid-baby knows what he's doing." He wiggles a gold-wrapped rod of weed between index and middle finger.

"This is my ship," I say between caged teeth.

"It is," he agrees, thick lips pursed. He inspects the smoking blunt. "Promised we could use it for the trip. Didn't say nothing about you being pilot."

"That's a double negative, you cock-biting cu—"

Reiki snatches my hand and our palms make a pop of air. Her steadiness contrasts my quaking.

"Christ's crack, Z," Jaal titters, fanning himself. "You're gonna get me all hot and bothered, talking like that."

His taunting wink sends me back into the hall, sweat pooling at the base of my spine. Insanity reaches the tiniest curves of this cracked body.

Reiki's hand is still molded to mine. "Don't give up," she whispers against my ear. I want to swallow her voice like a pill and wash it down with the steam in her eyes. "He's trying to rile you, so you'll mess up and give him an advantage. But you can't. You won't. His power is a delusion."

"Yeah, well, so is my freedom," I grumble, trying to shirk her. But she remains on me, devouring and empowering, a loving magnetar.

"The *lack of freedom*, for you, is the real delusion," she corrects, brushing my hair aside to kiss a temple. Re-sanctify the space that has been desecrated and abandoned. "You're free to be you. Whatever that means." With each kiss she trails down to my neck, weirdly, the calmer I

129

become. Until her mouth hovers over a thumping vein, an exposed secret, and my breath hitches.

A candle is lit in place of hellfire.

"Pleiades, Ki." I shake my head, pushing her off. She detangles, emanating a hopeful yellow light.

We exchange visual whispers, conveying confusion in crisp, twinkling irises.

It's not that I dislike her affection, but in the shadows, pupils cold and dilated, I aim to avoid falling for the same tricks that got me into this horny, gemless mess.

We reenter the control room and take seats farthest from the others. Chills decorate my spine.

We're enveloped in silence, which is unusual for these idiots, let alone a take-off. While the walls still wiggle in anticipation, the typical purr and rumble is muted. The floor sparkles like a panel of comets from our scattered energies.

They've done so much to Syzygy, but I know he's still my ship. Fancy tech, a new voice, and a mediocre replacement captain won't change that.

To prove it, his gentle, sexy voice punctuates the peace. "Ascent commencing. All systems operable. It's lovely weather for a trip, Captain Zenith." When I close my eyes, I can feel his warm metallic smile.

Obsidian goes about his business, beginning our journey with more finesse than I gave him credit for. His feathery faux-hawk wisps in silver-and-red tendrils while his head bobs to check each camera. As we continue to rise through the atmosphere, nervousness grips my feet, forcing toes to tap against the floor. With each beat, a thermal lightshow plays.

"Everything's so quiet," I muse, biting a hangnail. "Did you add a damper to the fuse or something?"

Jaal's tongue slides over the roof of his open mouth. "Interstellar dampers are for pussies."

Unable to hold still, I swivel my eyes and cross my legs. He knows how much I've hurt, but now I want him to know how little I care.

My mouth runs without the brain's consent. "The only impressive part of this is the fact that we've already transcended the thermosphere with barely a peep from the engine. Everything else is extra."

On every inch of the wall, screens display fields of stars. Like lost children in a makeshift pod, we push through exospheric mist and drop our jaws with the baggage at our feet.

All this divine timing and scenery, and Onyx puts on her S-Com, hiding herself from the magnificence.

"You got something against beauty?" The words leak too quickly for me to sop up.

A finger to her lips, she shakes her head. "You got something against a person doing whatever they want?"

"You seem tense, Z," Jaal cuts me off. "If you need more fuck-fests, don't let us spoil your fun. Could join you, if you'd let me." Another wink sprinkled with salt.

A vicious smirk picks up my lips. "Oh, J." Condescend. Deflect. "It's cute that you think that would please me." Tongue curled between my teeth, I rise and make for the door. Reiki stays on my heels, the loyal angel to Jaal's obedient demons.

"What're you doin', 'meegs?" Obsidian calls, spinning the chair. Behind him, the screens sizzle white and black, a comforting symphony of proof that G still has some autonomy. I'd find Obsidian's ignorance to Jaal's true nature sweet if it didn't impede on my sense of freedom.

"Not any of you, that's for damn sure." I use Jaal's implications like a knife against his throat before the door slides shut.

"That was…bold," Reiki says, but it hangs like a question.

"C'mon."

On the slick hallway floor, socks slip. I bang my knees on the door when we reach it.

Reiki helps me gather myself. "You're literally beating yourself up." Her whispers reverberate down the hall.

A toxic mantra plays in the tunnels of my inner ear. *Don't let them know I plan on hurting myself before they can hurt me.*

"Password?" Syzygy asks.

I lean against the wall to peel off the socks. "Anulos."

"Access denied."

"Oh, right." My face heats as I scrunch up polyester. "Something else you changed."

Reiki's blush rivals mine.

Clearing my throat, I unscramble my mother's name. "Soluna."

The door opens wider than my heart. Entering, I tear off my shirt and throw it on the bed.

"I thought it would help." Reiki sits on the bed and cradles my shirt. "Remind you what we're out here for."

131

"Yeah, but now Jaal can come in whenever he wants."

She shrugs. "He doesn't own your voice, so even with your mother's name—"

"Not in the mood for logic, Ki." My palm runs over a hidden panel next to the bed, which emits a whistle tone before opening. "Let me sulk."

I rummage through a cupboard lit by tiny red lights. Colorful bottles and vials clink—empty old habits I haven't touched in months.

"Thank the planets they didn't change anything in here," I whisper, wiping sweat from a cinched brow.

"I told them to maintain your privacy."

I snort. "Is that why they think I'm masturbating every five minutes?"

A shower of rose petals dot her aura and prick her face. "Well. I'm not sure that's exactly it, but. Anyway. Who cares what they think?"

I turn back to the cupboard, stomach clenching at the sight of more empty containers. "This is the only sacred place I have left."

"I wouldn't call alcohol sacred," she giggles, but the warmth leaves her voice as quickly as it came. "Zenith. What are you doing?"

"I'm not doing anyth—"

"Zen, stop!" She launches at my forearm.

Breath snagging, my fist clenches a little too tight, and I crush a vial as if it was nothing more than aluminum. Glass pieces protrude from scripts of blood and raked skin. Rivulets rush down my wrist, creating candied patterns with purple veins. The tiniest shards crumble like snowflakes onto the navy carpet.

"It tickles."

Reiki kneels beside me, cupping my hand. "You're not even drunk yet."

A pout replaces mad giggles. "If only I was strong enough to crush Jaal like this."

"He's already doing that to himself," she reminds, guiding me onto the bed. While she holds the bloodied hand, coaxing me to focus on breathing, I sit next to her and watch intently as she goes to work. But it's not energy she works with, yet. First, she plucks the chunks of glass and deposits them on the bedside table. A snap of her fingers causes the lamp to go on, ushering more light into the space.

"Ple…" I sigh, suppressing the swear. "Thanks, Reiki."

"You keep hurting your hands," she whispers, clearing her throat. "Do you know what kind of omen that is?"

Silvery dots speckle my vision. "No."

132

A heavy sigh sends energy rolling off the tendons in her neck while she inspects the wounds. "It's a sign of self-hatred, but it also means you're a natural-born Conduit."

A smile cracks me open. "What?" I laugh, shaking my head. A gasp zips through teeth as she extracts an oblong piece. "N-nah, Ki. That's you."

Head bowed, her eyes meet mine. I melt under such a shadowed look. "I knew from the moment I saw you, how you bite your nails, crack your knuckles…you do a lot with your hands, to distract from their true purpose." A tiny bubble of spit forms in the side of her mouth. "Energy flows readily from and through you. You're a healer, Zen."

Still not entirely convinced, I tilt my head. "Well. I should take better care of my hands, then."

Irrevocable warmth floods the space between us. Cupping knuckles gingerly with one hand, the other hovering over blood puddles in my palm, she whispers an incantation. Royal sapphire symbols pass through flitting lips, shocking me to the core with magical and scientific awe.

"What are you doing?"

Bandages of light synthesize from her open palms, caressing the wound and morphing to my flesh-and-bone shape. Tendons tilt with pleasure, soothed by fluid energy. It shoots through my veins, replacing boiled blood with pure light.

"I'm tuning you." Her voice crescendos like a song. "You're ready to heal yourself."

"Tuning me, like an instrument?" I shake my head. "Wait…didn't you already do something like th—" I gasp at the accompanying pain that radiates from thumb to elbow to chest, forehead to nose to breath, curling like gaseous flares through all systems.

Words clot in my throat when throngs of musical fire braid my legs together, sending scarlet roots into overdrive. After prickly tension comes sweet release, and I'm a goner.

Thick, visceral light pools at the base of my spine, sifting between thighs as though I'm made of sand. Lovingly, seas part for this penetrating energy, dousing azure flames with new fuel. Nothing, no one—physical or meta—could touch me any better, or delve any deeper.

I moan, immediately covering my mouth with a freshly healed hand. All the fire coils to my face, sizzling in gaunt cheeks.

133

That sensation coupled with Reiki's laughter makes me shiver. She beams. "Never have I met someone so in tune with their body, that tuning their energy makes them—"

Harsh thumping against the door makes us jump.

I clear my throat and call in a high-pitched voice, "Who is it?"

Behind the door, Jaal fumes. "Using that voice ain't gonna make me go away. Get out here. Wanna talk. Man-to-boy."

I lean back against a mound of pillows. "Mmm... no thanks."

"Wasn't offering, Z. This is a command from your—"

"You're not my anything, Jaal. Please accept that before you hurt yourself."

Reiki goes rigid.

The monster in him only proves me right by banging on the door.

We sit quietly, waiting for the storm of Jaal's rage to pass. Even Reiki's decorative fairy lights shake from all his yelling and slamming.

Ignoring him, I raise my hands and scan the overlapping scars that fade to shadow. Even my natal chart is silhouetted, ever so slightly. She made me sugar-encrusted, puddled with stardust. When I look at her, she gleams.

The toxic strands give me an idea.

I reach over the side of the bed and hoist the sitar into my lap. The freshly healed hand feels raw against polished wood, but with Reiki's tendrils of light still licking, it's not so bad.

I strum. Each twang douses the air in sonic medicine.

The quality of sound shifts when I wrap a brass wire around an index finger, protecting sensitive flesh from tense threads. When I close my eyes, it's almost like raking my fingers over throbbing skin, wincing veins and cinched throats. Reiki's irises coat mine like contacts, bright brown and tinsel.

When I open them, Jaal's rebellion fades. He lumbers away.

"I soothed the beast," I whisper, pinching my chin thoughtfully. "I guess you were right."

"Well, think about it. If music does that..." She glances at my billowing root chakra, hiding a snicker in the crook of her arm. "Then just imagine what it does to other people, coming from you. You can arouse and tranquilize...you can make all kinds of remedies." Her snowy lashes flutter, swaying like tiny arms against a speckled backdrop.

Dropping the brass wire, I snap my fingers. "Hold up. Why don't you and I heal Mama?"

Her eyebrows bunch. "Zen. That's why we're here."

134

"No, not like this. I mean like, with our energy and our music. Just you and me. A proper, old-fashioned healing session."

More petals stick to her aura, but this time they're cherry blossoms, half-wilted. "I told you—even I can't heal the Fever. It's…beyond my capabilities."

"Right, but with both of us working on it…I mean, you could teach me. It'd be like…like Ayurveda, or something. You have your wicker basket witchery, but I've got, oh I don't know, sexy sonar."

She laughs so hard, she snorts. "You're precious. But no, I don't think that would work."

I rest the sitar on pillows, letting its neck brush the headboard. "That's uncharacteristically hopeless of you." Some silver-lined side-eye should shake her temperament.

But the mood doesn't budge. Even when I playfully squeeze her calf, all she does is frown and pat my hand.

Disappointment hits like a rock to the gut. I draw knees to my chest in protection. Self-preservation, which is better than self-destruction.

"I'm sorry, Cap." She sighs, elbows and hands up to re-do her top-knot. "Let's just. Try Jaal's plan first, and then go from there."

Betrayal, even on a smaller scale, bites me.

Seventeen

After many naps and snack-fests, I'm sprawled in bed, hanging my head off the edge. "Syzygy. Report."

A beat of silence, and then he sizzles to life. "Twenty-seven hours into the trip, Captain. Internal conditions are…less than ideal, if I am being honest."

"Really? Haven't noticed."

"You have already consumed an eighth of your weight in food, Captain. This is usually a sign of distress."

I burp. "Well. What about outside? Good weather, I hope?"

"External conditions are more palatable, at this time. For example, if you check the screens, you'll see that we are passing Ace's Comets, a bubble of perpetually falling stars that cannot escape their own gravitational capsule. Much like myself."

I grin so hard, my face aches. "Vast mood, G." Then, I rub my eyes and sit up. "Ace's Comets, huh? That's about…" I click my tongue and finger-count. "Thirty hours away from Mars?"

Silence plummets and mimics outer space. The only sound that breaks it is Reiki's and my collective breathing. She meditates on the floor next to my bed.

With a quirked brow, I turn to her. "Ki. You alive?"

Her mouth twitches. "More than ever." She eyes me through a squint. "Is everything alright?"

"Syzygy's being weird again."

"He sounds fine to me." She breaks her meditative posture and leans against the bed. "You, however, need to relax."

"You're right. Have a drink with me."

Her belly bounces with laughter. She rubs her solar plexus, cackle dying down when her gaze snags mine. "Oh, you're serious."

I throw my legs over the bed's edge and crouch in front the open cabinet. Dried blood spots litter the corner, from earlier.

Reiki clears her throat. "Is this a command from my captain?"

"Me? Commanding? Never."

I reach into the shadows with more tact this time and produce a full bottle of blueberry wine. "All the way in the back," I exclaim, popping my tongue. "This stuff is great. It turns your whole mouth blue, and then your vision."

Air puffs through her spluttering lips. "Why would I want that? I already see blue everywhere, with your throat chakra bleeding all over the place…"

I flourish a hand. "That's different."

"How old is it?"

"Oh, a few months," I fib, coughing into a fist. "Maybe a year. It's gotta be stronger than God by now, but that's how I like it."

I turn to rummage around for a wine-opener, but Reiki grabs the heel of the bottle. Instantly, lapis-colored energy makes the glass wobble. With a graceful pop, the silver cork soars and bounces off the ceiling and onto the bed.

"Oooh, she's an astrobat, healer, and wine-opener," I cheer, licking the rim to stop the spill. "How can we not be friends?"

She props her chin in both palms. "You keep using that word: friends." Her translucent brow rises. "Is that what we are, in this life?"

I take a long swig. "Uh, yeah. I think so."

Her aura electrifying, she pokes the end of the bottle while it's in my mouth. I cough and wipe my face, but blue juice sticks to my beard.

"Ki, what the fu—"

She smacks my head with a pillow, snatches the bottle, and guzzles.

"Oh, I see what you're doing—distracting me to get to the booze!"

Her stained mouth opens to let out a burp. "Wow. That's liquid candy."

"You know what else is liquid candy?" I tease, tugging the neck of the bottle. She keeps a hand on it while I sip. While our eyes lock, my other hand brushes her thigh, still buzzing with gold rings of energy.

"You're stupid," she murmurs, a dare lurking in her eyes.

"Look, we can't all be harmonious witch hazels like you, okay? I'm a hundred times more human than you. Every thought in my brain is dirty."

The dare in her gaze becomes wet truth. "That's not because you're human. That's because you're hurting."

"Is there a difference?"

"No, but I want you to recognize that…that it's okay to hurt, but don't use it as an excuse to—"

"The booze," I cackle, gulping another round. "It's already kicking in for you, isn't it?" My stomach sloshes, wave after wave, slopes of oak-pressed foam.

She drinks again, her hand over mine. "Maybe."

I was right—it's stronger than it should be. Probably older than I thought, too. But it stains our mouths better than ink and clears my shoulders of their burdens.

My fingers unfurl to embrace the flow, the violet fluidity of humanity.

Eventually, we lie on our backs, pretending to watch stars cross us. If I squint, everything sparkles.

"I can't see my own aura," she says like it's a scandal, spreading her fingers and inspecting the space between them. "Or maybe it's my body that's blurred. Colors, man…they're so confused."

I laugh between teeth and lip, making myself dizzy. "That's sad," I hiccup. "Your body's beautiful. I always wanna see it clearly."

"Really? I chose a good one, then."

"Yeahhh, mannnn." My eyelids merge, but what lies under them frightens me.

Inside my mind, there's one of those extra ancient paintings we can only see digitized, depicting the full spectrum of gods and hell-spawn.

Overwhelmed, I open my eyes and spout blueberry tears.

Reiki turns on her side, lower lip trembling. "Oh, my love. What's wrong?"

"Nothing," I mutter, blinking away the bad stuff and squishing her cheeks. "Just my demons. God. Your face is so plush."

Mirroring me, she puts a hand on either of my cheeks, making me giggle.

One of her eyes blinks before the other. "What are we, for real?"

My thumbs run over her mouth, tugging the corners up in a forced smile. Pink origami. "We're human, silly."

She sticks her tongue out. "No, I mean…" Everything's blazing, but her face is hotter than my hands.

"Whoa, you're burning up," I hiss, dragging us both into sitting position. The back of my skull tries to pull the rest of me intact. "Are you sick?"

"No."

I drift on a bouncy cosmic cloud. Her face is a sun holding the system in orbit. "I could take care of you, like you do. Pleiadeeees, that's gotta be lame, having to care for me even though you barely know me. 'Specially since I'm the actual worst."

She laughs so hard she cries. Or maybe, she cries so hard, laughter dives in too. "Shut up, impossible soul."

"Oooh. Do you know what else is impossible?"

Her face scrunches, hiding behind glossy tears. "Tell me."

My head detaches from its body. At least that's what it feels like.

I whisper in her ear, "That we make out 'til breathing isn't a thing. Like, we literally demolish the concept of breathwork."

"You're right. That *is* impossible."

"Oh, c'mon, I know you want to." I pout. "Everyone always wants to."

"You sound like Jaal." Her hair falls out of the bun, sheathing her head in copper wisps and waves.

More sobering words have never been said.

Sucking in a fruity breath, I bite my lip. Fuzzy brain tissue knits together. "Shit. Yeah. Sorry, Ki. It's the…wine…and I just thought…after New Year's…I didn't mean to be pushy." I peer over the edge of the bed at an empty bottle glinting in fluorescent lighting.

"I mean." A tap of her chin, a thoughtful glance. "There's nothing to celebrate." She hiccups and shrugs. "But if it makes you happy." She leans into my chest, pushing me back into the pillows.

Flecks of copper dust my skin, precious metals caressing.

But even while spilling onto me, she hesitates.

I slide my fingers between braids at the base of her scalp. An indigo mouth opens to take her in, to crosshatch myself into oblivion. Maybe it's the booze, or the fact that she is blurry, in every sense of the word, but I want it more than I've ever wanted anything else.

But the ship lurches defiantly, setting our lips off course. My stomach dips toward my knees.

Reiki looks around wildly, flicking hair in my mouth. "What the—?"

Syzygy bellows, "Position breached. Systems stabilizing."

"What kind of rhetoric is that?" I manage through a cough, detangling from the sweat-infused haze. "Syzygy, re—"

"Position breached. Weapons prepared for functioning. Fire at will."

"CHRIST!" I leap off the bed, accidentally kicking Reiki's ribs.

My clammy feet plop on cold flooring as I rush down the hall. Lights waltz past me. I've probably never run this fast down these halls, especially with booze-infused veins. Walls tremble when I fly into the cockpit, but I can't tell if it's my drunkenness or an oncoming attack.

"Who're you killing without my mission?" I shake my head. "*Per*mission." A lead tongue isn't fun in the company of space-scoundrels. They greet me with laughter.

Obsidian grips the controls like he's playing a game. I stalk up to him to shake the chair. "Hello? Earth to Obsid...oh my fuck."

The screens display a mosaic of destruction.

Gusts of flame-kissed rock hurtle past us, but larger pieces are aligned with our path. Not just rock, but metal and wood, singed and spinning in perfect harmony, like Tauris' ribbon-whipped dancers.

This isn't another meteor shower.

Not everything is charred, just scattered. Chunks of houses, sure, but also strips of clothing, showerheads, furniture, Sens-coms, open pill bottles, and more. An amalgam of people's lives, wasted away, warped by outer space's vicious maw.

Ahead, Mars is an orange-faced boy with a bruised eye. Broken and abused. Kicked and punted outside of his own orbit.

A throat-shuttering gasp sticks to spit, causing me to cough. "Pleiades, what even..." I shake my head, lurching for the controls, activating orbit analysis and various safety parameters. "This can't be real. You guys are fucking with me. We shouldn't be this close to Mars yet, and...my God." Blackened bodies are hurled from nowhere, circling the abyss of space, colliding with rocks and dissolving into bluish specks. Some are so mangled, they're barely decipherable from debris, stringed carbon smothered into oblivion by fate-driven hands. "Sweet Seven Sisters and Holy Pluto. What's happening?"

"You're the captain," Jaal jeers, slapping my back so hard I cough again. "Figure it out."

Brain fibers crank, break, and re-lace before his words sink in. Unfolding before us is the biggest crime he's ever committed.

"N-no fucking way." I zoom in, only to cover my face in shock. "And you want me to trust you? After everything, you think this is acceptable too? Justifiable, for the sake of science—"

140

"Zenith."

I can't even face him. "What are you trying to prove?"

Luckily, I don't have to look at him to hear the slap of straightened knuckles against cheekbone.

Jaal doubles over, almost hitting the controls. I swallow my tongue as a fierce-maned Reiki shoves him into a chair.

"That was my home in this life, my sacred space," she hisses, opalescent tears rolling. "Just because you never had one doesn't mean you can go destroying other people's, collapsing planets for the sake of your wounded mind's temporary pleasure."

He opens his mouth.

"No." She thrusts a finger in his face. This is a new facet of her, one I didn't expect. "You don't get to speak, Jaal, if it hurts those around you. You don't get to pillage a whole solar system because you can't take care of your own inner-child. Healing is a process. Revenge is popping pills to numb the ache, only to feel worse than before. You can't become the beast that bit you—that's not healing. Not true…freedom…" After the solar flare of an aura, her energy retreats, once again pushed to its limits by passion.

This part I recognize.

She faints into my arms, flannel pajamas pricking me with static electricity. My thumb brushes over her flushed lips.

Fuming, Jaal launches out of the chair and pinches my wrist between forefinger and thumb. He can't seem to find the words, but his aura is blistering. His eyes burn and toil with every changing color.

"Get off," I command, which earns me a thick fist to the face.

Boiling blood splutters from my nose. Reiki's unconscious body rolls away.

My spine crunches. An array of color-coded health issues litters the floor. *Erratic heartbeat, broken nose, high blood pressure, exhaustion, dehydration.* If Jaal was barefoot, it would probably add the ever-growing list of updates on his Fever. But I don't need a machine or six senses to tell me—

Jaal's fist rams into my cheek, and the pain radiates from my jaw to collarbone. Numbness overcomes pain neurons, trying to shut down, fueled only by PTSD. But I'm still conscious. I can't feel a thing but the huge weight that covers me.

With a knee on either hip, Jaal forces me down, as if I could sink any lower. A dozen more health issues pop up behind my head, circling us with light-labels.

Every part of me trembles.

141

Dizzily, I perceive Obsidian hunched over the controls, trying to steady the ship as it veers into clouds of debris. Toxic powders unfurl and blossom, dotting the screens in fluorescent hues. He needs to adjust the static shields.

"Jaal, ge'off. I deed ta fix the ship's—" His meaty palm clamps my bloodied lips shut. I can't even open my mouth to bite.

Jaal's body hits mine so hard, I worry that I'll crack open and he'll embezzle my insides.

But when he doesn't get back up, pressed into me like a wilted leaf between book pages, I sigh. He's unconscious.

Someone rolls him off me. With one hand rubbing my eyes and the other covering my gushing nose, I sit up and blink.

A silver syringe sticks out of his neck.

Onyx crouches over him, retrieving it and wiping fluid remnants on her jeans. "Sorry."

Eighteen

"*He* didn't know it would happen like that," Obsidian insists hours later, interrupting my glazed focus on our path ahead. "He wanted to leave his mark on Mars, with Tauris' death, but he didn't mean to injure the whole planet."

Monochrome space is laced with winking stars and neighboring solar systems of various shapes and shades, continuing to unravel like nothing happened. But this abomination will take its toll, and then some. Anything could happen. Our solar system is unhinged; it could send the whole Milky and Andromeda into peril too, or even worse. There's no going back from something like this. I'm still wracking my brain for a solution. As if I'm supposed to. I'm a lot of things, but I'm not a hero. Just like how Jaal isn't a fucking god.

On the bright side, with Reiki asleep in my room and Jaal passed out in a massage chair, I'm more relaxed, and therefore more able to handle people's bullshit. With my nose Sens-bandaged and soaking in rosemary salve, I sound and look even less threatening than before.

"Does't matter." I tug the collar of my gray bathrobe. It smells vaguely like pine and saltwater, probably because Reiki was sleeping on it. "Dehfuck are we gudda do?"

Onyx huffs, folding her arms and leaning against the wall. She hasn't sat down since tranquilizing Jaal. "Follow the plan. Stay strong. Be smart. Maybe he didn't know about Mars, but he knew his fever would get worse—that's why he gave me permission to..." She rubs her fingers, as if invisible needles are lodged under her nails.

I nod. "Thanks, by the way."

Her shoulders heave. "It's my job. Point is, Jaal's not far gone enough to forget what's important."

143

I'd love to know what he deems important enough to sacrifice innocent lives for.

Crystalline nebulae swarm outside—blue, copper, silver, and everything in between. I shift the cameras' perspectives, hoping to gain more clarity not only outside, but inside too.

I bite my scabbed lip. "Is it all true, what Reiki said...about Jaal?"

Clumps of mascara sprinkle onto her mocha skin, a failing façade. "How should I know?" Her orange eyes hurtle upward. "Idiota."

Just when I was beginning to like her.

The nebulae are cracked with color—blood-stuffed veins of precious metals thronged in gaseous light. All kinds of chemicals lurk under bright mandalas. Swirling galaxies flux to soundless music, stamped on the blackness of space like kiss marks.

"Ah, space...it's like looking at a beautiful man," Obsidian says, clamping a hand on my shoulder. "Or woman. If you prefer."

I massage my forehead with one hand, wrist arching to avoid knocking my nose. "Doe offense, Sid, but have you ever piloted a ship before this?"

"Nah." He leans toward me, grin tugging his sculpted face toward a receding hairline. "But I been trained." Up close, his paper-bag skin smells like talcum powder and black beans, but his aura has softened tenfold. "Really, I thought Onyx would play pilot, 'cause she's the best of the best, but uh..." He glances at his sister, who looks away. "J lets her do a lotta things...just not—"

Onyx hisses to shut him up, amplifying her reptilian appearance, and brings an index finger to her bared teeth. She stands in front of the chair, where Jaal is sprawled and coated in drool.

I lean back and stare at Obsidian's crinkled brow. His chakras are almost invisible.

Metaphysical energy has been a blurred whisper to my third-eye since my nose was jabbed, blood clots blocking clairvoyance. I'm lucky Jaal didn't stab my brain with fractals of my own skull.

I clear my throat. "What?"

"Nada," Onyx spits, arms folded.

Nothing, I think furiously, looking at the screens. *The universe could be nothing from this angle—just dusty pieces of ever-expanding space, all-encompassing distance, and consequently, division.*

I glance between the two of them. "I doe there's bore. Say it."

Onyx snickers, but her maliciousness is shallow. "Sorry, homie. I don't speak broken boy."

144

I mirror the smile, running my fingers through my hair and catching a knot. "Doebuddy ever does, and yet. Everybody is broken."

Obsidian thrusts a canteen toward me, gaze shifting between his sister, Jaal, and me. "Patience, 'meegs. Jaal can tell his own story."

"Aw shucks, Sid," I mock, sipping the water. "Cute. Unfortunately, we don't all have the luxury of being subservient little bitches."

Onyx whips toward me, acrylic claws drawn back and ready to rip. She'd probably turn both bandage and skin into confetti. But Obsidian grabs her wrist. "Nah, 'mana, he's right."

"He's not!" She yells, yanking out of his grasp and choking up. "We ain't a teama' flyin' monkeys or some shit. This is our job. Not like we like it, not like it's easy. But we do it 'cause we gotta." She scratches and rubs her palms. Her citric acid gaze sticks in my mind even after she hurtles out the door. I don't know where she's going, but it takes too much effort to care.

Pinned under Obsidian's wary stare, I turn back to the screens and marvel. But even arm-wrestling galaxies shrouded in amber aluminum can't captivate me for long.

"What's her issue?" I ask, unable to halt the words.

He reclines in the chair next to me, sighing. "Lotsa' things, Z. But mostly, she don't like talking about our past."

"I didn't ask about your past. I asked about Jaal's."

He giggles under an ivory lace glove. "One in the same, 'meegs."

I scan the twinkles in his eyes and the glitter in his outrageously uncombed hair. I smack my forehead. "Krodos. Did everybody doe Jaal before I did?"

"It's only been a couple years for you, 'mi—"

I glare at him.

"Zen." He nods. He cracks his knuckles on dark upholstery, nervous to let go. "What I mean is. You and Jaal were partners for a handful of years. Me and 'mana, well. We knew Jaal for ages, but only recently got back in his good books."

"Huh." I slouch. "So, you two weren't always fuckbuddies?"

Chaotic laughter erupts from his lungs. "Nah, Zen. We were more like…hermanos. You were his first real—"

"Toy?"

"Love."

"He doesn't love," I guffaw, spinning the chair to face him. Pulse climbing, my facial wounds thump. "He doesn't doe how."

145

"Cierto." He clears his throat and shifts positions, a chunk of pink fringe falling over smoked eyes. "But you came close to teaching him."

"So, you were… Brothers to booty-calls, huh?" I taunt, and I don't care that it's mean.

Obsidian licks his lips, removing half the gloss. "It's complicated, and nunna' your business."

I scoff, sending trickles of drying blood back down my throat. "You got that right."

"But you gotta know—I ain't here just to fuck him. Or even fix him. I'm here 'cause I believe in his work. Heart, mind, and soul."

My moms' voices trickle back and forth between my inner and outer ears. I turn my chair completely away, but I still feel him looking at me. Judging me.

"Zen, you ain't the only one hurting. We all got our baggage. Hell, you and me? We ain't so different in our pain. I see it now. We're mixed paint, 'migo—all sad and brown." He forces a giggle.

I shoo him away. "Okay, whatever."

I don't know why everyone wants me to empathize with the son of a bitch. It took me long enough to realize he was the reason I hurt even worse after leaving Moms. Now I'm supposed to justify all that just because he's hurting too? Come on.

Despite her compassion, Reiki's the only one who bolstered my resentment with her rage, but that defiant act only made Jaal clobber me, proving us both right.

He probably would've raped me in front of everyone if it wasn't for Onyx. The whole thing makes my head spiral into my gut.

I rub a pounding temple. "Why won't he let Onyx pilot?" Curiosity is the worst form of self-harm.

I envy Obsidian for his ability to breathe so smoothly in and out through his nose. A feather glides from his hair piece and lands at my feet.

"The reason we was outta his good books for a bit," he explains, scratching his chin. After throwing a glance at Jaal, his voice drops, lower than I've heard him yet. "Nyx got him into a lil'…accident. He don't like when she has the controls."

But he lets her tranquilize him with needles.

Everything hurts, but that won't be helped by continuing to point out Jaal's obvious flaws.

146

Without another word, fidgety from my rapid-fire questions, Obsidian stands and trails after his sister. Jaal's snores rattle my insides in their absence.

Every part of me is still vibrating, trying to shake something I can only feel and never see. I burrow further into myself, blissfully glad to hide.

Even the streaking galactic rainbows outside appear fake and flat to depersonalized eyes. Threads of debris from God knows what other cosmic tragedies pass without lingering. In my world and others, no one is safe.

A light buzzing erupts from under me, and I rise so fast, knees and ankles pop. There lies my forgotten S-Com, blinking red-and-green.

"Incoming signal from 11 Bridge Bend, San Fran Isle, RSA."

Syzygy's manly voice announcing my childhood address is chilling, to say the least. With shaking hands, I don the goggles and inhale cardamom, salmon, and white wine vinegar. My brain tricks my bandaged nose into picking up the extravagance of Uncle Lutfi's cooking.

Curled up on the couch like a kid, he nurses a mug of black tea. Steam swirls, blending in with the white spots on his face. A leathery smile starts behind a pair of copper, crescent-shaped spectacles.

"Evening, Nephie." It sounds so disgustingly cordial when he says it like that.

"Christ. Hi."

His smile lines deepen. "I have convenient news for you."

I can practically feel the rug scratching my toes. "Spill."

But then he leans forward and blinks rapidly, cleaning his lenses with oversized sweater sleeves. "Sweet glittering stars. What happened to your face?"

"I was born this way," I deadpan, mocking his accent as best I can with clogged nostrils.

"Jaal finally snapped, did he?"

Like he hasn't already. I shake my head, self-consciously petting the bridge of my nose. "It was an accident. No big deal. Just. Tell me the news."

Our matching mercurial eyes hold one another for a moment before he clears his throat and grips the ends of his beard braids. "They're in the Saturnine sector, your mums."

My heart pinches itself. I fly out of the chair. "No way."

"If you make good time, there's still hope after all."

"Really?"

147

"Well, I checked the timing of it all." He scratches a twitching tendon in his neck. "Astrology doesn't lie. Planets are prime and ready to shine, as they say."

"Doebuddy says that, L," I laugh despite my clogged nostrils.

He waves a dismissive hand. For the first time, I realize there are no rings on his fingers.

"Lutfi. I meant to ask. Are you and Prue—"

"Happily separated." A sad wink accompanies the fallen smile. "I'll spare you the horrific details." Drops of tea cling to his beard after he swigs it. "Focus on getting to your mothers. They're waiting for you."

"You spoke to them?" I clutch my nose, stunting hot blood flow in the nasal cavity. I should change the bandages soon, but I don't want to move.

"Of course, my boy." He exposes his stained teeth. "How else would I know where they are? Your mother considers this a vacation. They look forward to seeing you." His throat bobs on a cube of energetic blue ice.

I bite my cheek, head tilting. "They didn't wanna talk to me?"

Awkward silence smothers me. He holds the bottom of the mug and loses more drops in frenzies of beard hair.

I swallow. "Lutfi. What is it?"

He wipes his mouth on a trembling sleeve. "Ah, well. You'll see."

Nineteen

Over the next week, healing hurts more than usual—which is saying something. Sense-crippling aches and Lutfi's haunting harbinger plague me.

Reiki tends to my wounds inside and out, but I can't look her in the eye. Every time I do, her eyes remain, but the body changes, warped by a dozen different genders and generations. Desperately, I meditate whenever I can, which she doesn't mind.

Onyx watches Jaal diligently, but there's only so much a bunch of non-gods can do. I cannot stress that enough.

Each of us has their own spectrum of mundane efforts and divine inklings. But most of us are tipping the scale with our loud mouths, especially Jaal, who's been bursting at the seams since rising from a forty-eight-hour comatose.

He's the one I should avoid. Not Reiki.

One artificially-created morning, she and I hide in the storage pod, leaning against the dome windows with our hands in a bag of granola.

"I'm going to need a bite guard instead of bandages." I rub my jaw.

"So you won't bite us?" Her crooked smile etches my view. Teasing each other has helped us cope with the chaos. If you can't laugh at a mess, you're going to hate cleaning it up.

Despite that, I nudge her. "You know what I mean. My jaw hurts worse than the bruises and broken bones."

"At least you're healing well."

"But I haven't slept well in days."

"Aw, even with me in your bed?" Pinkish light leaks from the corners of her mouth. A delicate hand sweeps my thigh. Onyx painted her nails cobalt during one of their frequent bonding moments.

I wipe my mouth and run my fingers through clotted curls, averting her persistent gaze. "You don't get it. You're always zen."

She giggles.

"Oh, you know what I mean." I shove her harder this time, and her body heat imprints the glass with fog. "You don't even have to meditate to feel at peace."

"I think my drunken rampage on Jaal the other day proves that theory to be incorrect." Laughter loosens the blanket around her shoulders, exposing moon-kissed collarbones. The hem of her satin slip clings to slender hips and the peach fuzz on her knees.

I shake myself out of the urge to tease her, or worse. "Reiki." My tongue mashes the roof of my mouth, restless. "I'm not just scared for myself anymore. Mars is in shambles, kicked out of its own fucking orbit, and my head is in the same sad state. How am I supposed to help anyone?"

"Well, first of all—breathe." She rubs my back in firm circles. "It's okay to be anxious, Zen. You haven't seen your moms in four years. Your mama, technically more, since she wasn't herself when you left."

But it's not enough. The saccharine voice I've become obsessed with isn't functional for talking me down right now.

"How are you not constantly full of rage?" I blink back tears, crunch on peanuts and granola even though it hurts, and swallow thickly. A sandstorm rises in my tight throat. "You hit Jaal. Obviously, you're not happy with all this."

Reiki pulls her auric vines out of mine, pink from beige. Her sigh is more of a croon. She rubs her thighs, nervously playing with static electricity. "Honestly, the further we move from the sun, the hollower I am. My outburst came from a dark place. I had to let it go, of course, but not like that. What I did…it's despicable."

"Jaal deserved it." I shrug.

"It's not whether he deserved it—it's how I feel now because of it. And I'm." An intake of breath gives her more time to choose a word. It huffs out in a blue gust. "Empty. My actions have been destructive for everyone. First you, now Jaal…How am I supposed to heal when all I do is hurt?"

"Join the cult," I hiss, but immediately take it back. By freaking out earlier, she has emptied herself to make room for my shit. She's undoing herself, because of me.

I touch her wrist, eyes flitting to hers. "Sorry. What I mean is—you're not alone."

Instantly, a trickle of indescribable color warps not only her aura, but her face, and she looks like someone I've seen but can't remember. Again.

When I touch her face, the illusion vanishes. She nuzzles into my palm. "You apologize too much." Her whispers trickle down my wrist.

Self-conscious, I pull away and check my nose with both hands, prodding each side to busy myself. Bandages are off, but it still bleeds now and then, knobby and puffy.

Reiki rests her head on my shoulder. "Have you thought about what you're going to say to them?"

"To who?"

"Your moms." She taps the top of my spine. A swirl of cool energy seeps into rutted vertebrae.

I shrug, which turns into an attempt to roll the knots out of my shoulders and press out inflammation. "Does it matter?"

"Talking about it might help," she advises, face hovering inches from mine. In the dim, cascading light, her pupils grow and shrink, unable to settle.

Twiddling my thumbs, I shrug again. "I guess I'd start with…an apology."

"Shocker," she giggles.

"I ran away, ignored all their coms, tried so hard to sever them from my life." Cool air tickles nose hairs when I inhale. "I don't know. It's hard to feel out…who knows what state Mama's in. She probably doesn't even remember me, or Mother, or herself…" I let the words drip over an invisible pool on my trembling chin.

Another moment of pupil-dilated consideration passes. Blowing a stray hair out of her face, she squares my shoulders. "Alright. Take off your shirt."

"Um, why?" I try to squirm out of her grasp.

"You need to relax." Her thumbs circle to flatten biceps, ringing out tension.

I snort. "A massage from you won't help."

Expecting her to be offended and give up, I try to rise, but the heels of her hands dig into my knees, stretching thighs and rooting me to the floor. Unlike Jaal, she anchors me, but not out of dominance. Instead, she emanates aggressive compassion and firm wisdom, aura and irises glowing pink.

With gathered breath, I bite my yellow-bruised lip, unbutton the flannel shirt and turn around, giving her access to my back.

A leg slides on either side of me. Her body forms snugly to mine, better than any expensive massage chair. Slowly, with hot energy and cool skin, she works the balled bone of her wrist into my muscles.

Knots tie into double knots before they loosen, spasming in rebellion. She digs harder, and it hurts so good, like hot rocks spilling over and combing straight to the bone, melting marrow.

A long moan dissolves into a yawn, spraying spittle into my lap. Flickering dwarf stars reflect in the tiny beads of water, rusty rouge like blood opals.

I might be taken care of, but my ship's engine is still plagued by the Phoenix shit, and our solar system is still fucked up. Aware of my breath but not knowing when it might stop is equal parts depressing and thrilling—more so than usual—as I swim through the great, crossfaded paradox of human existence. Sitting and floating. Healing and dying.

I tilt my head back to peer at soaring comets. Physical light streaks our metaphysical blush in an autumnal swirl of burnished gold.

Reiki stops massaging. For a moment, I listen to the sound of her breath, acutely aware of her shaking exhalations skidding down my spine and her hands resting on my waist.

She sniffles, and I turn to look at her.

Rosy tears draw stripes on her cheeks. "It's just. I can feel your trepidation." She wipes her nose. "You don't know if you know me, if you can even trust me, or..." Her face presses into my ribcage. I can't tell if the ache is the bruises, the muscles, or something deeper.

Syzygy has held a lot of my breakdowns, and now he holds hers too. Spinning coins of energy roll down from brain stem and clink in my gut.

"It's difficult," I concede, rubbing what's left of the knots, "to know if I know myself, let alone anyone else. Just. Be patient with me. I'm still getting used to you."

She sits up. The wide whites of her eyes ignite in buttery afterglow, cheekbones glittering like half-baked meringues. A crisp halo circles static-strung red hair. "So, you don't remember me?"

My thumbs swipe her cheeks. "What do you mean? I remember you hanging from my ceiling two weeks ago." I shrug, a lopsided smile playing. "And since then, you've proven yourself a Conduit, warrior, and everything in between. It's a lot to take in. Cut me some slack."

This is the life I want—drenched in confused bruises, holding her face in my hands, removing her tears, knowing she'd do the same. Waking up with her, bantering like we made love the night before even though all we did was sing and talk. Details are meaningless if I could always feel this understandably misunderstood.

But I'm a sieve for euphoria.

I stand, unlacing myself from her grasp. "C'mon," I say, wiping crumbs from my stubbled chin. "I wanna check the screens."

Stubbornly, she holds my hand, even while squeezing through the trapdoor.

In the bedroom, dozens of brightly patterned blouses, leggings, and hair accessories are splayed on the floor from an impromptu fashion show the other night. I won't pretend the aftermath doesn't look incriminating, but the only thing it proves is that we suck at cleaning.

We wander through the maze of my possessions, dodging a few particularly gnarly hair clips and piles of used makeup wipes. Fluorescent pink fingerprints dust the doorframe, laden in spectral highlighter and eyeshadow.

"Is everyone still asleep?" I murmur as we leave the room, bare feet pattering on tinny tiles. Our morning breath ricochets off auras and light-speckled walls.

"All but one." Eyebrows raised, she nods toward the open door ahead, in which the floor glimmers and streams like holiday lights.

Jaal sits in the center of the cockpit, knees bent and eyes closed. I think he's trying to meditate, but he looks like a child, all wound up and unable to be still. The balls of his feet jiggle, sending waves of light splaying anxiety diagnoses across the floor. He's wearing velvet pajamas and his locks are pulled into a fat bun.

Inhaling quickly, I attempt to smoothen the energy. "Morning."

Spearmint incense tickles my flared nostrils.

At first, he doesn't respond, and I wonder if he's mastered the art of sleeping while sitting. But then Reiki—ever the shocking goddess—sits in front of him.

An artificially sapphire eye opens. "Is it?" His voice sounds like sludge.

"Ha ha," I deadpan, plopping into the captain's chair and scanning the screens. Blackness swarms the view, barely blemished by stars. I ignore the monster in my gut that screams for Reiki to get away from him.

"Guess I meditated all night." He cracks every joint methodically, releasing pressure from neck to ankles. His eyes flicker between blue, violet, and brown, trying to pick a reality.

"Using S-Contacts isn't meditation," I snap, desperately searching for a distraction. I'd even take another broken planet over this discussion.

"Took a page out of your book, Z. Escapism clears the head."

I pinch the bridge of my nose, staring past chapped fingers at the unfolding universe. She's still a few sizes too big.

But then, the air shifts. Jaal clears his throat. "Z. My man. I get you're mad, and I'm s—"

"I'm sorry." Reiki's words overlap his.

I swivel to gawk at her. *The nerve of someone, throwing around words like they mean something to the other person!*

Blinking away false colors, Jaal wrings his hands. Old scars on his palms and wrists have been hacked open, thinly bandaged but bleeding through. A buttercup-tinted aura highlights them and makes him look even more sickly. My heart climbs into my throat, waving a burnt white flag.

"Don't be the big man, bruja." It sounds like a grave warning, but he snorts and shakes his head.

In each corner and dip of the room, where there should be tension, I only sense puddles of regret. It floods and stains like bruises.

While Reiki tries to take Jaal's hands and heal self-inflicted wounds, I tap the control panel. Shift the subject, clear my throat. Stuff the heart's surrender back into slimy guts where it belongs. "Jaal. Enlighten me. Where's Jupiter? We should be headed straight for it, but there isn't a sign or spec."

"Think you know the answer to that, Z."

"Well." My teeth smother each other, rubbing away enamel. In the back of my nose, wetness forms, so I sniff, hoping it's not blood. "I'm not a math warlock, but I can calculate on my fingers why Jupe isn't where it should be." I hold up a peace sign. "Two words: Your. Fault."

Scowling, Jaal slaps Reiki's hands away.

I glance again at the black vastness of space. "I don't wanna hear Reiki's apology. I want to hear yours."

He rubs his scraggly six o'clock shadow, yearning to itch off the metaphysical mask. Part of it fades, only for a second. "Sorry for hurting you," he sighs, "and everything."

I'm not sure if he realizes what *everything* should mean. What the punctuation of his words implies. *Everything* is another discrepancy, an excuse to ignore the obvious. It's like *collateral damage* or *sacrifice*. Meaningless until it hurts someone.

But I hang my head, spine crunching. "Apology accepted." Their eyes drill into the back of my head while I straighten and continue to scan the cosmos.

It's a strange thing, being encapsulated like grainy contents of a pill, but just outside my synthetic home there are layers of dark matter and energetic fabric, cleaving skull-shaped caves of light with shadow. Every ounce of life has another pound of death. But with orbits off-kilter, the skyscape cracks and wobbles—indefinite reality awoken from a nap.

"I still can't find it," I whisper, fiddling with camera controls.

"If Jupiter's dead, then our solar system will cease to expand," Reiki blurts, dicing our attention. When I look, mist overtakes aura, shrouding her in prophetic hail.

Jaal puffs air from the corner of his mouth. "Planets don't die." He glides a hand across sweat-drenched brows.

"You're lying to save your skin," she observes, brushing symbols on her left palm. "But you don't need to. I'm not here to attack you again. I just." Her hiss of frustration sounds like meditative breathwork.

"Want validation?" He leans in, confused.

"No, Jaal. Not everyone wants validation from you. I want a revised plan. No, actually, what I really want is for you to—"

"Wait." I rise, knees shaking. "What do you mean—the solar system will stop expanding?"

Reiki sighs, struggling to hold patience. "Not the solar system. That was bad wording. More like, um. Your bubble. Human consciousness."

"Aw, stop cock-blocking the cosmos." Jaal rolls his eyes and cracks knuckles, feisty spirit settling back into grizzly body. "Celestial and terrestrial bodies die all the damn time, sure. Doesn't matter. The universe still gets what it wants, even in the end." A side-smile reveals the intentional pun, but under black pajama pants and a white tank, his muscles squirm.

"Humanity stopped expanding a long time ago," I reason, grasping for the bigger picture.

155

Reiki shakes her head. "Neither of you are listening, big surprise." Neck tendons clench when she clears her throat, casting away gentleness. Under bare feet, the floor reads: *headache*. "Humanity is always pushing beyond their limits, not just physically but mentally, emotionally, spiritually. Your entire consciousness depends on ever-expanding premises. Without the expansive influence of Jupiter, minds decay. Hearts close. Horizons shrink."

"So…you're saying we'll cease to exist?" *It's official—I'm part of a Sens-show.*

"I'm saying you'll exist, but you won't be aware of it. Conscious decision-making is already evaporating thanks to the demolished Mars. Now, our awareness is depleted too. Stars only know what awaits us in the Saturnine sector."

You can say that again, I think miserably. There couldn't be more pressure on this stupid mission than there already is, but at least she's expressing how she really feels. Her wisdom is the only thing keeping our "team" together.

I don't know what's more antsy—Jaal's body or strobing aura. All I know is I'm grateful to be on the other side of the room because he stalks toward the blank wall and punches it, knuckles popping like spark-dusted firewood.

While he howls, apparently surprised by the wall's lack of give, Reiki throws hands into the air. "Violence isn't helpful."

I choke on my spit, snagged between laughter and shock.

But she doesn't smile. Her whole being is ablaze, waltzing in terrific multicolored fire. In this moment, there's no doubting who she is. "Our task was nearly impossible enough, and now we have to—"

A choked sob spills from Jaal's fat lips, spiraling up the wall. The floor is sprayed with lit-up diagnostics—high blood pressure, spinal inflammation, Fever, depression, PTSD.

Reiki straightens. "Jaal. Breathe."

He shakes his head, punches the wall again, reopening knuckle scrapes. "Everything was fine when we kept moving. We never stopped, kept going, l-like we asked, like we wanted…"

I tilt my head, thoroughly baffled. "What the holy Io are you talking about?"

"Ah, fuck," he whimpers and sniffles into his hand. A thick string of mucus stretches like putty out his nose. "Stopped so many times, fixed points in time, never changing, always erasing…"

Eyes wide, I look at Reiki, begging for help. I've seen Feverish breakdowns before, but now the energy is there too, a vomit-like slosh

156

of confused fear. Our doctor-floor can't handle the number of symptoms gusting its way.

I try to be neutral. Gentle. "Hey. Maybe we should—"

An invisible force brushes the top of the ship, sending us spinning. I'm flung back into the chair, which vibrates helplessly in response. Jaal splays against the wall due to misplaced gravity.

Nausea slings from stomach to throat, and all I can think is: *What fucking else?*

Obsidian and Onyx stumble into the room, eyes swollen from interrupted sleep.

While the ship stabilizes, Obsidian tugs the ribbon of his sherbet robe. "More meteors?" he yawns. An arm stretches to rest on his sister's naked shoulders.

"Not quite." She points, and although it takes us a few seconds to look away from her fuzzy pajama pasties, we follow her gesture to the screens.

Syzygy's perfect body is pulled into a thick sheet of gravity, a silvery atmosphere that glitters.

A tourmaline horizon expands in the cameras' lopsided view.

Twinkling satellites and moon bases greet us in the distance, somehow still hooked to Jupiter's trembling belly. The poor beast sneezes globs of luminescent gas and weeps streams of faltering light, literally at the end of its orbit.

My jaw hangs, but behind me, I can feel a deep blueness pooling at the base of Reiki's skull. As usual, she cries with the planets.

Jaal peels himself off the wall and furiously massages his lower back. I'd laugh at his uncanny chicken appearance if we weren't being sucked upside-down into Jupiter's haphazard atmosphere.

Instinct kicking in, I hastily reach for every control I can tweak, mind unraveling through my teeth. Words chatter in a desperate frenzy. "G can stabilize us inside for the time being, but there isn't enough external energy, thanks to Jaal's jerry-rigged engine scheme."

I expect a blow to the back of my head, but instead, the oaf plops his steroid-puffed ass onto the floor and whimpers. "Nyx, it hurts. Everything hurts."

Onyx rushes toward him. She sits behind him and cradles his head in her lap.

I stare, both disturbed and entranced by his infantile state and the way their chakras shift together. A thin sheet of slushy empathy forms in my stomach, glinting in gold light.

157

I try to stand, but the ship flinches, confused gravity rifling me out of the chair. Fingernails scrape pleather, friction fizzing between synthetic material and collagen. Blood leaks out my nose, shaken free.

Obsidian lumbers to my side, one hand sweeping controls, the other yanking me to my feet. "I'm at your loyal service, 'meegs. Tell me what to do."

Helpless, wheezing laughter causes a bright bubble of blood to splatter across my face. I plug my nose with a squeeze. "In the words of our a'cestors, shut up a'd drive."

With shaking knees, I spin to face Reiki, who stands tall, cold and composed except for briny stains on her freckled cheeks. A soundless prayer swims through bobbing lips and throngs of melodic energy.

I want to soak her in, but first I need to soak up all this blood.

Twenty

With my shirt bundled and tied around my face like a flannel ninja, I meet Reiki in the room's center. Sacred shapes and interstellar hues continue to drench the ship's interior, but for now, the rush of my blood slows.

I don't know what compels me to mirror her outstretched arms, palms hovering inches from hers, but doing so feels powerful. Our identical poses generate blankets of vibrating light and shadow, swaddling the room.

Holding and spinning stardust like it's chi, we recreate our sense of gravity, pulling everyone who fell back on their feet and shifting the ship's center. Below, the engine rumbles with gratitude for our aid.

Reiki hasn't taught me how to do any of this, and yet, here I am, flaunting purple astral fingers and rewriting physics.

It's both easy and difficult, like trying to remember a second language. Sweat settles in my cupid's bow. Reiki's eyes are closed, but her butter-slice mouth curls.

My body bursts to capture her in an embrace, however small and fragile, but the rest of me—fractals of a sketchy mind, heart, and soul— root to the spot. Whatever this is, it's important, and I need to focus.

A whistling groan whirs past our ears, spitting into our simulated star-engine. It takes me a few beats to realize it's Jaal.

While the ship recalibrates, he only spazzes more, unaffected by his topless friend's consoling. A stray chartreuse burst from Reiki's trembling wrists turns Onyx's eyes a brighter, more toxic orange.

"Jaal!" She begs, clinging to his shirt while he tries to stand. But he tears it off and barrels for the hall, wrapped in newfound, stumbling silence.

Onyx follows him, obedient prey becoming the hunter. For a moment, my mind peels away from present drama and into memory's throbbing darkness.

Past-me peers through the bathroom keyhole. (Another pointless aesthetic detail that was probably Lutfi's idea.) My parents talk quietly over a compost toilet bowl.

"Meditation can't cure shit," Mama says between dry heaving and wiping her mouth on a towel. "I ain't singing hymns and lying on carpets anymore."

Mother's honeycomb eyes are as purged as Mama's stomach. "I'm not asking. I'm telling."

A smug snort produces a bubble of snot, which she wipes on the back of Mother's hand. "Where were the demands when I wanted you to play dominatrix?"

Usually, Mother would blush, wrap the ends of her headscarf around shivering wrists, and giggle. But she only sighs and slumps against the wall. Her lips barely move. "You keep bringing that up. I didn't realize it was such a crucial part of our relationship."

"It's not, if you don't mind being fucking bored all the time." Mama laughs like it's a huge burn, and high-five slaps the toilet seat. It clatters from the force, sending me running.

Past-me barely understood.

Present-me still doesn't get it. If the Fever can turn Mama into a horrible person, what the hell is it doing to Jaal?

Somehow, Obsidian maintains control of Syzygy even as we work with energy. Like yanking hair clogs out of a drain, we pull the whole ship out of Jupiter's consuming gravity and back into outer space.

Safely away from atmospheric suction, the engine settles back into a deep hum-and-thrum, music for my ears and soles—which, by the way, are causing an eruption of strange symbols to be cast on the diagnostic floor.

Energy slithers from our grasp, fading from opaque to transparent in a matter of seconds.

I fall to my knees.

Reiki opens her eyes and squeezes my shoulders. "How are you?"

I clear my throat. "Tired, but…" Stained flannel falls from my face. *Healed.* Hardened blood coats my nostrils like paint chips. I shake my head and blink. "What did we do?"

"Think of it like motion sickness medicine."

"Mmm," I chuckle, resting my head against her thighs, letting her play with my hair. But then I rise, eye-level with her mouth. "I have

160

another question. It's gonna make me sound crazy, but I figured you're all for that."

"Oh, definitely." Her thumb and index finger catch my chin.

I snag her hand, focusing on the blots of sweat between her lower lip and chin. "Ki. When I look you in the eye, you change. You shift through a dozen different faces, all of them familiar, but I've never seen them before. Is that wicker basket witchery, or...?"

Silence spills. I muster the courage to meet her garnet eyes, hazy moons circling boulders. Something's there that wants to be released. *If I could just tease it out...*

Her lips part, but Obsidian interrupts, panting. "*She* shifts through faces? Did ya see J? Looked like a fuckin' child, and no help to us. Dios, I haven't seen him like that since..." His face scrunches and he returns full autonomy to Syzygy.

"Systems stabilizing. Balance restored, for now. Thank you, pilots."

I drop Reiki's hand and kiss her cheek.

A violet veil passes between us, leaving her with a smile. "Everything I do is wicker basket witchery. But all I am is You." Electricity crinkles at the top of my head and shuttles down to my feet. Suppressing a giggle, she throws a thumb over her shoulder. "I'm gonna check on Jaal and Onyx." Aura rose-gold, she tiptoes out the door.

I face the screens. Jupiter dons different colors in one sweep like titanium quartz.

Catching his breath, Obsidian sits in a chair and reties his robe. Unfortunately, I can tell he's gone commando. "Ship's tipsy, Zen, but we're in the clear. Can you believe it?"

"I'll believe anything at this point." I sit next to him, rubbing my knees. "Which is why I want to know."

"Know what?"

"What you're all hiding from me, about Jaal."

"Zen—"

"Obsidian." It comes out hard and dark like the rock he's named after. Thick energy rolls over my aching muscles, empowering loose words. "Gemini Fever brings out the worst in people, but it's not just insanity. It's like getting crossfaded while having the flu, losing every ounce of inhibition, so the truth spills and stains. It is them, and it's not. So, like. I want to know—no, fuck that." I throw hands in the air, done with passivity. "Planets are dying. If you insist on me forgiving him for being the popped cherry on top of my ruined life, I need to know. How do you and Onyx know him? What will his Fever bring out?"

161

Obsidian's mauve eyelids sink and flutter, as if searching for answers behind his skull. He wrings his wrists. "Better to hear it from his mouth. He's prolly close to telling you by now."

I roll my eyes. "He's close to letting his brain leak out his ears and nose. At this rate, we'll all die before I know. And I need to know."

He dabs his mouth with the side of his thumb, staring into space. "You don't, though. 'S'a lot to explain."

"I already know Mama was his teacher, and that he's fucked a lot of people over, including me. What's left that doesn't take five minutes to tell?"

He chuckles into a sweaty palm. "You sound like our mama adoptiva. She thought everything was black and white. How wrong was she, eh?"

A sickly green snake of energy constricts my throat, pinning me into a weird, hunched position. My body begs to turn toward him and be open to the novel idea that I wasn't the only traumatized child in the Milky, but my eyes stay on the screens. Jupiter floats further out of our range, technicolor cloak billowing in cosmic breeze. Pockets of atmosphere burst, causing dusty, multicolored ringworm on the planet's skin.

Metaphysical scales loosen and my vocal chords twinge. "You were adopted?"

He nods, scratching his temples. Long pieces of hair drift into his lap. "All three of us. Jaal didn't come 'til later, though. Foster homes."

So, that's it.

Space debris whizzes past the screen, snagging my attention. I want to find peace in the pieces of this mess.

Instead, I find a yellow dot.

At first, I think it's one of Jupiter's moons, tossed from its node and sent for galactic hills. But I squint, and the dot grows. It rolls toward us, a perfect sphere of ignited gas. From every angle, it should be impossible—a star engine without a ship's body.

"The hell is that?" Responding to the curiosity, my forehead tingles, third-eye twitching to get a good seat for whatever happens next.

Obsidian hurtles to his feet, bunching up the end of his robe. "Big yikes, 'migo."

"No shit." My eyes can't roll far enough.

Approaching us from just outside Jupiter's atmosphere, the star twirls and spins.

162

"HUGE YIKES!" Obsidian amends, collapsing over the controls, searching in vain for a way out of the incoming ship's beam. He fumbles with buttons and pads, struggling to gain control.

I grip the chair's arms, rigid with shock-thrusted laughter.

The strange celestial body dwarfs Syzygy. A bolt of raw light rockets into the control room. Every particle inside dances and ignites with multidimensional color, liquefying into cosmic jelly.

"Dematerialization process triggered," Syzygy announces. "Your attendance is requested, pilots."

The accompanying pain is unreal. It digs through the whole nervous system, turning cells into flaming swords that sting and banish the senses—sixth, fifth, fourth...

My brain throbs against a crackling skull, splashed with inky ash, until each spinning neuron commits suicide. Third, second, first...all senses knocked onto the floor, where Obsidian writhes and rants in Hisphindi.

Then suddenly, we're scooped. Plucked. Sucked from our ship at incomprehensible speed and blown into a bowl like sand through tubes.

Shifting particles splinter for a millisecond longer, and then crush together all at once. Solidified. Calibrated. Sand mashed with pure heat into smooth glass.

Slippery carpet rubs against freshly materialized skin. My pupils dilate to catch a lick of light. Stomach acid lingers between teeth and tongue. My ears ring, but then Obsidian's voice falls from the shadows.

"Velour rug? Dios, someone has shitty taste."

I reach into the darkness, stumbling on all fours. My vocal chords crack. All that comes out is a whimper.

"Zen? That you?"

Turning to sit, I sniff bloody snot back into sinuses and catch the briefest scent of cedar and lemon. From the curling echo of his voice, I deduce that this room is like G's control room—circular, medium, and with high ceilings. But I catch myself spiraling through a fit of thought in which we're stuck between spirit-worlds and the physical. It's like Syzygy, but not. I'm like myself, but not. I'll be so pissed if I end up in purgatory with Obsidian.

A firm shake of the head forces me back. *Breathe. That's what Reiki would do. Oh, God...Reiki. Where'd she go?*

I emit a hatched whisper. "We've been dematerialized..." I wipe my mouth with a sweaty palm and continue the sensual inventory. *Okay, pants are still on. That's something.*

163

Obsidian rams into me, quaking with terrified laughter. His rough fingers wrap around my wrists to stabilize. "Ah, shit, sorry. This is all too familiar, eh?"

"Why's it so dark in…?" On cue, a soft click sounds and warm light pools above us in a circular ceiling of glowing crystal.

His jaw drops so far, it cracks. "Oh, man." He accidentally elbows my groin, causing the nausea to circle back, and plays apologies on repeat.

"Shut up," I hiss, inching away. Aches dissipate everywhere except my throat. "Where are we?" I can't warble a decibel higher.

Luckily, I don't have to talk much. Panels above continue to flick on, stealing any words we could muster, until the ceiling triples in size. As shadows lift, our eyes adjust and shed any illusions we had.

To my happily rehabilitated sixth sense, the room feels too different to be anything in or near Syzygy. It's more oblong than circular, and obviously larger.

At first, the walls appear plain white with falsely wooden Sens-windows, but then they shift to star-spangled, fake-paint iridescence. Windows disappear, along with the citrus aroma. Illusion after illusion shattered, leaving ironclad pillars and patriotic murals.

An empty chair sits behind an old desk at the other end of the room, accompanied by nothing but a quill and ink. I crane my neck to peer at the carving in its strange alloyed surface—a diamond-shaped seal that reads proudly, *E unum pluribus*. I crawl toward it and reach out to check its legitimacy, then retract for fear of leaving fingerprints. But it's pointless because our sweat and slobber is all over this rug. DNA for the taking.

My limbs move without me, flailing for a loophole. Every chaotic thought begs for an epigenetic shift, inside and out, so that the government won't know me. Can't own me.

The room is vast, but it shrinks with every wheezing breath I take.

Obsidian takes his cue, grabbing my wrist again. "Breathe, 'meegs."

A door's outline is zapped into the wall behind the desk. It slides open effortlessly, propelling a new gust of smells. Roasted marshmallow, leather, coffee lager, maple syrup, and Martian department store cologne.

I don't recognize the man who stands there, at first. His skin is another translucent star of paint against the shadowy blue wall. When he steps into crystalline light, his dagger-straight hair shimmers, framing

164

indigo eyes in a snowy dome. I know this charming face. Everyone on Earth does.

Usually, he's seen in slacks and a button-down, hair combed back or plaited so tightly his hairless browbone juts. But in front of us, in the middle of a mock oval office, he dons gray sweats and rainbow toe socks, letting down more than just his guard.

"Hello, Mr. Lin." His plastic, boyish face pinches to one side when he smiles. The accent is thin, but familiar. A curt bow and rhythmic clip of the ankles solidifies the strange façade. "Pleasure's all yours."

Twenty-One

My knees crunch on the floor as I spin to scan the perimeter for a real window, another door, anything. But there's no escape. Just white-on-blue stars and blood-striped paint.

Obsidian wobbles to help me stand and leans against the desk, gawking at the newcomer.

I rub my eyes and blink hard. "President Samson?"

"Don't be shy." The icicle-man shuts the door behind him. "It's been a couple weeks since we first met. You can call me Micah." His nails are as glossy as his hair, the same melty material as my wardrobe's contents. "Howdo. It's delightful to see you again."

"*You* were the cop?" I blurt, acid rumbling in my throat.

Micah's splotchy eyelashes flutter. "Aw. What happened to flirting? Are pleasantries behind us already?"

"Zen," Obsidian mutters. "This man's half our gov's 'zecutive branch." As if that's supposed to impress me.

"One-third," I mumble, peeling his sweaty fingers off my forearms. I clear my throat. "What are you doing here, uh…Micah?"

Lowering an octave, Micah answers by mocking his husband's inauguration speech, the same one I listened to a year after leaving home. "Everything I do is for the good of my people."

In the back of my mind, I wonder if Reiki ever brushed up on American history, what she'd say if she witnessed this patriotic surprise. Three segments of States, reunited after centuries of discord. Three independent presidents working together. From one, many.

"But really," he continues, shaking his head. "That gig with the coppies was a side-hustle. We've been on vacation, Bey and I. Our

166

thirteenth honeymoon, or something like that. It's been rough, thanks to you rocket-rousers."

I scramble to defend myself. "Christ and Kronos. Jaal's the one you should sentence to be strapped on a satellite, not me!" More word-vom, threatening to induce real-vom. I splay the classic I didn't do it jazz hands. "The whole project is his, not mine."

Micah's lips form a tight line before bursting with laughter. "This isn't an interrogation, Mr. Lin. If it was, Beyon would be here and I'd have a beer."

He has a point. Relief starts in my chest and spreads.

But facing the president of mid-RSA—without a shirt nonetheless—sets all my bones on edge. He's a new unknown, another variable in this giant experiment. Another space-tourist peering in on chaotic environments, watching me revolve and squirm.

I cough and massage my neck. "Well. Don't get me wrong, I'm jazzed to meet you for real this time, but uh, what's with the fireball?"

"The one thing I don't drink." He laughs again, head tilting to reveal bulging blue veins under liquid plastic skin. He sniffs and wipes his eyes, realizing nothing about his joke is bringing me joy. "Oh, you mean my ship. Well. You're inside her."

I rake a hand through my tangled curls. "So…what is it, a giant external engine?"

"While your ship is a ball of energy protected by strong materials, our ship is a collection of matter protected and charged by an energetic super-aura." Micah plops into the chair and rests his elbows on the desk. "I'm sure Mr. Nadir told you—he sold us the design." A frosty wink.

Of fucking course. The bastard makes weapons, not medicine. Thanks for reminding me.

Hair on the back of my neck spikes, energy fluxing. Reiki could have walked her fingers up my bare spine and it wouldn't give me as much of a chill as this.

Squeezing the edge of the desk, I lean forward, only able to tower over Micah because he's sitting. "Level with me, Chief. Do you think working with Jaal is a good idea?"

Plush silicon gives him a great poker face. "I don't know, Mr. Lin. Do you?"

I could ask, threaten, plead, and it would all be valid. But it wouldn't go anywhere. I've been on this rampage of a mission for nearly two weeks, and seldom have I said the right thing. So instead, I push off the desk and turn away, rubbing my itchy palms.

Micah sighs like a whistle through his pencil nose. "At least show some gratitude. Not only did I let you slide back home undetected last week, but we just saved you and your ship from Jupiter's all-consuming crotch."

Obsidian's curiosity has its own metaphysical theme song. Techno strings glide up and down, echoing from aura to mouth. "Pres—er, Micah. Honored to be in your weird, evil-eye mothership. But Zen and me single-handed this ourselves. We good pilots. Coupl'a the best." He tugs the robe's collar proudly.

My eyes narrow and so does the space between heartbeats.

Micah's lower lip bubbles, unconvinced. "Meh. How do you know you didn't fail, that you're still falling into a colorful abyss?" He tilts his head and slaps both hands on the desk. With an invisible, ungodly force, he sends Obsidian and me reeling onto our backs. The floor cradles me, but not for long. We dent the carpet, which liquefies and inhales our bodies like a ragged black hole. Our yelps are smothered in supple, rippling velour.

In a sweep of tumbling suction, we slosh out the ship's bottom, skin searing, and hang like astrobats from fiery strings. Flaming hoops flick into black air, miniature solar flares and demonic forked tongues.

This isn't real, I think, and repeat it like a mantra until the words ooze from my pores. *It's a mind-game. Probably an expensive one.*

I cast around for Obsidian, aiming to use his stupid face as an anchor for my sanity, but to no avail. He dangles even lower, from his ankles, every inch of his skin lit up by volcanic glow. Peeling my gaze away, I try to reach for the celestial rope that holds me captive. But my fingers brush through scattered particles.

"Okay!" I yell over the furious winds. Good to know there's still oxygen in this cruel simulation. "We get it. Very funny!"

A shadowy puppeteer drops me lower. Yelping, I spin until rope cinches my wrists, kicking for a semblance of momentum.

I tuck my chin toward my chest to peer below at the endless chasm of space and time, uncurling in a grand, toothless smile.

In this psychological torture chamber, a blue bead of clarity hits my forehead. My jaw cracks and my shoulders slump. Struggling does nothing for me, and everything for Jaal. It's not Jaal this time, and it never will be again. But there will always be a piece of him in me, and me in him if I keep twisting the bonds tighter.

Fuck. This.

A sigh like an angel's cry leaves me breathless. Every muscle collapses into cosmic ether.

I blink and we're back in the mock oval office. Sitting cross-legged on the very solid floor. My nostrils flare, welcoming the scent of beach sand cologne. In the same moment, Obsidian turns away from me and upchucks all over the floor.

Despite that, I laugh because now it really looks like an interrogation, but we're not the men in question.

Donning a gold and navy-blue suit, Beyon Ycarimus holds Micah's flimsy wrists behind his back with a white-inked hand. Even though they're only inches apart in height, Beyon dwarfs his lover due to sheer posture, the look on his face bellowing, *what were you thinking?!* Swarthy as hell, with square shoulders and a level chin, he makes Micah look like a flake of selenite.

"I'd be lying if I said this doesn't turn me on, President Y. Watching you two together is like witnessing mid and west RSA merge." I beam with restored confidence, throwing a sideways glance at Sid. He wipes his mouth on a quivering sleeve. "But I would downright soil my pants if you let us go and continue your vacay without us." I get up to leave, but Beyon places his free hand on the desk.

Reinforced gravity plunks me back down. A rock sinks in my chest. "This is a Sens-Room, isn't it?"

"Newest and best," Micah preens.

Of course our government has a whole room for Sens-powered mind control.

Beyon's eyes are so dark, they're almost black, ringed in a thin outer crust of hailstorm blue. His lips take up a quarter of his face. Both presidents have the same synthetic gorgeousness, but he meets my gaze with an even better mask.

Obsidian hides a gag in his sleeve, breathing deeply to calm himself. I pat his thigh.

Just when I think it'll be eons 'til we hear him talk, Beyon's buttery lips part. His voice is like water boiling in a trembling metal drum. "Zenith Lin. We're interested in Project Galaccine. We'd like to help."

My instinct is to lean back with laughter, but he remains grave. Icy stones of energy form under his eyes. He loosens his grip on Micah, who slinks back into the chair with pinkened cheeks.

"We don't need more funding," I insist, staring at Micah's yellow-inked hands. If he touches the stupid desk again, we're screwed.

A knotted smile strokes Beyon's face. He shakes his head and cracks callused knuckles. "You misunderstand. Thanks to President Samson, you're properly confused."

169

"Yeah, you should keep your husband on a leash," I snap, but a fist of remorse tightens in my gut.

Obsidian hacks up acidic phlegm again before raising a finger. "Uhum. Señores. I don't think you know what we doin' here—"

"I don't believe you know the magnitude of stress this Geminine problem has put on the solar system. Have you seen Mars?" Beyon's booming voice makes every electron in the room buzz.

I shiver and scowl. "That was all Jaal. His stupid bombs—the ones you keep funding for some unknown reason—killed thousands and now they'll kill trillions more in some fucked up, cosmic chain reaction."

Micah stretches his neck to peer at Beyon, who raises an eyebrow.

"What?" I demand, glancing at Obsidian. "I'm not wrong!"

"Actually, you're wrong on all counts." Beyon clicks his tongue and rubs his chin, scanning me like I'm an anomaly. "You truly believe your silly heist is to blame for all this?" He shakes his head. "You and Jaal are wildly self-absorbed."

Regaining a swath of sunlight-in-water energy, Obsidian raises his voice. "Hey now, Señor Pres. That ain't fair. Jaal and Zen work hard to get a solution to problemo Gemino." He raises fingers in air quotes. "We tryin' to heal the system, and sometimes we make mistakes."

"They still aren't getting it," Micah murmurs, as if we can't hear him.

Beyon's eyes roll like polished marbles. "I love you, Mi, but please shut up."

"Why aren't you telling them outright?" Micah starts to rise.

Beyon's firm hand pushes him back down by the shoulder. "They should be able to put the pieces together themselves."

I snort so loud it echoes off the high ceiling. "You kidnapped us by dematerializing our bodies and then played with our minds like they're putty. We can barely put ourselves back together, let alone the pieces of your sketchy truth."

Beyon nods his bald head as if to say *fair enough* and brushes the desk with pianist fingers.

Immediately, our minds are crunched into a tight compartment of semi-sensual vision. Sucked through a psychological straw. Nothing but third-eye, picking up faint signals. Our consciousness projects out of this ship, into another.

Voices chatter under the low rumble of an engine. My engine. Reiki, Onyx, and Jaal are huddled in the engine room, lit by dim auras

170

and Syzygy's core. Shadows etch and swell on their faces, displaying an array of mutual confusion.

"I don't understand," Onyx grumbles, peering through stellaglass and running a hand over buttons and knobs. Syzygy's engine thrums. "It's functioning perfectly, but we're moving way too fast for it to keep up." A flash of harvest moon eyes. She looks at Reiki, tugging her sweaty shirt collar.

At least she's dressed.

"Someone's taking us where we need to go," Reiki says dreamily, tracing symbols onto the engine's capsule. "He'll be fine, we'll be fine, and Zen and Obsidian will be more than fine." Her lips split in a dry smile.

She turns and sees me with all her being, and for once I know how she feels when I see her through dozens of faces. Without logic, or physical sensation, we recognize our presences through time and space.

Something clicks in the nether of my mind. I reel back into body and swallow the urge to throw up.

Obsidian scratches his head frantically, as if trying to shed the visions, and then flops onto his back with a gruff sigh, perplexed.

"Ugh," I lean forward and tuck my head between quivering knees. "I think we just astral projected."

"Close," Micah giggles into a hand. Throat chakra energy drips over the buttercup stain of his natal tattoo.

"We can do a lot to the dormant human mind," Beyon explains, brushing his hands off and walking to the other side of the desk. He's so irritatingly tall. "That was just simple quantum reverberation. The next step in Sens-technology. When the mental links ignited simultaneously, your mind lurched into your ship, which we're currently ushering to Saturn at full speed." His brows arch and he leans toward me, raising my chin between rough fingers. "Rest assured—we're here to support you."

Why me? I wonder, but then consider the possibility that he means the collective "you."

"Powerful verbiage," I mock Beyon, tongue clicking. "Too bad that speech wasn't public. Or are there hidden cams in here too?"

Beyon squeezes my jaw. Scarred divots and dry caps of his flesh snag my stubble.

"Alright, alright." I pull away. "We trust you. I guess. Just tell me. If the solar system collapse isn't our fault, then whose is it?"

The husbands exchange glances, the first spiritual string I've seen between them glowing like a silver lining in electric clouds. Beyon clears his throat. "We don't know."

"Perfect." I hobble to my feet, backing out of their collective aura. "Everyone loves hiding crucial information from me, so why should RSA presidents be any different?"

"Oh, shut up," Micah guffaws. "Do you really think we're out here just for another honeymoon?"

I cross my arms. "Uh, yeah. That's exactly what I thought."

"Oh my Gahhhd." He smacks his head. "Even dead matter isn't that dense."

Beyon slides a heavy hand over his face, aura like dried blood. "You're not the only one with a mission, Mr. Lin. Our goals are aligned."

"How?"

Micah snorts. "We'd show you, but your friend already ruined our favorite carpet. Who knows what'll happen if he sees the sick solar system?"

Beyon rolls his eyes, but his lips tremble. A crack in the mask. "Listen. Mars didn't explode because of Jaal's bombs. Do you really think we'd let that slide?"

"Our country has a craptastic history. I don't know what to think." I chew my lip furiously, gripping my bare elbows. The temperature plummets, but no one touches the desk to change it.

"You were kind of right before," Micah chimes in. "About chain reactions. You're just wrong about where it started."

"Mars disintegrated," Beyon continues, sweat glimmering on his cling wrap forehead. "Not because it exploded, but because it shifted out of orbit, due to Jupiter shifting, due to Saturn's sudden...boundlessness."

"Boundlessness? You're saying Saturn's the origin of this mess?"

Then he does something marvelously unsettling. White ink puckers on the edges of his palms when his fingers curl into a mudra—a meditative hand symbol I haven't seen in five years. He's working with energy, not only to calm himself, but to amplify an energetic mask. It's not just plastic surgery that thins his facial lines and polishes a nude scalp.

When he catches me gawking, his hands crunch to crack knuckles, ruining the mudra. "Usually, a solar system dies when its sun supernovas."

I nod. "Which has been humanity's concern for millennia..."

"Until your generation was born."

I squint and raise my eyebrows. "Excuse me?"

172

"Scientists noticed abnormal changes in the outer rings during that time." Beyon mashes his hands together like he's molding something. "And ever since...even our newest rogue planets have shifted all orbitals drastically. It seems...after years of research, a popular underground theory is coming to fruition."

His stainless teeth ripple with light as he speaks through a grimace. "A solar system—or a whole galaxy, in fact—can be so overwhelmed with planetary bodies that it destroys some of the older ones in favor of the new."

An ache like knotted wire settles in my throat. "So, you're suggesting—"

"It's Spring cleaning," Micah sings, counting his wiry fingers. "A couple months early for our planet, but..."

"The damage started with Saturn, and it's moving inward." Beyon tears up. "There isn't enough energy in the outer rings to sustain so many planets. To save itself, the solar system is...switching it up, as you might say." A vein in his temple twinges and he lowers his head, hiding another desperate mudra in his lap.

I roll my neck. "What about Pluto?"

"What?"

"You said 'starting with Saturn, moving inward,' which implies Pluto and the Rogues will be safe." I shrug, struggling to hide a sadistic grin. "That sector could make a nice home for twelve billion homosapiens, plus some Others."

Micah cackles. "There is no planet as lovely as Earth."

Lies, I think.

Beyon presses his lips together so hard, they turn light pink. "This isn't a famous Jaal-Nadir-joke. This is...regrettably...real life. Mars is obliterated. Jupiter is dying. Saturn has lost its rings."

"No way!" Obsidian yells, creaking into standing position, balancing on my shoulder. I don't even care. I'm too distracted by the energetic cleaver in my brain and heart.

"Show me."

"All in good time, Mr. Lin." Micah clasps his hands with Beyon's, a mutual love mudra. A summer sunset coats their aura.

Beyon heaves a sigh. "It's been a mess for everyone, Zenith. You must understand. I've seen galactic war and thievery, but this is...far beyond anything we could've predicted. The solar system is compensating for some kind of...energetic imbalance. Eventually, Earth will be destroyed too. Gods and goddesses know what will happen to the whole Milky..." He crumples into his lover's lanky embrace.

173

Micah looks at me, marblesque eyes soberer than I've ever seen on that gaunt face. How quickly these two switch roles, no substances needed. Stingingly, it reminds me of Jaal and Onyx mere hours ago.

"See, we're on the same path," he insists, rubbing Beyon's shoulder. "If we take more aurorae and disperse it ourselves, there's a chance the process will slow. Balance can be restored. We've proven time and time again that humans can work with Earth's environment, and now we must work with interstellar environments more prudently. Who better to team up with than people who know energy fields inside and out? And…if you don't mind me saying, Zenith, your speed at completing Jaal's tasks—as dangerous as they might be—proves your adequacy for this mission."

My stomach swims in venom. But then I stare at my hands and the coiling ink patterns. Saturn's symbol is nestled at the base of my ring finger, emerald-black in this lighting.

I imagine Mama and Mother, staring at Saturn's mess, blowing fog onto their old-fashioned windows to draw the planet a new throng of rings.

My knees buckle. My lungs stretch for more breath, unsatisfied. I almost cry with my president. Almost.

For once, Obsidian is speechless.

I rest a hand on Beyon's shoulder, then Micah's. They're so much younger when they look at me, and not just because of plastic surgery. Pastel and navy-blue mesh to plea for help. It was only moments ago that they arrogantly offered their aid, and now they admit to needing mine.

Twenty-Two

*H*ours later, atoms aching from one more dematerialization, I approach Jaal.

I focus on my breathing, a gelled Sens-pill clasped in my sweaty palm. Everyone watches me with clipped breath. The room's energy balances on the thin thread of his sanity.

He sits in the captain's chair—I only let him so he's less likely to argue—and stares at me with grizzly eyes. The crazier he gets, the more pitiful his sagging face, and the more I recall how difficult it was to take care of him when he had a regular fever, let alone this one.

Onyx stands next to him, a hand on his velvet-swaddled shoulder. Her citrus irises spurn each word that comes from my mouth.

"Well, Jaal." I extend my hand, to which he raises a brow. The rest of his facial muscles continue to hang. "You've been given a message." Any clever wordplay or smooth diction I had prior is tossed into electric ether.

As soon as my hand unfurls, Jaal snatches the blue-green pill and holds it up to a lazy eye. From his suit's breast pocket, he produces a copper monocle and squints through the glossy lens. What he's inspecting, I'm not sure. He knows what it is, and that when he swallows it, everything will be relayed immediately. *Why is he hesitating?*

"Message is for you." He tosses the pill back to me and bites his pinky nail.

I catch it and scowl. "Take the damn pill." Another step closer, and I thrust it in his face between forefinger and thumb. "It's important."

He nods quickly, gently pushing my wrist away from his face. "Important that you take it. Tell me about it later."

I roll my eyes so hard, they sting. "I'm not your secretary. In fact, I'm your captain. And as your captain, I command you to take it."

Drums beat in the sporadic dilating of his pupils. His brows shift together like tectonic plates. "As your friend, I advise you don't make me."

Friend. That's a new one.

Sighing, I glance up at Reiki, who's wrapped in pink and purple rope, dangling from the ceiling. Loose red hair expands in a cloud from the static. She throws me a diagonal smile and shrugs.

"Fine," I grumble, and swallow the bead dry. It sticks to the back of my throat at first, but with another gulp of saliva, it sinks into stomach acid and spreads throughout my body. Neurons fire frantically to keep up with chemical release. Psychotropic truth unfolds.

It's all so much, I plunk onto the floor, aching to be grounded.

My vision is overwhelmed by an apocalyptic montage—*Saturn loses its natural star-splashed glow, rings crumbling into dark energy and dying matter. A long, gnarly string of ice-encrusted rock bashes against the others, dotted in red eye-like sparks. Like a huge snake, it turns to me and hisses.*

From there, I pan over an orbit. *Jupiter is smacked by a gust of dark forces, an invisible tsunami sprinkled with ice clusters and flaming comets. It rolls out of line and subsequently turns Mars' gravity into a sick joke.*

Helpless without a warrior's shield, Mars collapses. There isn't a J-bomb in sight.

Venus swallows itself, creating a temporary black hole. Earth explodes magnificently like starworks.

Indefinitely, our solar system spins out of control, spitting on passing galaxies. The Milky's arms outstretch in pleading, bellowing prayer. Why, God? Why do we do this to ourselves?

Stars weep and drift apart, shaken from their quantum bonds by ferocious beasts of lava, hydrogen, and rage.

Despite their efforts, blackened planets we've collected over the millennia thaw and shatter like glass, coating cosmic homes with silver confetti.

With that pleasant simulation passed, leaving a pin-prick sensation on my skin and the scent of burning alcohol in my nose, a new face appears.

Sitting at yet another presidential desk, an oil-eyed woman smiles with scarlet lips that match her suit. Instead of hair, black-and-blue ribbons burst from her honey-colored scalp and drape over the desk. She flickers like a hologram but solidifies when I look directly into her eyes.

"Hello, Zenith Lin. I'm President Elisha Sye, Commander in Chief of Eastern RSA. It's a joy to meet you, if only briefly." She laces her blue-inked fingers over the desk and leans forward. "I speak to you, on behalf of my people, from my home in the Hand Lakes." Her smile swells. "Since I'm currently working on domestic affairs, I regret to say that I cannot be with you on this crucial journey. For the good of all, Presidents Beyon Ycarimus and Micah Samson will assist you with Project Galaccine, but make no mistake—you are the project's leader. Official documentation has been filed, copies of which will be stored in your brain at the end of this message."

How did Jaal know this was meant for me, and why are they giving me such a huge responsibility? I inhale, preparing to speak, but she raises a firm hand. Her nails change color from every angle.

"It's come to our attention that Jaal Nadir is no longer suitable for this position. You, however, have proven more than capable of carrying out orders."

Ah, so they don't mind my ramshackle mental health, but they love my obedience.

"After much deliberation, the boys and I have decided to help you, under the following conditions."

The fact that she calls her co-presidents "boys" brings me tears of laughter and makes up for the fact that I'm shaking.

Elisha clears her throat and cracks her knuckles. "Firstly, the professional contract between Jaal Nadir and the RSA government is hereby suspended. All research funds cease for the time being, while manual aid remains."

Her words are so ambivalent, they slosh around her throat chakra in puddles.

Her overly smoky eyes fan left and right while she reads off the list. "Secondly, the RSA government is not responsible for any injury, illness, or death that may occur during Project Galaccine. That responsibility is yours."

Classic cop-out.

"Thirdly, all parties agree to work toward the best possible outcome for all living beings, including those not yet discovered by humanity."

Weird flex, but okay.

"Fourthly—and this is for the best possible outcome for all living beings—you must begin with the redistribution of Saturnine aurorae. Energetic balance is key for our survival." Her nostrils flare and twitch. "There will be no need to make the original Galaccine. That personal project goal has been deemed…unimportant. For the good of all, not just the few, our goal is to restore our solar system to its natural harmony. Extracting planetary energies would hinder that goal."

Unimportant? My mind screams. *People are drowning in your precious Hand Lakes because the Fever made them forget how to swim!*

Honestly, I should have expected this. The Galaccine was a great theory. But if the solar system is killing off its oldest counterparts, then the picture is much grander than Jaal or I ever imagined. Flying too close to the sun is a problem for people who ask too many questions anyway, in the eyes of the government. As usual, Icarus falls.

"Lastly," Elisha concludes, leaning back in her throne-like chair. Gold light catches and streaks her brown eyes copper. "All of this is classified information. For now, the details of our agreement are strictly confidential and stay between the boys, you, and me. No one else is to know until further notice. For the—"

"Good of all," I say, coming back into the room as the pill wears off. "Yeah, I get it."

My crew flocks around me with wide eyes. Reiki unravels herself from her exercise rope and offers her hands, waiting to absorb the knowledge she expects to rush from my trembling lips.

But my mouth is a desert. The whole room closes in on me.

I tear away. Feet fling down the hall before my brain can catch up, thumping past blinking green lights. Frantic panting echoes off chrome walls, and it isn't until I reach my bedroom door that I realize it's mine. Every sense detaches, aching to stretch past the walls into outer space.

Heart caving in, I rub my eyes and harbor a thick sob. So, even the government wants to use me. Because I'm obedient. Unlike Jaal, I do as I'm told. I don't make my own ideas, or tiny rebellions. The whole fucking human race knows it. And now they depend on it.

When I look up through a blurry spectrum of tears, I realize no one followed me. Alone, lower lip trembling, I lean against the door.

A soft chime goes off and Syzygy asks, "Password?"

But I'm too weak to speak. Or even cry. Instead, I slink to the floor, skin and mind bruised, and burrow my face in sweaty palms. Vein-colored embers of energy glow in my throat and sink down to my stomach.

All of this is confidential.

One truth orbits the rest, expanding as a bubble, refusing to sink.

When I touch my throat, a memory unfolds before all three eyes. Chakras sprawl to release it.

The last time I saw Mama, the morning after she tried to kill Mother, her face was as colorless as the whites of her eyes. Intense tranquilizer gushed through her, turning blue veins silver and gold. She smelled like a litter box and her breathing filled the air with tremors.

Sprawled on the sofa, she watched me leave, but I didn't think she really saw me.

Little did I know, that was her final grasp for clarity. A last-minute attempt for Mama to push through the fog of the Monster, to save her baby boy.

The door was half-closed when she called out: "Take the ship."

Coming back to the present, I wring my wrists, wondering if she knew just how far Syzygy would take me. And now he's different, reprogrammed.

So am I.

With heavy shoulders, I rise and turn to face the bedroom door. "Soluna."

It zips open, revealing the product of Reiki's stress cleaning. Clothing piles removed, recycled back into the freshly dusted wardrobe. Makeup and glitter stains have been buffed out.

On the freshly made bed, next to fluffed pillows, lies an outfit. At first, I assume it's Reiki's, because of the dragon scale printed leggings. But it's on my side of the bed, paired with my favorite jacket. Plus, a black harness, equipped with my kyanite knife and a gun holster.

I bite my lip and pet the leggings' scales. Thermodynamic, they fade from green to reddish pink.

Soft knocking comes from the doorway. I know it's her before I look up. She smiles tentatively, arms folded over a skin-tight black jumpsuit. Her bare hands and feet are crisscrossed in rope markings. The door slides shut behind her.

"I figured we could relax and have one more fashion show," she offers. "Before our arrival." She spins on the balls of her feet and bows. A flicker of the dancer I first met weeks ago.

Something between a whimper and laughter falls out my dry mouth. I still can't say much. But I can feel myself running away again, out of my body. Away from anything solid.

Her aura fluctuates between sea green and opal. "I know you're stressed, but I also know it's not the time for big speeches or crazy energy work, so…" She wiggles her fingers. "I just thought…maybe. We could have fun. I could watch you strut your stuff. Y'know?" A shadow

179

crosses her chocolatey eyes, and she waves both hands. "Wait, that sounded weird. Not like I *want* to watch you, but I thought, like, with the Leo in your chart, you'd probably want to...oh, stars."

An apple blossom aura emanates from her. Understandably so. I'm climbing out of my pants. Anything to get out of my own head. *I'm already naked to the rest of the galaxy. What's the difference?*

Our eyes meet. For once, her face is still hers, a sunset I can't look away from.

But then, my senses are skewed. Vision, smell, touch, taste—the throb of fluid and air through my body tilts, imbalanced. Foreign substances still leak through neurons, playing with my perception of reality.

My heart drums.

The ceiling tilts like a canopy.

Rusty rivulets of hair tickle my neck. Volcanic, salty petrichor flirts with my nose. My face scrunches up.

Reiki's on top of me.

I lurch to move, but her cool fingers trace my hip bone and anchor me to the mattress. Red light ripples between skin and sheets, glowing like a bodily lantern under us.

No, this isn't right...and not just because of the obvious. This isn't her energy. This isn't real. It feels like someone else...like a memory.

But my brain can't figure out who or what it is. It's too busy trying to remember how to hide a boner.

My jaw drops so I can speak, but everything's clogged with light. Nothing leaves me, and everything floods in.

Without warning, her mouth smashes against mine.

Spluttering for breath, I try to sink through the mattress, or tuck and roll, but she hooks a thumb in either hip and pushes. It's not the same as what she's done with me before. There's no freedom here—it's all forced like a mosaic of stolen trauma.

While her mouth careens down my neck, one hand rakes between my legs and the other spirals to my arching lower back.

Of course, there's a part of me that craves her every touch. But this touch isn't hers.

This is someone else's sexcapade, a homemade project leaking into reeling braincells.

It could be so lovely, if I could just tweak a few things. It could be perfect, diamond-like, etched in the fabric of our collective being. This is too jagged, reminds me too much of someone I used to be, and so much that was forced upon me.

180

I flash in and out of present time. Still choked by wet nightmares and demanding hands.

My lungs compress under the weight of her mouth on my chest. *I can't breathe.*

I grapple with control, eager to reclaim my fantasy. *She would want me to breathe.*

Fire rains down as each neuron remembers itself. My nervous system reboots.

I said—I can't breathe! I restore light to the truth—something that was never able to come before I did. Until now.

In a gust of pearlescent smoke, the false image of Reiki scatters. The whole room shifts and solidifies.

I return to reality like coming out of a hangover.

Somehow, I haven't moved, sitting right where I was before losing it. Still naked, but untouched. Safe, but not alone.

Reiki sits at my side, fully clothed, eyes bulging. Caricature shattered. "Earth to Cap?" She waves a hand in my face, oblivious to my mind's crimes.

I flinch.

Her lower lip puffs out. "Zen? What's wrong?"

My heart bangs on cage bars. My aura curls inward, hiding in its exposed body like the ocean's rhythm tucked in a seashell.

She leans over the bed to snag my leggings. "You're shutting down because you're stressed." A deep, thoughtful sigh. "That's fine. One thing at a time. You don't have to strut, or anything like that. Just. Get dressed." Her giggle turns to another concerned frown. "Please?"

Whining, I roll off the bed, onto the other side. Sheets reek like her. Us. But all we ever do in this bed is sleep.

Sucking air, I peel away from the bed and press my forehead against the wall.

Tears boil behind my scalp. "W-wicker basket..." I mumble, but the words are constipated. Maybe it was all a production of my perverted brain, the broken organ that can't stop, the flesh-prison always craving more.

She follows me, and now I realize she might be the one person more obedient—foolish—than I am. I glance at her through blurs of blue and white.

Even though she's clothed in black, white, and a yellowing aura, all I see are layers of wiry ribs under rose petal breasts, curling wet lips, and hungry eyes. Another entity who wants me. Who I want...

"Zen."

181

I shake my head. Words burst. "Please leave."

"What? Why?" Flustered, she reaches out.

Ice smothers a heat storm, ready to take me in. Her fingers brush hair behind my ear, trailing the side of my neck. Tendons twinge in revolt. Bumps scatter over my skin, ripples of fiery rain.

"Don't touch me!" I hurtle away from her, creating a safe zone between the bed and wardrobe.

My joints pop and quake, terrified to release. I curl up and cover my face, so that we won't see each other cry.

Twenty-Three

A confused, cosmic tundra is all we see while Syzygy is dragged through stardust by the presidential ship. Since Obsidian and I no longer have control, the best we can do is sight-see, scrolling through various camera displays. My fight for being captain is sucked into oblivion with all my other initial stipulations.

"Do you think the RSA ship can handle itself and protect us?" I muse, sipping electrolyte water from a plastic champagne flute. Taking care of both ego and soul, I try to ignore the squeeze in my gut.

"Unclear," Syzygy responds, even though I wasn't asking him directly. "So far, so good."

Obsidian only shrugs and continues to scroll through panorama shots.

Potential black holes rumble and flux under us, the kind of swirly, blood-pudding substances Jaal would use to make bombs. Or maybe another dangerous, pointless, nonexistent vaccine.

Heaps of bruise-hued nebulae crackle on the chalkboard scape. Light energy and dark matter mix and slosh in thirsty throngs.

We shift the view back up, toward an array of split cosmic murals. Far ahead, a crumbling planet tilts on a new invisible axis, trying not to fall.

When zoomed in, we can just barely make out fragments of Saturn's blue-and-yellow rings. More cuts and bruises on a broken boy's mouth.

The whole universe must be chortling at our shared trauma.

"Zen." Obsidian shoves my shoulder. Calluses scrape my collarbone, bringing me out of an existential wormhole.

I flinch, adjust my unbuttoned collar, and smack him away. He smells like patchouli. "What?"

"You're not listening."

"Sorry." I wave dismissively, wincing to focus on what looks like a waterfall of ice in Saturn's distant atmosphere. Glitter drops from the planet's body like mystical stairs. "I, uh…I mistook your mumbling for the fireball's rumble."

Obsidian clears his throat and chews a freshly painted pinky nail. "I *said*—Pres Micah sent a Sens-message. He wants to know if you liked his gift."

"What?" I turn my head so fast, cracks ripple from my neck to skull.

"Dunno what he meant, 'meegs," he claims, flailing hands in front of him.

With a smeared scowl, I turn back to the screens. "I swear, if he—" And then it hits me like a rogue comet. The sexual hallucinations weren't my own; they were Sens-instilled. Part of the fanfare. I squeeze my temples.

"What is it, bud?" Obsidian pats my back. "Migraine?"

"I believe it's pronounced 'Micah.'"

He laughs, only stopping when he catches the drift of my singed aura. "Yikes, 'meegs. Only known the guy a few hours. What did he do?"

My brain and nerves buzz, the music of my soul blaring and belting notes I didn't think it could hit. Burned in my vision are Reiki's dark eyes, distant and overflowing because I pushed her away.

"Sweet Jesús, was it the pill?" he speculates, wiping overdrawn brows. "What did it show you? What did they say?"

"Pan, I hate Sens-tech," I groan into my folded arms, leaning against the control panel. Grizzly rouge sparks form and fizz under my skin, energy corroding. I lean back quickly, throwing Obsidian sharp side-eye. "Let's fight. Er, train, or whatever you call it."

His broad, falsely freckled nose wrinkles. He clutches his feather-encrusted elbows like a spooked bird, frozen in front of ship lights. "I dunno, 'meegs…"

I've given up telling him not to call me that, but I won't give up on this. "Oh, c'mon. Please? I need to shoot something." I grab the kinks in my hair and tug.

"Oh, so shoot me. Perfecto." He shakes his head, but a smirk pins his lips back.

Flinging to my feet, I feel the same fire behind my naval that drove me to trust Reiki. Now, in the span of a blink, that flame settles into igneous rock. I gesture at the screens. "See all this? Target practice."

Mocking me, he gestures to my outfit with a sassy wave. "See all this? Sad cry for help."

I stick my tongue out. "Lay off. Reiki picked this out for me."

Remarkably, we laugh together. I don't know what made us friends, other than an unfortunate taste in men and a common goal. Maybe our dematerialized bodies shared particles, and now we're forced to be pals.

Whatever the reason, I sift through annoyance to find gratitude. Weirdly, this might be the closest I get to having a brother. "Seriously, Sid. Let's shoot the rocks."

His false lashes flutter. "Is that code for somethin'?"

Buzzing with electric joy, I shove him and produce my gun, spinning it on twiddling fingers.

He only laughs more. "'Meeeegs. Come the heck on. Ain't no electro-gun gonna take out these bad boys." He throws a hand toward the screens. Huge rows of ice and rock plummet toward us, organized in super-magnified crystalline patterns like cocaine lines. Thanks to Syzygy's static shield and the presidential ship, we slide by icy spirals with ease. Knowing that we'd probably be space-dust without the RSA's fireball makes my tongue sour.

I tuck the gun back in its holster.

"If you ain't opposed, we could break out J-bombs," he suggests, a wicked crack in his eyes. "You hated that, though."

I space out on his strange facial features, from dusty makeup particles clustering in wrinkles to the unique genetic paint—ancient Mexican American and splashes of Indian—in his crispy skin. I don't know where the stories end and he begins.

Maybe we are similar after all.

Aching to watch something scatter to pieces other than my sense of identity, I snap finger guns in his face. "That isn't a terrible idea, Sid. I *am* fucking bored." I lean forward, only to realize that I don't know how to control the new weaponry.

Obsidian scoffs, peeling my hands from the control panel. "You ain't bored, 'meegs. You're pissed. And you got a right to be. Shit keeps coming at you like comets. Believe me, I know that feel."

"Do you?" I spit, words shocking my mouth like lightning. "I haven't seen the extent of your empathy yet." Which is kind of a lie, but I'm too wound up to care. "You won't tell me what I need to know."

His deep sigh splits the space between us, splintering our bonding auras. "'Bout the others, yeah. I ain't gonna speak for anyone else. But if you have a question 'bout yours truly." He shoves me and smiles. "Hablamos."

My lips part to ask a tundra of questions, mostly to distract myself from the aching in my chest, the wounds that I put there in Reiki's name.

But before sentences can even form, a huge force like no other tackles the ship, causing us to rumble and tilt. Floor and walls creak, impossibly loud.

"Oh, what the hell are they doing now?" I cry, rubbing Syzygy's walls. He heaves from the force of another blow, which jumpstarts adrenaline and whips me to my feet.

"Position breached," Syzygy booms, mechanically enraged. "Systems stabil—"

He's cut off by bangs and scrapes. Something beastly is trying to get in.

"Pleiades!" I yell, reaching for toggles. "Whatever that is, it's nastier than drunk Jaal." I pan through camera angles, searching for the perpetrator, only to settle on tons of floating rocks. They clot the screens in angry, icy torrents, obscuring our view of Saturn. There's barely any space left.

Obsidian yanks his colorful hair extensions into a bun, shawl billowing like a storm cloud as he flies to his feet to reach more controls. "Maintaining static shield, but doesn't seem to be helping," he updates, eyes flicking back and forth in a stretch of gray light. "Issa damn storm."

"Keep it going, co-captain." Despite struggling to stand, I toss him a crooked smile.

The floor trembles and shifts through various colors, unable to tell if upcoming ailments belong to the ship or the people.

Syzygy practically coughs. "Some systems unable to stabilize. Recommended course of action: prepare weaponry against opposing force. Fire when ready."

"Some?" Obsidian repeats, doing a frantic scan of the room. "Which ones?!"

Behind us, the door slides open and the rest of our crew floods in.

I'm too distracted to look at them, but Jaal slaps the wall and bellows, "You heard him! Fire at will, bitch!"

The back of my mind stamps a red IGNORE sign on his stupid, leathery forehead. Keeping a hand on each steering toggle, trying to

186

balance the ship, I raise my voice. "Sid? Please send Micah a message—one: no, I did not like his gift." The room sways, knocking my hand off a circular set of buttons. I readjust. "And two: we're being attacked. Send help."

"Bit busy, 'migo!" He yells over another bout of rumbles. "Only got two hands."

An absolute thumb tack in the skin of existence, Jaal wedges himself between us, pressing a random combination of buttons. "Got several hands, crotch-lodger."

I yank the steering system to the right, trying to dodge a vast ice cluster. It scrapes the side of the ship and I feel it in my ribcage.

"Hey, J," I practically snarl. "Why don't you find another blood opal so I can shoot you again?"

Whether he heard me or not is irrelevant—he clings to the controls like a child playing videogames. I can't tell if he's helping or making it worse.

Obsidian's eyes widen. His hands drop to his sides. "The fuck you mean, Zen?"

My lack of tact is short-lived when an ethereal roar clangs through alloys and collides with our ears. Sound becomes color to my overstimulated senses.

I grab my head, but everything spins on a spiral axis. Jagged bursts of light are skewed across the screens.

Jaal roars to match the sound, beast against beast. I focus on his brazen, bronze aura 'til the dizziness fades and I'm anchored in something new. Deep, bloody energy swims up legs and keeps me from fainting.

I've handled worse. This is nothing.

But it *is* something, and it's destroying my ship and possibly the presidents'.

"Weaponry activated. Fire at will." Even G fits as a war hero in the RSA's scheme. We have no choice but to be sucked into the new plan, armed and afraid.

Jaal's manic aura crackles with metallic fire. "Don't have to tell me twice." His brown eyes glow red in a sheath of exploding light.

"No!" Reiki calls from the doorway.

I want to turn to her, scream apologies in ancient languages so maybe she'll come close to understanding, but there's no time.

Somehow, the mass of rocks dodges Jaal's blow, animated by a thread of ruby light zapping through it. The light settles in hollow stony sockets, where dwarf star eyes glow menacingly.

187

Beast indeed.

The massive, serpentine creature unhinges an icy jaw and swallows every bomb Jaal throws. Smoky blue ice and yellow stone shimmer like scales.

Dark energy dissolves. Black matter swells and breaks, scattering into the cosmos to be violently recycled. It's the spitting image of the presidents' Sens-message, playing in real time for all of us to cower under.

The dragon leers, stone pillar teeth bared, ready to lunge. I stare at the screens, mesmerized by the suprabiological, cosmic anomaly.

Jaal aims to fire again, but Reiki snatches his bulky wrists with blanched knuckles. "Stop. Now."

It must be the Fever, or her wicker basket witchery, because Jaal's eyes widen and his sweaty lip trembles while he backs up from the controls. Under his feet, the floor continues to diagnose.

Reiki pours her energy into the panel, casting the ship in colors I didn't know existed.

Static clings to her body and aura, lifting each copper hair. She matches the creature's magnificence with steady breath and open arms. Separated by layers of stellar alloys and fancy shields, they are angel and demon in one hot second.

When I touch the wall again, it has the same warmth of the engine room, as if stardust lingers in every particle of the ship, supplementing and strengthening. As usual, Reiki surprises us with her weird alignment of technological and organic systems.

A collective exhale emerges, and so does an extra shield on the ship's exterior—an impenetrable wall of diamond-white light.

"Defense is for pussies," Jaal grumbles, but he's sedated by Onyx's embrace. He shrinks in her presence, crumpling and nuzzling against her shirt's faux fur collar.

The serpent rams its head into the shield, only to be blocked by brightness. Upon head-butting the energy, it bows and closes its smoking mouth.

"He respects our boundaries," Reiki announces breathlessly, wiping fresh tears on the back of her hand. "We should respect his."

The beast turns to fly away. At a distance, it becomes less of a dragon and more of a garter snake, tucked loosely around Saturn's crumbling hips.

I blink, noticing the tears in my eyes and wiping them with shaking fingers. I could kiss her.

Obsidian reaches her first, wrapping her in his shawl and squeezing so tight she coughs. "Diosdiosdiosdios," he laments, facing the unraveling heavens. "I don't believe what I see."

"Join the cult," Jaal growls, wiping his sweaty chin. He nods at Reiki, the only sign of respect I've seen him give her. "Looks like you were worth the trouble after all."

I take a step, ready to swat and watch his tongue bleed from clapping between teeth, but Obsidian releases Reiki and gathers my hands. A grave mist settles in his eyes and aura. It hisses: *Hablamos*.

I pull away and fall into the captain's chair. Between sweat and tears, I'm drenched.

Reiki sits in the chair next to me and pulls her knees to her chest.

Onyx presses mauve lips together. "Um? Is anyone gonna explain the fuck that was?"

Making me jump, our S-Coms go off in a choir of beeps and pulses. I'm still skittish when I put the goggles on, leaving the sight of the shrinking ice dragon behind. The balls of my feet bounce on the floor.

On the other side of our call, Beyon and Micah sit on the edge of what I assume to be their bed—a California king mattress laid on stacks of paper money. I can almost hear the old men crying for help in their dry, crumpled graves.

"So, that's what the gov does with ancient bills," Jaal jeers.

Obsidian's voice is painfully cheerful. "¡Los presidentes! Buenos días."

Micah grins with wine-stained teeth, chin bobbing to balance on his hand. "Zenith Lin, did you like my—"

"No." It takes tons of willpower to slow down the adrenaline still coursing through me, and to prevent me from ripping off the goggles and tossing them into a black hole.

Micah's bluish lips part, but Beyon places a hand on his shoulder. "We apologize for not aiding sooner." He adjusts his aviators. "We were...preoccupied."

"Clearly." I cross my arms.

"The fuck was that thing?" Onyx blurts, burying her face in the nape of Jaal's neck. Possessive ropes of light float between them, and my third-eye rolls.

Unfortunately, the presidents aren't much different. They exchange yearning glances. Tiny tingles of electricity the color of deoxygenated blood move between their clasped palms.

Beyon's woody eyes are just barely visible behind navy shades when he dips his head. "We don't know."

"That's rich," I guffaw, shaking my head. "If you don't know, who does?"

"That implies people in power are knowledgeable," Reiki adds her two-gems, both to my delight and frustration. "Which, unfortunately, isn't always true."

Beyon rolls his neck and shoulders. "Since we're a few hours from our destination, perhaps this conversation would be better held in person."

"Pan's ass," I swear, like I hadn't thought of it. "You think?"

Micah's skin is so frosted with highlighter, it practically blinds me when he tilts his head. "Bey doesn't trust Sens-tech."

My eyebrows crinkle. "Ironic." I pause to let that sink in, but they seem unfazed. A blustering sigh spews from my lips. "Okay, sure. But you're coming here. I've scrambled enough atoms for a lifetime, thanks."

I cut them off, sliding the goggles to the other side of the panel. My incompetent crew members wear their S-Coms like kids playing dress-up, except for Reiki, who catches me looking at her and quickly makes for the door.

With igneous rock still rolling in my lower chakras, I run for her. With each step, a chime goes off on the floor.

I snag her as the door slides open, pinching her wrist. Her breath slips between clenched teeth.

"Ki, listen." Behind us, the crew continues to chat, senses still submerged in the RSA ship. I shake my head, willing myself not to be distracted. "I'm sorry."

Her brown eyes bulge, sending fresh tears rolling. "Nothing to be sorry about." She wipes her face and sighs. "You've got work to do, Cap. Don't worry about me." Forced laughter scrolls her facial lines, pressing pieces of her together. "I'm gonna use your shower, okay?"

Words are right there, cradled in the bed of my tongue, but they won't move. I nod and let her go, but the subtle sound of skin brushing and releasing echoes moments after she's gone.

I zone out on the floor where new inscriptions and prescriptions blink.

Patchouli smacks me in the face. A harsh hand clamps my shoulder and spins me around. "Hypocrite," Obsidian whispers, while Jaal and Onyx follow Reiki's leave. The door shuts with a soft, air pocketed zip.

I clear my throat. "Hey, uh, what's—"

He smacks the back of my head, where knotted hair makes a dragon's nest. I bite my lip.

"Ain't the only one holdin' secrets, am I?" He grips my shoulder.

It takes me a moment to remember what he means. I roll my eyes. "Oh, please. Don't act like you didn't know about the opals. J wanted to prove his idea would work. I'm sure he asked you to shoot him too."

You'd think I aimed a gun at *his* heart. Every wrinkle that doesn't belong in his face deepens. "He *asked* you to?"

I pull away, digging my thumbs into the pressure points under my jaw. "Look, I have several difficult discussions to perform today, including one with two of three RS presidents. So, if you could, just. Please. Pretend I didn't say anything. It's really not that important."

"¡Es importante para mí!"

"Then you should talk to Jaal." I point to the door. "Leave me out of it."

I expect him to keep fighting, to display his fire through fits of turquoise and lapis in an overused throat chakra. But he's malleable to my words, shut down and reshaped by my sudden lack of compassion.

He exits the same way everyone else did, with less confidence and hope.

I stand in the center of the room, hoping this bewitched floor will read my fate like Tarot, so that I can prepare for even more ego-crushing blows.

At the thought, I revisit what it was like to be in Tauris' live presence. She breathed down my neck, lustful and mistrusted, and read me to filth. I was a constantly crumbling skyscraper, choosing to fall.

Pulling away from that archetype, new feelings bolster me. I think of Reiki, and how I was so quick to fall for that stupid hallucination, how it terrified me.

If she would talk to me, we could work through these feelings together, even the dirty darkness that made me push her away. The stuff that sticks, but can't be explained—quick kisses, breathless jokes, drunken embraces, and all the melodrama my body and brain can muster.

"Shadow work," I test the words on my tongue. Mother talked to me about it a few months after Mama first got sick. But it was different for them.

"We've been married for twenty-two years," Mother explains over a pot of simmering ramen. *"Still, I've yet to learn how deep our shadows go. There's always more to learn, more to share and dive into."* She waves the wooden spoon like it's a wand with magical steam. *"Don't worry about us—we're fine with our shadows. Yours is young, though. You must live your life with an abundance of faith."* Her apple-blossom cheeks pinch. *"And that comes from knowing your shadow well."*

Tears would come if they weren't blocked by splotches of crushed violet behind silver irises—only the cusp of my shadow. The rest hides in slippery chemical mixtures of self-hatred and fear.

Snapping my attention like a twig, the door slides open and Beyon ducks his head to enter. I slide a hand over my face, tugging skin and overgrown facial hair. Everything aches under my touch.

"I can see why you dislike materializing," he confesses, rubbing his neck. "Micah's stuck in the ventilation shaft."

I squint at him. "I'll try not to take that as a metaphor."

He offers no further explanation and sits in the captain's chair. Khaki-wrapped legs cross and he stares at me so intensely, on a normal day, I'd melt. But this trip has been anything but normal.

Sighing, I plop into lotus position on the floor. Diagnostic settings shift and flicker for both of us, but I don't care about what problems lie beneath his coffee bean skin. He coughs and rubs his neck again.

I roll my eyes and cup each knee with a mindful hand, playing mantras on repeat in the back of my mind. "So? What do you have for me?" I cross my arms. "Besides an intrusively crude rendering of my innermost sexual fantasies."

His brow scrunches. "I beg your—"

"Pardon?" I smirk, scraping dirt under my fingernails. "Granted, but here I was thinking you were the monarch granting pardons."

Rings of black energy around his neck tighten. He clears his throat again. "Zenith, please. You were brave and kind to accept our help with open arms, but we're at a world's end. Anything could happen. I need your full focus."

I lean back on my hands, spine curling and forgetting posture. "Mommy didn't pay enough attention to you when you were little, huh?" I feign a delicate pout. "It's okay, me too."

His knuckles crack and crunch, folded in his lap. "Your cooperation would be sincerely appreciated."

I press my palms together over my heart, Anjali mudra, and stare at the floor. Inhale deeply through the nose, exhale through the mouth. My eyelids merge.

It takes him a minute to comprehend that this is what my cooperation looks like.

My third-eye watches his bruised third-iris flit back and forth, reading invisible, incomprehensible words. Grasping for tools.

"This mission is of the utmost importance. With the solar system out of balance, the whole galaxy is at stake."

In silence, I squint one eye open to see him leaning toward me, his chin propped on laced fingers. "I take it you were, ehem, unsettled by President Sye's request?"

I snort. "It was more of a command, but yeah. I was."

He scratches his shiny head thoughtfully, a king trying to be a philosopher. "We know about Jaal's condition, you see. It's imperative that scientists who work with us stay objective—"

"That's not what I found unsettling, Presidente." I mock Obsidian, partially because I'm still bitter that he left me alone.

Realization dawns first in the navy-blue rings around his eyes and settles in his twitching mouth. He nods firmly. "Ah, well. Your team's original goal is a delicate matter. We know about your mother, too."

"Mama."

A deep bow of his head shows a sliver of respect. "Due to the ailment both she and Jaal possess, President Sye almost dismissed your leadership as well. Micah was the one who vouched for you, after viewing your courteous character a few weeks ago."

If I wasn't drowning in self-deprecation disguised as meditation, I would slap my knees with laughter, but instead I emit words like broken code. "I've been called a lot of things, but courteous isn't one of them. Thanks."

He rubs his bristly chin. "Zenith, you are many things. That's why we need you. And we're so grateful for your participation."

"Well. At least someone is."

His voice lowers. "Listen. I concede—we have a theory about what you saw. But it's a...sensitive topic. Only you can know."

"Sure. Give me more psychological weight to carry. It's my pleasure." I flourish a hand and open my eyes. Our auras darken and solidify, opaque halos. His slumps like wet clay.

The door slides open, burping up a crazed Micah, who could be a prisoner with his lime green jumpsuit and sweat-plastered hair. He points a pale finger at me. "Your pleasure, Mr. Lin, was the delectable nugget of sensory ecstasy I gave you hours ago."

In my mind, another fantasy plays: *I knee Micah Samson in the balls so hard, he faints.* But then, I blink and the amusing illusion scatters.

A sound like clinking ice squeezes through Beyon's throat. "Mi, again?" He lurches away from the chair, opening his arms.

Micah slinks to stand behind his lover, a winding vine stuck to a tree, and hooks a thumb in Beyon's belt loop.

"Bey," he whines, hiccupping. "I thought it would be a nice gesture, a token of gratitude."

"I didn't want it." Nuclear explosions roll in my stomach. "Not like that."

Ever the harping husband, Beyon gestures to me emphatically with both hands, eyebrows spiking. "See?" He shakes his head. "Stop spreading mischief. Tides are tight. We have our species to save. Possibly others."

"But he clearly likes her," Micah laments, elbowing his beloved's ribcage. "If they get together, they can make beautiful babies for us. Er—you know, for humanity. In case everything goes to shit." He flicks a wrist.

Beyon snatches Micah's wafer-thin waist and draws him close. I can't tell if he's aroused or enraged.

"Excuse me." I raise a surprisingly steady index finger. "As much as I'd love to overthink the conspiracies forming right now, we are—like you said—trying to save humanity. But that has nothing to do with Reiki fucking me."

Beyon's voice balances on the edge of cackling. "I know you mind me saying this, Zenith, but it's plain as sun—most of your identity has been morphed to fit certain schemata. Perhaps you're afraid to be yourself."

Obviously, moron.

"You can be yourself with us, without concern." He ruffles Micah's hair. "I didn't speak about that publicly for nothing."

I rub my dry eyes. Dust clinging to fingernails burns them. "Everyone thinks they can be my therapist, but only one person has managed to fulfill that role, and even she isn't meant to." With a clenched fist against my jaw, I tilt my head side to side, cracking my neck. "Fuck the feels and tell me your theory."

Micah cackles. "Our theory is that you and Reiki are—"

"About the ice dragon. Pleiades." I roll my eyes.

When the presidents turn to exchange looks, the stark differences in their profiles make me chuckle—Beyon's dollop nose clashing with the sharply spun sugar of Micah's. I remember why I ever

194

watched their interviews or paid any attention to their scandals. Even though they were hot messes, at least they stuck together, and looked good doing it.

Beyon sits back in the chair, bites his upper lip, and drapes laced fingers over crossed knees. His pants ride up slightly, revealing mismatched socks in gentlemen's shoes—a sliver of chaos in a control freak.

"We believe the creature you saw…" He clears his throat into a curled fist. "…isn't a creature at all. It's Saturn's defense mechanism."

"Sorry, what?" I was so focused on expanding and deflating my lungs, I'm not sure I heard correctly.

"Saturn was attacked," he reiterates, "and now it defends itself by manifesting something new and destructive. Much like a human's immune system, actually."

"If a human had god-like powers," Micah chimes in.

"Wait, so the solar system is breaking Saturn down, but it refuses to die?" I struggle to hold their weightless theory.

Beyon heaves a sigh. "Look, Zenith, it's a seemingly fast-approaching doomsday, but with you and your crew, it won't be." He glances at Micah, exchanging a fractal of sky-colored energy.

Strings form between them, none of which come close to touching me. I get the same vibe I got from Lutfi. They're keeping secrets, acting like I'm the confidant, and I hate it.

I scratch my temples and tug tufts of hair, ready to unravel and spill on the floor. "I'll tell you what I told Jaal—I think you're crazy, but I'll help you. Partially because I don't have a choice, but mostly for Reiki. She's not talking to me right now, but…" I tap my head knowingly. "She still cares about everyone, even those who've hurt her. That's the real goal, boys."

Light and darkness dribble from their third-eyes, rusty metaphysical pieces starting to move again. I wouldn't strike chords more if I pulled out my sitar and plucked literal chords. Their lips twist into desperate grins.

"I was right about you," Micah preens, sky-blue eyes shimmering.

"Ah, Mi." Beyon loses his fingers in Micah's slick hair.

Thanking stars that I put autopilot on, I stalk out in a mental frenzy, trusting Syzygy not to crash even though he's got a potential porno in the control room. I move so fast to the captain's quarters, my feet barely hit the floor.

"Here I am, just trying to make a living," I mutter, "and everyone and their sister wants to ram a hand up my ass and play shadow puppets, construct bullshit plans for a—*Soluna*." The bedroom door zips open and shuts behind me. "For a bullshit…universe." But all the toiling energy and bountiful hatred evaporates when I see the bathroom door. It's cracked open, lavender-laden steam curling out.

My shoulders fall, but my heart tightens. I knock. "Ki? Can I come in? I've gotta shave."

As I open the door further, her aura breaks like an egg and a gush of fluorescent pink energy enters my chest. A whimpering laugh echoes off tile and metal. "Sure, Cap. It's your bathroom."

Inside, her naked body is sheathed in ignited water. The lights aren't even on—it's all her, glowing like a centerpiece under my personal waterfall. Her aura and body blur in marvelous androgyny.

My heart hugging itself so hard it could burst, I shut the door behind me and head for the sink.

"You've got to breathe," she says sultrily. I don't dare look at her. I know it's the hot water making her fuzzy in mind and body, not the Sens-pill that's long been out of my system. But now the only system in the way is my own. Relapsing neurons firing trauma where there is none.

"I'm fine." I tug on stray curls and out-of-bounds brow hairs. In the mirror, my aura trembles from the power of hers. My hands shake when I slide open the glass and grab a rainbow-handled razor.

"Are you?" She shuts off the water and leans against the wall.

Soap sloshes from between thin blades when it hovers over skin, motion sensors detecting hair. I say a silent goodbye to the obnoxiously patchy beard.

"I…um." I scratch my forehead with the other hand. "I don't know."

The scalp-tingling shift of her moving behind me glues me to my own gaze.

Her soaked toes patter on tile. "I think you do know."

"You think too much," I snap, almost cutting my quick jaw with the razor. Licking my lips and repositioning, I gather the courage to meet her eyes through fogged glass.

Contorted and turned away from me like an ivy branch, she looks over her shoulder. "We're both guilty of that crime, Cap. The worse offense is to withhold your thoughts. So, tell me—what's on your mind?" With globes of white energy circulating her hands, she dries her

196

body. Water molecules are scooped from her pores in a swath of windy witchery.

"Um, well. I know I was weird to you yesterday—"

"With all the advanced tech we have, you use that." Her eyes follow the sudsy razor gliding over my jaw.

"It works, so I use it." My hands tremble as I try to segue. "I'm sorry for treating you like…*that*, even though I trust you."

"Mmm, do you though?"

I look up for a second to watch her run a finger over pursed, glistening lips. Giggles spill and she turns away again to wrap her hair in a damp top knot.

Foam covers my blush, but unable to hide my blossoming aura, I continue. "W-whatever, I mean I care about you. More than anything or anyone else. More than myself."

"You should love yourself," she drawls, shimmying out of the mist.

"I'm trying."

"I know."

I catch my reflection smiling and roll my eyes. "You and I…we're…weird and complicated, but so is everything else in my life, and like—you aren't Jaal. You couldn't possibly be…it's against your nature. And so, this…you…you're the only thing keeping me close to sane."

Waxy and full like a sun-spotted jade tree, she sits on the floor. I glance at her crinkled eyes, scanning her wingspan as it swells over her chest, back, and the magnanimous glow in her solar plexus. Her crumpled dancer legs rest in a puddle of sunsets.

"I want to embrace you, not push you away like everything…everyone else. So." Air in, air out. Heart pounding. Stars brimming, leaking through metal into scalp, skull, gray matter.

I gulp. "You should know. The presidents have tech as crazy as Jaal's. Materialization rays or some shit, Sens-tech on crack, and that ship, I mean come on…" Rinsing the razor, I laugh and shake my head. "But uh…that Sens-pill was the weirdest. It made me see…and feel you."

"Like an astral projection? Sid said they could do that."

"No. Not really." When I glance at her again, she's in downward dog pose, spine perfectly sloped.

Fierce blush and a freshly shaven face match too well, stinging when I hang my head under the running faucet.

I spit into the sink after turning the water off. "It was like a hallucination." Water droplets tuck and roll. "They uh…programmed it to…make me think you were having sex with me."

"Oh." She doesn't cower or curl up in embarrassment, but she doesn't laugh either. If anything, she sounds relieved. "Was it good?" Pale blue energy swarms her upper chakras as she slowly moves into Vriksasana, tree pose.

I duck so low into the sink, my neck cracks. Laughter chases a cyclone of wet hair stubs down the drain. "I, uh…yeah, but it…wasn't, at the same time. Because…it wasn't really you." I swallow and look back up at her through the mirror. "It felt like they took my memories of Jaal and…copy and pasted you in it. As if…" Anxious chuckles continue, causing my lungs to ache. "As if that was what I wanted."

"What *do* you want?"

I clear my dry throat. "Um…well. Really, I just want to be happy. And you make me happy, as you are. Not with anyone's expectations or add-ons. Y'know?" I can't help but wince.

She ponders this for a while, and then her nose scrunches. "Do you think that's how the presidents got elected—manipulating the populous with collages of their innermost fantasies? That's lower than low."

Gripping the edge of the sink, I turn to face her—the real her—and wipe my mouth. "I don't know." I shrug. "I'm not a politician."

Twenty-Four

Little spots of joy keep me mindful—from my freshly shaven jaw and trimmed undercut to Reiki's sunflower lashes and the hammock of understanding between our gazes. Even though not much more has been said, the energies passing between us bolster my peace.

Despite what Reiki might preach about souls, she and Jaal are as different as light and shadow.

Meanwhile, she and I are aligned like a planetary stellium, and sometimes I forget we're different people. I hate looking at myself in the mirror, but it's not as hopeless when she's the reflection.

Even when our sweet collective energy is impeded on in the cockpit, I stay cooler than ice.

"'Bout fuckin' time!" Jaal barks. "This ship needs its captain."

I squeeze Reiki's hand before letting go. Our auric fields are indivisible. "Sid can handle a lot more than you give him credit for." The back of my mind wonders if they spoke about the blood opal situation.

I scan Obsidian for any sign, but his aura is so foggy, all I can make out is a faint indigo knot strangling the base of his skull. He dons a butternut yellow robe and an array of ancient American jewelry, piloting Syzygy like a silent shaman.

For once, Onyx ignores Jaal and comforts her brother, one hand on Obsidian's uncomfortably straight spine and the other on her twitching temple, grasping for balance.

Ignoring the beeps at my feet, I stalk up to Jaal, who stands with open palms sprawled like the new Christ.

One awkward discussion down, God knows how many to go. I open my mouth, but Jaal cuts me off.

199

"Ain't talkin' controls." He rests a hand on my shoulder. His forgotten stubble gleams unnaturally white. I can't tell what's bleached and what's Feverishly modified. "Engine room. Now." Sliding to my bicep, his grip tightens.

I toss a wince at the other three while Jaal pries open the trapdoor below us. Reiki follows us closely, fingers laced in a tranquil mudra.

Itching with anxiety, I hold my breath on the first step, ears straining for abnormal crackling or whizzing. But thick stillness is worse—it stands like a wall between Syzygy and me.

Halfway down, I breathe normally. A clunk-and-whooshing sound assaults me, breaking through the invisible barrier, and I almost miss a step.

"Careful," Jaal calls up to me, like he gives a shit.

I blow a hair that escapes my elaborate braid crown. It zaps my vision, a fuzzy black lightning bolt.

As we approach G's core, a stench like burnt rice and boiling mercury clogs my nose and lungs, wrenching wheezes and coughs. Coupled with violent silence, it seems too terrible to be true.

I cinch my nostrils with shaking fingers. "Syzygy, report."

"Regrettably, this *is* what it looks like, Captain. Apologies. My systems were meant to be stronger than this."

"Don't get too close," Jaal commands, fully descending and stepping on one side of the ladder.

Reiki and I take the other side, still clenching the rungs. Our pupils and energies shrink away from the overwhelming light.

Most of the room is coated in vaporous lava. It seeps from a huge bundle of fried wires. Syzygy's engine swells to fill the stellaglass, hissing and spinning dangerously fast.

Clusters of juicy blood opals gather in the broken tank. The Phoenix Compound makes a rotten traveling companion, forming a huge crying mouth that splutters and spills on fractured stellaglass and metal, taunting G and stealing his energy. They look like siblings who fight for attention at a party, champagne bubbles sloshing in a glitterfall to the floor.

The closer we get, even by inches, the more silence pounds. While the visual is too intense, the quiet fills and negates.

"What…happened?" My brain slurps for oxygen that's barely there. The liquid-and-vapor massacre swarms.

Syzygy's voice is crackly, admitting defeat. "As it so happens…I am not…the most efficient…channel for this energy."

200

Simulating agreement, the Phoenix Compound raises a blood-orange hand.

Jaal clears his throat. "Messy, eh?"

"How long has it been like this?" I glare through twisting, creamsicle light. A strip of something unnatural that could be so beautiful, if it wasn't wrecking my ship.

He shrugs, massaging his brick jaw. "Since we got closer to Saturn. Think the beast set it off."

"This is fucked up, even for you," I manage through a cupped hand. Smells leak through and shoot up my nose, the sting of a poisonous sneeze.

"Wasn't my fault." Jaal folds his arms and shakes his head. His metal boot heels clink together, a sound that irks me in this vacuum-packed space.

I tug the beds of my braids. "Pleiades, J. My ship is dying because you hooked it up to your broken moral compass. It was *all* you. All of this has been your crackpot design."

He shakes his head hard and fast, dreadlocks flailing like tentacles in retreat. "This ain't that. The planets are going to shit. Right, bruja?" He looks at Reiki for confirmation.

Puncturing his words, I snag an old tool from the shelf, not even checking what it is, and hurl it into an oil-colored puddle. Green gas spews from it, swirling the color of bloodied snot. "SHE'S NOT A PET. USE HER NAME."

Jaal stretches his sweaty collar. "Reiki," he amends. "Technology's shambling 'cause of the planets. Energy dispersing. Right? Our work had nothing to do with it."

She wrings her hands. "I…"

"Oh, sure, and I guess you subscribe to every piece of metaphysical information she gives, as long as it fuels your ego," I seethe.

While he remains silent, chewing a fingernail, my teeth grind. I gesture wildly. "You're loving this, aren't you? You love to see me unravel under your stupidity."

Shrugging helplessly, he sighs and coughs an ashy blue cloud. I can't tell if it's toxic chemicals or a terrible aura.

"You expect me to fix this, don't you?" I yell through the nausea, just as a spiral of light pops and coils toward us. I duck my head, but keep a finger pointed at him, unwavering. "I've *always* cleaned up your shit. With no pay raise other than a quickie in your drug cupboard.

So you could bang one out, and I could go back to feeling loved and valued, even though I wasn't."

Jaal squints and taps an ear as the engine's crackles and flares rise in volume and brightness. He's oblivious to feelings and emotions, even when they threaten to burn us both.

I throw on the best pairs of work goggles and gloves I have. Which, in the grand scheme of things, aren't even that great.

Reiki's aura glides over mine, but she doesn't try to stop me.

"I *will* fix this," I speak calmly, staring at the bodily fluids of a dying star. "Not because I owe you anything—and certainly not because I know how—but because I want you to stop playing God. Every pathetic apocalypse you create in my world and the next one over. Every terrorist act you claim to be a contribution to science. It all ends now."

Behind grimy lenses coated in metal flecks and oil stains, the mess doesn't seem so intimidating. In fact, it's like the venture of confronting Reiki, releasing truth even though it stings. Even though I don't know what it means. But it's promising.

I cough. "All I need to do is remove the faulty wiring. Right?"

"Told you, it wasn't that. Do you ever listen?"

Scanning the mangled wires, I shake my head. "*You* should listen to me. Saturn's nervous breakdown might've triggered this, but your shitty energy theory finished it off. So now I'll remove the damage." I spit on my shirt collar and bite down, hoping to breathe through it like a wet rag.

I approach G's engine, scanning the area for a way to reach the clusterfuck of wires without getting singed.

But Jaal's fancy swing is broken, unhinged like his mind.

Upon closer inspection, his unethical lava mutant has grown with the engine, shaped more like a person than a fetus or child. A heart made of blood opals thumps in its deformed chest, glowing fiercer the more it screams.

The Galaccine. In the flesh. Kind of.

The humanoid glob casts itself through its cracked shell, trying to reach and spill itself over the engine.

"G, c'mon," I mutter. "Don't be like me. Don't give up your power."

Staring 'til half my vision is bleached, I take another step.

Fingers snatch my sleeve, tugging me to face Jaal. He waves meaty arms at me and calls my name, but he's not close enough to touch. Neither is Reiki. Maybe it's the spiritual presence she mentioned, or her strong astral arms. If I wasn't so focused on killing myself—I mean, fixing this—I'd be spooked.

One hand pressing the damp collar to my nose and mouth, the other reaching up, I stand on tiptoes. Sizzling red and green wires have fallen from their high spot and hang just above hyperextended fingers. The bulky gloves add half an inch at most.

Why am I so short?

I launch upward by pushing off the Compound tank, but my sneakers slip and stellaglass trembles. I catch one wire with a furling fist, and when my feet hit the floor again, several strings of metal and rubber tumble down too.

Sparks soar, but nothing is more threatening than the wailing lava-person, who breaks through the cage and aims a swirling hand for my face.

Diving to the floor drags a couple thicker wires with me, slashing the Compound and momentarily misshaping it.

I gasp into salty fabric, tucking and rolling away from puddles of singed fluid and toxic gas. In one swoop, the rest of the wires are yanked from their structure, hitting the floor with a pop and thud. I pull the bundle toward me, causing a thread of sparks to decorate my jacket sleeves.

Stellaglass splinters down the middle, sending a stream of flares out from the engine. Death mixes with life force, the star puncturing its own auric field and vomiting fire.

Someone drags my collar, sending me flying backward toward the ladder. In the chaos, I barely notice the tap of my skull against metal. Jaal lurches in front of me, taking the flaming hit with outspread arms.

Reiki lifts me up by the armpits, peels the jacket off, and tosses it onto the floor. Flames crackle and curl from the dark, synthetic surface, melting plastic fibers into mud. She stomps them out with platform Mary Janes—something an FBI agent's bot-daughter would wear.

"You ruined your favorite jacket," she remarks, kneeling next to me and swiping ash off my chin.

"And you...scuffed your new...shoes," I laugh and wince, scratching the back of my head. Blood leaks from my scalp, matting hair. I groan, not because of the pain, but because I'm so sick of being wounded.

An inhuman clatter sends both our heads turning. Jaal falls onto the engine and his whole body swells up in flames, coursing with a deadly sunrise.

"Oh God," I croak, but it's obscured by louder clanks and Onyx's bloody scream from above. She must recognize the scent of her best friend's burning flesh.

As usual, he evades the expected fate. He doesn't even burn. Somehow, his body receives the flames like the blood of Christ, communing with impossible quantum designs. More powerful and intimidating than before. Each cell switches like flicking on a light.

We shield our eyes from fluorescent tremors.

Bathed in colorless light, Jaal's hair blanches completely, frosty and splayed in static like Reiki's was when she worked with powerful energy. Back uncurling, he turns to us, grin ablaze. This is worse than when I shot him, worse than when he forced me to sleep with him, worse than anything I ever imagined.

Broad shoulders shimmying in firelight, he waltzes toward the Phoenix Compound and thrusts a greedy hand through the glass, into its concave chest.

Energy I've never seen bubbles between them, color and depth rewriting physics. Suddenly Jaal is the channel he tried so hard to make.

He's forcing his body to become a Conduit...

Both beasts weep for each other, momentarily connected by empathy beyond science.

But fire kills their tears.

Jaal's gigantic hand dwarfs the blood opal heart while he inspects it from every light-glinting angle. Hunching his shoulders and tilting his head, he crushes the cluster. His eyes change color without the aid of Sens-tech.

I lean into Reiki and clutch my stomach.

Ignited blood rushes through Jaal's clenched fingers, and he licks the remains, piling every opalescent drop into his thirsty maw.

Without opals, the Compound shrinks down to a small vat, lifeless.

Syzygy retreats too, auric engine sucking inward to fit its original space. An inch-wide crack remains in stellaglass.

Under dimming light, Jaal becomes somewhat human again, fading flames leaving no clothes, darker skin, and stark white hair. Dreadlocks fluff in nebulous patterns around his polished face, but his body hair was zapped with his clothes. Rings of melted metal and plastic spiral down his bulging muscles.

My ears ring.

He stumbles to lean against the wall. His trembling lips eject smoky laughter. "Who cleans the messes now, bitch?"

204

When fire dies completely, he hacks up bloody phlegm into his elbow, slumps against the wall, and faints. Gusts of ash fly in his wake.

Stray pools of magma cool to black domes, sped up by natural processes in an unnatural environment. Shambles of a shitty experiment.

Rock-encrusted boots click-clack down the ladder in a panic. Siblings who share too much in common with the igneous rocks gasp into their palms. They trip over each other, struggling to reach Jaal.

"He's not dead," Reiki announces flatly while they fawn over his unconscious body.

Obsidian's lower lip trembles. "W-why did he…?" When he reaches for Jaal's hair, static electricity nips at him, frying the feathers on his sleeves.

Whispering Hisphindi prayers or maybe incantations, Onyx rolls her shoulders back and holds Jaal's face.

I shake my head, bitter laughter encroaching.

Reiki ushers a stray hair behind my ear and looks up at the ceiling. "Syzygy, purify."

In the same moment that G activates and opens the vents, I lean over the plastic bag of a jacket and throw up.

Reiki rubs my back but continues to watch the others try to hoist Jaal to his feet. "He's not dead," she repeats. "But you can't move him right now."

They grumble responses, but I tune them out and wipe my mouth. "Ki," I whisper. "He turned himself into a J-bomb."

"Yeah, Cap." She bites her lip. "And he saved your life."

Twenty-Five

Micah sighs through his teeth and touches my shoulder. "How are you?"

I shrug him off. Their fancy, cologne-ridden ship has me more on edge than before, if that's even possible. I didn't want to come back, but at least this time they materialized doors to walk through, instead of my body.

President Samson and I are alone, which is both a blessing and a curse.

"A few thousand miles above Saturn, on the brink of humanity's end, and that's what you ask me?" I scratch the back of my scalp, where an amalgam of clotted blood is stowed in neuron-tricking Sens-bandages. When the wound aches, fake numbness spreads, tricking the brain into thinking pain is nonexistent.

"Your well-being is important, too." President Samson wrinkles his nose and spreads a hand across the Sens-wall, displaying our surroundings in brilliant, touch-activated HD.

From Saturn's gaseous surface, the icefall projects on one side but the other is coated with starwork-like splatters. More chemicals and powers we've never seen. The sight of it makes me shiver.

"So. Jaal went even crazier and accidentally hurt you? Again?" He slaps the screen, leaving a watery mark on Saturn's turned cheek. "Aren't you tired of being his punching bag?"

"Wow," I drawl. "It's amazing you weren't a psychoanalyst before the presidency; you read people so well." I cough into my elbow, ruining the well-thrown shade. "But seriously?" I toss my tongue around my mouth, tasting remnants of iron. "Yes. Everyone thinks this chaos is the work of suicidal planets, and I'm dabbling in metaphysics myself, but I'm not an idiot. Jaal set this whole thing up, clearly." I wave a flippant hand. "His valiant act of stealing engine-exhaust-aurorae and eating blood opals wasn't to save my ass—it was an attempt to save his."

I expect a classic drunken cackle, but his overstuffed lower lip retreats under his flawless teeth. "So, he's dead."

I laugh and shake my head. "He should be." But it dawns on me—the way sunlight drips into Saturn's lopsided rings and torn auric field—I'm glad he's alive. I don't know how or why, but the realization starts in my head wound and sinks down into a contorted ribcage. Death would be too simple for him. "No, he…well, we think he jacked himself up with a makeshift Galaccine. Last-minute effort to prove his experiment works. But I…don't really know what happened. Or what will happen."

"Puddles of Jesus, that's not part of the plan." With his elbow propped against the wall, Micah gawks, sipping apocalyptic gossip through a straw. His celestine blue eyes blanche in Saturn's light.

"There is no plan. Not anymore." I slap the wall, making another visual indent on Saturn's slippery icefall. Shapes blur and scatter, weak and offended by our touches. "I don't care what Sye says. We can't save humanity the way you want to."

"What do you mean?"

I shut my eyes to stop the surge of emotional color. "I mean– Jaal's mechanical conduit system is shot. It can't perform his plan, or yours. He was so determined his idea would work, he overdosed on it. He doesn't even know you all vetoed his Galaccine. If he finds out…" I thumb the Sens-goggles hanging around my neck, considering calling Lutfi.

Micah elbows my ribs. "Well, our plan might not be his Galaccine, but it's the Galaccine this solar system needs if it's going to be strong again." His vanilla cheekbone twitches. "For the good of all."

"You know, I'd never heard you people say that until Sye did. What's that about, anyway? When has a phrase like that ever lead to success?"

He rubs his pale throat, leaving pink splotches, and changes the subject. "How do you know Jaal won't die before he has the chance to ruin our plan?"

My brows pinch my third-eye. "I told you: he already ruined it. If he dies, we're screwed, because we depend on his knowledge and now his…experimental body. If he lives, we're still screwed, because he's a fucking mess."

207

His bluish chin hikes to the ceiling as he laughs. "C'mon, Zenith," he whines, producing a mini vodka bottle from his fake chainmail sleeves. He's the first person I've met who has worse fashion sense than Sid. "Don't let Sye and me be wrong about you. You're braver than you look."

My voice spikes a couple octaves in a mocking child's voice. "Gosh, thanks, Mister. But I ain't sure what you mean." If I keep joking like we're good pals, maybe this whole thing will become hilarious.

He opens the bottle; it glints faintly purple in the screen's waltzing indigo light.

Before he snogs the nozzle, I pluck it from him and swallow a shot. It tastes like pine needles and stings my throat, but I'm determined to enjoy the rest of life—even if that means getting trashed during the last few hours.

"Thirsty?" Micah snickers, throwing me a robotic wink. The apples of his cheeks swell, struggling to fit his stiff face.

"Just for that comment, I'm drinking all of it." I toss back the rest.

Beyon enters across from us, through an archway made of old copper pipes. It's the only flourish of decoration in the bland room, except for him now, of course. His bruise-blue and silver suit are alien against the beige Sens-screen, but the room senses his arrival. Faint, shadow-like starworks are projected in his honor.

"We have more palatable drinks in the foyer," he offers, adjusting his crunchy, metallic lapels.

"And by palatable, you mean…?"

"Ice wine and fire cider." He bows, revealing a crown of sweat on his inky scalp. His stature is stiffer than Micah's face. "Courtesy of President Sye and her Canadian neighbors."

I nod and slap the wall, surging past him. Everything's ending, but I'm just getting started. "Then that's where I'll be."

Each president grabs a bicep. I flinch, but their Yin-Yang eyes are swarmed with veiny desperation.

"What's wrong, boys?" I ask, embracing Elisha Sye's power-by-proxy.

"Aside from the obvious?" Micah raises his eyebrows as much as he can with a plastic forehead.

"Hush." Beyon's free hand strokes his lover's jaw.

Cringing, I wave both hands in their stupidly privileged faces. "Yes, hello, I'd like to go five minutes without being sexually har—"

208

"You've got to kill him," Micah blurts. Decorum is thrown aside, along with any sense of dignity. His smirk morphs, pink silicon bubbles protruding from a tucked grimace.

"But he's your husband," I gasp, hoping this is a stupid joke. For an alcoholic, he sobers up fast, donning a dark aura and heavy, sulking eyes.

"Not me," Beyon snaps, his forehead vein popping. "Jaal Nadir."

Sickening silence is followed by blubbering laughter. I can't stop it—my belly shoves manic cackles out in vomit-like colors, 'til tears stick to my lashes.

Losing patience and an auric front, Beyon sweeps a hand over my mouth. "As much as my husband enjoys joking, we are not." He removes his hand, pulling spit strings from the corners of my mouth.

I inhale with the shuttering lungs of a child who's been reprimanded, tears skiing down one cheek. My brain toys with the idea of insanity, how simple it would be to submit to its clutches. But then they'd want to kill me too.

He wipes his hand on a rose gold pocket square, nostrils flaring. "I'm sure this is difficult for you," he reasons, tilting his head back and forth. "But it's also a great opportunity. As I said before, we know you. We know your motives. We know your talents."

I follow his flitting eyes to my hip, where the gun and knife rest snugly. My gut shrivels.

He clears his throat. "You have plenty of reasons to kill him—"

"I have plenty of reasons to do a lot of things."

"—least of all being the fact that you're in his will for a hefty gem sum."

"I'm sorry, what?" I strain to break away from them, and they only let me go out of confusion. My hands slide from my wet eyes to dig into my braid crown, plucking bundles of wire-wrapped shock from my aura.

"You didn't know?" Micah rubs my shoulder. This time, I let him. Numbness ties skin to muscle to bone. Knees weakening, I sit on the floor in crumpled crisscross and stare at his snakeskin sandals and Beyon's velvet loafers.

As if I could contain any more emotion or thought, as if it didn't sting enough to know nothing about my ex-boyfriend's past.

Beyon nods. "We have access to all his legal documents, which he updated shortly after coming down with the Fever. He may be a mystery to you and the rest of the country, but to us, he's as simple as any man. All he wants is security, and that includes leaving you with…mutual benefits."

"B-but I'm…I'm not…he doesn't even…" The words spin in my head, refusing to leave, tracing dark energy lines behind my eyes. I could cry again, but it would probably break the Sens-bandage's numbing hold on my neurons. I bite my quivering lip and imagine cells stitching themselves together over my parietal lobe.

"Don't worry about it." Micah kneels next to me. A stinging waft of lavender beer and sauerkraut siphons a couple more tears. "You'll get the compensation you deserve. That's all that matters."

"He could just give it to me now. I shouldn't have to…wait 'til he's dead."

"It's safer this way," Beyon assures. "If he dies, the system can be safe again."

"Oooh," I breathe in wet mockery. "Can't have the *system* in danger, can we, Chief?"

I know I've hit hard because his irises ignite like rolling coals.

"Everything's changing fast," Micah explains clumsily, wringing his wrists. "Jaal is a wild complication, especially now. He wants to take more energy and condense it further, which ruins any hope we have for reestablishing balance. His plan is obsolete, and so is he."

"He's already tried to kill himself, at least twice." My teeth clench and grind. "If he can't, no one can, and I won't. Not again."

"Again?" Batting his lashes, Micah tilts his head. He's got that look that other gaybies used to give me in high school, when I knew something I shouldn't and they wanted hot tea.

Meanwhile, Beyon couldn't care less about my personal trauma. Or maybe he's not as clueless as his brain-fried husband. He towers above us and pats Micah's fluffy head, unwilling to bend to our level. "We know you've been through more than one person should be able to handle, but this is crucial to our cause."

"What cause?" I accidentally rip a hair out of my head. "There *is* no cause, I said that. First you want me to snub Jaal's leadership, and now you want him dead. Don't you have assassins for this kind of thing? Leave me out of it."

I don't look up at Beyon, but I can feel his frustration dripping over my scalp like a cracked egg. His pent-up rage practically peels the bandages off me, but I refuse to be manipulated by anyone or anything else.

He starts to pace with his hands clasped behind his back.

"We thought you'd want to do it," Micah murmurs, still peering at me hopefully. "After everything he put you through."

"Yeah, and you also thought I'd wanna be fingerbanged by someone I just met." I roll my eyes despite the sinking ache. Cement sits behind each eyeball, pressing against gray matter. I cough and tuck my knees against my chest. "You think you know me 'cause you know what happened to me. Record upon record of scandalous stories probably sit in your filing cabinets. But you don't know anything. My desires and preferences aren't yours to explore and exploit."

While they cool each other off in hushed tones and slushy auras, I play a mental song to the beat of my heart against chest and thighs. With each shifting vertebra, a different note echoes behind my inner ear, healing physical and mental punctures. It's not as powerful as real music—fingerprints kissing metal-wound chords—but it's enough to take the edge off this dizzy, tipsy breakdown.

Remembering the promise of ice wine in the foyer, I stand, rub my eyes, and sway. They move to catch me, but I thrust a hip to the side and regain balance.

"I won't kill him," I announce, raising a loopy index finger. "You'll have to find a new asshat, I mean—assassin."

Twenty-Six

"You're drunk," Reiki notes upon my return, wrapping a thick coppery braid around her gold-inked forearm. The natal tattoo glints in my bedroom's dimmed light, drawing me in. She rests against the headboard with a pillow in her lap, waiting for my swirly skull to retire there.

"That's how we get shit done around here," I reply with a perfectly timed tongue-pop.

She covers her face, mostly to hide amusement. "Only you would get drunk while concussed and claim it to be productive." Her teeth flash like a wink. "Did they harass you again?"

I lean on the door frame with a hip and elbow, tossing freed curls to one side. "Not in the way you'd think." The bandage on the back of my head loosens. "But they did make more outrageous assumptions about my personal life." My gaze sinks to her ichthyic legs crossing and uncrossing over the sheets.

"Well, they can join the cult," she says, smiling crookedly.

I clear my throat. "Y'know...I should've known it wasn't you in that Sens-vision...you didn't have your natal tattoo..." Words slip and slide, a song played on wine glass rims.

With her mouth drawn taut, she nods and folds her hands. "Also, I wouldn't have kept going if you asked me to stop."

"Mmm," I agree, sloshing onto the bed. The room tilts, making me giggle. "But what if I asked you to keep going?"

Silence fuels lingering ideas that fill the space between us. Our pink-and-blue auras sink into each other as spongey clouds.

"You're the monarch of mixed messages, you know that?" She chuckles while I curl into her lap.

"You're one to talk," I giggle, tugging her forearm into my line of sight. Freckles scatter the natal chart, making it vibrantly emotive.

She pulls away so hard, I almost scratch her wrist.

"Sorry." My clammy fingers retreat.

"It's okay." She shifts slightly, adjusting the pillow under my head. Coolness leaks into my scalp.

She clutches my skull and faces me back toward the wardrobe. Poetic songs written in eyeliner scrawl its side, some from years ago and some from our recent sleepovers. My neck muscles unravel and my head gets heavier in her lap.

"Stop fighting," her voice cascades into my ear, coupled with the rustling of the bandage being removed.

"I'm not," I protest, craning my neck to look at her.

"I was talking to myself."

"Oh." One side of my mouth cinches up. "I just outed myself, didn't I?"

Her laughter falls frothily into my ear, sliding over pressure points behind my jaw. "A little."

I close my eyes and imagine clockwork shadows cycling each golden notch in her irises. Booze makes visualizations ten times more vivid and confusing. "What are you fighting?"

"Feelings," she says through a pinched throat. "For you."

"Oh." A tornado tickles my stomach. "I'm sorry."

A nervous cough escapes her. "Now I hope you're the one talking to yourself, because you don't owe anyone else an apology." Her breathing shifts with the discussion topic. "Don't mess with your own head and heart just because everyone else does."

"They all think they know me so well…" I cringe and shake my head, frizz clinging to blankets. "But no one does…I'm not even sure I do." My chest aches.

"Not even me?" She cradles the back of my head, but instead of the usual ice-tones, a cluster of heat explodes.

I curl further, neck begging to sever so the rest of my body can ignore the pain. But even as I think that, stabs scatter, morphing into a dull simmer.

"I…don't know."

"Of course you do. You feel it with every part of yourself." Her vibrating throat draws my energy closer, revitalizing the need to heal.

While one numbs my skull, her other hand plucks energy from my forehead, unraveling black threads from a sobbing third-eye. Aches are expelled from back to front, and I can't help but think about the crude sexual fantasy, how that was also back-to-front-and-all-over-the-place. Subconscious fiction and mindful reality collide. But where I'd usually find crusted guilt, there's only a deep-seeded calm.

The space between my overworked mind and hurting heart shrinks, but at the same time, walls dissolve and leave endless fields in their place. I feel okay. More than okay. I feel like I belong.

Her pale, steady fingers pinch a metaphysical dust bunny in front of me.

"This," she explains with the same patient teacher's voice she used weeks ago, "is everything you hate about yourself, everything you resist, everything you don't want to see." A rising wave of tears overcomes her, but she blinks them away, no longer harboring energy that isn't hers. "You've hid it for so long, it's gone dark. Can't see itself, or anything else. If you're going to save the solar system, you've got to save yourself first." Her light laughter sprinkles, polishing the words so they seem less grave.

"No pressure," I deadpan, biting the inside of my cheek. The mass shifts from physical to metaphysical, a hand-sized black hole. "What's it made of, specifically?"

Rose gold energy leaks from the corners of her smile. "See for yourself."

Ushered by some divine force—or maybe just her bolstering gaze—I sit up and cup my hands, ready to receive without question this time.

With her aura overflowing green and gold, she hands me the dark sphere.

In moist palms, it doesn't feel terrifying. It barely feels like anything, at first, lacking weight or temperature or texture. Yet, it's so fully present, staring me down, challenging me. Somehow, it's both me and not, a superfluous energy-tumor created from overthinking and underfeeling. Self-hatred as the lack of self-love. Everything and nothing balanced in shaking hands.

Truth is siphoned from my lips without full awareness. "This is what makes it so hard for me to trust you, isn't it? All the fuckery that ever happened to me, turned into..." I try to meet her gaze, but the sphere's swirling faces make me zone out—a memorial space meant only for me.

I'm hit with a plastic stench, the kind that Sens-nails reek of. The ghost of Jaal's fake nails raking up my spine, leaving marks with the heat of lit matches and the hardness of diamonds—not because I asked, but because I didn't say no.

214

The sphere swivels and so do I. I'm only vaguely aware of Reiki's hand on my back, replacing the scalding scars with love. Senses shift with the wind.

Muffled at first, there's yelling. Berating. Not Jaal and me—although that plays in chorus with the rest—but Mama to Mother, the night before I left. The night she tried to strangle her to death, and I just sat there and watched in horror, until Lutfi broke down the door to save his sister.

My taste buds recall flavors—blood when I bit my tongue too hard, spicy chocolate on holidays, cottonmouth when I poorly tried to make friends, wine all the time, vodka with Jaal (Jaal with vodka). I taste the self-hatred, smell the regret, hear the fear, see the pain, feel...everything. All this toxicity I consumed like medication—morphed into several lonely selves. But these senses are vessels for experience, not identity. My memories aren't my shadow.

My shadow is depth and expansion and chaos. It's the act of growth itself.

It turns crookedly like a planet or star, and fond memories of Syzygy come to mind. I start to love the damn thing and all its spindly insecurities. Not only because it needs love, but because I need to give love.

Immediately touched by the lighthearted spark, it crackles. My chest rises and falls like tidal waves, continually neutralizing the energy until it feels like a micro-sun. Warmth puddles under my curved fingers and swims the span of life and love lines, chalky wrinkles, and permanent ink.

When I hunch forward as if leaning in for a kiss, the silver globe floats over flexed forearms, trembling biceps, past swelling lungs, and settles in the center of my being—the soul's throne. Absolute heart-space.

Shadow and light integrate. I'm whole.

Inhaling deeply, I blink and adjust to stabilized lighting, spots dusting my vision. Reiki's aura washes the room with color. It could be dark in here and I would still see everything clearly in her presence.

My lower chakras relax into acceptance of my ancestral wisdom, pain, and sexual fluidity. Energy flows upward to fuel my sense of identity and love, combing my throat and all the wounds there. My upper chakras hum like tuning forks and crystal bowls, matching harmonies 'til the urge to sing is yanked from the depths of my being. "I make music without music. Like, I can feel it..."

Through cyan tears, Reiki laughs and rubs her hands together. "Primordial sound. You are music. Heart-centered vibration. It's how you heal—recognizing that who you are isn't the same as your experience." Her hyper voice lilts with my rhythm.

Unable to hide overwhelming gratitude, I scoot forward and snag her in a hug, burying my face in her neck. Her aroma takes over, one step into freshwater.

Our arms squeeze so hard, we both shake. Shoulders and ribs clench as our hearts leave scarlet ink impressions on each other. Chords strike again, more fitting, reaching upper octaves to capture existential oddities—like my attraction to all genders or the way she has a different limb in each multiverse.

Incredible peace settles between us, knit by auras and physical touch.

As we part, I reach for her forearm, but she pulls away. Our eyes flit back and forth, and while mine land on her mouth, hers steady themselves on the bridge of my nose.

"Can I—" we begin in unison.

Awkward laughter ensues. She gestures for me to continue, her aura splitting open.

"Can I see your tattoo?" It's not the question I planned on asking, but it feels right. "I haven't had my head out of my ass long enough to really look at it."

With a stony face, she nods.

I lift her tattooed forearm with shaky hands. She flinches but moves in closer so I can examine it. Her energy gives in, the same way mine did moments ago.

Now, I'm decent at astrology, thanks to Uncle Lutfi. But where I expect to see an illustration of Planet Earth dabbling with Mercury and Jupiter in Pisces or even Aquarius, I find a few speckled asteroids. Instead, Earth flirts with Venus on the brink of Cancer, which means her sun resides in the beginning of Capricorn.

"Hey, this is cool…we have the same…" Everything. Down to the last degree, our tattoos have identical orbits, shapes, and planetary positions. Everything except for the ink color.

I search her bursting blush and haywire aura. "I don't…get it."

But then I look again. Mercurial points swim like tadpoles on her skin, shifting positions and angles. I blink quickly, but the mirage doesn't disappear. If anything, it enhances, rippling against veins and tendons. Confused and always shifting to match something— someone—else.

216

She cradles her arm close to her chest. "I'm sorry. I'm so, so sorry."

"No apologies," I scold gently, running my thumb over slippery ink. "If I can't, you can't." Soft laughter plummets from my tongue, still warped by alcohol. "So, that's how you broke in, huh? You can copy natal charts...What is it, some fancy ID-changing tech in your skin?" I rub the back of my neck and then my crown, grabbing a fistful of curls that aren't crusty with blood. My aura slinks inward sheepishly. Even though she's the one whose secret is revealed, it feels embarrassing for me to ask such personal questions, almost more embarrassing than my attraction to her.

In this mutable tattoo, I've uncovered a deep-set insecurity of hers.

Confirming, her lips curl into her teeth. She shivers.

I pull the skin under my eyes down with flat palms, exasperated. "Was it Jaal's tech? Another stupid experiment?"

She shakes her head, peering at her forearm like it's a curse. "N-no, it's...always been this way. It's not just you. It happens with everyone. It's how I can access Jaal's trove..."

"Is that why your face changes too?"

"No...that's different." She inspects the frayed ends of her hair.

"Can you teach me?"

"I don't know."

I pet her fluxing forearm. "Pan, Ki. You could start a galactic war with that kind of ability."

Twenty-Seven

My ego judges its spirit again. Every warning-story I know screams, *don't trust her*, but what I feel bashes those words to pieces.

After all, our pocket of the universe will collapse at any moment, and I'm determined to enjoy every second prior. Even if it means sitting in silence with someone who also struggles to express their truth.

Strangely, we switch places. She falls asleep in my lap the way I would have in hers, a soft blush painting her face. Copper hair dives out of her braids and swims over blue sheets like steampunk dolphins. Cuddling my thigh and hip, her warmth melts into mine.

Her crown chakra leaks silver and gold in a miniature celebration, relieved to have freedom in a safe space. I can't believe I told her she couldn't have both.

Peaceful silence is only disturbed by my noshing on the snacks she prepared for us. Dried mangoes, brownies, pretzel wands, protein bars, and cactus tea.

Am I eating my feelings? Probably. But I don't know what else to do, and a ship's captain needs fuel too—especially on the brink of existential breakdown.

I glance at her forearm, and my third-eye tingles with expectation. Theory and philosophy mingle in my monkey-brain, taking ideas and running. She could be a giant conspiracy, a distraction to keep me from finishing the job.

But there is no more job, I remind myself. *What drives me isn't what…or who it used to be…The Skyscraper has fallen. Now I'm rebuilding. Remembering.*

Her natal chart settles on a mix of mine and someone else's—maybe her own—and it shimmers like fish scales. Gray haze covers minor chakras on the loose tendons in her wrist—probably where acupuncture needles once gathered—making a steady link to her throat. It's not just the ink that's hiding something.

Adrenaline trickling, I retract a curious hand when she snores softly and rubs her nose.

The only way to know for sure if I can trust her—no, to remind myself that I can—is to use what she taught me, what my moms would've taught me if those roots hadn't rotted too soon.

Breathing deep, I focus on the flow of energy through my body.

Since the drunken shadow integration, I've felt more like a fountain than a person, able to flow through any blockade.

What's your shadow, Reiki? I rest a prickling hand on her collarbone. The words echo through my brain and spinal cord, firing neurons and spiking hairs.

I capture the feeling of song without physically singing, but this time I reflect it toward her. Blood rushes to my hands, supporting waves of vibrational incision. Awash in light, her energy is a compass, pointing out the blocked spots and chakra smudges.

Weirdly, when light sheds, grayness darkens in her forearm and throat, the intensity making her curl tighter against me. With a hand squashed between her chin and collarbone, I try to pluck the fibrous energy like she did for me.

But it's lucid and stringy, clinging to itself. Dozens of double, triple, quadruple knots choking back truth. It's so bizarre—I wouldn't have guessed she could be so hypocritical, but it proves she's human.

I wince from the sting of knots unfurling. White spots scatter over my natal tattoo. *If I could just loosen the vibration a little more, I could help her, like she helped me…*

Sweat stipples my brow as I hunch forward, cupping a glob of strings that refuse to be untied. I could tug them up from their tangled depths, but it would hurt us both. I could take them from her, but I've seen how that ends. It would be like swallowing a star, invigorating destruction.

But then I recall the music, the hum moving through each cell, every touch the strike of a chord.

My lips part, forming a bubble the color of dragon spit, throat and third-eye working together to create a new remedy. Silent song. It flows in rivulets, but looks more like Jupiter's swirling surface, oil spill on a crystal globe.

Screw the Galaccine, I think—no, feel. *We're the remedy.* Confidence swells, scooping out any doubt or worry I once held. I can't deny

219

something so visceral and pure. If Jaal can prove his ramshackle plans work, so can we.

Without reaching into her and hooking the energy out, it's transmuted. I feel every inch of chaos and calm around her, but instead of soaking into me it dissolves in our personal ether. A shared resource.

At first, it's a soothing experience. We have similar energies, streams that constantly evolve to fill space.

Brainwaves crash to enhance reconnected flow. Flavored sounds. Visual scent. Earth's finest Sens-drugs can't compare.

And then it shifts.

Again, my perception of present time is replaced by an artist's rendering, but this artist knows what she's doing. Waves of shapely color heave over us, collapsing and inflating bodies, raking souls of dried-up delusions. What's left is something unthinkable—truths that can be glimpsed, but mostly only felt. Movies shared inside a dull headache. One brain sleeping, the other awake.

In my perception, our bodies morph.

I'm larger than her, coated in fur. She's covered in layers of different cloths, shivering into me while I try to sing a lullaby that comes out in whimpers. I don't know where we are, but everything is frozen, and I'm so hungry.

Icy pine floods my nostrils, and then liquid iron. Heavy eyelids make it difficult to focus on her burnished face for long. Smoke coils in frightening pillars. Instead of drifting off, I open a toothy mouth and howl.

Beyond veiny trees, birds scatter.

The vision shifts, and what sound like vintage guns popping are fireworks—old ones that stay near the ground, littering lakes and cornfields. Ancient celebrations that costed way too much and lasted all night.

In this panorama, I'm human again. We're a pair of very naked teenagers, but this isn't the first time seeing each other that way. I'm stark white, and she's delightfully dark. Both without tattoos of any kind.

When I glance down, dysmorphia lingers in the taunting pink scars on my chest where breasts used to be. But when she looks at me, she doesn't see a lost boy in a girl's body. She sees me as I am. As I do now—soul captured in a body's ambiguous embrace. There is Love in this connection, too.

Grinning, she squeezes my hand while we count down to the firework finale. Our voices melt as good as I expect them to, soapy soprano and baritone united. On "GO!" we jump into water together, light-streaked shadow tugging us under.

But then a storm cracks inside our collective consciousness.

Rain pelts slender windows. We're in the kind of car you need all four limbs to drive. Gears slip into first, second, third, and I realize Reiki's-soul-inside-a-different-body is driving. Vessel inside vehicle.

220

Through wet smog and sheets of ice-water, she pushes the car further, shifting gears with each synchronized click of the controls.

He's one of many faces bearing Reiki's femme fatale eyes, with a boyish jaw, strong nose, and auburn stubble. Gold-encrusted skin and hazel energy in the mouth. When the gears hug fifth, a broad palm sweeps over my bare thigh. He throws a side-eyed smile at me, distracted by what I can only assume is a flawlessly painted face.

There's a quaint confidence between us, the sensational knowledge that our bodies have only known each other for a few hours but hooking up will be the best decision of our young lives.

A better decision would be to drive slower, but it's too late.

Wheels spin vainly on a dancefloor of water. The grip on my thigh tightens, and then his arm constricts like an extra belt across my chest. We slide toward a steaming underpass.

One of us—maybe both—lurches so violently we almost fall out of bed. My whole body clamps down on her, remembering the Now. Falling into itself. Myself.

Awake, she grips my waist and stares up at me. I hold her clammy hands and squeeze.

"It's okay," I lie through a stunned mouth. "Just a nightmare."

She shakes harder than I do, panting as if she's been running. Her whole body convulses, energy whirring without knowing why. Gray blockages leak onto the sheets. She rubs her neck. Truth unfolds in the form of bruises.

"What did you do?" When it comes out, it isn't her voice.

It's mine. From a long time ago. Vocals so dark and deep, they were hidden until now. Thunder splutters to be heard over the wind. Buried under eons of karmic shadow, another memory bleeds into the agony and confusion of this life.

"What did you do?" My blockhead of an incarnation demands, punching the wall and leaving a dent. Black skin on a white wall. Dirt stuffed under fingernails. Yin-yang manifesting improperly, dysfunction unfolding.

I've caught her doing something she shouldn't. I can't remember what, but it doesn't matter. The rage is palpable, rock and fire twisted in the pit of my stomach and up my neck.

Half-dressed, caramel-colored, her beaded braids wild and dirty, she lies at the bottom of the stairs, where my feet will be in five, four, three, two—CRUNCH. My heel jabs her jaw like bomb shrapnel.

This time, she wails, and it crushes me, but I keep going. I know who she is, I know what she's done, the families we've made and the moments we've shared, and still I smash her bones like glass, beckoning decades of bad luck.

My perfectly imperfect reflection. Shattered.

Self-hatred turned homicidal.

In the present, I gasp.

When consciousness returns to these skinny limbs and aching head, realities set in. Each a different pill for a different sickness. So many in so little time and space—my hypocritical spirit experiencing trauma from various angles, in endless loops.

That wasn't me...that could never be me. That...that's Jaal.

But this isn't science or psychology—it's the kind of fact I know so deep within, it's not a fact anymore. Even quantum mechanics can't touch it. Only my soul can.

I went into this, wondering if I could trust her soul, when it's my own I feel betrayal from.

Every bead of energy in my body screams to be released, bonded by the memory of action.

In the room, here and now, we're sitting across from each other, foreheads locked. One steady hand on each of my shoulders, she tries to console me. Energetic petals wrap me and tie bows with bandages.

My body folds and shutters, feverish in its own way. Balling the collar of her romper in my fist, I can't speak. I just stare at her throat, where grayness is gone. Then down at my hands, where the grayness went. Skin, ears, eyes, mouth, nose—drenched in mercurial paste.

"You remember." Her voice is plunking rain.

"R-remember what?"

Her mouth canopies my eyes, catching muted tears and blowing them away like dandelion seeds. She holds me. "What we share." No hint of pain or remorse lingers. It almost sounds like ecstatic relief. "What we've learned together."

I didn't mean to hurt you...myself... Thoughts echo, aching to solidify. I can't remember whose life is whose.

The room spirals. I lean over the edge of the bed, gagging. Instead of vomit, I eject, "Hurt people hurt people." The lesson that clatters against my ribs and peels skin to reach spirit.

"Yeah," she concedes, tears mirroring mine. Steadying me to face her again, she adds, "But healing yourself heals others, especially when they reflect so much of you." Another kiss dots my third-eye. "And here we are."

I know now why having a sixth sense for the first time made me lunatic. Not only does it open you; it reconnects you to everything you've done and everyone you've been. It's true, what the Conduits and quantum mystics say—we live more than once.

222

"I've been channeling these memories for a while," she continues, brushing sweat and tears off my jaw. "That's why my body shifts. My cells scatter to find Truth. And they found yours...ours."

While my lungs expand and shrivel, stuttering with every puff, I meditate on the memories I just witnessed, searching for more meaning. A sign in her consistently muddy eyes, or an omen in the familiar curl of my toes.

"I...I think—"

Her icicle thumb smudges my lips together. "Hey." Our foreheads tap one more time before she pulls away. "You've worked the upper chakras enough. Let's work on grounding." Her empathetic wince flourishes into a proud grin. She glances at my lips and settles on my eyes. "Just...stay sober, Cap. That's how we get shit done around here."

Twenty-Eight

*S*weat coats my nose and chin as I poke my bubble-masked face out the emergency pod door. With the rest of my body still safely under stellaglass, I yank one of the controls upward, activating a false gravity field around the top of my ship—another surprise feature Reiki added when we were on Earth. Unlike an aura, it's invisible, but as a bodily anchor, tangible. Instead of feeling like I'll be sucked into black-satin-oblivion, I breathe recycled oxygen with a dazed sigh, settling into this new gravitational dome.

Reiki waits below, donning gloves and a suit that match mine and carrying a satchel full of—apparently—"grounding tools."

Obviously, there's urgency in the air, but I'm hoping that whatever she's got for me will help our cause.

I elbow-crawl onto stellaglass before standing and spreading my arms across the sky. Still carrying a wish to sing with the stars, she follows me, finding her way through the metal rungs and glassy porthole more easily than I did.

The only thing uncovered is our hair, which we let loose in honor of mutual freedom. Edges of the bubble masks morph to our hairlines and temples, suctioning to our jaws and drooping like whipped egg whites in a long tube of the ship's oxygen supply. Our black and copper locks rise and snag, only to fall when gravity regulates.

From this angle, we're in the pews of an arena-themed cathedral, viewing Saturn through the eyes of a worshipping audience.

The ice dragon emerges from shadow and circles the gaseous ball, attempting to hold chunks of frozen rock and vapor together with sheer will. Its ruby eyes glance toward us, but it shows no desire to

224

move, too focused on the task. We're not alone in our mission to harmonize and heal.

Our voices careen the inside of the bubble masks before reaching each other—a trick between regular and Sens-tech.

"You know," I murmur. "A year, or even a month ago, if someone had told me I would save the solar system by saving myself, I would've smacked them…"

She watches me, one eye swimming in glitter, the other shielded by condensation.

My throat curdling, I gesture to Saturn. "I was…ehum. Skeptical when you said planets have personalities, that each is alive. But you're right. Even when he's falling apart, Saturn's still a control freak."

"You're turning into a mystic, like your uncle," she teases with a mischievous wink. "Or even worse—me."

"Too late," I confess, picking apart a couple frizz-glued hairs dangling at her masked jaw.

"You're right." Her gloved fingers surround mine. "You know truth before you think you know it, don't you?"

"Is that a riddle?"

"No, it's a cosmic fact," she replies, twirling her free wrist while I hold her other at my chest. "As soon as you met me, you recognized me, but you reacted poorly because you didn't think you knew yourself…or could love yourself. But the truth is…you are love. Infinitely. You're love in action, playing a part. We all are…some are born knowing it. Others forget as soon as they penetrate the ether and hit rock."

My middle chakras stir, a black hole swarming behind my naval, consuming all the old concepts of what is true.

The presidential ship sheds light from behind us, casting a spooky spotlight, drowning our quivering silhouettes. I think about how ridiculous it is that my life—no, all life—is basically a form of entertainment. An endless power-play. No escape from the drama, because in some sick way, it's fun.

None of that scares me anymore, though. What quakes my existential core is the mere concept that there's more to living than just this moment, and yet at the same time, this moment is all there is. My head spins just from the thoughts. Cold sweat intensifies, a watery clamp around my neck.

"Remind me how this is supposed to be grounding."

Svelte and feather-like, she looms over me just enough to touch foreheads. Even in a skin-tight, papery space suit, her truth shines through and mingles with mine.

In explanation, she shrugs off her bag and produces a collapsible bo staff and a pair of clear quartz nunchaku. "If you can work with energy, you can work with anything." Smirking, she tosses the staff. Suspended in the dome's thinner air, it cracks open and unfolds fully, gliding into my hands as if designed to fit them.

I scan the bone-like bo, thumbing the tentacular ruby designs carved into wood. It looks like a petrified relic the way it wrinkles and bleeds on itself.

When I look up, she's handling the nunchaku too quickly for my eyes to keep up with. Quartz points spin around her neck, shoulders, and cinched waist, 'til she bends to snag them just below her knees. The motion's so fast and fluid, I don't know whether to be turned on or terrified.

"Don't freak out." Slowly, she whips the nunchaku in a figure eight at her side. "I'm not asking you to do anything you can't." Then, like a good little ninja, she bows. "Now that you've remembered...your body will remember too. We've fought together, side-by-side, in many lives."

I pucker my lips to blow hair out of my face, forgetting the mask. "There weren't any show-downs in the visions."

"You haven't seen them all," she confesses, smirking. "Some would drive you crazy."

"Show me."

Snagging the challenge in my gaze, she shifts her stance. A flame sprouting in each pupil, she comes at me with all she's got.

I lunge to the side quicker than expected, fully aware of how rusty my recent injuries and habitual drinking have made me. Luckily, meditation has kept my mind limber, and therefore lubricated enough to act fast—sending the right signals to all the right places. No mixed messages this time.

At first, the bo rests at my side while I slip past her flinging advances. She doesn't give me much time to figure it out, but rather than getting overwhelmed, I sink back into familiar mindfulness, focusing on each shooting inhale and sidestep. Every contact point on my feet to the floor sparks a new channel of flow—acupressure for a warrior.

In a second's fraction, the floor's earth-mocking energy radiates into my soles, ankles, and rockets to my wrists. Only we would find grounding peace so far away from Planet Earth.

I juggle energy between my feet and hands, preparing to strike. Ruby-infused wood clacks against quartz in defense. But on the offense, I lurch, and the bo catches the nunchaku chain with a *ping*.

Refracted light glints in her eyes, turning them from fresh coffee to old lava. I see pools of our lives together. Breaths shared over space and time.

With every wrist flick and bicep clench, her energy cools while her body heats up.

Blunted quartz brushes my forearm, leaving a hair-thin scratch. Our eyes converge for a millisecond before she peels back and hits me again, this time in the abdomen.

Sweat runs hot, but the pain isn't enough to take me down. If anything, it sends air deeper into my lungs, drilling determination into organs.

My body zips past brain, doing before thinking, wingspan unraveling to get the most reach out of this weapon. Even against Reiki's wispy willow arms, the bo gives me power I'm not used to. Her swings miss my face by a mouth's width, and I bend my knees to dodge the blow and tap her thigh.

"Good." She returns the nunchaku under her arm, hip jutting to the side. "Everything has a vibration, Zen, even weapons. We take them for granted and use them for monstrous reasons…" With the next serpentine flail, she knocks my elbow, forcing my fingers open with an electric pop. The bo clatters to the floor. "But weapons aren't really weapons. They're like bodies. Just vessels for experience."

On static-slick feet, she slides up against me, cupping my elbow with her free hand. Immediately, the zinging pain dissolves.

"It wasn't just poetry when I said, 'healing yourself heals others,'" she explains, teetering between student and teacher. "Since everything in the physical universe has a vibration, everything is a vessel. You, me, these weapons…that's why it can hurt so much and feel so good in the span of seconds…you get filled up and emptied again and again…" Her lips stay open at the last word like unlaced ribbon.

While space-proof cloth shuffles between us, I squat down to snatch the bo while keeping eye contact, aware of what my face is level with. "Are we talking about sex again?"

She whacks me in the shoulder.

"Agh!" Dropping the bo again, I lean to one side and rub my arm. "It was just a question."

Fog hides her exhausted smile. "Zenith. I'm serious."

"Same."

Another clack, this time against my wrist.

She returns to her original stance, one foot swept behind her, nunchaku at the ready. "Remember learning about all the different origin stories of Planet Earth? The creation myths?"

"Do you?" My brow lurches. "You didn't live there very long."

"In this life, sure." She beams and taps between her eyes. "But I know how it was created. I remember."

I scoff to cover up laughter over how adorable she is, glancing at the endless velvety space just outside our dome. It bleeds metallic dust and gloss. "You remember, huh? Okay, Adam, tell me, then—which story is true?"

"All of them." She shrugs into me, puffing a sigh through pink cheeks. "I wish you'd take this seriously."

"And I wish you'd have some fun," I retort, grinning. "We're gonna die soon. Again." Another giggle escapes me. "If you wanted to teach me a lesson, you could've at least done it in the bedroom."

"Why?" She teases. "Are you sleepy?" Her pearly teeth poke through a lopsided smirk.

I tuck and roll, scoop the bo, and whack her in the back of the knees. She doubles over. I have enough time to prod her spine with the staff, but not enough time to keep her from yanking it up with the chain.

Backwardly, she pulls me toward her, and I stupidly refuse to let go. Chain loose, she frees an elbow and decks me in the chest.

I unfold and topple onto my back, groaning. Laughter follows close behind when she towers over me, a powerful gold glow emanating in the shape of dragon wings.

"Ah, I give in…" My voice leaps an octave when I tilt my head back and splay my arms in cruciform. "Ground me good, Ki." I close my eyes, tilt my head back, holding in laughter 'til my face burns, and then squint open an eye.

Straddling me, she shakes her head. "Now you're just outing both of us." At her touch, the bo staff collapses and she returns it to her satchel, along with the nunchaku. "Not sure why I ever worry about you, Cap. Like I said, you know before you think you do, and you know we've melded before."

"I still think you're talking about sex." I sniff recycled air, only to find the muted stench of cold plastic and a hint of sweat. With all this Sens-tech, sensory deprivation is highly appreciated.

"You joke to cope with this life's trauma." Her body curls like an autumnal leaf. "But yes…our bond has crossed spiritual and sexual boundaries. After all, sexuality is an echo of spirituality."

"Both can be misused," I add.

She nods, her smile unbreakable. "People fight over sex, but they have all-out wars over whose creation story is true, and then they come up with new ones every millennium. Which means that creation isn't history…it's now, the only constant, ever-evolving truth. Forever unfolding before us, with us, as us."

Our masks brush and flux, bubbles turning rainbow from the physical and energetic tension.

"And?" I ask, distracted by the friction between fibers in her irises, and the way her body slopes over mine like lyrics on instrumentals.

"And," she bubbles, "it's only the most important truth for you right now because you glimpsed our souls, saw such seemingly finite things become…infinite. Why do you feel that is?"

My heart trips over itself. I crane my neck and gaze outside. Saturn weeps into the dragon's shoulder. New ailments sprout in its swirling skin—collapsed gaseous caverns, bursting icy ligaments, and toppled gravity that bubbles like phlegm as it dissipates.

When I turn back to her, my neck cracks. "Tell me." Just like that, I'm begging again.

"When Divinity created Heaven and Earth, They also made man and woman—humans."

"That's an outdated tale…overused…"

"Exactly, because it's a myth, and so is gender." She beams, running a finger over the bridge of my nose. "And so is disunity." Her voice lowers. "Ancient testaments neglect to express one fact that we all feel down to our DNA—man was not man before woman was taken from him. He…*they* were both male and female at once. All and one. Divinity made Themself."

I laugh because this tangent reminds me of long nights with philosopher druggies, but also because I'm stunned that it makes sense.

Her breathy voice drives me wild. "Creation began because Divinity emptied itself. One flame split into Two. Cellular division on a cosmic scale, patterned across the matrix of time and space."

229

Saturn's dwindling glow stains my vision, but it calls me the same way Reiki's aura does. A challenge that promises redemption. A similar wavelength.

"Source was genderless before manifesting. We're twin souls, after our schism. This life is powerfully confusing, just like all the others, because we're still so used to being together. The reason I love you…the reason you hate Jaal so much…it all comes from the same burning need to be One again." So much conviction, with barely a pause to breathe. Her cheeks match a pastel pink aura.

Switches click within me, turning on power I haven't felt in years. "You…you love me?"

Her soothing alto tickles my ear. "We are Love; kind of impossible not to feel it too."

Lifting her face with my gloved hands, I want to feel her fully, but bubbles of all kinds prevent it.

"Anyway, yeah," she explains through a mouthful of grins, peeling herself off me. "That's why humans are so fluid. We're light—a particle and a wave—split into many containers. The uncomfy in-between."

My body lurches as if waking from a dream. "Oh, my fucking stars." My glove snags hair when it runs through it. "Sorry. I mean, I'm. Not sorry. But just. You made me realize." A huge, all-encompassing sigh sends tingles down to my toes. "I know how to save the planets."

In the fluid falls of sparkling dust in Saturn's gash, I see my tears. In the weird energy-dragons that circle its belly, I see the dragons of my conscious dreams, brimming with lavender, petrichor, lime. Whether they're hallucinations, sensual side effects, or meta-reality…they're there, and they call to me—the original, cosmic Sens-message.

Light energy is celestial blood, circulating in her shrinking pupils while I explain. "If we give the planets more aurorae, then they'll regenerate and stabilize. Energy into matter." I clap in staccato, the same way I did during our fashion shows. "Balance restored."

She scratches her head and props herself up with the other hand, aggravation still playing on her lips. "Aurorae is more than light, Cap. It's…essence."

"Which we all have. Right?"

A light cough, and throat chakra bruises return.

"Ki, you're a Conduit. You of all people should know where I'm going with this."

"Sure, Cap, but energy can't be created. Only moved. It sounds like you're saying a person's auric flow can feed an entire planetary field…and by that logic, an entire solar system."

"I know it's crazy, but crazy is what got us here," I spew, grateful that she hasn't pushed me away again. Breath runs ragged. "Jaal was right to make a Galaccine, only he didn't do it right. There was too much emphasis on matter, on perfecting cellular immunity…He forgot about what lies beyond. Quantum fields."

Her hesitant wince slowly morphs into a shocked smile. Her jaw hangs and tilts like one of her astrobatic moves. "You want to return vibration to its vessel. Light to a dimming lamp."

"Theoretically, yeah." I thumb her throat, wandering over the blueness 'til it lightens. "But I'm hoping…just maybe…with our combined energy channels, and Jaal revved up with aurorae and opal juice, we won't need fancy tech or scientific experiments or even a conventional plan." I shake my head, hair rustling against glass. "C'mon, Ki. Let's do what we're meant to do, in this life and the next." My hands move to her face again. "Be unconventional with me."

As usual, my most badass and meaningful moments are interrupted by Jaal's fist hitting a hard surface. I look down to see him slap the stellaglass and flash me a curious beam.

Plainly ignoring him, I meet Reiki's gaze.

She's more distracted by the ruckus below than I am. "Jaal will think some kind of sacrifice is necessary…" She blinks rapidly. "After all, massive amounts of energy only move when matter dies."

"I know, but we have each other and—"

More rapping on the glass, enough to cause our bodies to vibrate.

I sigh heavily, clouding the rest of my mask. It only clears when I roll out from under Reiki, thrust open the trapdoor, and stick my head in to glare. "Y'know, Jaal, you're just like a demon, getting summoned at the mention of your name." An indignant sniff. "Y'look like one, too."

Twenty-Nine

*A*mong the ship's shadows, Jaal is ablaze with crystalline rainbows. While he could dye Saturn's body with his soaked aura, his physique is monochrome. Looping dreadlocks impossibly white, eyes mismatched, he seems fully non-human.

His calluses and wrinkles have vanished, replaced by a melted gleam. If I didn't know any better, I'd think he had an appointment with President Samson's plastic surgeon. He dons a slippery, cream pantsuit with an obscure logo—a pentagram made of penises—an empty weapon belt, and toe socks. His muscles press against plastic fabric the same way the Phoenix Compound begged to be released.

"Pan," I swear, grasping for an ounce of patience.

"Get down here." Jaal cinches his lips.

My jaw grinds between a smile and a scream. Reiki clings to me as we shimmy back inside, shutting false gravity off behind us. The dome collapses. The trapdoor seals tight.

I remove the bubble mask and wipe condensation off my cheeks. "To what do I owe this pain?"

He gets so close to me, I can feel his breath. Wafts of ash and pot on his skin have been replaced with burnt peppermint. The atoms of his body writhe with sticky aurorae, dying and regenerating constantly. He has one bronze eye and one silver eye, not because of Sens-tech, but because another side-effect has manifested. Instead of fighting the Fever, the makeshift Galaccine seems to be working with it, forcing him to scatter and be more pure energy than human.

"Aw, Tauris got your tongue?" I condescend. My heart flails in its cage. "I haven't spoken to you in hours…days…there must be something in that itchy throat chakra of yours."

232

"Honestly, thought you'd like to see me…now that I'm more…"—his marblesque eyes glide over Reiki—"your type."

Reiki sways out of the space garb like a snake shedding skin and hurls it back on its proper hanger. "I'd watch what you say, Jaal. Planets are famished. Overextending your energy out here is like a blood beacon."

Stifling my laughter, I return the masks to their compartment. "Y'know, this pod's a damn closet. I can't breathe in here." Sweat smears my temples, underarms, and lower back, making me shiver when I bend to strip. Clothing underneath settles back into its original shape. Rocking on the balls of my feet, I hang the suit next to Reiki's. "Let's talk in the cockpit."

Desperately, Jaal waves a blackened astral arm, but Reiki's and my auras deflect it. Where Reiki has energetic wings, he has tentacles. "Look at me, Z." His silver iris shrinks like a lunar eclipse. "Totally changed. No different than Reiki now."

"No. You two are universes apart."

"Maybe at one time, when I was careless…" He stands in front of me with open arms. "But now's different. We all know it. The past isn't real anymore."

"Really?" My voice spikes an octave. "Was it real when you seduced an eighteen-year-old and made him steal shit for you on the reg?" I crack my knuckles and create a protective mudra over my stomach, fingers laced. "Was it real when you called him your beloved in private, but to your rich friends, referred to him as a pet?" He opens his mouth, but I keep going. "Was it real when you gaslighted and coerced him at every turn? Was it real when you harassed him, even while he slept?"

He launches at me, and I raise my arms to defend myself, but Reiki strikes him in the wrist. The nunchaku wraps like a snake and yanks him back, glowing with her protective black aura.

Jaal's silver eye flashes. "Let go! He's mine; I can touch him if I want! He's not yours; he's mine!"

"I am my own," Reiki and I snap in unison, our voices barely decipherable.

He goes to swat me with his free hand, but a throng of dark energy holds him back. The same dark energy that damaged Reiki's vision a few weeks ago.

"Sid!"

Half-way out of the porthole, dressed like a damn cactus, Obsidian brandishes a dark energy crystal. He binds Jaal's wrists with nothing but pure force.

Jaal struggles against the flecks of bent shadow. "TREASON! MUTINY!"

Onyx follows Obsidian up through the trapdoor, speaking Hisphindi to try and calm their foster-brother.

"You always betray me, Nyx," Jaal spits. "Why do I ever trust you?"

I put my hand over my chest to slow my breathing. Reiki tucks the nunchaku back in her bag and hugs me. Her aura shifts from black, to silver, then pearl.

I now realize what Jaal meant by "my type." There's a reason why her tattoo shifts naturally; why her body feels like both gemstones and feathers; why she holds every life-memory we've ever shared behind a glassy forehead.

Even Jaal in all his blockheadedness begins to glow to match her, cells separating to seep luminescence, his body coursing with more energy than it's used to. For Reiki, that amount is nothing. She *is* energy. Conscious Light in a pretty, fluid flesh-suit.

I bend over and produce the bo staff from Reiki's bag. It lengthens and ignites at my touch. My chapped lips bleed from their grin.

Reiki keeps a hand on the small of my back. I stalk up to Jaal, through sticky static, and prod him in the chest. He breathes so intensely, he spits sparks.

I press the bo harder against him, creating a boundary between us. "You may be more energy than matter now, Jaal, but you haven't changed. You still think you can take anything you want. You're still sick with greed."

His silver eye shoots to Reiki, but the hazel one lands on me. Metallic fire bubbles a hole in his shirt, just above the penis pentagram. "None of you understand. None of you know what it's like to kill yourself over and over…and never die."

I think of what Reiki said about burning constantly with no resolve. "I know more than you think, and we can talk about it all. But first. Let's get out of this pod."

More than anything, I've got him curious. This is the first time I've successfully stood up to him. He wants to know more. Both of his eyeballs rotate back to me, fixated.

The staff's flames shrink to small coils of dull warmth. Satisfied, I stow it back in Reiki's bag.

Obsidian and Onyx continue to hold Jaal on our way to the cockpit, but some of their energetic cords have been cut. Bonds broken by bitter truth.

Are they feeling their pain, or mine?

I stride forward and clasp a hand on Obsidian's back. "Thanks, amigo." The vibes skyrocket at my command.

He flinches and chuckles. "Nah. Thank you, Zenith. I didn't realize how far gone he was…how much he…hurt you."

"Don't talk about me like I'm not here!" Jaal flails against the wall, where Onyx pins him with the force of dark energy. "Y'all talk like I'm crazy, like I lost my game. I ain't lost a thing!"

I scoff. "You know, Jaal. You meant everything to me when we were together, until I realized—I didn't *want* everything. I just wanted me. I wanted myself back, in a way I never thought possible…'til recently." My shoulder cracks. "I bet that's how the planets feel. They want their Truth back. They're trying to remember themselves. But they need all our reflections to do so. That's the only reason you're still…here."

President Samson's disembodied words swim through flashing neurons—*we thought you'd want to do it, after everything he's done to you.*
Kill him.

His cells collapse in on themselves, trying to decide how to act, where to disperse, or if staying together is the best option. His body's a pointillist painting, and his soul is even worse.

I see so much of Mama in him, it makes my throat burn. I'd like to detangle my vocal chords and display them in order of what hurts most.

Onyx and Obsidian exchange frantic glances, their grips on the dark energy bonds loosening.

Jaal rubs his dripping nose with a knuckle, where yolky light starts to buzz. His gaunt, papery face sags when he looks over Onyx's head at me. "All this time… thought…my happiness was your happiness."

"See, that's where you fucked up." My voice is its own choir. Truth rises with swarming vibrato. "Happiness is energy, and all relationships—human or otherwise—require reciprocity. Equal exchange. If you hoard all the energy for yourself, even the most empathic companion won't feel your joy; he'll just be hurt by the imbalance. Not to mention…you've never been happy, have you?"

"I WASN'T TRYING TO HURT YOU!" He bellows, and then crumples into Onyx's embrace. A dark energy crystal clatters onto the floor. "I was trying to fix it..."

"Fix what?"

"What she did. What a woman always does. Betray her family."

I halt in my emotional tracks, energy buzzing. "What? If this is about my mama—"

"She ruined herself, and then she ruined your family, and I...couldn't just stand around doing nothing."

That was what made me fall for him in the first place. That was his promise—to save me from impending familial disaster. But I know better now.

"You didn't save me, Jaal. You used Mama for your scientific success, and then—"

"That's what you think." The knot in his throat loosens. He stares at me over Onyx's shoulder, through layers of white frizz. "Project Sagittarius was meant to reverse—"

"And then you used me."

His guilt returns full-force, unable to be squelched by his fickle aura. "Didn't want things to go like they did..." He rubs his temples, pulling out fried dreadlock chunks.

Onyx tries to pull him back, but he shakes his head and saunters off toward the cockpit. Obsidian holds a crystal close to his chest but doesn't use it.

My voice chases Jaal down the hall. "Of course you did! You cling to control, and what you want goes. You kept me at a chain's length constantly, and to this day, even though we broke up, you still dangle me in front of people like I'm some Andromedin specimen." Then my body moves with my brain, following him to the ship's middle. "I've only ever worked for you, Jaal, not with you. So did Mama. You made us both sick." My teeth chatter with the desire to say more, but I'm out of breath by the time we reach the screens.

Sniffling, he leans on the control panel with his elbows and curls his head into his hands. Smoky liquid gushes through his fingers and runs down his forearms in veiny trails. "Been nothing but good to you. Given you everything. Got you outta her...our mess..."

My throat chakra rifles poisonous words at his head. "It's *still* a mess, Jaal. A few weeks ago, you stole my hard-earned trove so that I would keep working for you. When you first hired me, you could've had some bangled bots do your dirties, but no—that would've been too ethical. Instead you thought, 'hm, yeah, I'll take the child of my dying teacher and exploit him for thief's labor; that sounds stellar.'" A snarl sits between my lips and teeth. My body goes rigid like hardened magma, not letting him in—not his words, body, or aura.

"You've used me all this time, but even that's not enough." I jerk a thumb toward Reiki, who catches my hand in hers. "You claim Ki to be yours, like you own her, which is delicious coming from someone who shares my foundation shade." Ripping out of her grasp, I rub my dry eyes and drag skin downward, letting the world go blurry for a moment.

Onyx and Obsidian close the door behind us.

"You've been taunting me for weeks about this stupid blood opal thing, this scientific miracle, and now here we are—you guzzled all the loot and left me with none. Emptied me—our people—of all hope. So. Forgive me if I hardly think you've redeemed yourself by becoming a J-bomb." The taste of bitter earth drenches my tongue.

The liquid running down his arms is the remnants of his natal chart and other tattoos. Cosmetic cosmos awash in the heat and power of his auric center.

"Become a bomb?" He tilts his head. "What about a Pharmer? That's what I really am. Corrupt, piggish, drug-pusher."

"Mi amor." Onyx kneels beside him, trembling. "We talked about this…you are *not* our parents."

"I'm more like them than you'll ever be." For once, he isn't bragging; he's relenting.

The drum in my veins stutters. I lean back against Reiki.

Jaal covers his face and then points at me. "Yeah, bet you think that's real funny, don't you? Our parents were cosmic drug techs, who plotted against the Conduits. You probably think I wanted to fulfill their legacy, and I was gonna create hellscapes to do so. You think I'm evil. Well. Join the cult."

Onyx glances at me apologetically. "He did not take our parents' last name. None of us did…"

"The name died with them," Obsidian concludes, sitting in the captain's chair. He pinches the bridge of his nose, evidently tired of bawling. "We ain't proud, 'meegs. We just trying to heal, like you."

"You gotta understand." Jaal peers at me through grimy fingers. "Everything I did was for the greater greatness."

"Except me, Jaal. Nothing you did to me was right. Nothing you did to them—" I pull away from Reiki and gesture to his siblings.

"They sold me out!" He spits, snatching Onyx's wrist. Everyone holds a breath in quivering lungs. Obsidian scrambles for another crystal. "Before our parents died, Nyx and Sid sold me out every chance they got, when I tried to take the pharms down. When we ran away together, Nyx flew me right back into the pharmers' hands. You don't wanna know the shit they did…when a child misbehaved…what their idea of parenting was like…I was just a kid."

Jaal's foster siblings drown in guilt, but it reminds me why we're here in the first place.

Kneeling in front of him, I stare into his pulsar eyes, impossibly calm. "I was a kid, too, when you plucked me from the stars and made me do things I didn't wanna do."

His silver eye glints in reflection of mine.

I clear my throat, regaining composure. "You and I…we both ran away from toxic egos and ended up making our own. I will never justify your actions like you do, Jaal, but I see you, and I'll forgive you, when I'm ready. You will, too."

Reiki ushers me slowly into standing. From this angle, she's particularly androgynous—jaw more chiseled with shadow; eyelids heavy and sweeping; fingers freed and plucking my spine's ivories, holding me in her key.

I retie my bun and glance at Jaal. Curls snag on my clammy hands. "I'm not broken anymore, but our spacious home…the solar system—that's what's breaking now, and it's not…exclusively…your fault. The initial damage…it was Tauris, wasn't it?" As soon as I say it, I know it's true. Knowledge encases me, engulfs me, braiding my spinal cord. My hunch, in the back of my mind's eye, has always been right. "Her astrobats and clones…they were powered by aurorae, weren't they?"

"What gave it away?" Jaal pants, smiling bitterly.

"Your constant lack of trust in women, for one thing."

Onyx retracts from Jaal for a moment.

"Now, I'm no scientist," I confess, flinging up a pair of jazz hands. "But since Reiki started teaching me, I've thought a lot about Tauris…her toys, her schemes, why you sent me there at all. The astrobats weren't just powered by aurorae, were they? They were infused with it, against their will. She stole massive energy fields from planets, and probably thought it was her God-given right."

Outside, Saturn rebels for attention. The more it crumbles, the slower it revolves, gases losing color as they drift off. I space out on the solemn scene, tempted to get down on my knees and pray, when I realize the rock-dragon isn't circling anymore. The planet's bursting and twisting, with no gravitational caretaker in sight.

"Reiki. You weren't Jaal's token; you were a double agent. His 'in' with the woman who started this auric mess. Your body may have scattered its own cells, but being so close to her energetic experiments expedited that process. Why didn't you tell me?"

Glowing, Reiki shakes her head and squeezes my hand. "I didn't have to. You've always known, Cap. You just didn't say it aloud." Every dust speck passing her aura gets caught in soft strawberry light.

I crack my neck every way I know how, 'til no more bubbles hide in the joints. No more truth stowed away in subluxations. No more stifled neurons or starving engines. "I appreciate the honesty, everyone. Keep it up. But we're going to need more than candid chats to restore balance. Each of us is a part of a whole. Valuable and irreplaceable. So, essentially: no dicking out."

Jaal wipes his tears with inky hands, leaving war makeup on the apples of his cheeks. His body solidifies. Onyx gathers him in her arms again.

Almost knocking me off my feet, Obsidian hurls his green arms around me, plastic fringe prickling my skin. But I return the hug in full, letting him bury his puffy brown face in my shirt collar and rubbing his back.

"What's the plan, 'meegs? I mean—Captain."

This kind of smile feels foreign on my mouth.

"Zenith and I are Conduits," Reiki explains.

A collective murmur stirs. Even Syzygy seems to raise a chrome brow.

Reiki looks at our shabby crew one at a time, soaking them in. Through flared nostrils, she inhales. "We're going to teach you how to channel energy, on a grand scale, together. And then we're going to channel it right back to its source, like a fountain."

Thirty

"**I** told you: I don't want to kill Jaal, so I won't. His death wouldn't help us in the slightest." I disconnect the presidents' signal and pick up a hand mirror, bold voice shrinking to a mumble. "Besides, it would make him a martyr, and that's the gayest shit I've ever heard." I pinch a stray lash back into place and squint at the finished product.

"Your style is supreme, Captain," Syzygy preens.

Hours of placing microscopically thin falsies on my twitchy eyelids have been more fatiguing than expected. I've eaten two bags of dried fruit and pistachios during that span, while Reiki's been further cultivating our newest, greatest weapon—the crew. As Captain, I make it a priority to stay as far away from their wing of the ship as possible, but she insisted on working with each of them one-on-one to open their chakras. Not that Jaal needs it, but he does need the perspective.

Speaking of the angel herself, Reiki plops into the chair next to me, redoing her ram horn plaits. "I can't believe they're listening to me."

"Same. Makes it worse that this plan feels like a lie."

"It's not a plan, and it's not a lie." Loose loops of hair unfurl over her flushed ears before she weaves them back.

I chuckle and set the mirror down. "I know, that's why I said it *feels* like it…like we're distracting them with menial tasks. Meditation might save their mental health, but will it save a whole solar system?"

"Wait, are those Sens-lashes?"

"Yep." I blink profusely, and they shift through each color of the rainbow like hair-thin glowsticks. Light leaks into my cornea, shifting what I see. "Another gift from Samson. An apology for…well, you know." Words somersault into chuckles. I dab holographic gloss on my bottom lip, transmuting chaos into self-care.

Clearing my throat is easier than usual. "I just let go of their signal, actually. He was worried, as he has every right to be, but they're still supportive." With a heavy shrug, I glance at the tears she never wiped: saltwater crusting over her freckles. "Hopefully Sye agrees."

"I'm sorry; I can't take you seriously with those things." She waves her hands in front of her, snorting with giggles. "Your eyes look like they're flipping through TV channels."

"TV!" I cackle, throwing her a teasing lip-pop. Gloss on my mouth leaves a phantom kiss of menthol. "What millennium are you from?"

"All of them, remember?" She folds her arms and nudges my ankle with her toe. "Anyway. What makes you want to use something like that?"

Freshly shaven follicles raise at the touch of her skin, but my brow drops. "I don't trust the president's tech, but I thought I'd humor him, at least for now. He went to the trouble..." *Even though it's not any trouble, because he's got more gems than every crystal cave on Earth.*

"Well," she giggles, cradling her bouncing tummy. Vanilla silk wrinkles over a flexed abdomen. She's wrapped her bodice so tightly, it looks like binding. "Now you can have Sens-porn all on your own, without his help."

"Or yours." I scratch the side of my neck and peer into the mirror again.

One would assume she had the breeze knocked out of her. Auric tendrils curl into each other, so free of dusty blockades they don't know what to do with themselves.

"I only help when asked." She squeezes my elbow, fingers lilting over my forearm and stopping at my natal tattoo. "Conduit's honor."

Without looking, I feel her wink staining my turned cheek. Every vein pushes harder against my skin to reach for her.

Pleadingly grateful to be wearing harem pants, I cross my legs and snap the mirror closed. "Mmm, interesting. Tell me more."

Piercing the tension, a loud screech ricochets over the ship, metal against rock. The star-shaped ceiling shudders. Screens flicker and blur, replacing starscapes with pixels. Walls wobble like they'll splinter.

Instinctively, I duck, but Reiki draws me to my feet with a hand on either side of my face. "We only help when asked." She runs a thumb over my lip. "When the need is genuine. And our solar system is begging."

Hot, I think, but as soon as my lips split to say it, Syzygy jostles to the side, wedging my elbow against one of the toggles.

241

I reach for them in vain. The controls are unresponsive, but the engine shifts with the energy of an external source.

Angular rocks of woe sink deep in my solar plexus. Mood ruined.

"It's the presidents," I wheeze, brushing strung-out stress off my aura. "They're overriding Syzygy."

"You said they were supporting us!"

My laugh comes out more like a whimper. "I may have exaggerated just a...smidge!" The last word hikes up an octave when the ship lurches again. "Oh, Pleiades..."

Syzygy's epic voice echoes throughout his internal organs. "Breech attempted. Signal detected. Power remains."

"My life." Delirious and fed up with everything, I gaze at the star-shaped ceiling, my spine jiggling against the floor. For once, there are no diagnostics.

"Accept signal," Reiki commands with a barreling alto. The Sens-goggles slide over her face easily, even with the cornucopia of braids.

In the same moment, quaking slows and turns to stillness. A break between mini storms. A pause between breaths.

Instead of feeding the engine, starstruck gases glom onto our ship for dear life, probably wondering, like us, what the fresh hell is happening.

Reiki's lips are a parting sea. She freezes, face draining of pinkness to fill her aura with baby blue. Her cheeks sink under the goggles' edges and her shoulders slump.

"What is it?" I prop myself up on the elbows, funny bones aching in the most un-funny way. "What do they want?"

"One moment, please," she says to the other end of the com. Her body sways in the captain's chair, overcome with sensory confusion. Pulling off the goggles, she glances at me with desert-cave irises. "It's for you."

"Well," I respond, batting my new lashes and sitting up. "I am the Cap..." I falter when visuals blink into my sight. It's a perception much scarier than a tantrum-throwing power couple.

An earthy lemon scent plays with nose hairs and drenches my eyes. Steam rises from a hot pile of udon and veggies; the ceramic bowl almost singes my fingertips. Disoriented, I lean back, expecting a chair, but find the softness of Reiki instead. She holds me upright on the floor while the rest of my senses wander.

Breath stipples my lungs.

242

I know that smile, the way those polished morganite cheeks tuck and dimple high. Tufts of salt-and-pepper hair are gone, lost to the Fever maybe, or covered by the sunflower headscarf and tassels.

"Mama," I exhale, wiping my chin clean of tears. I didn't even notice them falling.

She sits regally in the captain's chair, hands tucked in billowing black sleeves, eyes and nose obscured by a kabuki Sens-mask. The color combinations are so stark, I could throw up, but with deep breathwork, I refrain. Her mouth's corners twitch further into their warm grin, pinned with uncanny pride.

She bows her head cordially, smile splitting to reveal disturbingly white teeth. When I last saw her, they were brinier than a smoking sailor's. Her skin is so smooth, the way it used to be before the Fever.

Sashaying right into dramatic conclusions, I stand, knees wobbling. "Mama, you look…did J give you the remedy? Are you…?" My inner child returns through quivering vocal chords, treading on thin, naïve ice.

I feel Reiki's hands, one on either hip, gently pulling me back, begging to ground me. I also feel her worry, creeping up my vertebrae, fingerprints and tattoos whispering warnings.

Mama is quieter than outer space. She bobs and tilts her head, beaming like a doll. I imagine, under the mask's pearly veneer, her nutmeg eyes scanning me like she used to after long nights. *Where've you been, stardust? A fun party, I hope?*

Instead, as if she's falling asleep, she's barely able to hold herself up, mirroring my weak knees, lacking a bolster.

That is, of course, until Mother appears to catch her in a silk-laden embrace.

I jump so hard and quick, I knock Reiki's chin with my shoulder.

Mother's curls are tied up with a rag and sweat pools in the divots of her collarbones. Gray dust tarnishes her ebony skin. She can't see me (their tech isn't presidential, after all), but there's a knowing glint in her purplish gaze.

"Leave him alone." Mother's not begging Mama this time; she's commanding. Her almost baritone voice stabs like shards of black tourmaline. "Get up and go back to the room."

My throat cinches at the sight of Mama's obedience. As if a switch clicks, she becomes fully conscious again, erects herself, and removes the S-Com, leaving me staring through a greenish haze of nothing. It fades, and when I open my eyes entirely, I swallow a gag and return desperately to my breath.

I wait on the edge of my seat, or rather, Reiki's lap. It takes me a solid sixty seconds to realize her face is buried in my twitching shoulder, kissing the spot repeatedly, apologetically.

More minutes pass, eager to break my expectations as always.

Time doesn't feel real, but it moves without doubt, just like it did when I ran away the first time. But I'm not the one running, or hiding, now.

"What is it?" I demand. "What's wrong with her now?"

The top of her palm dances over my throbbing throat. "It's...not what you think."

I unravel from her grasp, standing with wobbling joints. "It never is." Vertigo swirls, but I brace myself on the captain's chair and wipe my eyes with a fatigued wrist. I focus on that wrist, on each stunted hair follicle and thumping lapis vein.

Not long ago, I wanted to bite those veins and scatter the pieces, use the blood as fuel for other people's goals. I left hatches where there should've been love marks, and then I let someone else cover my tracks. But now, I've owned up to it, started the healing, and the scars are blurred back into ink vats, skinny ley lines, as if quantum portals opened in every cell and haven't closed. Never will close. It's a process. I'll be an open wound, bleeding old trauma, for this life and beyond.

Disrupting my meditative focus, the hallway door unzips, letting in a slew of stoked pheromones, cranking brains, and an astronomical amount of opinions no one asked for.

"Thoughts occurred," Jaal announces, stroking his slick chin. Without facial hair, he's even more infantile. He gestures wildly with the ends of a mauve feather boa.

Onyx and Obsidian stand on either side of him. Her eyes have gone dim, burnished gold instead of raw orange, and his are sizzling coals.

"How rare," I drawl, launching into the captain's chair before he can, swinging crossed legs to the side. "What's on your mind?"

Sid hooks a thumb in Jaal's jeans, preparing to hold him back, but the beast isn't angry. Instead, his puffy eyes brim with auric tears to follow physical ones. He collapses onto his knees, forcing dumbstruck Sid down with him. While Sid yanks his thumb back and wedges it between petal-painted lips, Jaal smacks his hands together in prayer.

"Know I wasn't the best savior before, but so much is different now..." With every erratic twitch of head and face, his eyebrows unfurl. He dons insanity so well. "Serious this time. Changed. Evolved. Gimme a chance to prove I can still save us, save it all. Let me be the one. Hell, if it thrills ya, let Reiki and I do it. Got the most power, she the most knowledge…let us be the ones.”

Sticking the edge of my tongue between my teeth, I lean forward to make sure my glare sinks into every neuron of his bulimic brain. “You’re making less sense than usual. Maybe you should lie down.”

“No!” He hisses, breaking free of Sid’s grasp. I flinch, expecting brick-knuckles to the face (or worse), but with a brawny hand on either shoulder, he stares me down. “Forget all the complex Buddha shit. Presidents want me dead, right? Make it easy for ‘em. Toss me in the auric fields, and I’ll restore ‘em myself. Payback for all the energy I stole, not from them, but you.”

My stomach sinks. “How did you—”

“Pure energy,” he breathes, gusting my senses with a smell-mash of citronella and sage. “It’s what I am, what Reiki is, what your Mama is, so we know what it’s like to rub up against the universe, be a piece of greater wholes. You gotta let me do this, Z. Please.”

There he is, begging again. It’s so tempting to let him commit suicide, to watch his silly body go up in sparks with new year starworks. But that desire burns up before he has the chance to.

Strength’s ghost inhabits my twiggy arms, and with a palm against his chest, I shove him off. He backs away, stuttering under his breath.

Body and spirit inflamed, I rise, auric field billowing like a solar storm. “We talked about this, we all did. As much as it pains me to admit, you’re no different than us.” He’s on his knees again, because I lowered him there, coaxing with hands on his shoulders, like he’s always done to me. His head is level with my heart chakra. “Nobody’s anyone’s ‘savior.’ We’re all reflections of each other. Nobody can die while the other is alive, channeling. So, take a deep, cleansing breath, and chill. The fuck out.”

Syzygy rattles again, hurling us both against the control panel.

Jaal snatches my waist, dragging me away from a broken screen.

I gawk at the shambles of my ship’s solar plexus, internal controls that compile his organs and wiring—failing miserably, crumbling like a Martian cave.

“Shit!” I scream, letting Reiki detangle me from Jaal’s grasp. “Shitshitshit. Why does everything just…break…all the time…”

Reiki’s hands are under my arms.

Sticking a trembling finger in Jaal’s face, I spit, “I don’t know what the fuck’s happening, but you’re the engineer—can G handle this? Tell me she…tell me he’ll be okay.”

From manic to helpless, inspired lion to pouting dog, he retracts any leftover words in a mouthful of silvery saliva. He turns away, teal with confused sickness.

Onyx meets him halfway to the floor, anchoring him like Reiki does for me.

Obsidian tries in vain to fix the controls. His coconut-shell shoulder blades are slicker than his lips, and the whiteish flesh of his palms leaves salty smudges all over the panel.

Sick and tired of holding onto someone else for security, I straighten and blink a new signal pattern in my Sens-lashes. My vision swirls chloroform green, and then black while I fickly choose a potential death sentence.

"Syzygy," I call over the chaos, batting the lashes and lowering my gaze. "Signal President Ycarimus."

Choppy and androgynous, losing his programming, G replies, "Signal out of reach."

Now I'm sweating, dragging sticky lips over chattering teeth, digging elbows into the back of the chair, trying so hard not to lose my shit like everyone else. Auras on fire. Bodies soon to be.

"Try again," I plead, but it's only followed by what sounds like static laughter—chunks of spliced programming falling out of gravity like Saturn's rings. "Fine. Syzygy! Signal Mother."

Without waiting for response, I bolt, trying hard not to fuck up the blinking patterns.

Lines of red lights zoom just under me, a runway for my haphazard plans.

Every time I ran through these circuit-like hallways before, I was charged by my own stale drama. All of that has been removed, washed, sprayed with chemicals like the floors of Mars and then lit ablaze.

Now, the cosmos is traumatized from holding humanity's issues. Blockages curl under alloy panels and fingernails, stardust and dark matter flirting with dirt, shadow, pain. A collective scream lodged in my ship, my experience.

It won't take one healer; it'll take a whole damn tribe.

Neglecting to see if anyone has followed me, I stow away in my bedroom, where the shaking stops.

Syzygy's crispy voice holds my hope and sanity in tandem. "Signal failure. I'm bored, Captain."

It's a beautiful, twisted glitch.

What he means to say is: the ship is being boarded. But the cheeky pun from crumbled programming jolts a grin back on my face.

If I have a shred of faith left in me, divine or otherwise, let it be used now to prove that my moms are in fact boarding this ship. That they'll help me.

While my soles crush foam and downy cotton, my torso stretches higher than it ever has, vibrations pushing past the ceiling and trapdoor. For once, I'm not small. I'm bigger than I've ever been, playing Nephilim in cosmic ridicule.

Heart vigorously combing through my ribcage, I pause to recall Tauris—her silly prophecies, and enchanting clones, her wasted, hungry body splayed at my feet—killed by the very tools she wielded to heal.

If she could see me now, she'd swallow her own tongue.

My nostrils flare with cool air. I pull myself up into the emergency pod, shaking with adrenaline.

The black velvet sky unfolds in rays of blue, yellow, and pungent chrome. I wince in the overwhelming cloud, struggling to focus on Saturn's rings splattered across a cosmic canvas. From Earth, it probably looks like nothing more than a smudge, but here, it's a terrifying masterpiece.

"Didn't I tell you?" Reiki's voice crawls into the pod before her body does. "What our third-eyes see in people, everyone sees in the planets. They're going to lose themselves to color, just like we do." A hand on the small of my back, she stands beside me, her cheek pressing against my square shoulder.

"You're awfully calm," I pant, peeling off Sens-lashes in defeat. Disappointment teeters on the edge of my blood-brain barrier.

But then I look at her, truly, with senses physical and beyond, tugging in focus. White fabric embraces every jutting curve and bone. A raspberry halo warps the outline of her material body, brightening when she returns my gaze.

"There's still so much you don't know," she speaks as if through a conch shell, waves caressing throat, air, and then ears. Salty-sweet vibrations I could get used to, would love to hear and feel for the rest of existence.

"Show me, then." I turn to her, cupping her face, freckles and ink. "One more transcendent experience before we save the solar system."

She shakes her head and kisses each palm. "It's already happening…look…"

I follow her index finger back past the stellaglass globe, toward broad draconic wings that hug our ship. Even from this distance, Saturn is dragging us in.

I wander through possibilities of escape. "We can…" But she tilts my face toward her, and I'm stuck. Not in pain or panic, but tranquility. Every fractal in her eyes bears a different spiritual memory, an imprint in time, space, and the mash-ups between.

Another sassy rattle from Syzygy knocks my lips against her chin, producing giggles.

I tumble into her, gripping her shoulder and hip for support, staring past copper mandala braids.

Beyond our little safety dome, a burst of flaming nectarine descends into Saturn's famished stomach. Light coils extend to high-five nearby moons.

My jaw hangs. "Sweet stars. The presidents fed their ship to Saturn's rings."

Her mouth balloons when she turns around. Our collective aura matches the presidents' ship. In its extra-ignited form, it still dons comet camouflage, rolling into the dying planet's embrace.

Now I've seen everything—RSA presidents sacrificing their lives for people like us…bandits, scientists, Conduits…

"It's not over 'til I say it is!" An uncannily deep voice bellows from under us. "The States didn't reunite for nothing."

I glance down, through the trapdoor. Shadow and light pool over metal edges. A starchy hand covered in wedding rings waves.

Beyon and Micah poke their heads up, still the epitome of Yin and Yang. This time, though, they don matching powder blue suits with pointed shoulder pads, sequined buttons, and award pins.

"It's not over," Beyon reiterates, throwing us a classic trembling fist. "Until we finish it."

Micah cackles, "and we *always* finish!" His pearlescent grin is more blinding than Saturn swallowing a fake sun.

I rub my neck. "Damn, Ki. Look who's trying to change my view of authority figures."

A sound like several starworks going off simultaneously reverberates through stellaglass. Above our petty craniums, Saturn burps with gratitude, momentarily satisfied. An energetic shot or two. Some of its rings have even solidified.

"Do you really think feeding him your trillion-dollar star-imposter will save us?" I ponder, approaching the glass and laying a hand on its foggy surface.

Beyon clears his throat. "Perhaps, but if you have a better idea, all my senses are on."

I stare ahead at pooling colors that infinitely create rainbows.

"Sye trusts you, Zenith," he continues, cracking knuckles. "Probably more than she should. She's not here, of course, but we are. Don't be afraid of your fate, after all this time…"

A double-handed slap on metal urges me to turn around and look at him. Reiki spins on her toes, in sync with me.

"Look!" Micah shoves Beyon out of the way, propping himself up on the floor. He points to the other side of the sky, where something infinitesimal emerges, drenched in delicate shadow.

"Friend or foe?" Beyon wonders, stretching to get a better look, only to be elbowed in the face by his flailing lover.

An older, beetle-shaped ship putts toward us, glimmering emerald in the aftermath of Saturn's bright binge. I recognize the symbols printed across its scaly surface—pieces of eastern and western cultures blended together in stellapainted graffiti. A delightfully homemade beast. A model I haven't seen since I was prepubescent—4400 Stellium Six.

Mother's ship.

One of their external lights blinks white and blue, the old-fashioned signal for a request to dock.

"Signal granted," I tell Syzygy, forgetting that his programming is in shambles. Technology fails us now more than ever, stubbornly drawing us back to a time when Earth was a child, like it knows its end is imminent.

Too busy to mourn the mechanical love of my life or ponder the universe's plan, I yank a crystalline lantern from the storage cupboard and hold it to the glass. With a thumb pressed to the bottom, activating sensors, I flick the lemon-yellow light in an off-beat pattern.

"What does that mean?" Beyon interrogates, still pinned between the trapdoor's edge and his lover.

I bite the corner of my lip, waiting for the signal to sink in on the other side. "Oh, this? It's the beat of Tiger Mom."

"The 4420's jam?" Micah squeals, accidentally slamming his chin into the floor. "Oof."

"One and only."

I can feel their bewildered judgement, the harsh gazes of critics who never knew my moms, never shared laughter with them before they fell apart.

Even through clouds of depression and across different realms, I can hear Mama's windchime laugh, feel Mother's blush. A phantom, but it's there.

Stellium rotates toward the landing dock, kissing Syzygy's shaken cheek.

Wiping sweat on the back of my hand, I set the lantern aside and clasp Reiki's hand. "Ki, come with me. We're gonna do something I never do—greet my guests."

While she tilts her head, I mutely cheer—no more anxious fire at my feet, or boulders tugging me under. I guess the universe was made for two, or even a plethora.

Thirty-One

Syzygy's guest bedrooms—which I've avoided like the Fever—are overflowing, not just with cramped chi, but an array of personal items. Various drug cartridges, perfume bottles, guns disguised as makeup components, and used tissues litter the corridor.

"Ugh," I wince into my elbow. "Was this from all the times Syzygy was jostled, or are they really this messy?"

Onyx's door is slid open halfway, enough for me to poke my head in and see how much of a minimalist she is compared to her brothers. She's perched on a high bed, hair-pocked legs dangling, eyes closed. Her pierced nostrils flare, but I can't hear breathing. The room is spacious, and most of what she expels isn't material—it's energetic.

Reiki nudges me with her elbow and points.

My jaw releases when I realize what Onyx is doing—the same integrative energy work Reiki had me do a couple days ago—cleansing her shadow fields. Soft blue light trickles from her bobbing throat, down into a jade heart chakra, brightening with every oxygen boost in her lungs. She's so tranquil, with one open palm on either knee, the watercolor lines between her aura and body are smudged. She doesn't even notice our presence.

A dark globe begins to swirl around her, cleaning and protecting from electromagnetic rampage.

I pull away from the door and gaze at Reiki, my eyebrows soaring.

"She's determined," Reiki explains.

"She's nothing like she was a few weeks ago."

"Life is simply energy inhabiting matter," she reminds, squeezing my fingers between hers and rubbing ink marks. "It moves when we

251

change, or we change when it moves. A shift always takes place, and sometimes that means old things end…"

"Does any of this bother you?" I pluck her gaze with mine. "The energy stuff, I mean. Everything you say…and what you said earlier about sacrifice…makes it clear what's gotta happen…what might happen to you."

"There you go again…knowing before you think you do." She tilts her head and blinks, sending spirals of saltwater down her pink face. Knowledge and wisdom dance between her irises.

I ball her hand up in mine 'til our knuckles crack. "I don't want you to die."

"Nothing dies."

"I don't want your body to die. I want you to come home with my moms and me, live a fully human life."

Her eyes wince in a smile. "There've been so many. But Zenith…you're focusing on the wrong ending. I'll be okay; I promise."

A few feet away, Jaal and Obsidian are doing Deimos-knows-what in their broken taco of a living space. All regular lights are gone, replaced with rotating hover-lanterns that cast multicolored beams on trash trails.

Their voices murmur over syncopated chimes. Lights stiffen at indigo, a color I don't see often in any of their auras.

"Light therapy," she clarifies, guiding us toward the end of the hall. "Arguably the oldest and most efficient way to transcend the physical dimension."

Another colorful distraction.

She eyes me, wiping tears from her face with a thumb. "Where's all this doubt coming from? Don't you know that if you have all the right pieces, the outcome is whole?"

Whether that's a metaphor or plain-as-sky truth, she's right. I cough into my wrist, burying nervousness under twitching tendons.

Ahead of us, the hallway swoops into a cave entrance of sorts, one that connects with other ships when consent is given. I've only avoided it because until now, guests have been a little less than welcome.

"I still think Jaal decorated this to mock Tauris," I muse, scanning the chrome-encrusted alloys he soldered to be rock-shaped.

Reiki jumps when an array of locks and hatches click and rumble from the other side.

The rock wall decomposes to absorb my moms' ship, angular fixtures shifting like origami to accommodate our guests.

Old and new technologies are forced to mingle, but the only complaints are whirs and creaks between structures. Synchronicity falls. Whole-ship power transmission.

For once, I've given someone else permission to materialize into my walls. Someone who I've been running from longer than Jaal, or even myself. I've opened all channels of communication, removed the insecurities and shadow-gags. There's no going back.

While pearlescent bits of Syzygy dissolve and retract further to make space for rickety Stellium, the floor quivers.

A makeshift door manifests to be more of a grand entrance than the previous one.

I don't realize I'm holding my breath until Reiki's hand wanders over my chest, leaving magenta light on a swollen heart chakra. Our smiles snag in the unwinding fog.

It'll be okay, her eyes sing, dripping honey-colored nebulae.

On the cusp of healing, I free my limbs of tension, my lungs from tight breaths.

Approaching the ship like a ghost, my arms lift effortlessly, hanging on air beams. A yogic greeting, saluting mantra.

But hope swallows itself. Thin layers of metal peel back like a blooming lotus, an open passage for yet another weapon to be launched at me.

Reiki yelps.

I catch the crystal tomahawk by its handle before it can split my third-eye, physical eyes so wide they burn. Hot adrenaline courses through me.

"Zenith," Reiki hisses, yanking it away from me while I freeze.

Just when I was close to befriending my trauma.

A gust of sea salt and turmeric pump my lungs, and without even blinking, the floor is nothing but spilled udon with a hint of blood and the walls shed themselves to reveal endless grassy fields and I can't breathe because between the pollen and the yelling there is no oxygen on Earth that can help this madness breathe.

We're not even on Earth, I remind myself. *That truth is old.*

My eyes are rubbed dry, worn out from days of tears, makeup, thrown punches and overdosed Sens-spells.

Resilience rushes in a hot flash.

Oxygen in, fuckery out.

Fluorescent gratitude hugs my trauma 'til it suffocates.

"Mama." The name scrapes tonsils as it passes. "I thought you were—"

"Dead? Or healed?" Her tinny voice strangles my ears. "They are the same." Silhouetted by flickering yellow ship light, Mama strides forward, bare feet snagging a sweeping blue and gold sarimono. A violet headwrap hides one eye and her sun-shaped nose ring is skewed, as if she haphazardly dressed for the occasion.

Miraculously, I stay calm, even after almost losing my shit.

"You're not Mama, are you?" I speak it before I know it, glancing at Reiki for confirmation.

Returning my gaze to Mama is a mistake.

Her gargling lips part, releasing grossly mechanical noises and tongue clicks. Unhinged, her head falls to the side, neck twisted so unnaturally she can't possibly be human. Pallid skin folds over itself in mockery of a scarf.

My stomach lurches. I clutch Reiki's silken bodice, aching for her powerful solar plexus energy to leak into mine. Golden hour in the middle of outer space.

Instead, my soul's mirror sighs deeply. She slides the tomahawk under her feet and holds it there for safety. Our shared light-bath hardens into a fuchsia glacier.

I could shake violently. I could scream. But instead, I crystallize, not erratic or in pain—but incredibly curious.

Breaking the tension, a heavy patter of feet on fake marble spurs toward us.

Mother approaches, wearing Mama's old work clothes that wrestle with her curves. She waves a dirty rag at me, panting, then uses it to wipe her forehead. Hair coils stick to her round face.

"I'm so sorry, stardust," she calls, clamping a shockingly calloused hand on Mama's shoulder. "I wanted this to be perfect, but I…ran out of time." Her cleared throat becomes awkward laughter, an unsung tune, and then all at once her voice stiffens. "Soluna. Sleep."

Just like over the S-Com, Mother's touch and words tranquilize her. Mania drains from Mama's almond eyes and she deflates in Mother's embrace.

"This is…" I murmur. "Not what I expected."

Reiki's the only one who hears me. She clasps my hand, knuckles clacking into mine, and shifts her weight off the tomahawk. "Look closer, Cap…what's she missing?"

"Aside from basic decency and sanity?" I snap, but my thumb circles the edge of her natal tattoo. The icing-like caducity of her skin squelches my frantic heart.

Mother hoists Mama into her arms bridal style. Royal blue fabric sweeps over her confident gait, but guilt corrodes the love in her hazel gaze. "We, um…we'd better sit, Zenith. I need…a peaceful place to discuss…"

Her true exhaustion bleeds through—oil blending with burnt melanin in her cheeks, sweat puddles under her thick lips and dimpled chin.

That's when I notice Reiki's distinction. Mother's aura overflows, equal parts passion and compassion, carried by colors that don't exist on this plane. But when I scan Mama, truly focusing on her, she's colorless. There's no life force, no luminescence. Just a shell.

More feet drum against the floor, this time from behind us.

The rest of our crew surrounds us, auras spilling into each other—burnt red, claustrophobic blue, and hazy silver.

The presidents stride like soldiers at our flanks. Their auras act as a barrier for our united cell. Breath catches in my throat. We're an energetic army.

Beyon extends a cordial, oblivious hand. "You must be Imani Lin."

Mother nods with a pinched smile, her gaze still on me. "I am, and this is—"

"Not who you think it is," Jaal spits, practically foaming at the mouth.

I glance at him over my shoulder. His aura becomes his skin again. In his eyes, tears brim, and above them, a cobalt spark goes ballistic.

Clearing my stinging throat, I gesture down the hall. "Ki, please take Jaal, Sid, and Nyx back to their rooms."

As much as I don't want to, I relinquish Reiki's embrace. She slinks away to join the others, tomahawk in hand like a baton to lead the way.

Amazingly, Jaal doesn't revolt, but he pauses at the cusp of his doorway, still gawking at the thing that looks like Mama. In his white cotton robe, he could be a priest, overgrown and wild from years of being isolated.

For a moment, I glance between them—Mother, Mama, and Jaal—and the shared suffering that lingers in the air where words should be.

I stiffen. My soul's mirror left, but here I am, finding more reflections in solar miscreants.

Reiki ushers him into the room, Obsidian following close behind. Onyx's Hisphindi whispers flood the hall with unintelligible mantras.

Beyon and Micah reek of pride, inching closer to me with crossed arms. Apparently, they even shaved for the occasion, wiping Yin and Yang chins clean before tossing their ship into Saturn's ether.

"It's a fantasy to meet you both," Mother forces the words out, knees wobbling.

Despite my rage and trepidation, I offer my arms. "I'm not as weak as I used to be." For once, it's true. "Give her...give it to me."

"We can do it," the presidents blurt in unison.

Mother bypasses the three of us with pursed lips and heads down the hall. "No, thank you."

I jog to catch up to her.

The presidents follow too close behind me, breathing further down my spine with every clack of their polished hooves—I mean, oxfords. Upon closer inspection, I notice Micah's stiletto cheekbones are streaked with ash, which I originally thought to be fallen mascara clumps.

"Your ship snag you before it fell?" I ask. "Was it a romantic departure, at least?" There's an apologetic flavor under my tongue instead of sarcasm.

His pasty brows contort, every angle of his face sharpening to cut my words. "It was my home, Zenith. One of many, sure, but it was my home. I...hope it buys us some time."

Quickly, I redirect my gaze toward Mother. Her right shoe is missing a sole, causing her to stumble every now and then. Mama's neck stretches like putty over her left elbow. Azure fabric skids the ground.

Solar plexus boiling, I sprint to her right side and lift Mama's plasticky legs, allowing Mother to better cradle her head. Mother stares forward, tiny green hallway lights reflecting in her honeycomb irises.

Our pace slows.

"Mother, listen," I whisper, stunned by how sharply it echoes through Syzygy's veins. "This...apparatus...it isn't Mama, right?"

Her gaze bubbles, not with tears, but trembling pupils that don't know which way to look. I wiggle my fingers over Mama's false skin 'til I can lace them with Mother's and squeeze.

"If I may," Beyon tries.

"You may not." While we approach a familiar fork in my ship's maze, I feign a cough. "What you may do, Presidents, is keep an eye on the controls while I speak with my mother in private." I scan their dumbfounded faces in bluish-black light with hardened brows. "Thank you. For your continual service." The words are hard to bite.

Mother and I turn right, toward my bedroom, while the presidents click their heels together like good soldier boys and obey orders.

Well. That's what I wish would happen.

Instead, Micah raises a pale, knobby finger. "Oh, no, no, we did not just sell our home to the devil to have you push us around like that."

Beyon clasps his lover's shoulder. Pins and rings clink. "Mi, he's right."

"He's not!" Micah peels away and punches the wall with a surprisingly loud clunk.

"Oy!" I bellow, channeling my uncle more than I'd like to.

Mother tries to press on, but I hold us in place. Fire hurtles through my guts. "If you've got a problem with me or how I run things, that's fine, but don't take it out on my ship. He's been through enough."

"We *all* have, in case you haven't noticed!" Micah wrestles against his husband's grip. They clamp down on each other.

"I'm sorry," I concede, shaking my head. "I *am* grateful for your help, both of you. But time's running out."

With a bowed head, Beyon's dark eyes flick up to me. "He's right, Mr. Lin. We have been through enough. Let's end it soon, shall we?"

It's one of those moments that embodies the millisecond before neurons fire and cells shift. So much of who they are unravels before me in perfect, divine time.

I nod and tug Mother to join me down the next hall.

When we're out of earshot, I emit a rattling sigh, aiming to splice the tension. "Lovers' quarrels, am I right?"

Bags under her eyes are heavier than the weight we carry. "I miss the quarrels. Sometimes." Her chest lifts and falls. "I miss their authenticity."

We lean against the wall, but before I open my bedroom door, I sigh even harder. Lungs shake, and I can feel it in her too. Our collective trauma slides against itself, blood under a scabbed wound.

"Tell me something," I say to her, tossing caution to the cosmos. "Was she worth all the effort and pain?"

She bows her head low to gaze at her beloved's lookalike. In her strained smile, I see a glint of myself—the haphazard way I peer at Reiki, with such brain-curdling devotion. Our contrast fades. The mirror has split and scattered in every nook and cranny of my life.

257

Without receiving an answer, I turn back to the door. "Soluna."

"Don't say her name," Mother blurts, but it's too late.

Alerted by what I assume to be code, Mama kicks me in the chin, releasing a haunting battle cry.

Stiffly, I collapse with a grunt, knees thumping against the floor.

Mother cinches her grip, but her weary arms are no match for this manic machine. While the fake Soluna flails, her sarimono tears at the seams. With each shred of the headdress and bodice, Mother's eyes fill with more tears.

"S-Soluna!" She tries, but to no avail—her password is sheathed in sobs.

Red-faced and wriggling, Mama yanks herself out of the dress and bolts, skin struggling to stick to flexing muscle and artificial bone. Without speech, she makes her way clumsily to the other end of the hall.

"Ugh." I rub my jaw.

At first, Mother doesn't even bother chasing her. She stands there, staring at the shreds of sarimono, bending to pick them up and rub them with her thumbs, like they're good luck talismans.

Dizziness threatens to tug me aside, but I shake it off. "Sweet Pleiades, that hurt. What is she?"

"A simulacrum," Mother weeps into a stray piece of blue silk, helping me up with a quaking free hand. "A...plastic mirage. That's all."

"So, she's not conscious?" Brain tissue strains around the idea of Tauris' toys, how blatantly aware they were of their own manipulative creator.

Drool bubbles at the corners of her puckered mouth. She shakes her head. "No, she...it's not her in the slightest. Lutfi wanted to tell you, but I made him swear he wouldn't..." A vigorous sniff. "We just wanted to make you happy...after everything you've been through, we just...but...no. No, Mama's not conscious, stardust. She hasn't been for a long time. At least...not on this plane. She's gone, Zenith. I'm so sorry."

There I go again, feeling knowledge before knowing it—every cell swelling with answers.

My mind retrogrades to weeks ago—but maybe it's been months, because time is like a trick of the light—when Reiki broke into my ship and used my shower, claiming there was a "presence" in the bathroom.

Is it someone I know?

No.

My fingers tingle, the confirmation scattering throughout nerve endings.

Relief makes a swimming pool of my stomach, softening everything. I stand and grasp her hands.

"It's okay." Swallowing chunks of ice and exhaling fire. "And if it's not, it will be." Luscious light trickles from my palms into hers, brightening when I squeeze. "I won't ever abandon you again." Speaking little truths into vast existence. "I'm just glad she's not..." *One of Tauris' playthings.* "...Hurting anymore." Tears fall, washing away my fear. "C'mon, we can't let a damn sim ruin our home, right?"

Thirty-Two

While rushing after the simulacrum, I hear a soft *thank you* and I'm honestly not sure which parent says it, but it reverberates, echoing louder than the sound of our feet patting on metal.

The ship seems to tilt on its own, like a mandala, but it's not vertigo for once. Everything I've learned or known before knowing aligns in a perfect swirl.

Instead of senses being faked, sense is being made, at the deepest and most transcendent levels.

"Where'd she—where'd it go?" I demand through pants, spinning around to make sure I didn't miss a room, compartment, or corner. It's a hunt for precious treasure all over again, and although it makes my stomach scream, this time I'm ready.

I touch the wall, lingering on the reassuring drum of Syzygy's engine. The human-made star beats like a heart, albeit a broken one. Alloys crackle, fibers straining when atoms vibrate quicker than usual.

My cervical vertebrae crinkle with the ship, equally electrified. I walk slowly and tilt my head side to side.

"You know that thing well," I assume, glancing at Mother. "Where would it go? What does it want?"

Her face is still gaunt, but she squeezes her elbows to juice some faith. I've seen that stance plenty of times—first in Sens-photos of the day I was born, then when I had trouble at school, and later when Mama first started Fever treatments.

In lofty hospital rooms Sens-designed to mimic nature's splendor, Mother coped. Even when the rooms wouldn't work anymore, when Mama's brain was too sickly stubborn for any well-intended illusion, Mother either squeezed herself like a lemon or

260

descended to her knees in prayer. Both caused aches in her ashy elbows and knees, but also pure hope that spread like a rash.

To this day, I wish my faith was that tactile.

"The simulacrum doesn't want anything," she replies dismally, after measuring long breaths. I could balance a knife on the hunched crook of her neck. She gazes down at her splayed, chapped fingers. "I couldn't figure out how to give it a brain, let alone a heart."

"You couldn't..." My teeth part so quickly, my jaw pops. "*You...?*"

Scanning her clothes and the extra set of wrinkles on her face, I get it. It all makes sense. But I never thought I'd see the day when Mother...

"Created a cheap copy of my wife?" Laughter punctures her mouth. "Yes. I missed her, Zenith, not who she was when she passed, but...who she was before Project Sagittarius." She clears her throat. "Which I'm sure you know all about now." Her eyes wander the corridor, and then fall again. "I wanted her to hold me...I wanted to remember what it felt like when she kissed me. It's selfish, I know, and so three-dimensional." There it is—the classic wagging finger, tick-tocking away minor and major sins. "But it's also pointless. Not even these hands, the ones who brought you into this world, could bring her back...or...even the experience of her. Life's not that simple."

I have the overwhelming urge to shove her, bust through her stiff shoulder blades, rip out her heart chakra and breathe light back into it. I have the words, but the actions slip through my fingers. I want to say: *It is that simple, Mother. I'll show you. You can experience whatever you want in your mind's eye.*

Thank you for being both wife and midwife to Mama. Without you both, I wouldn't be who I am. So. It's my turn to help you, raise you up...

Cutting off internal promises, a hollering duet erupts from the cockpit.

I jump, knocking a shoulder into the wall. But pain is just a nuisance at this point. Snagging Mother's hand again, I run.

In doses, thin tendrils of multicolored energy zip and encircle walls, floors, and doors. I can't tell if they're physical or meta, but maybe now that we're deep enough in this energetic playground, those labels are the same.

Beady hallway lights flicker in horror of their own dysfunction. Bright, vibrating forks sink into the air and lead us back to center.

In the control room's doorway, Micah waves us down. His overcoat is tied around his hips like a middle-aged woman's sweater,

261

buttons and pins clinking. Sweat beads at his blurry hairline, making him reek of gelled panic. His flailing hands are bound in white fingerless gloves.

"I apologize for what I said earlier," he confesses, wincing without wrinkles. "But this is insane, Zenith. You can hardly expect us to babysit your mama's defective clone while Saturn's about to swallow us whole!"

I brush past him. "I know, I know. But it's not a clone, it's...just a—"

My sneakers squeak to a halt, scuffing the floor. Nothing material or spiritual can hide the vibrato of my thundering pulse.

Silhouetted by a flickering wall of broken screens, the simulacrum stands with open arms and smiles. It reformed itself during its escape, almost perfectly crafted in Soluna Lin's image. Short storm-black hair, high cheekbones, a svelte frame, eyelids like gyoza dough.

Behind her, screens fade in and out to reveal chunks of the presidents' watered-down starship floating in Saturn's ether. There's still distance between us, but if its gravity loosens a smidge, debris will aim for vulnerable Syzygy.

I pull back sweaty strands of hair, redoing it again and again. Breath trips over itself. All my joints turn to jelly.

"Hello, friend," Mama's artificial voice slinks. "How do you do?"

"It doesn't recognize me."

"How could it?" Mother asks, shielding her gaze. "It's never seen you before."

I peer at the simulacrum, and she scans me, a mutual exchange between matter and energy. We can breathe energy into matter, of course—that's how life sparks. But there isn't a glimmer of vibrance in her. Still, I pursue hope, too sick of giving into doubt.

She cocks her head and coos, "Where's my tommy?" Jet black fringe sweeps over one eye. "You took it from me, didn't you?"

My heart dive-bombs into my stomach. Some small part of her must be there, under layers of jaded programming and fickle plastic.

"It doesn't speak like her," I hiss, my sacral chakra seething. "But it changed after we chased it, so that it looks more like..." I glance at Mother out of the corner of my eye. "What did you do? How did you make it?"

"I..." Warped clouds strangle her aura.

"It's like you made her in my closet," I guffaw. "And added Sens-layers."

Someone clatters into me from behind, rattling my core.

I flinch in Reiki's lanky arms as they tighten around my chest. Not in restraint, but an embrace. My muscles liquify under the soft ink-press of her frame.

To our right, Obsidian yanks the hem of my shirt. "Los mundos mezclan."

"What?"

"Worlds blend," Onyx translates, standing in front of us protectively. "Until they are one. We work together. All plans be damned." And then—if you can believe it—she throws me a wink over her shoulder. Her swooping sleeves brush battle-stance hips. Her luminescence spreads, a thick circular shield of silver and gold, caught in an auric cross.

Symbols, Reiki's voice enters my inner ear. *She uses religious language and symbols to clear the mind and open the channels—the way spiritual rebels did in the old days.*

Wobbling like a top, Jaal gawks at Mama's doppelganger, clutching his chest where volts of energy pound his heart. If I blink, his physical form fades, molecules spiraling out of control.

"It's not you." Jaal runs a hand through his deteriorating dreads and pulls out chunks. "It's never been you."

The simulacrum ignores him, frigid gaze still on me, seeking comprehension through clusters of corroded code. Maybe, deep down, she has an ounce of memory that Soluna left behind...

"It doesn't understand," Mother insists, willing herself to look at her wife's copy and the shaken crew. She dabs her eyes with cracked knuckles. "It can try, but it won't succeed. Zen, you were right...she's basically plasticloth. Made to be fluid, not fluent. Physically perfect, not mentally interactive. I know how it sounds, but—"

"All have needs, Imani. Even yours deserved to be met." It could be genuine, if Jaal wasn't grinning like that.

Mother spits into her hands and smooths frizz from her forehead. "You have no right to speak to me like that, Jaal Nadir."

"Speaking of rights," Micah squeaks, jogging up toward the front of the room, just behind Mama's copy. He clinks his knuckles on a presidentially sealed wine glass. "None of us will have any rights to do anything if we continue squabbling like scandal-slathered politicians." He's so blunt, I'm surprised it comes from him and not Beyon. In fact, the dark-skinned president sits in one of the farthest chairs, observing the drama through his many expensive rings.

263

"As one of many presidents on our planet," Micah continues, picking at the hem of his glove. "It's my duty to let you in on an overarching secret—*life* is scandal, my gems. Furthermore, Zenith Lin is captain of this ship and this mission." He titters and swirls the wine in its glass. "Which means we must treat him and his family with gratitude and respect." His grin glitters behind a wave of blueberry wine while he lifts his glass in cheers.

Like lost disciples, the rest of the crew follows the tilt of Micah's glass and gaze toward me.

Except Mama's simulacrum, whose head is turned a disturbing 150 degrees toward Micah's puffed-up chest. Her jaw unhinges; she might bite the bastard.

"Oh, no you don't." Mother's hips swing as she saunters toward her lover's monster. "Soluna." Flat palms ascend in high command. "Sleep."

The simulacrum's eyes darken until there's no difference between pupil and iris. "No," she chimes. "I don't want to, Imani."

Instead of biting the president, she chucks a fist at his heart chakra. He stumbles back into the screens, which flicker like starworks before committing to their demise. Blue wine splashes across the panel, drenching controls.

"No! Now we can't monitor the damage..." Hairs on my arms and the back of my neck raise, calling to the heavens for backup. The problem is—we're *in* the heavens, and we *are* backup.

Beyon rushes to his husband's side.

"Pleiades and Pluto!" I scrunch up my shirt in salty fists. "There's so much chaos in here...we're the perfect pill for a control freak like Saturn to swallow."

Soluna's doppelganger petrifies for a moment, triggered again by my voice. Her neck twists like licorice. "Let me die."

"Soluna, stop." Mother grabs it by the shoulders.

It shifts again, morphing steadily into a more romanticized version of Mama, a well-preserved Japanese woman who would do anything to restore balance. Beauty and justice manifest in sunflower butter skin. A bored sigh exits her flowery mouth. "Let me die already, Imani. Why can't you just let me die?"

Mother jolts back as if she's been hit, hands up and splayed in surrender. "Stop it. You're not her...you're just a ghost print..."

Mama's simulacrum absorbs the sentiment through perked ears and quaking eyeballs. "You know what your problem is, Imani? You'd like me better wasting away, so you can take care of me forever. You thrive on dead things. You're a maggot."

Mother slaps the simulacrum so hard, it twitches violently and backs into the monitors. Black and crystalline chunks rain to the floor in a chorus of glassy screams.

Behind the hand that delivered the blow, Mother whimpers.

Reiki unravels herself from me, all three eyes wide. Her violet wings return in clusters of fibrous light-feathers, peeling open while mine shiver blue.

She lurches forward but I snatch her wrist. "Wait. Mother can handle it."

"No, you don't understand what's happening…what she's trying to do…"

She knows something I don't. I let go of her like I always do, witnessing God's witty comeback to all my secret prayers.

Palms haloed in pure light, Reiki approaches Mama with more confidence than anyone in this room can muster. At first, it looks like her silken bodice unwinds, but then I realize it's her aura releasing ivory tendrils.

Mother lets her pass, sinking into a nearby chair and burying her hands in her mane of hair. *I guess she can't handle it…*

At first, Mama's simulacrum is warped again, faded into itself by the impact of its collapse. But when Reiki yanks it upright and grasps its shoulders, the copycat's mouth opens and light bursts from every cranial orifice.

I sway in the haze of energy, exhausted. Deep breathing urges all chakras to open, so that I might find clarity. My pulse settles its beat and my lungs find their home again in my ribs. When I let my physical vision go fuzzy, I see it. I see her—the irreplaceable, gushing gold of Sol's soul.

She impresses the measly simulacrum with technicolor heat waves, taking over its body after probable hours of previous attempts. Plastic, flaccid consciousness melts in pure, spiritual flame.

Light bends in a life-size kaleidoscope, so that I see every shade and shadow in our collective field. Senses heighten, making all realms of perception collide. I try to focus on the spirit's face, instead of the way the walls seem to crinkle like aluminum.

Her lotus bloom smile could birth a thousand nebulae.

Mama. For real this time.

Settling into herself, Soluna rests in a chair, temporal flesh simmering with the tasty sample of eternal life. She wipes her face with both hands and admires the way they fall into her lap.

265

"Sweet stars," Mother breathes through unclenching fists, hobbling toward her. "Sol. I…I'm so sorry."

I tear my gaze away from the miracle only to check on the crew. Since opening all energetic channels, I feel their scattered choir of heartbeats in my own.

Mama rises, meeting Mother halfway and cradling her elbows. "'If apologies were productive, I would've found a cure for Gemini Fever by now.'" She ticks off each word with a nod. "I spoke those words when I inhabited flesh and bone. Do you remember?" Golden flakes glint across each iris, a mere shadow of stellar substance. "In other words—you have nothing to be sorry for, sunshine."

As per Mother's greatest desire, Mama holds her. Mother curls to fit her small frame, huddling in the warmth of her rising and falling chest. Somehow, they fit perfectly, the way they did before.

Reiki sways, and I only just reach her in time to catch her. My knees scrape the floor. I look from her glossy eyelids and tsunami of copper hair to Mama's smile.

Her eyes crinkle so much, I barely see their several shades of brown, but they're identical to the eyes I saw my reflection in when I was small. The same gaze I had staring contests with and would lose to.

My inner child laughs hard and sharp. My belly bounces. Teardrops swell in the corners of my eyes. Everyone else's sensations fade, replaced by a stinging joy that stretches from my jaw to my toes.

"What do we do now?" I plead.

Recognition swarms Mama's gaze.

Wet laughter escapes Mother's trembling chin while Mama turns, pressing her palms together and pointing them at Reiki and me.

"Reiki's been solid for too long," she explains as if it's simple, tilting her head. "Without you, her body struggles to hold shape. It took her much longer than usual to find you, in this life."

"You know about that?" Bewildered, I adjust Reiki in my arms, turning her face against my breastbone. "What're you saying?"

"Karma's a funny force. It doesn't always act with balance, like everyone thinks. It has some fun on the way." Chuckles begin in Mama's trembling belly under sapphire fabric. "Zenith, I've been to the ethers and back many times now. I've seen you, her, all of it. Harmony feels a lot like dissonance, sometimes." She boops my nose. "Of course, you know what the power of recognizing souls can do."

"Can I ask…I mean, I just need to know…when did you…d-die?"

266

She sits on her knees and ankles in front of us, close enough to square my shoulders with surprisingly firm hands. Even her calluses have returned, imprinting fake skin with real memory.

"The Fever drew me farther from that body than I've ever been, but I'm not ashamed of it." Her bottom lip juts. Celestial light starts to dim, becoming comfortable with its current shape. "So, you could say I've been dead since contracting Gemini. But I didn't really leave. You know that, right?"

"B-but I did. And…I'm sorry for that." I hang my head.

Jaal's muffled sobs litter Onyx's sleeves. All his backed-up emotions seep through skittish molecules.

Mama laughs lightly. One hand scoops my chin and dabs the tears away, while the other remains on my shoulder. "I can't tell you how proud I am. Actually, fuck that—I can, and I will." Her teeth are starker than the whites of her eyes. "I'm proud of you, Zenith Lutfi Lin, for being strong even when I wasn't there to teach you how. And I love you, not because of what you've been through, or because you're my child, but because I am Love and I honor your Love too."

I glance down at Reiki, my heart shivering.

Mama's smile shapes her words. "I know you feel like it must be her, only her, and no one else. She feels it too. But that's only because you reflect each other so easily. Your energies are mirrors, one anchored and one floating. She pulled herself together—literally—to meet you at this vibration."

"Okay…but…" I try to match what she's saying with our current state, but chaos and order just don't add up right now.

"She's ever-changing, isn't she? So fluid, you'd think she's like this silly cloth-body." She gestures to her own fluctuating form. "Her molecules move faster than yours, parting like seas so that you can perceive her spirit. The time and energy it takes to get to know someone's body is irrelevant when you can see their soul in high definition." Her head bows, nose sloping like a chunk of rain off petals.

Reiki's breathing becomes shallower and erratic against my chest.

"Don't misunderstand, stardust," Soluna continues, brushing her hands together. Speckled luminescence descends. My root chakra tingles. She opens her palms again to sprinkle the leftovers on Reiki. "This is your soul's closest, most vivid reflection. So easily recognizable, you might as well be the same. One never without the other. But if you're going to keep this solar system alive, you've got to love all of it with every facet of your being. And trust me when I say—it will take every reflection you have."

Thirty-Three

The room breathes deeper again, slowly but surely. The crew settles into themselves.

Mama's soul leaves its makeshift shell with less than a breath to spare, but I feel her everywhere, even in the oozing green energy seeping through Syzygy's skin.

Fake flesh decks the floor. Silence salutes her.

My crew's sensations linger like ghosts in my body, but my soul's light burns through them all, awakened by Mama's words. Even though our meeting was brief, I come out of it with more clarity than Tarot or meditation could ever provide.

"Jaal," I command. "Help Mother send her wife back into the cosmos."

His irises flash shades of sun and moon.

Empathy in here is tangible, clouding our previous judgements with new colors. I can't help but gawk at the energetic network we've created, in barely any time. It must be a record of some kind.

Before he can answer, Reiki jolts in my arms again, clonking her head into my clenched bicep. She must feel the rise in vibration too.

With my other hand, I hold her neck in place. Our auric fields mesh like nothing has changed, two shades of fluorescent teal. Truths heal together, in peace.

I exhale, relieved to see her lavender eyelids twitch. Her breathing deepens with my understanding.

"Jaal," I repeat, and amend: "Please help Mother dispose of the simulacrum."

His gaze crystallizes. He nods, restoring a semblance of humanity in himself. As he approaches Mother, his apology rises in a tidal wave of light. Energetically, he's bold, but physically, he rubs the back of his neck sheepishly.

Mother sighs through laced fingers before clamping a hand on his shoulder. Forgiveness flows easily from her, as it always has.

Together, Jaal and Imani gather sheets of polyester dermis and fake bone. It's much lighter to carry when it's in pieces, unlike their hearts.

Micah clears his throat into a tight fist. Somehow the least subtle creature catches the most subliminal messages. "Shall we...give her a proper send-off?"

I meet his oceanic eyes and nod.

Maybe it's the traumatic transcendence, or the deep breaths, but my muscles don't strain a smidge as I rise, swinging Reiki in my arms bridal style. Her long calves dangle over my left arm, but she feels like a sleeping bird, hollow-boned.

Mother squishes simulacrum pieces in a last-minute hug as the scent of Mama's juniper spirit fades.

Onyx wanders after Jaal and Mother, plucking stray skin-shards off the floor, muttering mantras to herself. Obsidian opens the door for us.

I smile, feeling like a true captain. "Alright, bitches. We're about to save our solar system in a way no one has before. From here on out, humanity won't be the same. I can feel it, and I know you do too."

Beyon, our group's caboose, raises a concerned finger. Ash and sweat curl over his thick brows. "Forgive me for being blunt, Captain Lin, but what are your priorities here?"

The smile on my face must be manic, because when I turn to him, his chin tucks inward. "Why, President Ycarimus, I thought it was obvious—my top priority is and always has been the whole of humanity, as yours is. Or is the RSA's shiny reputation suddenly your sole concern?"

As we follow Jaal and Mother down the hall, Obsidian pats my back. "That's our capitán," he says, donning a fond beam. He leans in and lowers his voice, chin bumping into my shoulder. "Whatever the presidents' agenda, 'meegs, they *do* wanna help."

"I know. I'm just having fun." I glance down at Reiki, deciphering a smile behind sheathed shadows.

Micah skips to catch up to us, striding on my other side. "I knew you had it in you to pull the cogs out of your ass. You weren't acting like yourself, before..."

I can't help but snort. "Why do you people like me more when I'm a dick?"

Giddy laughter springs from his puffy lips. "It reminds us of our beloved hard-ass, Elisha Sye." He winks and rubs my shoulder. "She'll be pleased with how passionately you care."

"You haven't contacted her yet?"

He shakes his head and folds his arms, glancing back at his lover. His voice drops to a whisper. "We haven't hired an assassin, either. We don't have the time or energy."

I chuckle. Reiki's body weight lightens with each step, and so does the burden on my back.

I've walked these metallic halls so many times before, I should be exhausted by them. But while electromagnetic pulses linger, I soak it all in, to find that place where my body and mind align.

Instead of saying Mama's name to open my bedroom door, I press my palm against its glowing façade. It opens without question.

The crew makes a perimeter around my bed, unsure of what to do next.

"Alright," I announce, climbing onto the bed to open the ceiling's trapdoor. My knees quake, not from the lift, but in anticipation. The ladder spills out onto Reiki's sleeping face, and she squirms in my grasp while I shift out of the way. "C'mon, spacy dogs."

"I don't understand," Onyx confesses. "How do we all fit?"

"We'll just have to shrink our bulbous egos down a few sizes." I hand Reiki over to Obsidian and begin my ascent.

As my ankles dangle, I hear Jaal croak below, "W-wait."

On the storage pod's cool floor, I rest my belly and duck my head low to see all their faces—an amalgam of bronze, tree bark, and ash.

Jaal coughs and glances down at the armful of simulacrum skin. His pulsating lips are smeared purple. "For those of us who still wanna be scientific…what is it you plan—"

"I don't plan on anything," I interject, rubbing leftover tension out of my jaw. "Which is, honestly, the most scientific way of looking at things."

"Zenith." Mother uses the same voice she once carried when I took too much licorice from the candy jar, or when I fell asleep on the floor next to their bed. She smiles, but it's the kind of grin that warrants a grimace. She expects more from me than some well-crafted sass.

I blow a stray curl out of my eyes and wipe sweat on my shirt's collar. "Alright, well, you all heard Soluna, you just didn't understand."

"That's an understatement," Beyon mutters, wiping his scalp with a stretched sleeve cuff. Like the rest, he seems more youthful in the oncoming glow of planetary chaos, and this time it's not the plastic surgery.

"We're all simulacra, in a way," I explain, working some royal-blue-throat-chakra-realness. "Just bodies encapsulating souls. Where do you think those souls have been, and where will they go? No...where are they, in all times and spaces at once? A body only lives because of energy, but that energy flows everywhere simultaneously." My aura wobbles with the silent song of several strings. "There's never a lack. Lack is an illusion of matter."

They stare, unable to tear away, eyebrows mashed together.

"Jaal, you made J-bombs because they use invisible forces that cling to everything in the universe. They're...easily accessible. Our bodies...are basically capsules for the same kind of force. Well. Conduits."

"So, we're gonna explode?" Obsidian asks, squinting.

"No." It comes out sharper than intended. I get off my stomach and sit in lotus position, tapping the porthole's edge. "Just...get up here and help me. Then I'll show you what I mean."

Stars, I hope Reiki wakes up soon.

Saturn's tarnished light settles through stellaglass.

Mother and Jaal raise chunks of flesh into the pod before climbing the rest of the way, each having a completely different reaction to the sight before them.

"Oh, Allah's stars," Mother marvels as she stands beside me, arms sprawled, eyelids fluttering in the weight of terrifying beauty. "You couldn't see it as vividly on Stellium."

Uncaring that Saturn has in fact regained one of its rings, Jaal tries to gather all the simulacrum pieces himself, but Mother meets him halfway.

"You're not alone, stupid boy," she whispers, nudging him with her elbow and stuffing strips into the crook of her arm. "Stop trying to be."

"Amigo," Obsidian calls for me. I kneel to take Reiki back from his embrace. She curls into me again. Apple blossoms gush from her aura, into my jade chest.

After readjusting his hoodie, Sid climbs up with ease. "She's lighter than a leaf."

I shuffle on my knees toward one of the storage compartments and lay her there, caressing the back of her skull just before it knocks on the floor. Then, tucking into rhythmic breath, I return to lotus position.

When I close my eyes, Saturn's scarred light becomes sticky green, coating the insides of my eyelids. Lungs swell and deflate with shared air, a substance I've grown used to in more ways than one. Slinging my shoulders back, I draw my hands close to my heart and pray, not like my parents did—bent over in solemnity—but in all the ways, recalling religious devotions from unremembered lives. Without moving, I swim through a fusion of fire and ice, preparing my body and soul for what's to come.

"He's meditating," Micah giggles. I hear his overpriced dress pants slither against the floor. "The solar system is collapsing, and he's *meditating*."

"Saturn has a ring back," I counter, eyes still shut. "Our solar system is rebooting."

"Zenith Lin," Beyon utters, following his husband through the trapdoor. "Please tell me this isn't religious mass suicide."

I open my eyes. He stands above the porthole with arms locked over his chest. Micah sits cross-legged on the floor and leans against his towering legs.

"Have a pinch of faith, Mr. President." A cheesy grin smears my face while I stand, looming over Reiki. Light tattoo lines and faint scars begin to tingle, and I wonder if the process has already begun.

"Now." I clasp my hands together, somewhat aware of Reiki shifting at my feet. I clear my throat and gesture to the storage. "As you can see, there are only six bubble masks in here, and eight of us. Basic math determines that's a no-go."

Mother deduces where I'm going with this. She hoists the flesh-pile over her head with one arm like a woven basket. Strangely subservient, Jaal spreads the bubble mask over her face, and she does the same for him. They work together like soldiers, auras burning with the kind of emerald ferocity I never would've imagined them sharing.

"Jaal and Imani will ascend first, tethered to the ship by a false gravity field. They'll burn the simulacrum." I reach into a drawer and pull out a special lighter, the only kind that makes our material palatable for outer space. "The rest of my crew and I will join them. Presidents, I ask that you stay here while we…finish the job."

"And then?" Beyon presses, but he's the only one who does. Everyone else watches and waits for me, at-the-ready.

273

Was this how Tauris felt when she put on a production? But no…these aren't pretty puppets; these are people. Loving, fucking, frustrating people. Soon to be, possibly, the most crucial Conduits in human history.

"You'll wait for further instruction." I kneel and bend low 'til my lips brush Reiki's forehead. She wakes, shuttering, a faint blush swarming her freckled cheeks.

"I don't understand," Beyon mopes, while Micah rises to console him.

"Do you remember the Schism?" I ask.

He tries to move past Micah, who anchors him. "How dare you. I'm not that old."

"No one is," I laugh, shaking my head. "But you should know that there could never have been a Reunion of the States without a schism in the first place."

"What are you implying?"

"We're all split at birth." I glance at Reiki's awakening body. "In Spirit, we were one consciousness, but in the physical plane, we're many segments. Fractals of the same light. I need you, and you need me, and it's not a game. It's not a radical religious stance. It's existence and consciousness acting as one Bliss."

Puzzled but calm, he relaxes into his husband's embrace, giving into whispering wisdom. Not mine, but the universe's.

"Thank you for helping me," I say, gripping Reiki's hand to help her up. I keep my eyes on the men, but she knows I'm addressing her too. "I mean it. I really wouldn't be able to do this without you. We're not going to fix what Tauris has done; we're going to *heal* it. I promise."

Thirty-Four

"**O**n this fated occasion, we say goodbye," Reiki announces through a bubble mask. Silhouetted in shifting light beams, she's godlike, able to capture lightning in her irises. "Not to who she is—a soul stronger than solar flares—but to who she was in physical form."

It might be odd, but I wouldn't want anyone else conducting Mama's makeshift funeral.

Out here, on my ship's snow globe surface, Saturn's vacuum becomes so intense that even protective energy fields leak. Gravity garners us close, and synthetic suits protect our skin, but energetic motion is unable to resist.

I squint past sheets of blurred gold, toward Saturn's lopsided body and ramshackle rings. From the rings' shadow, a massive bluish cluster reemerges. We've caught the ice-dragon's attention again. To be honest, I'm surprised it's still there. It's a good sign; it means the system still has enough energy to be conscious.

Our auras gasp for light, flickering like candles under exhale. To the casual observer, we're being consumed, but to us, a transcendent process has begun.

The presidents, who sit in the storage pod under us, were right—this is all a bit culty, but at the same time, it brings us together in a way we never thought possible.

Reiki clears her throat, fogging up the mask. "To help her final vessel rejoin the stars, and to fuel our energetic processes, we'll use four symbolic Earthen elements."

Despite his shaky frame, Jaal holds most of the flesh pieces in bulging arms. His veins are the color of smoke. He keeps glancing at me, not in the way he usually does, but with a trembling lip.

275

Onyx bears the smaller pieces of Mama's temporary capsule.

"With fire, we say goodbye to her passion." Reiki nods.

On cue, Mother raises the coil-shaped lighter with ashy hands and ignites it. One by one, Onyx dips pieces into the flame and rifles them toward Saturn's ether-creature. Out of gravity, they soar willingly into the planet's famished auric field and the dragon's mouth—not as sacrifice, but potential medicine.

When Onyx's arms are empty, she helps Jaal with the larger, more bodily pieces. They kiss them with fire and heave them up and out.

I start to hum an old hymn my moms once sang to me. My gaze is bleached by carnelian firelight, but I'm sure Mother is crying.

"With water, we remember our shared healing," Reiki continues, spraying a bottle after the floating pieces. Most drops float away, but a few scatter back onto us like holy water.

"With air, we breathe new life into old." Collective sighs emerge, but I keep singing like my life depends on it. I almost hear Mama harmonizing beyond clouds of ash.

Reiki makes a respectful mudra with both hands over her head. "With our bodies, which are made of earth, we release and renew, so that we may be better channels for all."

Each of us follows her example by forming a mudra. Mine rests in front of my belly, thumbs and index fingers hooked in an infinity symbol. My song fades into the stars, echoing long after she asks us to bow our heads and close our eyes.

In the space between inhaling and exhaling, I remember something long forgotten.

The first time Mama holds me, after seven hours of song-induced labor, she tucks a sweaty palm stone in my cloth and sighs.

"You did so well, Sol." Mother takes off her glittering headscarf and drapes it over us, beaming. "Well. What do you think? What should we name our firstborn? My brother wishes to claim the middle name, of course…"

"Zenith," Mama says, sniffling. Her chest rises and falls. "That way we always hold this child high above us."

"Zenith Lutfi Lin." Mother kisses Mama's forehead, and then mine. "I like the sound of that."

A cacophony of heartbeats brings me back to the present. I sink into everyone's sensations, as well as my own—Obsidian's aching muscles, Onyx and Jaal's warm embrace, Mother's tears, and Reiki's hand in mine.

While my crew turns their prayers into tangible light, the ice dragon forms a spiral above. From its neck, another head extends. Instead of ice and earth, it's the color of Onyx's eyes—vibrant citrus—and blusters with gas. Both heads unhinge their beastly jaws and breathe a spectrum of rainbow vapors.

Everyone's syncing. All but one…

"Syzygy."

Reiki lets go of my hand, eyes closed but knowing.

I follow the tug in my gut through trapdoors, past fumbling presidents and useless technology.

In my room, on the bed, my sitar sits.

It's the only item that hasn't been broken by our scramble, but I bolt past it. The sitar isn't what calls to me.

Don't worry, I'll come back for you, I think as I pass.

Another energy, one that may very soon lose its vessel, calls louder.

I reach the engine room's trapdoor. Vaporous energy gushes from it, across every shattered screen and throbbing floor panel.

I tell myself that Syzygy's fine, he's not dead, and we're going to pull through this together. But despite the past four years of speaking and living with my ship, I can't help but doubt the consciousness of a human-made star. It's a simple creature, after all, tethered to the need to constantly create.

With a ballooning chest, I peel off my shirt and tie it around my nose and mouth. I splay my hand across the recognition pad and enter Syzygy's underbelly.

Strangely, the deeper I go, the less smoke floats. Cooler air glides over my skin, spiking hairs on the back of my neck.

When I step off the ladder and turn around, I'm stunned.

In its stellaglass globe, the engine-star rotates slowly like an astrobat dancer, soft light burning rouge. Contrasting its cooler temperature and dulled pressure, the color is redder and slicker than bloodied rose thorns.

Syzygy dwarfs, giving up their power to Saturn without having to be asked.

"You *do* know what's going on," I manage to whisper, stepping closer. "Clever creature." Icy gusts from surrounding tech knock me back, an impromptu warning system to keep me from losing myself in heat. "I guess Jaal was kind of right, about sacrifice, huh?"

Their neon tongues licking the inside of the container, Syzygy hums in response, highlighting frayed wires and fixtures the mad

277

scientist left behind. Toxins were cleaned, but an energetic imprint remains, motivating my ship to help us finish what we started. Somehow, Syzygy knows, and employs only the best energetic channel to aid our flow—a star.

If Reiki's and my vibrations are harmonic, Syzygy's alone is a symphony, but it didn't take them dying for me to know this. I've always felt a plethora of strings generating tingles through metal and fiber, calling me back when I wanted to be lost. No matter how badly I wanted to possess this masterpiece spacecraft, they were the one who possessed me.

"Ah, fuck," I lament, wiping my sopping eyes with bent wrists. "I wish I had more time to say it, but…Thank you." Reaching out, I wiggle my fingers, letting a smidge of my energy wander into the capsule to keep them company.

"Goodbye, Beloved." I bow reverently. "I'll miss you." Then, I readjust the cloth around my face and climb back up the ladder.

"Farewell, Captain." The voice is transcendent of gender, but it has never sounded happier.

The transition from underbelly to head is ethereal, to say the least—comparable to a chakra pillar meditation. Syzygy's rich root, depleted only to be replaced with love, glows red. Smoky, ever-shifting sacral and solar plexus come next, once under perfect control and now giving into chaos.

Tiny green lights sputter back on in the corridors, acting as the heavy heart. My room's the navy-blue throat, full of messy passion and avalanched truth, whereas the emergency pod waits and listens.

With the sitar cradled under one arm, I smush the bubble mask over my face and stretch toward Syzygy's crown chakra. Renewed oxygen pummels my lungs.

Reiki opens the porthole, washing me in light.

I launch into white sparks of stardust and then her arms. Breeze tries to play my sitar, whistling through fibrous metal and wood. Reiki's braids brush my mask. I grab the bulges of hair and squeeze light into them. It seeps toward her scalp and she laughs.

"Welcome back, Cap."

We sit in the center of chaos, but I pause for a moment to marvel. Never in this life have I seen or felt colors like these.

The best way to describe the conglomerate of energy is that moment just before falling asleep, when the world swirls into shallow breathing, and anything you ever worried about rockets in the subconscious to be translated and recycled.

Jaal has never looked so peaceful, standing with his foster siblings in a triangle, energy pulsating to a collective beat. I tap into their hearts. They're still scattered like pebbles, but intricately aligned by cosmic ley lines—magnetic fields as strong as neutron stars. Slowly but surely, each rebellious heart adopts the rhythm of the other, aching to be lead home.

Below, Beyon and Micah are pressed together like butterfly wings. Their communal energy is a fountain, mounting itself on heaps of velvety love and pride. It phases through stellaglass to join our aura, without even an ounce of technological aid.

Mother has finally stopped crying, and her mask clears enough for me to witness the remarkable. While she sits beside us in lotus position, her mask glows with her soul's mirror—Mama's face—in a terrific, metaphysical Sens-mirage.

Saturn's double-headed dragon makes an arc in the sky, sipping the very tip of our transcendental rainbow.

Shaky breath wrenches my chest open, centering my attention. I cradle the sitar, but don't bother playing it, as music flows from my whole being with stellar ease.

Across from me, Reiki's knees make a diamond shape with mine.

Our breath syncopates, careening the cusps of our masks before sinking back through the tube. Her lungs envelope my own. My trembling vocal chords encase hers.

Spines loosen. Fingers unfurl, spilling over reassembled chords and a song's innocent birth. Jaws drop, allowing cerulean energy to flow.

Our vibration breaks through to join the others, a tundra of tactile emotion and delicious memory. The song is different from any we've sung before, or maybe it's the first song our souls ever sang together at the spark of existence.

Among chalky light beams, grinding ice chunks, and bubbling flow, it's nearly impossible to differentiate notes.

Voices split at first, filling our harmony with photons. But then they meld, not as two different elements, but as reuniting flames that came from the same wick. Laughter bobs and weaves through the song, the same way our bodies trained, the exact way our Spirit reunites.

I don't know when, but I shut my eyes.

I am the same sound that gave birth to Creation, catalyzed life before there was even death, and divided pure light into an ever-expanding spectrum.

My ancestors called it *Om*. The unenlightened called it a whine, circling Earth's atmosphere in search of "more."

I feel it now not just as sound, or a spot caught in a telescope, but as a long and warm kiss.

While I'm singing, my mouth becomes Reiki's. Thinner, jade-leaf lips liquify and drip over my chin, tracing arteries and tendons.

Her slippery tongue ushers stronger notes from a quivering throat. Her legs anchor my hips, arms bolster my ribcage.

Hands wander over aching strings, bouncing belly, quaking chest, bubbles of spit caught between teeth—hers and mine. Mine and his.

I've always been able to sing and cry at the same time, but this is different. I am rivulets of tears, overflowing, and I am the eyelashes sticking together, and I am her body and soul chording with mine. I am all and nothing, giving and receiving, so that a tunnel of impossible particle-waves beams in every direction, on every plane.

Our tiny, fragile pocket of the universe is belting.

Reiki pushes my hair back from my eyes, but I don't dare open them because I know when I do, I'll only be staring at myself.

THANK YOU FOR READING.

MAY YOU BE HAPPY.

MAY YOU BE HEALTHY.

MAY YOU BE SAFE.

MAY YOU BE FREE.

ABOUT THE AUTHOR

A. Rose Mapstone is an astrologer, Catholic mystic, and Reiki master living in Upstate New York. They attended Le Moyne College and completed a bachelor's degree in Creative Writing with minors in psychology and religious studies. Currently, they own The Reikery LLC—an energetic wellness business—which can be found at www.thereikeryllc.wixsite.com/lolpop. Their hope in publishing the *ANANDA* series is to inspire—breathe life into—the idea that spiritual healing is always accessible to everyone.

SOCIAL MEDIA

patreon.com/arosemapstone
facebook.com/arosemapstar
instagram.com/arosemapstar

The Reikery:
facebook.com/thereikeryllc
instagram.com/thereikeryllc
For inquiries— thereikeryllc@gmail.com

You are Seen. You are Loved.

If you're in a crisis situation, please seek professional help
immediately.
National Suicide Prevention Lifeline:
1-800-273-8255